AN APARTMENT IN
Venice

To Laura,
I hope you
enjoy this tale —
Marlene Hill

ALSO BY MARLENE HILL:

Alone with Michelangelo:
A Woman Follows Her Dreams to Italy

Last Fling in Venice

AN APARTMENT IN *Venice*

Book Two of Venetian Waters Series

MARLENE HILL

Cover art by Kelly Kievit

ISBN-13: 978-1493786336
ISBN-10: 1493786334

Published by:
Marlene Hill Taevs Marketing
Milwaukie, Oregon

PRINTED IN THE UNITED STATES OF AMERICA

BOOK DESIGN BY RAQOON DESIGN

ACKNOWLEDGMENTS

Loads of thanks to my magnificent, dynamic, inciteful and supportive Tuesday-critique partners:

Jennifer Fulford, D'Norgia Price and Linda Smith

To Mary Alice Moore, my ever supportive Monday-lunch critiquer.

To Catherine Wilson, once again a goddess of patience in guiding me through design and production decisions.

To Kelly Kievit, who created my beautiful cover, depicting the mysterious, seductive essence of Venice.

To Dustin Keys, always there for me to sort out myriad techie problems.

And *tante grazie* to Elena Di Mattia of Pordenone, Italia for monitoring my Italian!

For George

who seduced me

with his unconditional acceptance

and outrageous flattery.

CHAPTER ONE

"Come in," came a sing-song falsetto voice with at least two vowels stringing out the last word.

It was late afternoon and Giulia couldn't put this encounter off any longer. She'd seen Oliver Ogle, Human Resources Director, only once, but without any doubt, she had recognized a sleaze. She lifted her chin, threw her shoulders back and grabbed the handle.

Last week at the orientation meeting for new instructors, he had looked soft, pudgy and seemed harmless. But as he explained his role as the overseas representative of the University of Maryland, he'd made slimy remarks about the lovelies working on the post who would need *his* services.

And there he sat like a fat toad. For an instant, she imagined him zapping her with a long tongue as if she were a helpless insect. *A desk is between us. Good.* She stepped to the large, metal government-issue desk and put down two sheets of paper.

"Mr. Ogle, I'm Giulia Cavinato. Here's the information you need for my personnel file." She turned to leave.

"Are those all yours?" he said, focusing on her breasts.

"Pardon?" she asked and barely stopped herself from pulling closed the blue paisley vest she wore over a long-sleeved blouse.

"I said, are those jugs *all* yours?"

Giulia was tempted to put her hands on her hips but didn't want to appear defiant or girlish. She drew herself up to her full five feet five and one-half inches. "Mr. Ogle," she pronounced in a soft, low tone.

He leaned in closer to hear her voice.

"I hadn't wanted to believe the rumors I've heard about you, but—"

"Oh? What have you heard about me?" He leaned back looking pleased.

"That you use crude language with the women you've been hired to serve." She backed toward the door. *And you're a dirty old man.*

"Now, now missy. Don't take me wrong. Come sit. I'll only keep you a minute."

"You will not keep me here one more second," she said, surprised at the vicious tone in her voice.

Faster than she'd expected him to move, he came around his desk and grabbed her upper arm. In a patronizing tone, he said, "Calm down. We need to get acquainted, that's all."

"Let me go."

He held on.

"I *said* let me go." But he gripped harder. She twisted toward him, kneed him in the groin and ran out the door.

That was a clever thing to do my first week here. As a newly-accredited Assistant Professor of English, she hoped to work on this base near Venice for a long time. This job would make her dream of living in Venice come true.

No one was around as she raced through the empty corridor, shoved open the outer door and dashed down the steps of the admin building straight into a large officer.

"Oof!" He put his hands on her elbows to steady her.

"Excuse me!"

"Can I help you?"

Her face was flushed but she said, "I'm fine but need to be going." She sucked in a breath and pulled away from him.

"Wait a sec. You don't seem fine. Could you use a coffee or maybe something stronger?"

"I… I don't think so." But she trembled and was short of breath.

"You're new here aren't you? A new professor in the adult education program?"

"Assistant Professor." Looking down, feeling defeated, she added, "After today, if there's a probation period in the fine print of my contract, I'll be shipped out."

"Let me guess. You've just come from Oliver Ogle. Right?"

She looked up in astonishment. He was so close she had to tilt her head back to see his face. That's when heat streaked along her spine. She hoped he hadn't picked up on it. That heat struck a spark long buried inside but a spark she intended to keep well hidden.

"What happened?"

He'd spoken quietly and it took a second before she could decipher his words. "I brought information he needed for my file." She sighed. "I'm not sure it makes any difference what happened. There were no witnesses."

"Oh, but it does. Did he make vulgar remarks implying you'd make a tasty sex toy?"

"Something like that." She wasn't about to repeat Ogle's words. "I should have left right then, but I called him on it. He grabbed my arm and wouldn't let go and… well… I sort of kicked him."

"In the balls, I hope," the tall officer said.

She nodded and a small grin crept across her lips.

He laughed and then stopped abruptly. "Come on. We're going back in there while he's enjoying the aftermath of your visit."

Giulia jerked back. "It will be his word against mine."

"I'll be with you. You need to confront him now. You know, the get-back-on-the-horse thing. And someone needs to be a witness to *that*, at least." He took her hand. "Ready?"

His huge hand felt warm and strong. She looked up again and nodded.

As they walked to the building, he said, "My name is Chuck Novak. And you are?"

"Giulia Cavinato."

"Italian?

"American. Italian parents."

They were at Ogle's door. Giulia took hold of herself again as

Chuck knocked. No answer. He pounded harder. "Oliver, are you in there?"

"Go away. I'm busy. Make an appointment."

"Sorry, this can't wait." Chuck turned the handle, but the door was locked. "I think you know me, Oliver. Major General Novak. I must see you now."

They heard a click and Chuck opened the door. Oliver was limping back to his chair behind the desk. With his back still to them, he said, "What's so damned important, Novak?"

"She is."

Oliver's head spun around to see Giulia. He plopped onto his chair with a grimace. His plump neck was flushed; blotchy red spots had appeared on his face. As he brushed strands of ashen-colored hair across a bald spot, he spit out, "What's she doing here?"

The ugly smirk on his face told her he was someone to be more than wary of. He could even be dangerous. *Another woman user.* She clenched her fists and felt her insides start to boil.

"We're going to have a little chat," Chuck said. "I have Ms. Cavinato's story. I want to hear yours."

"What did this floozy have to say?"

"Tell me your version first," Chuck said.

"Oh, so you're judge, jury and executioner?"

"May-Be," Chuck said. His menacing growl startled Giulia. He'd been so gentle with her. "I have to warn you, Ogle, she's not the first woman on this base who's complained about you. Let's hear your side."

"She sashays into my office arching her back to show me her boobs. She's just a flirt. Then—"

"Where were you when she came in?"

"Right here where I am now."

"Okay. What happened next?"

"I complimented her. She took offense. I asked her to calm down, and she assaulted me."

"How did she assault you? Did she leap over the desk and punch you?"

"Don't get smart with me Mr. Military Man."

"Well, Oliver," Chuck said in the same ominous tone, "what *was* the nature of her assault?"

"Don't want to talk about it. It's over."

"Mister Ogle," Chuck said as if the word mister put a bad taste in his mouth. "As you've often said yourself, we all need to work together on this post. Is there any way we can call a truce?"

"Sure. All she has to do is apologize."

Giulia said nothing. Chuck glanced at her. In trim navy slacks, pale blue, long-sleeved blouse buttoned to her collar bone and covered by a loose vest, her small body was rigid. Fury glared from her extraordinary eyes—one dark espresso and one piercing blue. Imperceptibly, she shook her head. Even without that slight movement, Chuck guessed she'd never back down to this bastard.

"Are you willing to apologize to her?"

"Hell, no. I did nothing wrong. She jumped to conclusions."

"I see," Chuck said. "Guess we have nothing more to do here… *today*. Thanks for your time."

As they walked away from his office, they heard the lock click into place. But they didn't hear Ogle growl, "Payback time, missy," as he opened her personnel file.

"When I get back to my office, I'll write up both stories and—"

"And nothing," she said. "Without a witness, it's a stalemate." She muttered under her breath, "But I still have to deal with him."

"You're right, but you won't deal with him alone. It's time things change around here for Oliver Ogle. If I can't be with you, someone else will."

They walked to the point where she'd run into him. "And now, how about that coffee?"

"No thank you. I appreciate your support, but—"

"Will you come if I promise not to compliment you?"

She hesitated and almost smiled. "If you put it that way, why not?"

They walked across Via al di Moro—one of the few streets on the post without an American name. He led her to a new coffee shop that sat between a Burger King and Taco Bell, only two of the several fine dining establishments on the post. Chuck kept up a running chatter on the way. He opened the door for her and said, "What would you like? Regular Drip? French Press? Latte? Cappuccino? We've been longing for decent coffee on this post for ages, and some of us have been over-loading on caffeine." Lowering his voice, he said in a self-mocking tone, "After careful research, I've found the French Press the best."

"Ordinarily, I'd go for French press, too. But something soft and creamy sounds good to me right now. I'll have a cappuccino."

Talk about soft and creamy, he thought, I could devour her on the spot.

"Guess you don't always worry about proprieties, right?" he teased.

"Do you think what I did to Oliver proper?"

"Damn straight I do. Would you grab that empty table in the corner while I place our orders?"

* * *

Chuck watched her move across the room. She was a slender little thing, but under that straight-laced outfit, he had no doubt voluptuous curves waited for someone's hands. Maybe his. And he'd bet his brand-new Rossignol T-4 Skis she was *not* a flirt. With those soft, dark curls framing her face, he could see why Ogle might put her in that category. Obviously, the old buzzard hadn't missed her shape beneath her buttoned-up outfit. Did she believe that vest camouflage really worked? Funny how women seemed to think they could hide their body from men that way. Only those damned burkas could do that.

This wasn't the first time Chuck had noticed her on the post, but he felt lucky to have her run straight into his arms. She looked too young, but after spending time with glossy, gorgeous-to-their-eyeballs Italian women, he couldn't help but feel drawn to her freshness.

"Sorry you had to face Oliver the Ogre so soon after arriving," Chuck said, joining her at the small round table.

"Ogre he is," she said.

"Look, Giulia—may I call you Giulia rather than Ms. Cavinato?"

She nodded. "And what shall I call you? Major General Novak is kind of a mouthful." For the first time since they met, she grinned with genuine enthusiasm.

"It is, isn't it. But it comes in handy sometimes. Please call me Chuck. What I started to say is that everyone knows about Ogle but not how to get rid of him aside from pushing him back under his bridge with no way out."

"That would be super. But aren't trolls the ones who live under bridges?"

"Hell, I don't know. What I do know is, he needs to go."

A waiter brought their coffees. Giulia noticed small spoons were served with her cappuccino and his press. They were on an American base, but it was Italy after all. In most shops in the States, she usually had to beg for a spoon and then got a plastic one.

"What do you teach?" he asked as if he couldn't find out.

"English Literature and Business English. And you?"

"I do a little of everything. Occasionally, I get to supervise pilots in the 173rd Airborne stationed here."

"Is that the group that operates like the Navy SEALS and must be combat ready at a moment's notice?"

"Some are. In the Air Force, the combat-ready personnel are called Combat Controllers. Our motto is *First There*. Most of our assignments are rescue missions."

"But can't those be a lot like combat?"

"Oh yeah." He leaned back, and his eyes searched hers. "How is it you know about the 173rd? Most people hear about the SEALS but not much about Special Ops in other services. Obviously their PR is better."

"Supposedly the SEALS try to keep their covert work *covert*, but that's only what I've read—mostly through fiction. You can learn a lot, though, from well-researched novels." She squared her shoulders as if expecting he might doubt "facts" learned from fiction.

He found her protective attitude toward literature charming. Hell, everything about her was appealing, but he wanted to change the subject anyway. "Did you grow up, like me, speaking Italian as well as English?" He sipped his coffee and watched her.

"Yes. My parents came from small towns in the Veneto north of Venice." She put her cup down and said, "Wait a minute. How is it you grew up speaking Italian? Isn't Novak a Czech name?"

"It is. But Mother was of Italian descent." For a moment his voice darkened, then he continued. "With a name like Cavinato, you won't have trouble fitting into Italy. Or do you live here on the post?"

"I'm in a pensione in Vicenza. And off the base I speak only Italian because it seems locals don't have much use for people from out here."

"You've got that right. Sometimes the young bucks go into town and forget their manners. And proper Vicentini resent having their perfect city disturbed. So, what part of the Veneto are your folks from?"

"Mom's parents are from a little town north of Venice called Vittorio Veneto. Do you know it?"

"Had supper there last Sunday night." And his grin revealed a sexy dimple on the right side of his mouth.

"Honestly?"

"Honestly."

"Is that a place people go for a special dinner?"

"Probably not. But there's an excellent *trattoria* specializing in venison. A friend and I usually stop on our way back from ski-patrol duty."

"At Cortina d'Ampezzo?" Giulia asked.

"Yeah. You know it?"

"Mm-hmm. My twin brothers and I often went there while visiting our grandparents."

"In what part of the States did you live? And by the way, as an English teacher, I hope you noticed I didn't end that sentence with a preposition."

"I did notice."

And he noticed her eyes brighten with an impish smile.

"I grew up in Portland, Oregon but the last several years I've been in Eugene."

"Ah. Ken Kesey's old hangout."

A young airman approached and saluted. He had a message for Chuck. Chuck had to leave but asked if they might have dinner either in Vicenza or Venice. "We could share our impressions of Vittorio Veneto and—"

Automatically, Giulia started to shake her head.

"Please consider it. I'd like your take on working at a military post, on this whole operation aside from Ogle. Sorry to remind you, but I'll need your help in making sure my report about his behavior is accurate."

She said nothing. He stood ready to leave, but leaned over the table to stare straight into her unusual eyes and said, "I will ask again."

* * *

She watched him stride away, tall and assured. Power there. Influential power at this insular post no doubt. I'd be better off to avoid involvement with this man—any man. If I didn't live up to his standards, he could send me packing even if he can't get rid of that idiot Oliver. She scraped the last of the creamy foam lying in the bottom of her cup and mused. Would Marlowe, the American woman also new to the program, know about this Chuck Novak?

Darn. Only two weeks and already life feels complicated. And of course, the complication would have to be a man with shoulders a mile wide, blue-black hair and eyes the color of the ice caves on Mount Rainier. And that mouth. Shew! His dark mustache defined the most voluptuous lips on a man she'd ever seen. With that masculine face all sharp angles and prominent Roman nose, those generous lips were flagrantly sexy. *I've worked too hard to get here and need to stay focused.* But her thoughts bounced right back to Major General Chuck Novak. They say that clothes make the man, but that crisp dark-blue uniform with the ice-blue shirt, the color of his eyes, didn't do this man justice. He'd be impressive in *or* out of that uniform. *Oh Lord. I'm in trouble now.*

* * *

A natural beauty, Chuck thought as he left the coffee bar. *No perfect makeup, no goopy eye stuff. Doesn't need it with those bewitching eyes. God I hope she's not as young as she looks. Can't be, there's too much presence about her, and maybe a past hurt hidden away? Lord, those eyes.* An elemental swelling in his body went beyond basic lust. He imagined carrying her to his hidden cave to fend off the rest of the tribe. That image amused him, but he *could* see his hands running over her smooth, olive skin.

He nodded blindly to people on the way to his office. He wondered whether Giulia wanted to stay in Italy like Marlowe did? *I'm overdue on inviting Marlowe and Marc to dinner. Maybe Giulia would accept if it was a foursome.*

CHAPTER TWO

Giulia had been tempted to not tell her landlords, Luciana and Gino Cavallo, about her position at the base. It would have been easy because Luciana had assumed from the first that Giulia had grown up in the Veneto. But no, she didn't want to begin her new life with lies.

"Signora, my accent is from my parents. They both grew up nearby."

Luciana beamed. She lifted her hands up, palms out, and brought them into a half-prayer position.

"My Italian professors at the university wanted me to get rid of my Veneto accent, but I refused."

Luciana's eyes opened wide and her mouth dropped. She turned to Gino as if to say what kind of woman is this who disagreed with professors?

"Don't look so shocked, Signora," Giulia said on a half laugh. "After I told them I planned to live here for the rest of my life, they understood but made me agree to use standard Italian when I worked with their students."

"Do you teach Italian?" Gino asked.

"No. English literature. But I hope to tutor American students who want to learn Italian while they're here."

Both Signora and Signor Cavallo smiled their approval.

After only a couple of weeks, Giulia decided she needed more room to work at home and told them she'd have to find another space.

"*Aspetta,* wait, signorina," Gino said. "I might have a perfect place for you, come with me." He showed Giulia an apartment in the rear of the large building. Several apartments were back there. On the internet, their establishment had been listed as a pensione, but that was only the front of their property. She was thrilled to see the apartment included a second bedroom large enough to set up a study with a corner niche for a fold-away futon. Maybe her best friend, Nancy, would visit.

The unit had the standard living/dining area, kitchen and bath and also a small balcony overlooking a quiet street. She liked the idea of having a separate outside entrance. Gino led Giulia to the balcony and they looked down a flight of steps.

"The number seven bus *per il centro*, to the center of town, leaves only a half block behind your steps." He pointed to a post with a bus-information sign. "And returning, it stops just there across the street."

"Signor Cavallo, put me down for this apartment! I'll wait until it's free."

Back in her room with it's tiny fridge and hotplate, she decided to try to catch Nancy Metz, her financial advisor in Eugene. But first, Giulia prepared a cup of coffee. A big part of talking to Nancy involved coffee. Like some love affairs, theirs had been "love at first sight," and in a short time, their relationship had developed from strictly business to being confidants and close friends.

"Hey girl," Nancy said, "it's about time. I wondered if you'd fallen into a canal never to be seen again."

"I know. I know. I wanted to call sooner but it's been crazy since I arrived, and because of the time difference, whenever I had a chance, it was the middle of the night for you. Have you had your morning coffee?"

"In my hand as we speak," Nancy said.

Giulia could hear the smile in Nancy's voice. "Good. Me too. Can you spare a few minutes? If not, let's plan a time when we can connect. With the nine hours difference, it's tricky."

"It's a perfect time. I'm not going in today. They're painting all the offices on my floor, and I'm free to hang on the phone like a lady of leisure. Remind me, though, what time is it there?"

"It's about four in the afternoon," Giulia said. "Oops, I mean sixteen hundred hours and that means it's oh seven hundred for you, right?"

"Right," Nancy snorted under her breath.

Nancy had pulled herself out of poverty by joining the army, which made college possible. She liked to use military time whenever they made plans and had often teased Giulia about her civilian status.

"Okay, give me all the news."

Giulia gave Nancy her impressions of the military base and her students. Told about her living quarters in Vicenza and ended her summary with how she had met Chuck.

"Ran smack into his arms after kicking another guy in the balls. Way to go, Squirt."

Nancy stood five nine in her bare feet and liked to wear high heels. Not long after they met, she'd begun to call Giulia "Squirt." They were opposites and had enjoyed their differences from the start. Ash blond with natural corkscrew curls, Nancy's hairdresser had highlighted the top layer. The result was a striking Valkyrie with brassy, blond corkscrews bouncing with each stride she took. With those blond curls and her golden-brown eyes instead of the expected Teutonic blue, people noticed her. Giulia admired Nancy and felt lucky to have found a true friend.

When Aunt Loretta's attorney announced she'd left a small bequest, Giulia had set out to find financial advice. Not only was Nancy stunning, she was smart, street savvy and had rescued Giulia from a money-grubbing "advisor." Her twin brothers hadn't done as well with their bequests.

"So," Nancy said, "you had coffee with him, and?"

"And nothing. You know I'm not looking for a man."

"If not now, when, for God's sake? You've lived like a nun long enough."

"What about you? How's your love life?"

"Roughly the same as yours, now that I dumped Gabe." Her big sigh conveyed to Giulia more than her brave words did. "No, that's not really fair. It was… a mutual thing."

"Aw, Nance, I'm sorry. The usual problem?"

"He wasn't as obvious, but yeah, I think so."

"Surely there's a guy who doesn't fade when he realizes you don't need his protection. Or was it having your own business?"

"Maybe both."

"Maybe next time you could be up-front right away about your sole proprietorship, huh?"

"And maybe there won't be a next time."

"Don't say that. You love sex too much."

"I could try casual one-nighters?"

"No, you couldn't! You *know* you want more than that out of life."

They chatted another half hour and settled on connecting next time when it would be nine or ten P.M. in Venice and twelve or one P.M. in Eugene.

* * *

Chuck saw Marlowe walk across the base and called out to her.

"Hi, Chuck. How are you?" She waited for him to catch up.

She seemed like a small doll to him. More so to Marc, her husband, who stood six four to her five four, if she was that. The first time Chuck and Marlowe met was in mid-December at a lunch interview in Venice. She'd worn a conservative black suit with white blouse and sensible pumps, and Chuck had explained the position for which she would interview the next day. Marc had told Chuck earlier, "Find anything to keep her here so she won't go back to the States where I might lose her."

Attractive and sharp, Marlowe homed in on pertinent questions about teaching business law to undergraduate military personnel. And she had a quirky sense of humor. Even though Chuck could josh in Italian, no matter how hard he'd tried with the Italian women he'd dated, not one had an ounce of humor in her bones.

He hadn't seen Marlowe again until the New Year's Eve Gala. When she and Marc had walked toward him that night, Marlowe had looked and acted like a red-hot sex kitten, dressed in a short shimmery dress. With "fuck-me" stilettos and tousled dark hair, she looked to him as if she'd come straight from Marc's bed. Chuck had felt envious the rest of the evening. Ever since New Year's, Chuck had longed for someone like Marlowe. Someone real, open and with a sense of humor.

Marlowe got the job and she and Marc married before classes started in March. It was obvious to the most casual observer they were living in bliss. More and more Chuck longed for a relationship like theirs. How weird was that? After all his years of believing he never wanted to commit again, and with only one "sort-of" coffee date with Giulia, he was leaning in the other direction.

"Do you have time for a coffee?" Chuck asked Marlowe, who was now conservatively garbed in a white turtleneck top, black slacks and jacket to match. He mused about how women could easily change their appearance. Maybe persona as well.

"Sounds good," she said, "but first I need to give a report to Oliver Ogle. Care to come along while I enter his den?"

"Delighted to stand guard for you."

Good. He knows about Ogle. After her first encounter with him, she'd told Marc about the obnoxious bastard who first stared at her feet, then let his eyes move slowly upward lingering too long on her crotch and then again on her breasts. She wasn't afraid of him, but he did his slimy scan every damn time she met him! The most basic psychology course taught that such behavior could escalate, and she was glad to have Chuck with her.

Marlowe knocked on Oliver's door. He opened it and invited her in with open arms.

"Here's the report you requested, Mr. Ogle," she said holding it out. "Let me know if you need anything else."

"Marlowe, baby, I always need more from—" he stopped when

he noticed Chuck standing opposite the door. His legs were planted firmly apart with clenched fists at his sides.

Oliver coughed, grabbed the report and slammed the door in her face.

She turned to Chuck and gave him a little salute. "Thanks, Sir."

"At your service anytime."

"But it's not that funny," she said. "Within one week of being here, I heard of a pact among other women instructors. When it's necessary to have a confidential meeting with Oliver, a woman brings a girlfriend to wait outside to listen for trouble."

"Hey, I know he's a menace for the women employed by Maryland University."

She nodded but continued to walk with her head down. "About that coffee," he said following her. She stopped and turned back. He almost ran into her and started to put his hands on her shoulders but thought he might be accused of harassment himself.

"Sorry, Chuck. I shouldn't take it out on you." She laid her hands on his forearms, "But Oliver's brand of covert sexual harassment is worse here than in other work places because women are in the extreme minority. And military types don't always see his behavior as a problem. I could ask Marc to catch him in a dark alley, but other women don't always have a Marc as backup."

"Marlowe, some of us 'military types' do want to get rid of him. Come on, let's get that coffee and talk more about it."

They went to the same coffee bar where he'd taken Giulia, but he wasn't sure Giulia would want him to tell Marlowe—or anyone—what had happened in Ogle's office. He needed to clarify that with her and obtain her permission to put her name in his report. Without it, the report would be meaningless.

"French Press sounds great to me," Marlowe said in response to his spiel about the glories of the new shop. They grabbed a table to wait for their coffees.

"Maybe we can figure out how to derail Ogle," Chuck said and looked squarely into her eyes. "First off, it will be an uphill battle.

Technically, he doesn't work for the military, so we have channels on top of channels."

"I see." She slumped against her chair. "Guess bureaucracy's in *his* favor. But maybe more intimidation like what you offered today could be a start. That seemed effective. I just hope he won't mess with my personnel file because I brought you with me."

"Surely he's not that stupid. What if we'd set up a reliable system to pull a man from another duty whenever a woman needs a guard to visit Ogle. Kind of like the night-time escort services Marc and I were involved in on Pepperdine's campus."

"Sounds interesting," Marlowe said. "But, you know… there could be a problem with that. A big one."

"Oh? What?"

An Oliver intimidator could also be an intimidator to the very woman who requested him."

Chuck ran his hand through his thick black hair and said, "God. I keep forgetting about the world you women live in day in and day out. And not only on our post." He placed both palms on the table and leaned toward her, "We need to remove him don't we?"

"As in *The Godfather?*"

"Maybe that's the only way," he said in a soft, gravelly voice trying to imitate Marlon Brando. She was laughing as the waiter brought their coffees.

Marlowe sipped the brew with her head down wondering if it would be a betrayal of her discussion with other women if she told Chuck of their hopes to entrap Oliver?"

"Marlowe?" he said. "What's the verdict?"

"The verdict?"

"The coffee?"

"Oh. You're absolutely right. French Press is the way to go. It lets you know you're drinking coffee. I can almost chew it."

"You were thinking of something else, though, weren't you?"

She leaned back and sipped more coffee. "I can see why Marc likes you."

"Really?"

"Yes. You aren't totally M and M."

"Okay, I'll bite. What's 'M and M?'"

"A term I picked up since I've been here. Military Macho."

He leaned back and laughed with gusto. She loved it when she could elicit a full belly laugh like that. His laugh wasn't as engaging as her Marc's mellow baritone rumble. Chuck's was a basso profundo. But maybe she was biased.

"Many women have been talking about Oliver. In fact, he seems to be the main topic whenever a group gathers," she said.

"And?"

"I've heard a lot of talk about catching him in flagrant sexual harassment, but so far, no one's volunteered as bait."

"I can understand that after the disgraceful stuff that went on at my alma mater. The honorable Air Force academy in Colorado Springs," he said. And a dark frown creased his ruggedly handsome face when he said honorable.

He noticed her glance at her watch. "You need to leave. But Marlowe, I did have another purpose for this coffee, other than Mr. Ogre Ogle." He smiled and a softening dimple formed. "I have a rather delicate question to ask you."

It was her turn to ask, "And?"

"The other day, I met a woman newly arrived who started teaching English Lit about the same time you started teaching law and... I worry she's too young for me. I wonder if you could help me out?"

"Since there aren't that many new women teachers of English on the post, I'm guessing you mean Giulia uh..."

"Cavinato," Chuck said.

"Yes, that's right. Chuck? What would be too young for you?"

"She doesn't act too young. I've only talked with her a short time, but she's quick and well educated and charming and beautiful and—" He stopped and Marlowe was blown away when she saw a blush creep across the big guy's face. She'd always seen Chuck as cool and controlled.

"How old are *you*? Is that too delicate?" she asked.

"Not at all. I'm thirty-eight... going on forty." He seemed almost shy.

"I do know Giulia. We clicked the first day. Don't know her age but considering what she told me about working before entering college and also working part-time right on through grad school, I'd guess she's not too young. But you could twist Oliver's arm and check her file, couldn't you?"

"Maybe. But I don't want to go behind her back." *Hell, with my Spec-Ops skills, I could be in and out of Ogle's office in a heartbeat.*

"But you'll come to *me* behind her back, huh?" Marlowe said getting a kick out of putting this self-assured guy on the spot. He even squirmed in his chair. She couldn't hold out any longer. "Oh Chuck, don't take it that way. All's fair in love and war."

"Thanks, Marlowe. I owe you one. But—"

"Don't worry, I can be discreet. I feel sure Giulia and I are going to be good friends for a long time. We have a lot in common. Like me, she wants to live in Venice the rest of her life."

Chuck rolled his broad shoulders, relaxed and sat back in his chair.

"I don't intend to reveal your thoughts and feelings," Marlowe said, " but I won't be a go-between either." She stood up. "Need to go, but thanks for the coffee and the talk."

He stood too. And Marlowe whispered, "I do want to work with you regarding Ollie the Ogre." He leaned down to hear her words amidst the rustle and chatter in the coffee bar. He nodded and she hurried out.

Chuck sat back down and finished his coffee with a silly grin on his face. *Giulia does want to stay!*

CHAPTER THREE

On the train to her grandparents' home, Giulia felt a shiver of excitement to see again the lush foothills of the Dolomite Mountains. They reminded her of the fir and pine forests leading to Mount Hood east of Portland. Leaving Vicenza hadn't tugged at her the way leaving the magic of Venice always did, but Vicenza did evoke elegance with its pale stucco glow of Palladian-style buildings. At Treviso, she changed trains and bought an espresso. Her grandmother would brew a fresh pot as soon Giulia walked in the door, but bars at train stations in Italy served excellent espresso, too. A flutter in her stomach reminded her she was beginning a new life—one she'd dreamt about since childhood.

This trip marked a huge change for her. Finally she had a way to support herself in Venice. She'd never be able to own a place, but in all other ways, she already owned the city. Within a year, she hoped to move into a nice rental. With a modest stipend to make this trip to Italy, she hadn't needed to shepherd a group of tourists to foot the bill. Before settling in Vicenza, she'd allowed herself four precious days to wander in Venice. Soon the city would be her home! Knowing this, cast a whole different perspective on how she saw its beauty *and* its flaws.

Going to Nonna and Nonno Tony's felt more like coming home than when she visited her parents in Portland. These precious two were the only grandparents she'd ever known—her dad's parents had died in an auto accident before she was born. Soon she'd be in their sturdy wooden house surrounded by trees where only good memories lived. It was mid-afternoon when Giulia caught the city bus that carried her within two blocks of their home.

And there stood Nonna with open arms at the top of the front steps. With her, Giulia felt completely accepted and unconditionally loved. And in Nonno Tony's eyes, she'd known the world was her oyster before she knew what an oyster was. The coffee pot was ready, and in no time, she was in the kitchen with homemade almond biscotti on the table.

"Nonna, it's wonderful to be in your arms again. *And*," Giulia said, "no one makes biscotti like you!"

"*Allora*, so, my little Giulietta, is it me or my biscotti?" They laughed and hugged again. She felt at ease with Nonna, her beautiful grandmother. Only a few silver strands wound through Nonna's luxurious dark-brown hair cut in a short, soft bob. Unusual for an Italian woman in her seventies—both the color and the style. Many turned grey in their fifties, and then as if an internal clock had struck, they became old. Most pulled their hair—grey or dyed—into a knot at the back of their head, lowered their hemlines and wore dowdy shoes. It seemed to Giulia they gave up on any life outside their immediate family.

But Nonna had a lively interest in happenings everywhere. Her soft brown eyes didn't miss a thing. She knew about world affairs as well as the Italian politicians' scandals, and of course, the local gossip. Nonna had been a beauty in her day. According to Giulia's mother, she could have had any man in Vittorio Veneto or in all of the Treviso Province, but she chose bad boy, Antonio Tuon. Giulia knew all about bad boys. Her own attraction to hottie-bad-boy Ricky Torres, ended up with an abortion at twenty-four. Was it time to tell Nonna? Anyone? Lord, she'd never told Ricky. Sometimes she felt a twinge of guilt about that, but it would never have worked—definitely not for the child. Already Ricky had been unfaithful while she worked and studied. At least Nonna's bad boy had stayed the course with her.

"Tell me, Nonna, what's new? It's been a long two years. My professors held my nose to the grindstone, and I've missed you. Any new weaving projects?"

"I'll show you," Nonna said with a lilt in her voice and led

Giulia into the large room near the kitchen. Ostensibly a guest bedroom with a double bed and dresser, but, in truth, a weaving room. Her loom and colorful supplies were scattered on every surface. Nonna displayed several wool shawls to Giulia and let her run her hands over fifteen wool scarves. Her new designs were intricate, abstract patterns made with vivid-colored yarns.

"These scarves are special, Nonna. I want to buy this one. The patterns of blue and old gold are smashing!"

"It's yours." Nonna draped it around Giulia's neck. "At least it matches one of your eyes—and one of your nonno's, too," she said smiling.

Giulia wondered if Nonna knew what Nonno Tony did for a living. Surely she did. She worried Nonna had been in denial about a lot of things. Over the last few years, Giulia had become attuned to men who manipulated women and feared Nonno Tony might be one of those. Giulia's two disastrous love affairs had taught her all she ever wanted to know about men who used women. Had Nonna been putting up with an unfaithful husband throughout her married life? Yet, when Giulia was around the two of them, they seemed to adore each other.

He did have that charismatic charm of men who believe in themselves. She feared Nonna wasn't the only woman drawn to his magnetism. Choices, she thought. We all make them.

"Come back to the kitchen, I need to add a few more herbs to your favorite rabbit stew."

"Oooh, Nonna. I thought I smelled that heavenly combination. I want your recipe. Please? Onions and leeks, garlic, of course, and lots of rosemary, but what else? Yum. Their essence floats all around us. Thank you for remembering."

Giulia hoped Nonno Tony would be late coming home from wherever and whatever he was up to these days. Could he be a petty crook of some kind? As far as she could determine, his income had always been sporadic. She knew he was involved with her twin brothers' import business in Portland. The last time she'd been in their warehouse, some of the items from Nonno seemed different from the usual costume pieces he shipped. She had a hinky feeling about that. Did the boys suspect anything? Were they involved? They seemed feckless to her, but maybe that was merely an older sister judging younger brothers.

As Nonna and Giulia sat down to eat, Nonno Tony blew in carrying a huge bouquet of white lilies, Nonna's favorite. Before she could find a vase, he crushed her and the flowers into his arms for a big kiss. Next he turned to make an equal fuss over Giulia. What a handsome man, she thought, as he filled the entry way of the side door with his broad shoulders and bursting energy. At seventy-seven, with thick white hair, bronzed skin and one brilliant blue eye and one dark brown one—he still radiated sex appeal. He mentioned having completed a good business deal and entertained both women all evening with one witty tale after another.

He asked Giulia to carry a small packet to a jeweler in Vicenza for him. Only a few rough gems, he explained, along with a few thin rolls of white gold.

"More and more jewelers are using white gold to simulate platinum. They can't get enough of the stuff for making their inexpensive items," he said.

"Do they charge more hoping to fool their customers?" Giulia asked.

"Some do, some don't. Not our problem *la mia bambolina*, my little doll."

"Why me, Nonno?" She felt wary about agreeing to his scheme. To her, the request had "scheme" or "scam" all over it. Would she be carrying stolen goods?

"Why not?" he said. "You are family, little one," and his brow creased into a small frown. He leaned toward her lifting his hands in supplication "And family helps each other, right?" His voice took on a pleading sound. Surely she'd want to help out her old nonno. Sure, he could ship them, but that would involve forms and extra insurance expenses. He winked, reminding her of all their good times when he took her to country fairs.

"Now Tony. If she doesn't want to—"

He plowed on. "Who helped you win prizes at those stalls full of toys and candies?"

Not phased by his histrionics, Giulia said, "I'll think about it. We'll talk in the morning." That seemed to satisfy him. But later, Giulia worried about his request as she lay in her bed in the small attic room where she always slept. She adored being up there in "her" room nestled close to the wood shingles and metal gutters where she could hear even the lightest rain falling. And before long, she drifted off to its soft tap, tap.

Shortly before dawn, Giulia came awake with a start. The rain had stopped. Maybe it was only birds clearing their throats, but there was something else. She held her breath, then heard a creak from one of the steps leading to her room. She turned on the bedside light and grabbed her sweater to cover her thin over-sized Tee-shirt moments before the door eased open.

"You're up early, Nonno Tony," she said.

"You, too, *la mia coccolina,* my little cuddly one. Been waiting for me?"

"What are you up to?"

"Oh, *coccolina,* how can you talk to your old nonno like that?"

She said nothing but sat there with her arms folded over her breasts.

"*Allora,*" he said sitting down beside her on the bed.

Giulia fought not to flinch because she was determined to show no weakness with this man who roused conflicting emotions within her. She loved him at a deep level but almost distrusted him.

"I must go on a little business trip and can't see you off Sunday, but I brought this small packet that you agreed to carry back with you."

"Agreed? When did I agree? I told you I'd think about it."

"And have you?" He asked, showing her his most devastating smile that had no doubt suckered in both men and women since he was a babe in arms.

"I love you, Nonno Tony. But I do not want to carry your contraband."

"Contraband!" He laughed aloud, but quickly softened the sound, probably not wanting to wake Nonna. "No, no. No contraband. Must I beg you to deliver a few raw stones? They won't burden you." And he reached out to her.

She started to jerk away but batted playfully at his hands instead.

He sat back amazed that a woman—any woman—would spurn his touch.

She took his hands in hers. "Nonno. I'll do this for you. But I have a few conditions. First—"

"Ah *piccolina*, little one, the two of us are alike. Not only do we have the same strange, captivating eyes, we both like to be in control. *Senta*, listen. If you do decide to stay on in Venice—"

"That's decided. I *will* live in Venice," she interrupted.

"Good. When you do, we could become terrific business partners."

She ignored that, "I'll do this for you, this one time, but," and she held up one finger when she saw him ready to interrupt. "Do not tell the contact I'm your granddaughter. And do not describe my curly hair or that my eyes are like yours because I'll be wearing a straight-hair wig and a brown contact lens."

He sat back with a wide grin on his face and said, "Si, si, we *are* alike. We think ahead!" And with that he placed a small packet on her dresser. As he reached the door, he turned and said, "I'm not sending white gold after all, but one of those gems is yours, for your trouble. You choose which one."

"Aspetta!"

He stopped.

"You must count out the diamonds and put in a note telling how many."

He brought the packet to her bedside. Pulling on a pair of soft, white gloves, he counted nineteen gems, each grouping was wrapped in a small square of jeweler's tissue paper. She didn't know how to eyeball their actual size, but three large ones were in red paper. Ten medium-sized were in green, and in the blue paper, lay six tiny gems. Each group went into its own small plastic bag made of tougher plastic than sandwich baggies. All the bags went into a soft-sided envelope that he laid back on her dresser. He turned and said, "*Va bene,* okay?"

"Not yet. Add a note verifying sizes and types with your signature."

"That's my girl." He made more notes.

"And I will not take a gem. I'm doing this for you. This one time," and she held up her finger again.

He blew her a kiss and was gone.

* * *

Saturday, Nonna packed a lunch and she and Giulia went hiking in the lush foothills near town. She admired her grandmother, who was so fit that Giulia struggled at times to keep up. As they sat on flat rocks overlooking a lake of brilliant green, she thought of camping with Jason Stamos beside Crescent Lake in the Olympic National Park. It, too, had gleamed like an emerald. In spite of the sharp stab she still felt about his dishonesty, he *had* left her with a few jewel-like memories.

Nonna turned to see a look of distress on Giulia's face. "My angel, what's bothering you? Can you tell me?"

Giulia nodded. She did need to tell someone, and who best but Nonna? First, she told her about Ricky and the abortion.

Nonna said nothing but put her arms around Giulia, holding her in a long, comforting embrace. "That's a long time ago, *mia cara,* my dear."

"It is. But I was also thinking of another situation," she sighed, "with another man."

Nonna, opened the basket and handed Giulia a bottle of water. "Take your time, we have all day."

Giulia began. "Jason had strong, masculine features from his

Greek heritage. He was gorgeous, Nonna," and Giulia turned to her. "Taller than other Greek Americans I'd known. We met during my first year of grad school. I thought he was the one until he told me he was married."

Nonna gasped but made no comment.

"In name only, he'd said. They were legally separated. His estranged wife was living in Chicago with another man."

"And?"

"I was crushed that he hadn't told me. I left."

"Of course you were," she said putting her hand on Giulia's shoulder.

"He persisted. Assured me his divorce would happen." Giulia inhaled deeply. Shaking her head slowly, she said, "I went back." She stared at the emerald lake below.

"Then?"

"His 'wife in name only' appeared in Eugene begging him to support her and their coming child. At first he doubted it was his. Later, though, he confessed they had slept together when he visited Chicago. And the man she was living with was not a lover, but a gay friend!"

Giulia felt uncomfortable. She'd never discussed these things with Nonna. Abortion. Living with a married man. Gay friends. Shew! But Nonna merely nodded and waited for the rest of the story. "The gay friend had urged her to go back to Jason and make it work. Jason always wanted children and, well, he chose to try again."

Nonna took her into her arms and rocked back and forth. Giulia had never cried about this. A few tears broke through. Then it was as if a dam had broken. After a time, Giulia stopped sobbing and looked at Nonna, "The worst part," she said gulping air, "I'm more angry with myself than him."

"Of course," Nonna said.

"Once again I'd chosen the wrong man and once again he'd let me down."

"But it's long over. And Giulia, not all men will let you down."

She stood up. "Let's walk." She took Giulia's hand and they moved across the meadow. After a while, Nonna said, "Remember, you're starting a new life now."

Later as they ate, Giulia discovered more about Nonna's full life with her weaving enterprise. Her brown eyes glowed as she told how her weaving group had attracted interest beyond their own small area. As they walked back, Giulia said, "Nonna, I've never told anyone about—"

"*Non preoccuparti*, don't worry. No one—not even Tony—will hear of it."

"Thank you, Nonna, but I'm glad you know." And she felt lighter than she'd felt in a long, long time.

Giulia didn't see Nonno Tony again on that visit. As to what went on in their marriage, she could only speculate. After the joy on Nonna's face when he'd swept in with those flowers, and his obvious adoration for his wife across their table, Giulia had to admit she knew nothing about relationships.

CHAPTER FOUR

Monday. Giulia set out at five P.M. for Hotel De La Ville to deliver Nonno Tony's gems. She allowed plenty of time to make her appointment at six even though she knew exactly where to go. Her first week in Vicenza before classes began, she'd felt lonely and restless and took a long walk into town. Bar La Ville had looked warm and elegant on that chilly February evening. Wanting to feel as inconspicuous as possible, she'd worn her dark-brown contact lens. She could almost feel normal. She'd also worn a tawny page-boy wig. She enjoyed pretending to have smooth hair instead of curls that fought any attempt at style. Some clothes hadn't yet arrived, and she'd worn a plain pink sweater, casual black wool slacks and jacket to match.

Tonight, though, she wore the most elegant outfit she owned, a rich dark chocolate-colored velveteen pant suit with a short jacket. Her pale rose silk blouse seemed to make her skin glow. Small pearl-drop earrings and a ring with a matching pearl mounted in a gold setting were her only jewelry. The earrings had been given to her by her grandparents for graduation to match the ring that Nonna had given her earlier. It had been Nonna's favorite until her arthritic knuckles made it impossible to wear. Instead of re-sizing for herself, she wanted Giulia to enjoy it.

Giulia felt good about herself and confidently walked to the hotel desk to announce she had an appointment with a Signor Botteri. Immediately, a large, burly male dressed in a black suit with a crisp, white shirt and black tie appeared. His hair, as black as his suit, was slicked into an old-fashioned pompadour. And tight lips were marked by a grim mustache. He bowed silently, led her to the elevator and punched the number seven. The hotel was known as the tallest in the city, where, as in most cities except Milan, skyscrapers weren't allowed. She figured they were rising to the top floor. When it stopped, the elevator opened directly into a foyer. The big man knocked on massive, double doors and another attendant led her to Signor Botteri.

Botteri, a man of sixty or so, was also in black, but his suit looked silky and custom made. Certainly, his blinding-white shirt was hand sewn. *His pale-blue silk tie probably cost as much as my entire outfit.* For a second, she thought he looked familiar. He invited her to sit opposite him in a wingback chair beside a small fireplace. The warmth felt good.

"*Buona Sera,* Signor Botteri," she said. "As you know I've brought a packet to you from Signor Tuon. I have not opened it, even though he offered me one of the gems as payment for this delivery."

As he took the packet from her, she noticed his beautiful hands. The skin was smooth and his manicured fingernails were buffed to a high shine. He leaned in, and the way he stared into her eyes with a puzzled look told her at once that Nonno Tony hadn't kept his promise. In fury, she dug her own nails into her palms but forced a smile and pretended to not notice Botteri's stare.

She cringed inside at Botteri's nod and patronizing smile. Then it came to her! That simpering smile. She wanted to slap it off his face because he'd been the man who sent her a drink in the hotel bar that first evening in town. Thank God she'd refused it. She would not let him know she recognized him and get the hell away as soon as possible.

"*Buona Sera,* Signorina. I didn't catch your name."

"*Io sono* Mirella Rizzatti." It was her grandmother's maiden name on her father's side, but Mirella was also Giulia's middle name.

"May I offer you a glass of Pinot Grigio this evening, Mirella?"

She thought he emphasized "this" trying to catch her, but she didn't bite.

"No thank you, but I *would* like a receipt before I leave."

"Of course." He got up and went to a sleek, mahogany desk set near a window that overlooked the piazza seven stories below.

"Please spell your name, Signorina."

She did. Then he snapped his fingers and the young man who had led her into the suite appeared. "Signore?" he said, waiting at attention.

"Franco, please make a copy of these two documents—while we wait."

He turned toward her. "How long have you been in fair Vicenza?"

Giulia wondered if Signor Botteri knew he was paraphrasing the phrase "in fair Verona" from Shakespeare's prologue to *Romeo and Juliet*, but she merely replied, "Long enough to enjoy its many architectural wonders."

"Are you sure you need to leave this soon?" he asked. Was he pleading?

"*Mi dispiace, signore,* I'm sorry, sir, but I have another engagement."

When Franco returned, she stood. Botteri took the documents, stapled the copies together and sauntered around his desk to hand them to her.

"Signorina Rizzatti, thank you for being so kind to deliver these items. Franco will show you out. Maybe we'll meet again."

She smiled but said nothing. Franco walked her to the elevator where the burly one waited to accompany her to the lobby.

Giulia strode through the lobby toward the outer door, but a tall, elegant woman—a Mediterranean beauty with smooth olive skin, large dark eyes and swept-back hair—touched her arm lightly. "Signorina?"

She asked Giulia to join her for a cup of tea. Giulia was apprehensive and almost refused. She wanted away from this place where Botteri and his minions held court, but curiosity got the best of her. She followed the woman, who might be forty—might be younger. What could happen over a cup of tea in an up-scale hotel? The sleek woman called herself Laura.

They entered a quiet tea room just off the lobby. It had six, empty mahogany tables that must have been hand polished through the centuries. In less than five minutes, Giulia understood that Laura represented an escort service in Vicenza and wanted to draw Giulia into her fold. *That fits—ancient tables for a discussion of an ancient profession.*

"You already have a client," Laura said smiling.

"What are you talking about?" Giulia asked.

"A distinguished gentleman noticed you awhile back and wants to be your exclusive client."

"I'd never want such an arrangement!" Giulia said, standing up and spilling her half-full teacup onto the table.

Within seconds, the waiter appeared with towels to clear away the mess. He must have been hovering behind a decorative screen in the back of the room. Laura put a shaky hand on Giulia's arm, urging her to sit down again as the slim waiter returned immediately with more tea and a fresh cup.

The woman deftly adjusted her sales pitch, saying that most women preferred to not be tied to one client. That idea reminded Giulia of her trouble in Eugene with a client who had wanted her exclusively. He'd pressed for more than the "arm candy" he'd signed on for. She'd refused, but after that encounter, the man had urged the company to let him set her up in an apartment in an exclusive area. Giulia had been scared out of her wits. It would have been a plush prison. She might not be able to finish school! The manager of the service seemed to think it would be a plum assignment and expected Giulia to go for it. Instead, she resigned. Later she'd found another service operating in a suburb of Eugene, but out there, she recognized two married professors. She'd quit that, too.

Giulia only half listened to Laura's continued sales pitch, but the more she heard her describe the lifestyle—a lifestyle she had once experimented with—the more sordid it sounded. Saying nothing, Giulia rose to leave—no upsetting of tea this time.

* * *

She had walked to the hotel to work off anxious feelings about meeting Botteri. After being around those people, she felt dirty and looked forward to a long, hot shower. Surely she'd be able to spot the bus stop she'd noticed on the way to the hotel. She guessed it was about five or six blocks away. In late March at seven P.M., the sun had set and the streets were quiet. Even before she heard the heavy footsteps, her stomach had begun to quiver, sensing something was off. She searched for a shop window to pretend to look at merchandise as she'd seen people do when followed in movies.

But most Italian shopkeepers cover their closed shops with metal rolldown shutters and lock them at the bottom to a fixture embedded into the sidewalk. Finally, a few feet ahead, a lighted window was uncovered. The shop displayed heat pads, support hose and yet one more way to rid oneself of cellulite. Giulia had never seen so many ads about the problem, but she stopped and pretended to read the details. A big hulk passed by. She couldn't see his face, but his size and the way he moved told her he was the burly one with the pompadour. She walked on, passing him while he studied a poster for a coming event. Was he toying with her? After another block, he dropped back. Maybe he remembered a rule in the Thug Manual about not following closely.

She heard a rumbling vehicle and hoped to God it was her bus. She didn't look back but power walked as fast as she could without running. When the bus pulled to the curb, she jumped aboard. If he should reach the bus in time, she decided she wouldn't get off at her building. She'd have to get off at another place and find a taxi back.

Giulia took a seat quickly but not before she saw through the rear window that the man had begun to run. He didn't make it!

Her mind told her he couldn't possibly get to her stop in time to see her go up the back stairs, but as soon as she got off, she dashed to the front of the pensione. So far, no one from the base knew she didn't live in the pensione part of the building. Her sweet landlords understood why she'd wanted to keep it that way in case a young man from the base should decide to follow her home. It was a safe setup. How ironic that she arranged it this way to protect her from an eager, young serviceman when instead it would keep her safe from a huge hired thug.

After Giulia left that tea party, Laura had caught up with her and thrust an "application" into her hand. *Application? Ha.* Giulia knew it would be construed as a contract, and she almost threw it to the lobby floor and walked on it. But the desperate look on Laura's face made her sympathize with another working woman and she jammed it into her purse instead.

Safe inside her cozy apartment with the doors locked and curtains drawn, she took a good look at the "application." No matter how legalistic the words sounded, they were still about sex for sale. Memories of stress and fear came back, reminding her she had once signed similar documents. Even though hers hadn't been for sex per se, the world saw arm candy differently. With a grim smile, Giulia carried Laura's contract to the kitchen sink, struck a match and torched the hateful thing.

After a long, hot shower, she called her grandfather.

"Nonno Tony?"

"Si, si, coccolona. Are you all right?"

"Yes, of course. I want you to know I made your delivery this evening. And we need to talk. Will you be home next weekend?"

"You sound upset. Can you tell me now?"

"It's complicated."

"I have to be gone all next weekend, but I can be in Vicenza a week from tonight, Monday, the thirty-first. Is that good for you?"

"Va bene," she said.

"Good, I'll call you next Monday morning. *Abbi cura di te,* take care of yourself."

"Give Nonna a hug for me." And she hung up.

She hadn't told *him* "to take care," and knew he would have noticed, but she was disgusted that he'd ignored her. That he'd told Botteri she was his granddaughter and had odd eyes. What had Botteri thought of that? Nonno Tony's chances to break into the famous jewelry business of Vicenza were probably not good. Not good at all.

CHAPTER FIVE

"*Pronto*, hello."

"Giulia? This is Marlowe. Are you busy on this beautiful Saturday morning?"

"Ciao, Marlowe. I'm on the train heading to Venice."

"Perfect! Would you join Marc and me for an early supper? Could you stay over that long?"

"I could. Sounds lovely. I've been wanting to meet your miracle of manhood."

"Jeez. Do I brag about him that much?"

"Not really, but whenever you mention him, your eyes flicker like the Northern Lights on a spring night."

"He is wonderful, but don't tell him. His ego is well and truly intact." And Giulia heard a contented chuckle in Marlowe's voice. "Do you have any specific goal for your day in Venice?"

"Thought I'd let my feet take me wherever they want to go." Giulia looked down at her comfortable sandals and was glad she'd worn something light for this gorgeous day. It felt good to be in her yellow halter sundress with its full skirt. She'd tied a pale blue sweater around her shoulders for entering chilly churches or walking through shadowy *sotoporteghi*, tunnel-like passageways carved out of buildings.

"Would you like company?" Marlowe asked. "Or is this your day to be alone in Venice?"

"I'm planning on a lifetime of being in Venice. Why don't you join me?"

"Super. Could we meet around two?"

"Name the place. I'll be there." Giulia felt excited about spending time in Venice with her new friend who seemed to love the city as much as she did.

"Have you been inside the old church of San Giobbe?" Marlowe asked.

"No. It's always been closed. You sure we can get in?"

"I'm sure. See you there, va bene?"

"Va bene."

* * *

She leaned back and looked at the marshy land as it became flatter and flatter the closer they came to Venice. Right on time, the train pulled into Venice at 11:07. When Giulia stepped down, she noticed that the palm trees growing in the open area near the tracks were still flourishing. Sniffing the Venetian air with a self-satisfied smile, she walked down the station steps to stand beside the Grand Canal and wait for Vaporetto Numero Uno. It'd be one of many lumbering water-buses that provide public transportation throughout the city and neighboring islands.

Vaporetto is a much prettier word than water-bus. But vaporettos are merely big diesel buses that happen to float on the water. At least two hundred people can crowd aboard—and do—during rush hours. Vaporettos may be powered by diesel now, but when they were introduced in the 1880s, their power source was steam, giving them the name vaporetto. Secretly, Giulia always thought of them as fat hens clucking their way up and down the Grand Canal rather than something as delicate as a "little vapor." Again she inhaled, and took in the essence of the sea. Soon she'd breathe this magical air every single day.

She rode the entire length of the backward S that shaped the Grand Canal and went to Piazza di San Marco. Today she wanted only a quick glance at the over-dressed old dowager, her private name for the church. With "her" exotic excess, she bedazzles and dominates all who enter the huge football-sized square. Only the old Venetians could pull off such an eclectic extravaganza. Five domes lift their humps to the sky. Spires and fanciful carvings cover every square inch of the upper arches of the sparkling facade. She admired again the gorgeous marble columns at the doorways, not one exactly alike. Visitors halt in their tracks the first time they see this spectacle. And when they leave, most turn back to take one long look as if they're not sure what they'd seen. Giulia remembered doing the same thing—more than once.

A golden lion holding the book of St. Mark stands front and center at the top of the building. Gold and colored Byzantine mosaics picturing scenes from Jesus's life are up there, too. What would the humble carpenter from Nazareth think about all this gold and glitter? Those sparkling bits of gold and colored glass fascinate any time of day—in any weather—but when the late afternoon sun strikes them, Saint Mark's church is a show stopper. And the horses! Those magnificent gilded horses, stolen from Byzantium centuries ago, watch the piazza from the church's balcony. Thank God the originals had finally been rescued from modern acidic air and now lift their proud heads in an upstairs room of the church.

She stood staring with the same delirious sensation she'd felt as a child on her first visit. The glorious glitter and exuberance were still working their magic. But this time, she would not be lured inside. Like Ali Baba's Cave, the golden walls and ceilings hold treasures beyond belief. Such excess and all so beautiful. She'd never pull herself away in time to walk anywhere else in the city this day, and for sure, she'd be late to meet Marlowe.

Giulia felt light hearted about her decision to postpone San Marco's. From now on, she could savor her favorites in the city at her leisure. She turned away quickly as if escaping the old lady's clutches and caught a vaporetto back up the S to the Ca' d'Oro stop.

She followed the long, narrow passageway leading from the vaporetto stop into Cannaregio, the largest *sestiere*, district, of Venice. This walkway had once been a private entrance to the most dazzling palazzo in the city. The massive wooden gate in the side wall had an eight-inch square peep slot looking directly into the water entrance. She could never resist stopping to peer through to the marble mosaic *pavimento* and the stone stairway leading to the main floor of the palazzo. This structure must have been built higher than many others along the famous waterway or maybe new owners had performed restoration miracles because the marble artwork looked almost pristine. Nowadays, water moving with the tides, swished farther into most entrances than originally planned. With the city sinking bit by bit and water rising centimeter by centimeter, most water-gate entryways were empty and useless.

She'd revisit The House of Gold another day. The reward for buying a ticket to enter Ca' d'Oro was to stand on the balcony overlooking the Grand Canal and speculate how she would have felt living in a house covered with gold, at least on the water side of the building—the side for important guests.

What kind of life did that family have? Were they content? Such speculation captured her imagination everywhere in Venice. If she could go back in time, she'd choose the sixteenth century, Tintoretto's century. His older rival, Titian, was—and is—more famous, but Tintoretto's work and life came across to her as earthy and much more exciting. Jacomo Robusti was nicknamed Tintoretto because his father had been a dyer of cloth and because Jacomo was said to be barely five feet tall. Thus, the little *tintore,* dyer. According to Melania Mazzucco's novel about his talented daughter, Marietta, Jacomo was crazy in love with his wife. Giulia liked knowing that.

She came back to the twenty-first century and noticed she was headed toward *La Chiesa di San Francesco Della Vigna*, the Church of Saint Francis of the Vineyard. In all of the city, Vigna was her refuge. Since arriving in late February, Giulia had been in a state of agitation partly because of Ogle and Botteri. But she had to admit, she also felt conflicted about how she would run her new life. Would she continue to avoid having a man in her life?

Nancy's words still sounded in her head. "You've lived like a nun long enough."

Getting settled in Vicenza, beginning classes as a bonafide professor hadn't allowed her much time in Venice yet. And today she needed time with Saint Francis. Although never really connecting to the faith of her parents, the saint's cloister had a way of drawing her into a prayer-like state. She yearned for a bit of his serenity.

She strolled through an immense *campo*, plaza, and passed beside the church of two saints, John and Paul, nicknamed *Zanipolo* by the Venetians. In the distinctive Venetian dialect, *Zani* is John and *Polo* is Paul. No matter how large a campo might be, in Venice there's only one Piazza, the Piazza di San Marco. Just another peculiarity of Venice that makes it unique, she thought. She'd drop into Zanipolo another day.

And one of these days, she'd speak the rather guttural Venetian dialect. Over the years, she'd persuaded Nonno Tony to share a few phrases, because of course, he knew how to converse when in Venice. No doubt his "business" contacts were old, chauvinistic Venetians who avoided speaking Italian whenever possible. Over the years, she had sipped coffee in bars away from tourist areas often enough to get the gist of the locals' conversations. Yes, she'd give it a try, soon.

She hurried into Campo Santa Marina, hoping Didovich's bakery would still be there. It was! Time for a coffee and a sinful treat. As she broke apart her flaky brioche stuffed with a dried-fig spread, she speculated about why this campo didn't have a church. What had happened to Santa Marina? Like regional malls in the States that needed at least one important store as an anchor, the Venetians always had at least one church per open campo. She was comparing churches to Saks Fifth Avenue or Macy's, but maybe that wasn't so far-fetched. Venetians had always been merchants first and Christians second. She leaned back for another sip, basking in the glow of being in Venice again.

* * *

Few tourists found this out-of-the-way treasure, but Giulia was enchanted each time she approached the large Vigna complex. The vibrant terra-cotta walls seemed to have been re-stuccoed recently. She wasn't sure she liked the fresh new look. Maybe she romanticized the crumbling, fragile condition of Venetian buildings too much. Stucco didn't hold up in the constant damp air, and had to be re-done frequently. It flaked and crumbled at her feet as she walked the ancient *calles,* narrow pathways. The buildings were most beautiful after a rain when the colors of the stucco deepened into rich, sensuous hues.

The church seemed empty and her steps echoed as she moved through the large sanctuary toward the small cloister. She stopped in front of Bellini's painting of a beautiful madonna holding her bambino. It was the most precious treasure the church owned because he had signed this one in 1507.

She shoved open the heavy door to the cloister and remained motionless, letting the silent reverence of the place flow over her. Saint Francis stood in the center, serene as usual, on his pedestal in the middle of an emerald-green rectangle of grass that might have been snipped by hand. Two dark cypress stood like sentinels one on either side of the diminutive saint.

Butterflies hovered around purple and yellow pansies that lined the four walkways leading to his feet. Francis would certainly have welcomed the beautiful creatures. Would he welcome her? Would he be able to help her? She didn't move onto the grassy area but instead, sat on the stone base of the structure that framed the perimeter of the cloister. Breathing deeply, she leaned against one of the columns supporting the arches overhead. Focusing only on the pansies and the grass, she let go and hoped for a sense of calm and clarity.

* * *

Giulia came awake with a start. *So much for clarity.* It was already 1:15 P.M. She'd planned to allow more time to find her way from Vigna to Giobbe. It was a long walk to the church of Saint Job, and she'd never gone there from this part of town before. After hurrying along narrow calles and crossing bridges, she decided to give Marlowe a quick call to let her know she was on her way. But when she reached Ponte delle Guglie, the bridge that crossed the Canale di Cannaregio, she realized she wasn't late after all. Her feet had remembered the way better than her brain.

She strolled beside the large canal that flowed between this out-of-the way piece of Venetian real estate and the famous Ghetto on the other side. Although people claim that area as the first place where Christians had crowded Jews into one place, Giulia figured Jews had been shoved into undesirable quarters long before the 1500s. But it *was* the first time such a place was given a name known round the world. All because the famous neighborhood was the part of Venice that had been a foundry, *il gheto.*

Most of the buildings on this side of the canal seemed drab and colorless, but people moved about with contented smiles on their faces. She also noticed a quietness. Strange. She'd expected San Giobbe's area to be noisy because of the cars rushing across the nearby causeway. Maybe she'd find a spacious apartment in this area for a reasonable price.

When she looked up, Marlowe was strolling toward her beside the same water's edge. Giulia liked this woman. And it seemed she, too, had trouble taming her hair. It was dark brown and cut just below the bottom of her earlobes in a thick, unruly bob. She wore little make-up or jewelry. Today Marlowe was wearing an electric-blue, short-sleeved top of boucle knit that shimmered in the sunshine, a black, circular skirt and carrying a light-blue sweater. Giulia hoped they'd become good friends.

"Got sucked into Venice, huh?" Marlowe said as they hugged.

Giulia nodded. "It's impossible not to. By the way, how do you know Giobbe will be open today?"

"The old sacristan is a friend from way back and arranged to be here this afternoon. Guess I haven't told you I was a student here for a year when I was fifteen and lived—"

"Incredible! That must have been marvelous," Giulia said.

"I stayed in a dorm in the convent behind *Madonna del Orto*," and she tipped her head across the canal toward Tintoretto's church hidden beyond the intricate maze of calles within the Ghetto.

"What a marvelous opportunity," Giulia said as they left the canal and walked on the long, narrow campo toward the worn-out old church.

"Yes," Marlowe replied, but Giulia thought she heard a dark tone in Marlowe's voice. Soon, however, Marlowe began to chat about the Venetians who dedicated churches to "saints" created from Old Testament figures. "*Giobbe*, Job, of course, and then there's *Geremia*, Jeremiah—"

"The first time I came to Venice alone," Giulia interrupted, "I stayed in a little hotel across from Geremia. I thought it was Santa Lucia's church." She laughed at herself. "All the signs inside the church pointed to her lying inside her glass case."

"I know. Little old dried-up Lucy upstaged Jeremiah when they settled her into his church after demolishing hers for the train station. At least she got her name on the station," Marlowe said and chattered on about other churches dedicated to fabricated saints. She ticked them off on her fingers. Moses, *San Moisé*, Samuel, *San Samuele*, and *San Girolamo*, Jerome."

"You're really up on this, aren't you?" Giulia said.

"Sometimes I get carried away with trivia. I became intrigued because of the Venetians' habit of going their own way for centuries. They must have been arrogant bastards to face down the powers in Rome. And they managed to give several popes giant headaches."

Giulia half listened enjoying the companionship of this open, friendly woman. She felt a kinship with Marlowe, and Lord knew she needed a woman friend here. She wanted to learn Marlowe's story. But all in good time, knowing how reluctant she felt about sharing her own.

* * *

The elderly sacristan gave Marlowe a warm hug. He seemed fragile and creaky as he bowed slightly to Giulia. But after a few words with him, it was clear his mind was not one bit creaky. As he showed the women through the church, he explained at great length—when he understood Giulia spoke fluent Italian—about the marble carvings done by the famous Lombardi brothers. After a while, though, he slipped away.

Marlowe took Giulia's hand and led her to a painting by Girolamo Savoldo. The label stated it had been painted in the early 1500s, and the colors were as brilliant and jewel-like as a Vivarini painting that was hanging near the sacristy. Vivarini, came from a glass-maker family on the island of Murano and was said to have had a secret formula to make his paints glow. Maybe Savoldo knew Vivarini's secret.

It was a manger scene, and Marlowe slipped quietly onto a bench in front of it saying nothing. It seemed this painting had a special meaning for Marlowe, and Giulia let herself be drawn into the ancient story as she sat on the edge of Marlowe's bench.

The baby Jesus lies on the floor of a rustic hut. Mary and Joseph stand over him. A foreboding sky hovers over the hills behind the hut, maybe a symbol of the agony to come for this child. At the rear, a shepherd lounges into an open window, observing the family. Another shepherd peeks around the corner. Mary wears a crimson renaissance-style dress with a sumptuous green shawl, and Joseph sports a bright red cloak—the usual renaissance anachronisms in religious paintings.

"What's funny?" Marlowe asked in a whisper.

Giulia moved closer to Marlowe and said, "The babe reminds me of my twin brothers when they were tiny. That chubby leg kicking in the air is exactly how they kicked covers away. They were such darlings at that age before they grew up to be major pests to this older sister."

"Sounds fun to me since I'm an only."

"Sometimes it was," Giulia said. "Compared to many renaissance painters, though, Savoldo knew what a real infant looked like except—"

"Except what?" Marlowe interrupted.

"That babe," Giulia said grinning, "is not a newborn."

"Yes, I noticed that," Marlowe said in a bare whisper.

Again Giulia sensed Marlowe's distress but hesitated to intrude. Then she took a chance. "Is this why you wanted to bring me here?"

"I guess so," she sighed. "Marc knows about my year in Venice and I'd like to share with you. I've kept this secret far too long for my own good."

Giulia felt honored to hear those words and remained motionless not wanting to disturb Marlowe's flow.

"That year *was* wonderful until I let one of my teachers seduce me into pregnancy."

Giulia noticed Marlowe examining her closely—expecting a critical reaction, maybe? Evidently satisfied, she continued with her story. Good, I want her trust, Giulia thought.

"The teacher was married. He suggested an abortion and *offered* to send me to Trieste."

"Send you! How old were you?"

"Almost sixteen."

"My God."

"A real prince, huh? I'm not a Catholic, never have been but couldn't do the abortion. Of course, the Padre and Sisters didn't encourage such a thing. So I had a son and gave him away... for adoption." Tears slipped out the corners of her eyes. Giulia moved to hold her. Between sniffles, Marlowe said, "The church found a 'good Catholic family' for my little Tomaso."

"It must have been so hard," Giulia said. "Did you get to see him before—"

"Once. He was perfect." More tears slipped down her cheeks.

"What about your parents?"

Marlowe sat up, wiped her face and sucked in a big breath.

"That's a long story for another time. The short version is that I believed I couldn't tell them. My Aunt Belle had arranged the trip to expand my horizons." Marlowe snorted. "That backfired for sure. But Belle came to see me through. And Padre Tomaso sat with me most every afternoon through my pregnancy. He left off being a priest shortly after that and works with organizations that promote sex education and choice."

"A priest left the church to support choice?!"

"He's an amazing person. We met recently, and he said what happened to me had been the tipping point for him. For too long, his colleagues had been eager to 'take care' of such mistakes. He wanted no more of it."

"Wow," was all Giulia could say. "How long have you kept that secret?"

"Twenty-seven years." They were both silent. "A long time, right?"

Giulia nodded. "What was Marc's reaction when you told him?"

"He'd been adopted himself. I was sure he'd drop me in disgust when he heard my story. Instead, he understood. Said he thought his birth mother probably suffered the same fate."

"Wow, again," Giulia said, thinking of her own secret. Similar story, different outcome. It had been eight years for her, and the only person who knew about Giulia's abortion was Nancy, and now, Nonna. But compared to other things, maybe her abortion should be shoved away into a dark corner.

"I spent hours in front of this painting trying to decide what to do," Marlowe said bringing Giulia back from her thoughts.

"Does the old sacristan know?"

"I didn't tell him, but he may. Venetians are voracious gossips and priests? Probably more so."

"Are you trying to find Tomaso?"

Marlowe nodded. "When I last saw Padre Tomaso—I can't stop calling him Padre—he had a lead. Marc and I followed up, but the man's age wasn't right. Marc's already registered with an agency to search for *his* birth mother, and we recently filed the paperwork for me."

"A formidable job," Giulia said almost under her breath.

"I almost doubt if legal work was ever done. The convent may have found that 'good Catholic family' after receiving a hefty donation for their efforts."

"What about *your* efforts?" Giulia said, then worried she'd been too flip.

But Marlowe laughed. "You've got a point there."

"Do you have other children?"

"A daughter, Mandy." Marlowe's face lit up. "She's getting a master's in the Urban Planning Department at Portland State University. Do you know it?"

"Of course. PSU is well known for their Urban Planning. But you're so young to have a daughter in grad school."

Marlowe laughed. "Thanks, but I *am* old enough, believe me."

"How old are you, if you don't mind me asking?"

"Not at all. I'm forty-three. Marc's thirty-nine and teases that he's always been attracted to older women. How about you?"

"I'm thirty-two."

"And you look about twenty-two, so here we are older women masquerading in Venice."

"That fits, doesn't it?" Giulia said. "Sometimes this whole city feels like continual Carnivale."

"Ready to go? Marlowe asked. "We can catch a vaporetto to Murano at Fondamenta Nuova."

"I'm ready. Thanks for getting me inside this little gem. It's been on my list for ages. And Marlowe, thanks for opening up to me."

"Thank *you*, for listening without judgment."

CHAPTER SIX

On the way to the vaporetto stop, Marlowe said, "Where'd your feet take you first today?"

"Pretty much straight to Didovich's pastry shop."

"My favorite, too."

"Since you're a maven on Venetian trivia, maybe you know what happened to Santa Marina's missing church."

"As a matter of fact, I do. In fifth-century Lebanon, she was called Marina the Monk because she entered a monastery disguised as a boy. Until the monks prepared her body for burial, they hadn't known they'd been living beside a woman. Can you imagine the shock to those sequestered old monks!"

They whooped with laughter. As each woman offered a different image of the improbable situation, they kept erupting into more laughter until they were staggering down a narrow calle. Giulia guessed they were both releasing tension of one sort or another. When she caught her breath, she said, "I assume poor old Marina's bones were brought to Venice in the usual way—by theft. But why was her church destroyed?"

"Napoleon, no doubt. It was probably one of those that he suppressed when he swept through demanding huge changes. Maybe the same time he ordered all bodies in Venetian cemeteries dug up and placed on the cemetery island."

"You could write a book for the tourists on Venetian trivia."

"Sometimes I drive Marc crazy with it. Let's turn left here onto Calle del Fumo. It's a nice, straight shot to Fondamenta Nuova. A relief from the twisty turns everywhere else in this city."

"I can't believe I've been in Italy for more than a month already," Giulia mused aloud.

"Me too. It's almost April," Marlowe said. "When classes began March fourth, I couldn't believe I had a job to support myself in Italy."

"But you were married before coming to work, weren't you?"

"Barely—we married in February. But what's that got to do with work? Are you implying that once I married, I'd drop everything and sit back to stitch Home-Sweet-Home samplers?"

"No," Giulia sputtered. "That was a knee-jerk reaction coming straight from my mom's knee through my mouth."

"I know about that. If Mom had known what I was studying, she would have done her best to discourage me from the Law."

"Why?"

Marlowe shrugged. "Because she feared I'd fail maybe? Or... jealousy? Thank God Marc came up with the idea of me teaching law at the base. I've never practiced, but in trying to make it understandable to others, I'm learning more than the students. Marc was intent on keeping me here, not that I minded. He called a good friend, Chuck Novak, about the possibility. Chuck arranged an interview for me. Do you know him?"

"Met him recently on the post." Giulia told Marlowe how they'd met outside Oliver Ogle's office. One part of her wanted to know more about the tall, dark, sexy man. Another part wanted to veer far away.

That problem was temporarily solved when they arrived at a row of *pontiles*—floating landing stages—lined up along the broad quay. Usually, one pontile was enough, but here, many water-bus lines left for all parts of the lagoon. *Il Cimiterio*, the cemetery island, seemed to float just across the way, and several flower shops crowded this particular quay. Marlowe stopped to buy a small bunch of brilliant, red poppies.

"I've been lusting for these beauties lately," she said. "Today I have an excuse to celebrate. It feels liberating to have shared with you. It seems silly to have worried about what happened long ago. Marc reminds me of this whenever I begin to brood. But letting it go still feels scary."

"I can imagine," Giulia said as they moved toward pontile number twelve.

"After I told Marc, I'd about decided to not tell anyone else. Of course, good friends would sympathize, but they'd also pick away at every detail. It'd be like opening up an old wound. But with you, it didn't feel that way."

"I'm glad," Giulia said.

They stepped aboard the floating landing stage and waited in a semblance of a line for the vaporetto chugging toward them from the cemetery island. After they boarded, it would turn back to repeat its route.

"How do your parents feel about your job and plans to stay on?" Marlowe asked.

"Well, they *are* Italians from towns north of Venice even though they're in Portland now. But they have mixed feelings. Mom thinks I'll be disillusioned when reality sets in. The thing is, I've been here enough to see the downsides of living in Venice. I'm sure you know what I mean." Giulia began to tick off items on her fingers. "The physical difficulties of carrying everything on foot and no elevators in most buildings. The dampness, the *acqua-alta*, the high-water times, and the mobs of tourists almost year round."

"Don't forget the glut of shops full of masks and doo-dads at the cost of real shops for real people," Marlowe added.

Giulia sighed. "Mom's glad her parents are nearby, but no matter where I'd land, she'd worry about me still single and going on thirty-three."

"And your Dad?"

Giulia inhaled a breath through her teeth with a little frown creasing her forehead. "Dad? Not sure. He's always been there to listen—I think he listened—but he, too, worries his little girl has no big man to take care of her."

"Speaking of big men," Marlowe said. "Yesterday, I ran into Chuck. He waited outside for me while I delivered a report to Oliver the Ogre." She laughed as she told Giulia of Oliver's reaction when he saw Chuck standing against the wall. "He looked ready to slit Oliver's throat. He didn't mention your run-in with Ogle to me, by the way. Probably didn't want to say anything without your permission. And, I didn't know about it yet either."

Giulia felt pleased that Chuck hadn't mentioned her encounter with Ogle. The two women sidled forward as the vaporetto nudged against the pontile and came to a stop with engines roaring in reverse to hold it there. The gatekeeper held newcomers back while passengers disembarked, then dropped the loose rope to let them step aboard. Both women donned their sweaters for the ride, preferring to stand in the outside space between the pilothouse and the enclosed cabin that held seating.

"Chuck claims some officers want to get rid of the guy," Marlowe said, "but it's complicated because of layers of protocols within the University of Maryland and the Military. He also said that all males on the post have been warned about serious career damage from *any* form of sexual harassment. But if women don't report it, how effective is the warning?"

"I know. Many guys don't get it at a gut level. I've preached to my brothers about the horrors of harassment and the dangers of escalation. Oh, they were protective IF they happened to be around when somebody hassled me. With their wives, though, they're more aware, but . . ." She shook her head.

The water bus stopped at the cemetery. As soon as people stepped off and others got on, it moved toward Murano. In two minutes, they arrived and got off in front of the Barovier palazzo. At a door marked number four, Marlowe said, "Here we are. We can talk more over a glass of wine. Okay?"

"Absolutely."

* * *

Marc's family palazzo was an enormous, grey building abutting the quay. Marlowe explained that traditionally, a glass-blowing family lived close to its ovens because they often needed to run twenty-four/seven. No automatic controls back then and family members took turns tending the fires. Marc's family company—the oldest and most famous of those in Murano—kept their ovens at the rear of the complex. Each family member has a separate entrance. To Giulia, it looked as if most units enjoyed marvelous views of Venice.

Marlowe unlocked a door and they started up a steep stairway to the first floor where another door opened into a living/dining room area. They stepped onto golden flooring. Straight on through was the kitchen with two casement windows that looked toward the inner buildings of Murano. In the distance, a church dome reflected the setting sun. A dining table sat in the center and to the right were two large, leather couches with a smaller loveseat forming a comfortable grouping around a fireplace.

"The floor, is it bamboo?" Giulia asked impressed with the layout.

Marlowe nodded.

"It's exquisite. That bright orange and yellow Rya rug near the fireplace is a brilliant touch. Yours?"

"Not at all. Everything here was chosen by Marc. Once I overheard his mother say 'that woman'—me—'would be making big changes in his beautiful design.' But I haven't had any desire to change a thing."

She was obviously in his thrall, Giulia thought. "Could I use your bathroom?"

"Of course," and Marlowe led her toward it. "When I first saw this tub, I lusted for it. As you well know, most rentals only have showers. But later, when I saw the jacuzzi in Marc's master-bath, I set my sights higher. Truth to tell, my sights were already set on him."

Yep. She's smitten.

When Giulia saw the sleek, blue-grey pedestal sink with toilet and bidet to match, she longed for such elegance. *Someday.* The mirror over the sink gleamed and its beveled glass sparkled. "I could get used to this," Giulia said. "Was that mirror made in Murano?"

"Don't know. It's gorgeous, isn't it? Always something new to find out about this place and my man."

"That would make you his woman, right?" Giulia said with a wicked grin.

"Yeah. Jeez, I sound like someone out of a Mafia novel."

When Giulia emerged from the bathroom, Marlowe was taking lasagna out of the fridge. "Marc's Nonna gave strict instructions to let it come to room temperature before putting it in the oven. All we need is salad and Marc will do that. His Caesar's far superior to anything I'd put together. He'll bring a couple baguettes from my favorite bakery on the short calle near Zanipolo. Do you know that one, just across the Rio dei Mendicanti?" she said bringing out a bottle of red holding it up. "Red good?"

"My favorite. I think I do know that bakery, their homemade bread sticks are to die for," Giulia said.

"I know. They always sell out early. I should have called ahead." She turned around with the bottle opener in hand holding it in front of her like a weapon and took a mock stance. "Now. Back to the Ogre. I really want to get him out of our hair," and she twisted the corkscrew in the air with a vengeance.

"Ouch. He better stay out of your path," Giulia said.

"Would you hand me a couple of wine glasses while I open this?" Marlowe asked.

Giulia opened cupboards until she found them.

"The trouble is," Marlowe continued, "we're the new kids on the block. I can *not* understand why the other women have put up with him this long!"

"I agree. They act like abused wives."

"I wish I'd been a fly on the wall when you kneed the bastard." Then she mentioned her talk with Chuck and his thoughts about setting up a system where a woman could call for backup when visiting Oliver. "Frankly, I can see a flaw in that idea because—"

"Me too. The guy who's sent to protect could be another predator."

"You know what Chuck said when I pointed that out?"

"What?"

"He ran his hand through that thick hair of his and said he keeps forgetting about the world we women live in. It's clear where his heart is."

Giulia relaxed, noticing she'd felt uneasy about his possible response.

He asked about you," Marlowe said as they carried their wine to the fireplace corner.

"About me?"

"He wondered if I knew you. I said I thought we'd be good friends, but I know he wanted more. Listen, Marc and I often have Chuck for dinner. Would you come by sometime when Chuck's here? I'm no great cook, but . . ."

Giulia stiffened. "I'm not in the market for a man." *You sure, girl? Your life sucks.* "But it sounds nice. Particularly in your beautiful home."

"And I'm not in the matchmaking business. But the four of us might cook up ideas on how to get rid of Oliver other than Marc's idea of bashing his head and tossing him in a canal."

"Put that way, why not?" Giulia said smiling. The wine was delicious and she felt herself unwinding as she sat on the couch.

Then Giulia heard a key in the lock, and Marc came in. She saw immediately why Marlowe called him her Viking. Absolutely gorgeous, he was big and blond with large, grey eyes and a smile that could light up all of the North country. A white paper bag was in one hand which he tossed to Marlowe—the bread no doubt. He turned to someone behind him and said, "Coast is clear, Chuck, come on in."

CHAPTER SEVEN

Giulia sucked in a breath and felt off kilter. Had she been tricked? The wine sloshed in her glass, but she managed to steady it as Chuck stepped through the door.

The contrast between the two big men was amazing. Not in size, Marc was only a couple of inches taller than Chuck, but with Chuck's dark color, they were a matched pair of opposites. His pale, ice-blue eyes struck a deep chord in her again. Then a crazy image came to mind. She was six years old standing in front of the shelves that held her mom's dog collection; Giulia's favorites were two magnetic Scotties. One black, one white. As soon as her mother left to check on her baby brothers, Giulia grabbed those Scotties, turned them back to back, and watched them snap around face to face.

Had Marc and Chuck sniffed each other out before deciding to be friends? She almost laughed aloud. That jerked her straight back into the room. At least a smile wiped away the frown she surely must have worn when Chuck entered.

Marc struck the side of his head. "You must be Giulia," and he strode across the room. "I apologize for forgetting you were coming tonight. When I met Chuck over in Venice, I dragged the *povero diavolo* back with me. He stopped kicking and screaming when he heard Nonna's lasagne was on the menu." Marc stuck out his hand. Giulia set her glass of wine down and stood up to greet him.

"Ciao, Marc. Glad to meet you. I've heard only good things about you."

"Whoa." Marc beamed. "Has she been telling lies again?"

"Maybe," Giulia said with a little grin.

Chuck hung back looking worried. And well he should if he had anything to do with this "surprise."

"Come in, Chuck. Have you met Giulia yet? She teaches at the base, too."

Chuck seemed to regain his composure and moved forward. "Ciao, Giulia. It's good to see you again." When they shook hands, she felt the same heat race through her as before.

Marlowe gave Chuck a welcome hug. "Maybe this is as good a time as any to begin plotting against Oliver," she said. "But Marc, let's get Chuck a glass of red first, and I'll put the lasagna in."

Marc brought wine to Chuck, and left to work on the salad. Giulia still felt disoriented. She looked into the kitchen and saw Marc grabbing Marlowe's rear as she bent over the oven. He reached under her skirt and pulled her into a backward hug, but she whirled around to give him a kiss and whispered to him. Giulia looked away but heard a rumbly chuckle from Marc. *That sounded like marital bliss.* She had to admit, it looked appealing. Then she noticed Chuck eyeing the couple with what seemed to be a deeper longing. She turned to stare into the fire and sipped her wine. She felt side-swiped. Her emotions were all over the place. Even though she tended to believe Chuck's unexpected arrival was accidental, she needed time to compose herself.

* * *

What a beauty she is in that girlie yellow dress showing her smooth shoulders. But damn. Does she think I'm stalking her? A couple of times I did happen to pass her building about the time I thought her class would let out. Maybe she'd seen me. And , yes, I was in the cafeteria a few times when I thought she'd be there, but only once did I stop by to say a few words. Something stupid no doubt.

He took a seat facing her from the other side of the coffee table and blurted, "Giulia, I hope you don't think I've been stalking you.

I admit I've been in the same place as you a time or two, but this was not my doing."

"Unless Marc is a consummate liar, I've figured that out. But," she allowed herself a small smile, "your spying skills could use some work."

"Was I that obvious?"

"Probably not. Maybe my anti-stalking skills are working overtime."

"My God, has someone else been following you?"

She nodded. "Last week when I delivered a package for my grandfather, someone skulked behind me, but I lost him."

He hadn't missed her smug smile and wondered if she enjoyed a touch of danger, but he said, "What'd he look like? Have you seen him since?"

Before Giulia could answer, Marc and Marlowe joined them and the conversation took a different turn.

* * *

The affectionate bantering between Marc and Marlowe helped lighten Giulia's mood, and when the lasagna's aroma rose from her plate, she realized how little she'd eaten all day. She tucked in like an Oregon lumberjack and devoured the huge serving. When Marc brought the large baking dish to the table offering seconds, Giulia took more. She wasn't alone in her appreciation of the savory dish, everyone around the table made satisfied humming sounds. She felt embarrassed when she couldn't finish until she noticed Marlowe had taken too much, too. Giulia hopped up to help clear plates while Marc began working his magic with the salad.

Marlowe brought chilled salad bowls from the fridge and Marc cracked a fresh egg over greens already mixed with crushed garlic in a large bowl. A quick toss and with a squeeze of a large lemon half in his huge hand, he dribbled the juice all around. He tossed the greens again with a flourish, scooped them into the four cold bowls, and they all dived in to enjoy its tangy freshness after the rich, cheesy lasagna.

"Fantastic meal. Marc, you can twist my arm any time," Chuck said wiping his mouth with a napkin.

Giulia watched the napkin slide across his full lips like a soft kiss and felt her insides clench. She couldn't pull her eyes away. When he turned toward her, she grabbed her glass. After a swallow, she also thanked their hosts. "I haven't enjoyed a meal this much since I've been in Italy—too much going on I guess."

"That brings to mind that creep Oliver Ogle," Marlowe said. "I've decided to take the initiative and be the bait. How shall we set him up?"

A furrow creased Marc's forehead and his mouth flattened into a hard line. "Is that the only way to get the cowardly wimp to leave?"

"Wimps can be dangerous," Chuck said. "Marlowe, I don't like the idea of using you—or any other woman—as bait. We don't know what he's capable of." He took a sip of wine and looked at Giulia, silently willing her to tell her story.

"Marc, you may not know yet what happened in Oliver's office," Giulia said and related the story with Chuck nodding his head. "I should have restrained myself."

"Whoa," Marc said. "Sounds to me like self defense. If more women would react that way, he might slink off into the sunset."

"How did he ever wangle his status as Director of Personnel?" Marlowe said. "He's such a faker. When I first visited him and complained that he had closed the door, he said, 'My dear, your personnel records are like *Arcana Imperii*,' then translated the legal-latin term for me as 'state secrets' making sure I knew *he knew* what it meant." Marlowe sighed, "It *would* be lovely if he'd drop off the face of the earth."

"No such luck," Giulia said. "Whoever is the 'bait' needs to be very sure of good backup."

They all agreed.

"In spite of your valid objection to an escort system," Chuck said turning to Marlowe. "I still believe a constant intimidation might work with him. We could handpick a few good men to take this on, and I think—"

"And just how would you vet this 'elite' corps of men?" Giulia interrupted. Her eyes hardened, and Chuck felt his cock react. Unrelenting, she continued, "Do you have access to their background information?"

There's fire in that curvy body, he thought, but calmly replied, "Info from their military records, of course, but my unit isn't the FBI. We aren't trained to do profiling. Yet, when men and women work together in combat, they learn fast who can be trusted. I don't doubt we could form a dependable group."

"How about we move to the living room for coffee," Marlowe suggested.

They all carried their remaining dishes to the kitchen counter and settled around the fireplace where Marc was already coaxing the fire back into flames.

"As an outsider," he said over his shoulder, "the only way I see a group of protectors could work is if all the women buy in."

They batted that idea back and forth while sipping coffee. No one accepted offers of sweets. Giulia noticed it was eight forty-five already.

"Sorry, but I should go. After the 10.05 train, I don't think there's another to Vicenza until midnight."

"That's right," Chuck said. "I'll walk with you. But while I've got all of you together, I want to invite you to dinner at Corte Sconta. We can finalize our plans there. Next Friday evening, everyone?"

Marc and Marlowe looked at each other, nodded and she said, "My mouth's already watering for their zabaglione."

Chuck turned to Giulia, "Can you join us? Have you eaten at Sconta?"

"I know of it but haven't been there. Zabaglione? Maybe I'll try it too."

"It's heavenly, and they're not stingy with the Marsala," Marlowe said.

"We might have to order ahead to make sure they have enough

for this little glutton." And Marc picked up Marlowe's hand and kissed her palm.

"Good, it's a date. I'll make reservations. By then, I hope to get recommendations for an 'elite' group, as you called it, Giulia." Still looking at her, he added, "Maybe you two could poll the other women on the idea."

"Yeah. That gives us almost a week to check them out," Marlowe said.

"Good. With more facts," Chuck said, "we can put a plan into action."

* * *

At the station, Chuck walked with Giulia to the designated track for the train to Vicenza. The Venice station wasn't large, considering the city's popularity, and the dull 1950s-style architecture offered none of the elegance of other *stazioni* in Italy. To Giulia, the lobby always seemed cluttered with large glass cases stuffed with glittery doo-dads for last minute buys. But why not? Venetians had been merchants for more than a thousand years. The bar, however—separated from the lobby by glass doors—was well appointed and efficient. When traveling alone, Giulia had often been able to buy a delicious coffee or sandwich at the last minute and still make her train.

This morning she'd bought a train pass because she expected to be coming back and forth a lot—her classes were only three days a week. It would save money and time. Chuck already had his because he commuted daily. Giulia pulled her sweater closer on the way to the proper track. When the train pulled in, he boarded with her.

"You live in Venice, don't you?" she asked. "You don't need to go with me all the way to Vicenza and back."

"I won't. I keep a studio apartment for times when I have to stay over."

"Really, Chuck, you needn't do this. I'll be fine. My *pensione* is on the bus line a short distance from the station.

"That may be. But tonight, you are *not* going home alone, especially since someone followed you recently." His voice, though firm, had taken on a velvety, intimate undertone that brought her gaze up to his face. She felt a familiar tremor in her belly. Maybe she'd seen better-looking men, but never one that oozed more masculinity.

They found an empty compartment large enough for six passengers on bench seats three on one side, three on another. Chuck wanted them to be alone and pulled a scarf out of his coat pocket for covering one seat, put the coat on another and looked around. Giulia caught on and found a notebook from her knapsack for a third seat and her scarf for the last extra one. They looked at each other and laughed.

"An old trick, but it usually works," he said.

Chuck raised an armrest between two seats near the window, and they sat side by side. He had noticed her shiver and took the window seat thinking it could be drafty.

"Okay. Tell me about what happened when someone tailed you."

She did, but her story seemed contrived to sound like a frivolous event.

"I don't think the creep who followed me knew what I'd given the old gentleman at the hotel."

"Hotel? Which hotel?"

"Hotel De La Ville," she said. "Why? What's wrong?"

"It's an elegant place, but I've heard rumors about shady business there."

Giulia stared at him, but in truth, she'd begun to suspect the same.

"Why did you deliver gems to a hotel rather than a place of business?"

She sighed. "It's complicated."

The conductor opened the door and they showed their passes. He observed the belongings on the other seats but said nothing. When he left, Chuck repeated her last words, "It's complicated and...?"

"I love my nonno, but I've thought for some time he might not always be on the right side of the law. Maybe he's just dealing under the table to avoid taxes—an Italian pastime as you know." Again she sighed. "I hadn't wanted to do the delivery, but Nonno Tony's a charmer, and I agreed for this one time only. He mentioned avoiding shipping costs, forms, and the like."

"Your nonno's probably not involved in syndicated crime, but the mafia *has* been operating all across the Veneto for years. Not only are there home-grown gangs but even the dreaded *'Ndrangheta* from Calabria. First they were in Milan and then spread over this way into Verona, Vicenza and maybe Padova. So far they're not in Venice. *So far,*" he added.

"I'd heard a little about that, but the 'Ndrangheta?" She shuddered. "This far north?"

According to the *Carabinieri,* they're definitely entrenched." He turned toward her. "Sometimes the federal police in Italy get a bad rap—kind of like the FBI in the States—but they do a great job with statistics. Would you do me a favor and not go to that hotel anymore, even its beautiful bar?"

"I appreciate your concern, Chuck, but surely the hotel is safe."

Turning her to face him and taking both of her hands, he looked into her eyes. The rims around his pale irises darkened. She thought of a photo of a magnificent Siberian wolf a friend had hanging on his office wall. Chuck said, "Please, Giulia." She reacted with a little intake of breath. His scent held a hint of an elusive fragrance. Whatever it might be, its basic essence was warm man.

He didn't press her further. He trusted she got his message. She liked that. The train began moving, and it was clear she wouldn't be returning to Vicenza alone. She felt a flutter low in her belly realizing she didn't mind having someone worry about her. The compartment's overhead lights dimmed as well as those in the corridor running along one side. A reading light over each seat was available, but they sat quietly both in their own thoughts.

CHAPTER EIGHT

"*Stupida sgualdrina,* you ignorant slut!" Botteri snarled at Laura. He rose from his desk in his elegant suite and began to pace.

Laura flinched and sat immobile in her chair, staring out the window behind his desk, not daring to move a muscle. She waited for his next explosion. Finally, she stammered, "I'm sorry, Signor Botteri. But Mirella did listen to your generous proposal and knew what I was talking about. Then she seemed angry about an exclusive arrangement and stood up to leave. But I talked her down and for a moment—"

"She'll come around. I want her in my private stable, *nella mia scuderia privata!*" he roared, and strode back to his chair, sat and swivelled around to stare at the scene from his window. The room was still. Botteri seemed motionless. Laura waited. Abruptly swinging back to her, he leaned across the desk and said, "You were saying 'for a moment'. . ."

"Si, signore. For a moment, I thought she was about to join the Service. Then all of a sudden, she changed her mind."

"And you have no clue as to why?"

"No. She seemed to drift away while I was explaining how our service works."

"In other words, you talked yourself right out of a contract. Again!"

Laura *had* managed to thrust the application into Mirella's hands, but in Botteri's mind, that, too, would mean failure, so she clamped her mouth shut.

"Where does she live?" he asked.

"We don't know. She hopped a bus before Bruno could get on."

"Did he notice the bus number? Name? Where it was going? *Any thing?*" He raised both arms and looked up as if in supplication to the heavens.

"I'll ask him, signore."

"You do that. You have one more chance, Signorina Laura," he said drawing out the word signorina in a low, menacing growl. "You will find a more competent tracker—at your own expense—and let me know the minute you locate her residence. I need to know who she really is. Why is she in Vicenza? What is her weakness?"

He strolled over to his private bar, chose a shot glass of leaded crystal and poured himself exactly two ounces of CM Sicilian Grappa made in the foothills of Mt. Etna. He took a sip and turned back to her. "Who's seen her besides Bruno the idiot?"

"Franco."

"Heh. Franco's best for shuffling papers. Who else could recognize her?"

"Vitale. He served us tea."

"Vitale, yes! My handsome Viking. He's wasted on tea. Get him on it right away. And now? *Vada via!* Out of my sight."

* * *

Giulia hadn't shared everything with Chuck about that hotel delivery and felt uneasy about that. She needed to talk with Nonno Tony.

"Be back in a minute," Chuck said, bringing her into the present. He stepped out and smiled as he carefully closed the glass door to the hallway where the heaters weren't working. Giulia watched him leave and knew she'd be learning more about this gentle military man, but soon her thoughts drifted back to her encounter with Signor Botteri. She shuddered remembering the hoodlum who'd trailed her from the hotel. Chuck knocked on the door with his foot. He held two white ceramic cups and saucers of hot tea. She got up to open it for him. "Their coffee smelled burnt, maybe this will take the chill off."

"Thanks. I do feel shivery."

"Spring is struggling, but I guarantee it will make it," he said.

She nodded and sipped the scalding tea, thinking he sounded as uncomfortable with small talk as she did. The train rolled along and they both slipped into their own thoughts again. Tasteless, but hot, the tea reminded Giulia of her encounter with Laura at that damned hotel.

The conductor announced the arrival at the Padova station rousing Giulia from her reflections. They'd come about twenty-five miles. She was still holding her half-finished tea. Chuck roused, noticed her cup and eased it out of her hand, placing it on the small shelf under the window.

"Only fifteen more miles. You okay?" he asked, wishing he could hold her in his arms for the rest of the ride. She nodded and settled her head against the cushion. He sighed and followed suit as the train moved on into the darkness toward Vicenza.

The last escort service Giulia tried was a strictly arm-candy arrangement. She couldn't stop her mind from re-playing a part of her past that still haunted her. She had earned good money with that service, catering almost exclusively to visitors who attended University functions. Men who wanted attractive women on their arms for an evening or two. She had stayed on her student budget and invested all of her escort earnings. With the money from Lettie, it might be possible to live in a beautiful Venetian apartment soon.

Aunt Loretta had supported Giulia's dream to live in Venice. When Uncle Giuseppe died, she moved to Portland, and they'd become almost like sisters. Giulia had always wanted a sister and still missed Lettie, wishing she'd lived long enough to see all this happen. Then again, she was glad Lettie had never known about her activities in Eugene. Arm candy or not, she'd sold herself. But when she'd stormed away from Laura and burned that application, she'd felt liberated—free. The train jolted Giulia out of her reverie.

She inhaled and sat up straight feeling encouraged. Maybe it was time to live a real life. But did she even know how?

She glanced at Chuck dozing beside her. He was truly a tall, dark and handsome man. And fit—that had been obvious when she'd slammed into his hard body coming out of Ogle's office. But he didn't display overgrown biceps, triceps, quads and whatever else all those muscles were that many admired. His thick hair was fairly short—no doubt military regulations—and cut in layers, probably to control what appeared to be strong, natural curls. She wouldn't mind running her hands through it. She noticed the dark shadow of a whisker grain along his jaw. Nice. It had been ages since she'd thought about the sexy rasp of a beard on her skin. Most of all, though, she imagined how his sensuous mouth would feel. When she was near him, dormant sensual feelings kept working their way to the surface. If she didn't control them, she'd land in trouble fast.

What were *his* thoughts while he snoozed as the dark night flew past the window? As if he knew she was back from her trance-like withdrawal, he turned to her and said so softly she hardly heard him, "How're you doing?"

"Fine. A little tired is all."

For a moment, she'd been sure he'd offer his shoulder. It would have been welcome, even though she hadn't let anyone this close for ages. Her chest felt revved up and her heart was racing. It did that a lot lately. They weren't touching, but she felt heat radiating from his body. For all his military bearing and take-charge manner, not once had he crowded her with sexual innuendos. But she wanted... My God. She wanted more.

Did he sense her emotional wariness? Whatever it was, she felt at ease beside him as they rolled on into the night. She relaxed against the back of her seat and sighed. Wrestling her twisted thoughts had been exhausting, but for the moment, she felt at peace. The movement of the train lulled her into a more comfortable drowse. As she drifted off, she felt an over-powering urge to scoot close to his heat-charged aura.

* * *

Chuck looked over at the enticing woman beside him. Could she be for him? He felt hopeful for the first time in a long time. Seeing Marc and Marlowe again reminded him he couldn't do the superficial stuff anymore. At this moment, Marc was probably spooning his large body around Marlowe's soft curves. *Dammit, I want some of that in my bed. Namely, Giulia.*

Most women were attracted to a military man, and he'd shared his bed with plenty of sophisticated European women. But too often they were more interested in his position at the American base than him.

God. Tonight he'd been turned on watching Giulia eat with a lusty appetite. He wanted to know what other appetites she might enjoy. She had fire. He wanted to turn that fire into an inferno burning for him. Oh yeah. But with his fey sensibility that he'd learned to accept over the years—and which had kept him alive a time or two—he was certain she'd been scorched. She was too cautious. For once, he was taking it slowly.

Her head nodded. He inched slightly closer and her head bobbed again. Finally, it fell against his shoulder. For now, it would be enough. He sighed and inhaled her heady, female fragrance.

CHAPTER NINE

It was mid-afternoon and the friendly bus driver stopped on the outskirts of Vicenza for Giulia. He pointed down a lane lined with tall Mediterranean cypress, saying, "*Sempre diritto,* straight ahead." Those words were often offered in Italy, and she expected a turn or two or having to ask more questions along the way to Villa Rotonda, Palladio's most famous building. She'd meant to come several times before, but it had been closed or *in restoro.* This time she'd been told it would be open all day until five.

It was pleasant walking among the dark, sentinel-like trees, but it seemed strange to see no one on a Sunday afternoon. In spite of the driver's directions, she felt drawn to take a right and followed a flight of broad steps bordered on both sides by rows and rows of cherry trees. She remembered Nonna taking her to local orchards when she was little. Cherries grew in the Willamette Valley of Oregon, but her only visits to cherry orchards had been in Italy with Nonna.

The steps looked so grand, surely they led to the Villa. When she was about one-third of the way up, she noticed someone coming down. Her breath caught until she deduced it was a woman. *Maledizione! No matter how self confident I feel traveling alone, there's always the possible danger from an unknown male.*

The young woman worked at a large estate on the hill and knew of no famous villa, but she said her boyfriend waiting below might know. He did and led Giulia to the heavy, wrought-iron gate surrounding Palladio's famous landmark. She started to tell the couple about Thomas Jefferson and his architectural copy for the Rotunda at the University of Virginia, but noticed their eyes glaze over as they stood with polite smiles. They had other ideas on their minds and could scarcely keep their hands off each other. Ah yes, Giulia thought, some women do know how to trust.

She bought a ticket and followed the broad path lined with oleanders, not yet flowering, but their glossy leaves held promises of abundant radiance. The cream-colored stucco of the stately structure glowed and the red-tiled dome seemed to be polished by the sun. Giulia felt thrilled to be here. Whoever had commissioned the Villa four hundred years ago would be surprised at how famous their home had become. Palladio's design included four equally-proportioned arms opening out from the central dome. From her vantage point, Giulia saw only one elegant porch with its six dazzling-white, ionic columns waiting at the top of fifteen—she counted them—white marble steps. Giulia thought of Tara and Scarlet O'hara. She had always admired her fiery courage.

She wondered if the inside of the Villa would be as beautiful as her view from the approach. She noticed a tall man in a pale-blue turtleneck, dark pants and jacket start down the steps. Two young guys dashed out of the building heading straight for him. They were up to no good and she yelled, *"Attento!"* just as they shoved him. Her warning was all he needed. He swung a blow at one man's upper body then rolled over onto his shoulder kicking the other in the knee. They both fell, scrambled up and scurried away, cursing. Giulia ran to the fallen man.

It was Chuck!

"Are you okay?" she asked bending over him.

"I'm fine," he said and looked up to see Giulia. He almost wished he'd been injured so she'd hover longer. As he got up, his ankle gave way. He sat down on a step to examine it. "Thanks for the warning."

"Is your foot hurt?"

"Twisted my ankle, no big problem. They weren't willing to fight for my wallet. Damned low-lifes out for easy pickings," he muttered.

"How'd they get inside? Surely they didn't pay."

"Yeah. Maybe the ticket seller gets a cut," he growled.

"Would it help to lean on me until you know for sure about your ankle?"

"Thanks, Giulia, but I can make it." Then he thought better of that decision and limped heavily reaching for her shoulder. "Maybe I'll take you up on your offer. My car's not far."

He didn't put his full weight on her little shoulder. She was small compared to his six-foot-two frame and didn't look all that strong. But she was surprisingly steady as they hobbled out the gate toward his bright-yellow Fiat Punto. He began to think fast, determined to not let her get away today.

"I'm lucky you came along when you did."

"They came at you fast. Your reflexes were amazing. All I saw was a blur, and they were gone."

"I wasn't as quick as I should have been. Out of practice." He shook his head in disgust. "I should have heard them before you shouted."

"You mentioned Special Ops. Are you still involved?"

"Not actively. That's a young man's profession and I'm pushing forty." *Damn. Hope that won't turn her off.*

"Are most people forced out at that age?"

"No. No one forced me out. Some guys stay in much longer; they merely train harder. As for me, I took a look at my life and decided the cold sweats that strike in the middle of the night aren't worth it anymore." *She didn't need to hear that either.*

"I'm sorry for asking."

"Don't be. I've been away from all that for three years and life's improving." *Much more since I met you.*

They were at the car where he opened the door and eased into the little auto and looked up at her. "Giulia, you saved me from a lot more grief than a twisted ankle. You know don't you, that in ancient Chinese tradition, you are now responsible for my well being?"

"Is that so?" she said grinning and put her hand on the top of the little vehicle. "You don't look the least bit ancient or Chinese, especially while wearing that miniature yellow automobile."

"We never do know our true heritage, do we?" he said ignoring her comment about his car. "I mean, if we go back far enough—"

"You could be right."

"Of course the tradition doesn't include daily care and feeding, but it does mean that when I'm in need, you will rush to my rescue. And what I need most is to have dinner with you."

"You're good," she said putting her hands on her hips. "It's tempting to say no just to hear what other plan you'll come up with, but—"

"But you'll say yes, right? I know of a Chinese restaurant in the northern part of Vicenza called *La Muraglia*."

Giulia wrinkled her nose in distaste and said, "A Chinese restaurant called The Wall. How clever of them."

"Uh oh. Guess I hit the wrong wall with that idea. How about a Pugliese restaurant? I know a good one, *Zio Zeb*."

"Uncle Zeb, huh? That does sound better than Chinese cuisine in Italy. I haven't enjoyed Chinese food anywhere except San Francisco or Seattle."

"Neither have I. It just popped into my head. You see, Giulia, I'm not nearly as slick as you might think."

She liked that touch of vulnerability about him or was it? A man like Chuck would surely know women like a touch of vulnerability in a man. She could go back and forth on this forever and hated feeling so cynical. She smiled and let it go knowing that once again she'd miss the inside of the Villa.

"How'd you get here today?" he asked.

"Bus and feet."

"Could I offer you a ride in my limousine?" He started to get up to walk around to the passenger side.

"Save your ankle," she said. "I can open the door." Once she was in and looked around, she said, "There's a lot more space inside this *piccola macchina* than I ever expected. I'll take back my remark about you wearing it. But," she stifled a giggle. "I have to admit it did look as if you were putting it on."

He laughed, too. "It's surprisingly spacious for long legs, and it offers more head room than some larger cars."

After a couple wrong turns, they arrived at the trattoria, and this time Chuck was out of the car and around to Giulia's door before she had located the handle. His ankle seemed no worse for that quick action, and she questioned just how bad that tumble had been. She felt warmth spread through her body. It had been ages since someone had seemed genuinely interested in wanting to be with her—only for her and not what she might do for them.

As they entered the restaurant, traces of garlic, oregano and rosemary wafted from the kitchen. "There's nothing quite like the aroma of Italian cooking," Giulia said.

"It's one of life's greatest pleasures," he said. But not the only one, he thought, while he watched the natural, feminine sway of her hips as she followed the waiter. Her slacks weren't skin tight but still, they fit her round ass perfectly. *Down boy.*

People were chatting and laughing at nearby tables. Chuck spoke to the waiter and soon they were taken into a quiet, dark alcove. "Hope this corner suits you. The other diners are having too much fun."

"Oh yes. I like it more quiet, too. What's good here?"

"I haven't eaten here much. Usually eat in Venice or at my own place, but they have an interesting specialty, *Ricci di Mare,* sea urchins, with pasta. No oil, no cheese, just the taste of the sea with maybe some parsley thrown in. As you know, 'Pugliese' cuisine comes from Apulia which is pretty much one long seashore down there on Italy's heel. Everyone grows up eating lots of raw fish. Sashimi isn't new to Apuliani, they just didn't know what to call it until the Japanese told them."

"So the ricci di mare aren't cooked except by the hot pasta?"

"That's right. Does that bother you?"

"Not at all. But what do sea urchins taste like?"

"The truth?"

"Of course."

"In my opinion, they taste like lobster liver."

Giulia wrinkled her nose again. "Isn't that the green stuff that's really the lobster's digestive tract?"

"It is," he said with a lop-sided grin that deepened his right dimple.

"Hmm. Any other recommendations?"

He burst into laughter leaning back on his chair. Then he held the menu under the lamp curved over their table, pointing to *Orecchiette Barese*, little ear-shaped pastas, Bari style. It was described as including rapini and sweet Italian sausage. "This one was delicious the last time I was here. My mouth's already watering."

"Sounds good to me," she said.

"Red or white wine?" he asked.

"Red please."

The waiter took their orders for Orecchiette, to be followed by green salads. Now what, Giulia wondered?

* * *

With another half grin, Chuck said, "Thanks for taking the first step toward your commitment."

"Is this for life?" she said, raising her voice in mock amazement, wondering if he knew how sexy he looked when that dimple appeared.

"We aren't eating Chinese food but you're not off the hook."

"Next time, maybe I won't shout when you're being attacked."

"Would you be that cruel?" He asked, engaging her eyes.

"Maybeee." She hadn't bantered this way for… how long? Maybe never. "Have you been to Apulia?" she asked, hoping to switch attention back to him.

"I have. My mother's family's from Apulia. When she was alive, I took her to visit her grandparents and cousins and aunts and second cousins. You get the idea. And you?"

"All my relatives are in the North and not one big family. Until I was an adult, our trips were always to the Veneto. I've often thought about visiting the South, but family constraints held me back. I *have* been as far as Rome and Naples. Now though," she lifted her glass but didn't drink. Her voice trailed off as she focused on her dream of life in Venice.

"Now though?"

"I drifted didn't I?" she said smiling. "Since I was about seven—when Mom first took me into Venice—I've been determined to live there. Finally, I think it's going to happen."

"Why didn't you take an apartment in Venice right away?"

"Financial reasons. It will take awhile yet before I can afford the apartment I want. As a student, I accepted cramped quarters with lousy plumbing and leaky roofs, but with savings and an inheritance from my Aunt Loretta, I'm getting closer."

"You'll be buying an apartment?"

"Oh no. My dreams aren't that lofty. I have student loans to pay, but a spacious rental with a water view might be in my price range. Do you know anything about rental apartments near San Giobbe? Marlowe and I were there yesterday. Because of her, I finally got inside that little church. Apartments might be less expensive in that area."

"I know where you mean," he said, "but I'd think the noise from the causeway would be a problem."

"I thought so too, but for the short time we were there, it was blessedly quiet. I'd need to check it out at other times of the day and night. For sure, one reason I want to live in Venice is the quiet." *Great job of getting him to talk about himself.*

Their wine and bread were served and when the waiter left, Giulia said, "You know where I grew up, how about you?"

"You want a resume?" he asked with a full-fledged grin.

She took a sip of wine, her eyes focused on his mouth and waited.

"Okay, fair enough. I grew up in the tenements of Elizabeth, New Jersey. One sister, two brothers. Dad worked in a refinery—when he wasn't drunk. Mom worked in the factory when we kids were old enough for school. At seventeen, I had an opportunity to get out by entering the Air Force Academy but..."

This time, he was quiet as he broke off a piece of bread and held it mid-air instead of eating it.

"Obviously, you took advantage of that chance."

"Yeah, I did," and he laid his hunk of bread down still looking at it. "I hated to leave Mom in that situation, but she insisted I go. With hindsight, I know she had cleverly convinced me I was doing it for her."

"Seventeen. Isn't that too young?"

"Not with parental permission, at least at that time."

"Was that a good experience going from New Jersey to Colorado?"

He let out a strained snort. "It took serious adjustment, but I saw it as a great opportunity for someone like me. I got my education, applied for as many training programs as I could, and felt I'd hit the jackpot when I was accepted into Pepperdine's graduate business school in Irvine. Not a bad drive from the March Air Force Base near Riverside where I was stationed. But talk about adjustment. The Pepperdine environment was the most difficult. It was a whole different world."

"How so? I've heard it's a respected institution."

"It is. But... it's private and costly. Mostly well-heeled students from other expensive colleges attend. Pepperdine was originally founded by conservative Protestants. Even though my family didn't observe Catholicism except for holidays, the strong Protestant influence felt like being in a foreign country. Marc and I met in the MBA program. He felt like a duck out of water, too. As you might have guessed, we stayed in touch and both ended in the Veneto. And that's enough about me." And he turned eagerly toward the approaching waiter. "Here comes our pasta."

They ate in silence. He noticed that she enjoyed the combination of strong garlic and spicy sausage with the braised green rapini.

"Are your brothers and sister still in New Jersey?" she asked.

"Relentless aren't you?" he said, but didn't feel upset. Lord how could anyone be upset with her? Those intelligent eyes, her smooth olive skin and brown curls with tawny streaks in them. "Do you realize you have two colors in your hair as well as your eyes?" he said.

"Well, uh yes, I think I do."

He laughed. "Of course you do. We've only met but I can't believe you would sit with strands of hair pulled through holes of diabolic headgear."

"You're right. I don't go through that torture, but how in the world do you know about that?"

"My ex-wife," he said, flattening his lips as firmly as a closed door.

They both dipped their heads and continued to eat.

"Sorry," he said. "I'm enjoying myself too much to pursue that story. Maybe another time?"

"We all have uncomfortable baggage."

"We do." He laid his hand on hers for a moment and let his thumb move back and forth across her knuckles.

After a few moments, she withdrew her hand. *Damn. She's uneasy again.*

They spent the rest of the meal in light conversation. He answered her questions about how the two separate military groups functioned on the base—the Army and the smaller combat-ready members of the 173rd Airborne. She sparkled as she told a few amusing incidents in her classes, and Chuck wondered if he was falling for her. He'd played the smooth operator for too long, and now, it felt strange to not be playing games—to feel tongue-tied.

* * *

He parked in front of the pensione and, without a limp, made it to her side of the car as she opened the door herself.

"It's only fair that I take you back to the Villa since you barely got past the ticket shack."

She didn't answer.

At the door, he put his hands on her shoulders, leaned down

to give her a light—a very light—kiss. She didn't flinch. He was tempted to deepen it but instead, took her hands and looked into her eyes. As he turned to go, he swung back to remind her of the dinner on Friday evening with Marlowe and Marc. "I'll come by to take you to the train about six. Okay?"

She hesitated, then nodded. "Six. Yes. I'll be here. And thanks for dinner. It was fun."

When he was gone, she made her way to her apartment, touching her lips and remembering his sensual touch along the back of her hand. She wondered why he'd been at Villa Rotonda.

CHAPTER TEN

"I will not meet you at the Hotel De La Ville! I will never go there again."

"Coccolona, what's wrong?"

"You know what's wrong. I'll be at Osteria il Grottino having a glass of wine this afternoon at four thirty. Come if you want to discuss this. It's *sotto*—"

"I know where it is. Under the Palladiana. Calma, calma. I'll be there, little one. I'll be there."

She felt shaky after yelling at her nonno. But thought maybe she was learning how to deal with him. Maybe he'd never had a woman tell him where to be and what time to be there. He'd seemed almost nervous. Hunh. It's about time I stand stronger against men like Nonno Tony. He's a rogue who comes in and sweeps you off your feet. *Is that why I was drawn to bad-boy charmers like Ricky and Jason?*

* * *

Monday afternoon, she watched as Tony rushed through the door of the cave-like café located beneath another famous Palladio building. He stood silhouetted against the light from the entryway at the top of the stairs. She admired him, always had. At seventy-seven, he still cut an exciting figure. Suddenly, he spied her and dashed down the steps to her table. He leaned down to give her a kiss—she'd thought—but instead, he lifted her out of her chair into a big bear hug. And, of course, she laughed and hugged back.

"Ah, you are as beautiful as ever, piccolina. Now, what are you having? Prosecco?"

She held up her glass to show him its ruby liquid. "A local Valpolicella, Ripasso style, but this one's not too sweet. Try it, you'll like it."

"Is that an order?" he said grinning.

"Of course not."

"Who's buying?" he asked.

"You are."

He burst into laughter and went to the bar to request his order then joined her again. "Allora. Why are you upset with your old nonno?"

"You didn't keep your promise. You told Signor Botteri I was your granddaughter. Don't try to deny it. The way he leaned over to stare into my eyes was a dead giveaway."

"But I'm proud of you and also wanted to make sure he would trust me."

"Why do you need *me* for him to trust *you?*"

"This is my first time to deal with him—he's a big dealer in the region. I heard he's a family man and thought sending my own granddaughter would convince him."

"Well, you blew it. He may never trust you again since I didn't have eyes like yours or dark curly hair."

He sighed. Short of apologizing outright, he took her hands and held them to his heart. "You are strong, piccolina. How did you get that way?"

"Life, Nonno Tony. Life."

"*La mia dolcezza,* my sweetie, did someone break your heart?"

Thinking of Jason's lies, she sighed. "A long time ago."

"That's lucky for him or I'd break—"

"No need for rough stuff. He said one thing, I believed another."

He nodded. "Now. Tell me how your life in Vicenza goes. Surely with all those young *stalloni* at the base, you'll find your Signor Perfetto."

"Hunh. They're too much like my brothers."

"The officers?"

"Maybe. When I'm ready. But Nonno, do you know much about this *jeweler*, Botteri? I fear he may deal with human beings more than diamonds."

"*Dimmi, dimmi,* tell me, tell me." Nonno leaned close, cupping his hands around her face.

"Let me back up. Before classes started, I walked into town and stopped into Bar La Ville. He'd been sitting in the back and sent a drink to me via the barista. I sent it back and left."

"*E così?* And so?"

"Last Monday, I remembered where I'd seen him."

Tony nodded, "And?"

"After I gave your gems to him and was walking out of the hotel, an elegant woman stopped me and invited me for tea. Seemed strange, but I was curious. Turns out she was a solicitor for an escort service. If I agreed to join her service, a certain gentleman, who had noticed me earlier, wanted to be my exclusive client!"

Nonno sat back astonished.

Finally, he's taking me seriously. "I think your big-man jeweler is more than a gem dealer. Nonno do you want to be *il mio ruffiano*, my pimp?"

"*Dio mio,*" he groaned. "No! I cannot believe this." He scooted his chair next to hers, pulling her into his arms. They stayed close a few moments.

"Good," she said. "I knew so, Nonno. With all my heart I knew so." When he released her, they both had tears in their eyes. She trembled. He pulled her close again, moving his hands in soft circles on her back as he had done long ago when she'd been afraid of shadows in her attic room.

"I will ask around about this man. Of course when he first saw you, he didn't know you were *mio angelo*. And not being blind, he was attracted to you." He kissed her forehead.

She shook her index finger at him. "But I told you," then she poked him twice in his chest, "that I'd wear a disguise."

"You did," he said grasping her finger. He kissed it and hung his head like a school boy caught in a lie. She wondered how often he was contrite like this with Nonna. "I admit, piccolina, I didn't take you seriously."

"By the way, I didn't take one of the gems as you had suggested. In fact, I didn't touch any of it. Not at all. When I handed over the packet, I was wearing the black kid gloves you and Nonna gave me last Christmas. From the start, I didn't feel good about this, and now I worry about *you*. A friend said that suspicious deals go on at Hotel De La Ville." She lowered her voice, "Maybe even the 'Ndrangheta are involved. I will not go there again."

"Good, that's good, *bambina*. Stay away. And now, we'll have a few bites before I leave for home."

After they ate, they stood and hugged again. "I'm glad we had this conversation," he said.

"Me, too. Take care of yourself, Nonno Tony. Think of Nonna, she loves you so much, you know."

"Si, si. *E lei è la mia ancora di salvezza,* and she's my anchor, my salvation."

"And *you* are hers. Give her a hug for me."

* * *

Dusk dropped gently as Giulia left the open piazza and walked down Corso Andrea Palladio where shadows seemed to follow her every step. She had lied to Nonno Tony. No, not lied, but she had *implied* that she was lily clean. When in truth, she hated what she had been. A whore—almost a whore. She knew she had contracted as a decorative companion, but in the eyes of the world, she was a whore. Hunh. Also a whore in the eyes of those men who didn't want to abide by their agreement. She walked faster at the thought of the smarmy ones who wanted more and offered her secret cash. At first, she'd been terrified but had learned to persuade them to keep their bargain by appealing to their overblown sense of honor, a trait those types often bragged about. Back then, she had justified her action. But still, the truth was she'd been a woman for sale.

As she hurried toward her apartment, she replayed her conversation with Nonno. The stricken sound he'd made and the tears she saw when she'd said "pimp," pierced her own sense of honor. That wasn't fair. She felt guilty for saying that. She knew he adored her, but for the first time, she sensed a mature connection with him. Her inner compass had shifted during their encounter.

Her built-in guidance system had been shifting ever since she arrived in the Veneto, but when she strode away from that woman, Laura, it was as if she had stumbled out of a forest fog into a bright clearing. Now the street lamps came on one by one as if welcoming her into more light. Yes, her compass had set itself right.

She skipped across the street and raced up the steps to her door. But the moment she stood inside her apartment and her new life, she shivered with uncertainty. Was it possible to wipe the slate clean and become authentic? Did she have the courage to be genuine with other kinds of men? Chuck, maybe?

CHAPTER ELEVEN

Friday morning Marlowe caught up with Giulia and asked what she'd wear for dinner that night. Giulia hadn't thought about it but didn't want to dress as a come-on to Chuck. "Not sure yet," she said. "And you?"

"I'm thinking girlie," Marlowe said. "I want to wear a flippy skirt with the expensive spikes I bought to go with the dress Marc gave me for New Year's. Why don't you go girlie, too?"

"It *would* be a nice change from our somber duds out here," Giulia said gazing at the grey utilitarian buildings around them and the drab barracks in the distance.

"With all the testosterone floating around, we ought to be teaching in burkas. But tonight, let's go for it!"

Giulia's lips tightened into a small grimace. The idea of "going for it" put her nerves on edge. An actual date after all this time? With Chuck? Or any man. "I'll see what I can find. Gotta run, Marlowe."

* * *

Chuck leaned against the curved banister at the bottom of the open stairway in Giulia's pensione. He looked up and saw her walking beside the upper balustrade toward the top of the stairs. Her back was to him, but he sucked in his breath. God, every thing about her stirred him. Not only the surge in his groin, but the mysterious pain he sensed she had hidden away. It brought out an instinct to protect her. *But from what?*

Yeah. He could watch her swaying hips for hours. It wasn't that exaggerated hip-swishing walk that certain women affected whenever they thought a man was watching. She moved with an easy grace. People could take lessons in good posture and coordination by studying Giulia Cavinato. Even her name sounded graceful.

All the colors of the rainbow mingled in her skirt. It was made of some kind of crinkly cloth and whirled sensuously around her slim body. The predominant color was bright turquoise, and she wore a matching silky-knit sweater with three-quarter sleeves. The skirt touched the tops of her low-rise black leather boots. Damn, he hadn't yet seen her legs but had no trouble imagining how her skin would feel as he ran his hands slowly from the top of her boots upward. He felt a quiver race through his veins as they headed south.

She reached the top of the stairs and turned to come down. When she saw him, her face brightened. "Ciao."

His breath caught in his throat at her smile, but he swallowed and said, "*Buona sera,*" pulling out of his erotic fantasy to watch her descend toward him. As she drew closer, he couldn't take his eyes from the scoop neckline that was modest enough to visit the Queen of England but still low enough to show a hint of cleavage. That hint would drive him crazy the rest of the evening.

"You're looking particularly beautiful tonight," he managed to say.

"Thank you. It feels good to dress like a woman."

"It feels good to see you that way, too. In fact, it's a pleasure to look at you... whatever you wear."

"Thanks again," she said with a slight flush on her cheeks.

"I'm glad you brought a jacket or I might have to do my gentleman thing and give you mine. It's April fourth, but—"

"I wouldn't dare take the coat off your back," she teased.

But I'd like to take every thread off yours. "The car's around the corner," he said as he touched her shoulder.

* * *

When Chuck and Giulia entered Corte Sconta, the waiter led them to the courtyard. She'd never been here but had wanted to try it. Over the years, her visits to Venice had been on the frugal side. But with her first real job, she could relax a little, knowing she'd soon free herself of the student loans.

Marlowe and Marc were already sitting with their heads together laughing about something. Their table was directly under an intersection of four strings of chinese lanterns criss-crossing the enclosure. Terra-cotta pots holding dwarf boxwoods formed the border of the outside dining area, and a pale, peachy glow shed a warmth over the courtyard.

Marc stood up making a point of checking his watch. "Glad you two could make it." He continued standing until Giulia was seated.

Chuck stepped behind Marc in a lightning move and twisted his arm up and behind in a mock hammerlock. Marc faked agony while Chuck took his time looking at Marc's watch. "Hmm. That tin watch of yours is off, old man."

"Enough of the machismo games, guys. We get enough of that at work," Marlowe said laughing.

"This is delightful," Giulia said. "It's almost like a *festa* out here."

"It is, isn't it?" Marlowe chimed in. "Marc and I had our first date right here, last October."

"Is that when you met?" Giulia asked, amazed how quickly their love affair had moved.

"We'd known each other from years before back in L.A. but hadn't dated. It's a long story, Giulia. I'll fill you in sometime. Chuck already knows, and I *think* Marc understands how it happened," she said grinning at him.

"Sometimes I still wonder how I got so lucky," he said.

"Flattery works every time," Marlowe said.

They all laughed as the waiter came to take orders and the evening got off to a merry start.

* * *

They had finished their pastas and entrées and were waiting for salads when Marlowe suggested they get down to business. She still insisted on being the bait to catch Oliver. Marc arched his back at this and laid his hand on her shoulder, but said nothing.

Chuck leaned in toward the center of the table. In a low voice, he said, "I've got a good group of men who understand the situation. Each one has a sister or a cousin, a girlfriend, and one, has a mother who's gone through rough times with people like Oliver. A colleague and I interviewed every one. They're solid."

"That's great," Marlowe said, "but will that be enough intimidation to send Oliver back under his slimy rock?"

"I'm inclined to think so," Chuck said, "maybe he'll ask for a transfer."

"I doubt it," Giulia said. "Not until he's forced out. He enjoys his power trip, but I may have a quicker solution."

The other three turned as one to stare at her.

"Since the altercation I had with him, he's been sending me emails. They—"

"Sending you emails?" Marlowe screeched then covered her mouth.

Giulia nodded. "The powers-that-be want to make the American presence in Vicenza more palatable to the Vicentini. Evidently the military thinks it's a good idea for service people to learn Italian. Ogle must have been re-reading my credentials. He's such a creep." She rolled her eyes. "Always trying to sound like one of the literati. In one email he mentioned a book of Cantos by Ezra Pound that he's reading in Italian. I'm guessing it's one with Italian on one page and English on the facing page."

Marc let out a boisterous laugh. "A faker, huh?"

Marlowe nodded her head in agreement.

"Absolutely," Giulia said. "Pound lived in Italy for about twenty years before being arrested for treason in the 40s. He came back and stayed in Venice until his death. A plaque hangs over the door where he lived that calls him a titan of poetry, *Titano della poesia*. He's difficult in any language, and I have a dual-language book of his Italian poetry, too."

"But Oliver implies something else," Marc said.

"I know," Giulia said. "There's probably not an honest bone in his body. It might be his way of apologizing, but I don't trust him. He's pushing for a meeting. So, it makes sense that I enter his office again. I've saved all his messages in case he might claim entrapment later. "

Now it was Chuck's turn to stiffen. But before he could say a word, Marlowe said, "We've got a new problem. One woman told me that he locked the door by turning the dead-bolt lever after she sat down. When she asked him why he did that, he fluffed it off as a habit and unlocked it, but she got out as soon as possible."

"That lock problem can be remedied," Chuck said.

"How'll you get in without alerting him?" Marc asked with a grin.

Chuck smirked and said, "Same way you would. I'm guessing you've known how to pick locks since you were eleven." Both men chuckled.

"It'll be taken care of. From the inside, he'll think it's working, and it will lock as usual when he leaves. After all, personnel records are in there."

"How shall we do it?" Giulia said. "Should I let you know as soon as I have an appointment?"

"Are you sure about this?" Chuck said, catching her eyes and holding their connection an extra beat.

"Sure. Sure. Sure," and she jabbed her fist in the air three times. "With your team of gallant men, what could happen?"

"Probably nothing. But a colleague and I will be nearby anyway. How about making the appointment late in the day. Fewer people will be around in case we need to take him down."

Marlowe and Giulia looked at each other and mouthed "take him down."

Their salads were delivered, and as they ate, they tossed the pros and cons of Giulia's idea back and forth.

"It seems to me," Giulia said, "that you and your commandos need to witness his bad behavior."

"Bad behavior?" Marlowe said. "You make it sound as if he'd been throwing spit balls."

They all laughed, but both Chuck and Marc agreed she had a point. "If we could rig his door to accidentally ease open while you're inside," Chuck spoke as if thinking aloud.

"You might want to make sure the escort service happens at least a couple times before Giulia's appointment," Marc said. "To avoid his cry of entrapment."

Giulia's stomach flinched at the term "escort service." She inhaled through her nose, eased out the breath and stabbed a piece of lettuce.

Marlowe piped up, "Each time a woman goes to Ogle, the man with her ought to make sure Oliver sees him. He could say, 'I'll wait here for you.'"

"Yesss," Giulia said, "but we don't want to put Oliver on the alert. We might have a long wait, and I need to move on this to make it work."

"Okay," Chuck said taking charge. "Two things need to happen. One. Giulia, you'll need to stall Ogle on the date until our system's up and running. Two. Other women involved need to have at least two telephone numbers for requesting backup."

"How many women are involved?" Marc asked. "Could you call them?"

"That's tricky, Giulia said.

"Yeah," Marlowe added. "The only way to get those names and numbers is through Oliver."

"Before I applied, I saw a list of teachers," Giulia said. "I counted about forty female faculty. We need to prepare enough info sheets—or better yet five by three cards they can carry—and personally hand them out. I'll take care of that as soon as I have the data." And she glanced at Chuck, who nodded.

"I'll help with that," Marlowe said. "When we gather the women, we should never suggest entrapment, the aim is to prevent harassment."

"Maybe we could invite them to the women's gym. It's the only place for privacy," Giulia said.

Marlowe said, "Great idea. Let's post an announcement offering news about a girlie event that no one else will pay attention to. Then, when we do the face-to-face inviting, we can let them know what the meeting's really about."

"We may miss a few, but word-of-mouth will reach them," Giulia said.

"So, we have a plan," Chuck said. "Until the women are informed, we'll need to wait and watch. How about changing the subject? Who wants dessert?"

They all passed.

"What? No zabaglione?" Marc said.

Both Giulia and Marlowe shook their heads.

"Giulia," Marlowe said. "Let's come back for a light lunch and indulge in their zabaglione."

"I like that idea," Giulia said.

"Espresso?" Chuck asked. After all, he was the host here and wanted to wrest some control back from all the bright ideas floating around. All three raised their hands on espresso and Chuck signaled the waiter.

Giulia and Marlowe excused themselves for the ladies' room. Chuck watched them leave. Marlowe wore a short, kicky skirt and high heels reminding him of how sexy she'd looked at the New Year's Gala. That had been when it hit him how lucky Marc was. Not only did he have an adorable woman, but from her interview and resume, Chuck knew she was witty and damned intelligent.

That same night, after making love in a detached way—with the woman he'd taken to the Gala—he had lain awake a long time thinking how empty his personal life had become. He'd broken off with her shortly after and hadn't bothered to find another woman. He'd lost interest in shallow relationships. Or—God forbid— maybe he was getting old. Then he ran into Giulia, or rather, she ran into him. Ever since all his senses had been working overtime. *This old man ain't done yet.*

"Marlowe looks lush tonight, doesn't she?" he said to Marc.

"Oh yeah," and Marc beamed. "Said she needed to amortize those expensive heels she bought for the Gala. Then worried about walking from the vaporetto to this place! She brought comfortable shoes along. Hell, I'd have carried her because I never tire of watching the way her calf muscles flex in those stilettos."

"Yeah, I'd carry Giulia for the same reason, but so far, I've never even seen her legs."

"She looks good enough to eat anyway. Right ol' man?" Marc said punching his shoulder.

"Right."

"Hey, what's wrong?"

"I hope nothing, but I get the sense that she's been hurt— undoubtedly by a guy—and I'm guessing she might have trouble trusting me or any man."

"Or herself?" Marc asked.

"More like I don't trust myself. Since I broke off with Tina, it's like I've forgotten all my moves to snare a woman. I haven't been this gun-shy since I was thirteen."

Marc said nothing.

"No! That's not it. I don't want to *snare* Giulia."

"She's different?"

"Oh yeah," Chuck said in a soft, breathy voice.

"And it doesn't help that you've had a dry season?"

"You could say that. The thing is, haven't tried. *Niente.* Nothing since New Year's."

"Oh man, you do have a problem," Marc said.

"One thing I know. I've got to take it slow."

"Well, as Marlowe often reminds me, slow is *jes' fine,*" and he smiled as if reliving a recent slow session with her.

Bastard, Chuck thought, but snorted in agreement.

Marlowe arrived back saying Giulia was working a pebble out of her boot and would be along in a minute. Chuck turned to watch for her. Through the full-length glass windows into the inner restaurant, he noticed a man seemed to be holding Giulia against her will. He rose out of his chair and took off.

* * *

When Giulia came from the ladies room, a man called out, "Julietta, what are you doing here?" She shuddered, and pretended to not understand English.

"*Mi dispiace, Signore. Non capisco bene l'inglese.*"

"You understand me, baby. I'd never forget those eyes."

She tried to walk away, but he grabbed her hand.

Her one and only time to forget to wear her brown contact lens was on an assignment with this man. In her employment with the first agency she tried in Eugene, she had chosen what they called Level A. Level A's were sent out on jobs that did not involve sex. To go with men who had to appear at business functions or maybe to attend seminars at the University. Men who thought they needed a pretty woman on their arm. The A service didn't cost as much for the client and served as a way for "new girls" to break into the business.

The agency expected new recruits to move into Level B, which included whatever kind of sex the client wanted. Of course, the women could refuse any request that sounded dangerous or repugnant—and that was written in the contract the men signed. Giulia had been tempted to move to Level B—it paid a lot more—but each time she came close, she backed off. Level A paid far more than she could ever make waiting tables near the campus. And the cheaper level was dangerous enough. She'd almost been raped twice. But the agency kept urging her to move "up."

She never teased men into thinking they'd get sex at the end of an event, but occasionally, someone decided to change the rules and wanted to pay her cash under the table. She'd been able to re-direct most of them, but when it had seemed impossible to dissuade someone, she could call a taxi service set up to come fast when given a special code.

The details about this man came back to her. At first he'd seemed to be a decent sort. He hadn't paid for sex but confessed she was too cute, and he'd always had fantasies about school girls. That thought had given her cold chills. She'd explained she wasn't prepared and reminded him of his contract. With a wink he had assured her he'd be gentle. She repeated she wasn't prepared. He said he carried protection. Again she insisted he stick to his agreement, and finally, he'd backed off. Good thing because she'd been about to kick him in the crotch that night—in public. After out-maneuvering this creep sitting here in Venice, she'd left that service.

* * *

Chuck appeared as Giulia pulled her hand free. Before he could say a word, she spoke in rapid Italian saying this man thought she was someone else and that she'd told him she didn't understand English. Chuck caught on and stuck to Italian, putting his arm around her shoulders and walked her away. He wanted to punch the guy out but knew better.

The man's parting shot was, "Oh, dolly, those gorgeous eyes."

Chuck flinched, his arm tightened around her. "You do have gorgeous eyes, you know," he whispered.

"Thanks," she said huddling close to him.

"Do you ever wear a colored lens?"

Sometimes.

"Don't wear one with me."

CHAPTER TWELVE

On their way to the train back to Vicenza, Chuck wondered if it was too soon to invite Giulia to his apartment in Venice. His gut said it was, but, just in case, he'd put a fresh sheet and duvet on the bed and spruced up his place.

"Chuck, you don't need to go all the way to Vicenza tonight. If it'll make you feel better, I promise to take a cab from the station."

"I know, but my—"

"Oh, your car. I forgot."

"I was hoping I could persuade you to go back to Villa Rotonda tomorrow."

"By the way, how is it you were out there last Sunday?"

"Honestly?"

"Of course." And her smile made his throat catch.

"I hadn't gone for years and wanted to check it out before inviting you to go with me. So. Tomorrow?"

"Well . . ." Hearing the echo of Nancy's words, she said, "Why not?"

Chuck felt as thrilled as he'd been at fourteen when the girl he'd fantasized about agreed to go to a movie with him. He held Giulia's hand all the way to the train station. Once in a compartment and on their way, he said, "We ought to exchange cell numbers in case something comes up. Okay?"

"Sure."

"Sure" she says, as if it hadn't felt like getting an overburdened plane to lift off. But it seemed like he'd made it over a huge obstacle.

At the door of her pensione, he gave her a small hug and

brushed his lips lightly across hers not knowing what to expect. To his surprise, she raised her arms to the tops of his shoulders and kissed back. He wrapped his arms around her, pulling her closer. Then leaning back to look in her eyes for a moment, he traced the outline of her lips with his tongue. They parted for him slightly and he pushed inside for one sweet taste. Desire burned hot and began to melt away his plans for restraint. Her tongue met his, and he thrust farther into her delicious mouth, but then, with a tremendous effort, he relented and released her. In a throaty voice, he said, "I'll be here at one."

She nodded and went inside but watched him through the oval glass of the door. When he turned back, she waved. *God.* He caught his breath. He almost kicked his heels in the air to leap over the stone banister. He liked that she'd waited to wave. When clear of her sight, he did leap over two bushes in a row, one after the other, as if running hurdles on the old Academy track.

* * *

Giulia touched her lips and thought about his. They'd felt sexier than they looked. Not even with her first lover had she felt such an instant reaction to a man. His erection had pressed against her during their embrace, and she sensed he was straining to control his emotions. Had she closed down for so long that she came across like someone trapped in a hair shirt or worse—frigid? Nancy was right, it-was-time-to-ease-up.

Within weeks after she and Jason had split, she'd thrown herself into graduate studies and eventually into the world of being a woman for sale, anesthetizing herself from all males, even from harmless smiles. My God. It had been more than three years since she'd allowed herself to respond to *any* kind of sensuality. Not a tremor until now.

* * *

"Pronto," Giulia said into the phone, wondering who was calling at eight o'clock on a Saturday morning.

"Giulia! You've got to come. It's my Tony! They attacked him."

"Nonna. What happened? Who attacked him? Where is he?"

"In Ospedale Vittorio Veneto on Via Forlanini. He's asking for you. Last night. Late. The police found him on the street beside his car."

"I'll come. Of course I'll come. Do you have your cell phone with you? Are you there now? How is he? How are you?"

"Si, si. I have my phone here at the hospital. He says he'll live but keeps asking for you. Me? I'm fine."

"I'm on my way," Giulia said, pulling an overnight bag from the closet and opening drawers to stuff underwear, night shirt, and cosmetics into the bag. "I'll let you know what time I'll arrive as soon as I know. Keep your phone on. Are you there alone?"

"My friend Angelina's with me but must leave soon. I'll be here. I'll be here. Come straight to the hospital. Please. He's half out of his mind and says do NOT go to the house."

"Tell him I'll be there soon as I can. Nonna, get coffee and a bite to eat."

"Si, si. Angelina fusses over me, the same." She chuckled out a little sob.

Giulia felt relieved that Nonna could laugh, but why was Nonno Tony asking for her? And why stay away from the house?

As she flipped through the local phonebook looking for a taxi number, she remembered her date with Chuck and dialed his number. As soon as he heard the problem, he said he'd pick her up in twenty minutes. He could get her there in an hour and a half. Much faster than the train. She made a feeble effort to argue but let her pride go and thanked him. The important thing was to get there. She had visions of the cruel 'Ndrangheta going after her nonno.

"Bring your hiking boots and warm clothes," Chuck said. "Spring storms come up fast in the foothills."

She pulled on a pair of dark brown corduroy jeans, a heavy blue sweater, wrapped a matching scarf around her neck and decided to wear the hiking boots instead of filling her bag with them.

Chuck arrived on time and saw her standing inside the door almost as if she hadn't moved since last night. At that moment, it struck him how much he wanted her. How much he wanted to take care of her for the rest of his life. *Geezus, where'd that come from?*

"Have you eaten anything?" he asked as he put her bag in the space behind their front seats along with his own duffle. He wore black jeans, grey sweater and black leather jacket and had decided to wear sturdy boots, too.

"No, but I can eat later," she said.

"I called ahead to Enrico's, a little shop on the way out of town. We'll swing by and get brioches and coffee for now and sandwiches for later. You'll need energy to deal with this."

"Thanks. Usually I feel self sufficient, but I'm scared for him, for them. I'll take any help I can get."

"Good. Not good about what happened, but good you're accepting help."

"I know." *This man understands my reluctance to accept anything from anyone.*

After making the stop at Enrico's, they were at the outskirts of Vicenza by nine-fifteen. Chuck said, "Now, tell me why you're so frightened."

She took a sip of hot coffee. "This coffee's perfect," she said. The aroma of fresh-baked brioches filled the little car. She took a bite and sighed with pleasure.

"Good, huh?" he said.

She told about Nonno Tony asking her to carry what she had feared might be contraband. She told of how her eyes were like Nonno Tony's—except his left was brown and her left was blue. She also told about wearing a brown lens and a wig to the meeting.

He looked over at her.

"What?" she said. "I've always wanted straight hair so I like to wear a wig sometimes." He remained quiet. "And… well… this time, I wanted to look different because I didn't feel right about the whole thing." She told about insisting that Nonno count the diamonds and sign a paper verifying their size. Again she hesitated.

"Is that all?" he said.

"Not exactly." She told of the man who had sent her a drink a few weeks before and that after she delivered those gems, she knew Botteri had been that man and maybe it had been more than a simple gem delivery. "And now, I think someone from an 'organization' attacked Nonno."

He reached for her hand and laid it on his thigh. He kept his hand over hers as they drove on in silence. His leg felt firm and strong and warm.

"We'll make a quick stop at Treviso, it's about halfway. Forty more minutes after that, we'll be there."

"Chuck, thank you for doing this. I might still be waiting to board a train." She was quiet for a while. "I wonder if I should go to this man Botteri and explain why he didn't trust Nonno and say I was embarrassed about my different eyes and that's why I wore the brown lens—"

"Would Botteri think *you* didn't trust your grandfather?"

"I think I could convince him about the eyes because sometimes I do like to pretend I have normal ones."

"Ah babe." He squeezed her hand. "You needn't hide anything, and not your beautiful eyes. They—you—are perfect the way you are." *Perfect? How about enticing, beguiling, fascinating, ravishing, tempting, and completely irresistible?*

"Thanks."

Strong rays of sunlight pierced through the dark forest reminding him of the ramped-up strobe light in a dirty disco joint in Uzbekistan. That operation had almost blinded Chuck, and the memory of the explosion that killed Harv, one of his best men, still jolted him. It had been their last covert rescue mission together. After that, he'd requested a change of duty. He'd seen enough.

Been through enough to last a lifetime—more than a lifetime.

Giulia sensed a stiffening in Chuck's posture and looked over at him. He sucked in a deep breath and reached for his wrap-around sunglasses stashed in a holder above the rear-view mirror. "Damned flashing lights drive me crazy," he muttered.

They remained quiet in their own thoughts. After a while, he slowed and pulled into a road-side petrol and snack shop on the approach to Treviso. "Want to stretch a bit? Use the facilities? More coffee?"

"Nothing, thanks, but I'll look for the *gabinetto*, restroom."

They were on their way in twelve minutes. He asked Giulia to hand him a sandwich. She also took one herself. "I didn't think I could eat a thing but guess anxiety makes me hungry."

"Yeah. Adrenalin does strange things." He knew what it could do to men in combat. Fast heart beats. Incredible thirst. Hunger. Not to mention that over-whelming adrenalin gave every guy a hard-on that wouldn't quit.

He'd brought bottles of water, and after they finished eating, she opened a bottle of Panna water and poured it into two cups. "I like Panna best," she said, "but many markets don't always have it."

"Are you a connoisseur of water?" he asked grinning over at her. *By damn, the Force's shrink had been right, joking with Giulia was helping to neutralize the power of that flashback.*

"Hardly. I'm not a connoisseur of anything I can think of. Until I drank Panna, I'd never noticed the difference in waters, but this has a smooth, slick feel and tastes so fresh." She poured more for him. "If the truth were known, a horrible additive probably hooks poor suckers like me."

Smooth. Slick. Jesus. Every word she says gives me a hard-on and I'm nowhere near combat.

"Back to Botteri," Chuck said, "how would you explain the wig?"

"That's easy. Women wear wigs to change their appearance all the time."

"True," he said. "The most worrisome thing is that you didn't touch the bag of diamonds."

"You think that might make him think I didn't trust Nonno?"

"Possibly. But that's only if they'd test it for fingerprints against—" he stopped.

"What?" she said.

"Did you have a drink while talking to him? Hold a glass or touch anything?" He ran his hand through his hair. "It's a long shot, but—"

"I wore gloves the whole time I was with him. All of five, ten minutes. They're beautiful kid leather my grandparents gave me for Christmas. I don't think I sat down. Oh yes. I did, briefly by the fire and then when I asked for a receipt, I sat while he wrote it."

"Jeezus! Does he have your name?"

She shook her head. "I used my other grandmother's name—she died many years ago."

"Hmm. So that wouldn't connect you to your grandfather Tuon."

"No. My name couldn't be Tuon anyway. Mom was a Tuon until she married. Would Botteri do all that research on my name? My fingerprints?"

"God. I don't know. So you gave the maiden name of your other nonna?"

"Yes. Mirella Rizzatti. I thought I was being so clever."

"You *were* clever. Rizzatti's a popular name in the Veneto. They'd have to go through hundreds of families to trace it to you."

"What can I do to convince Botteri that Nonno Tony's not a thief?"

"Maybe he is."

She stiffened and leaned away from him. "Maybe we need to hear his story first."

After an uncomfortable silence, he said, "You're absolutely right, Giulia. We need to hear your Nonno's story."

CHAPTER THIRTEEN

The grey-stucco hospital in the small town of 28,000 was easy to find.

"I'll drop you off and let you be with your family. You can call when you need a ride," Chuck said.

"Oh no you don't. You're not getting off that easy. I want you with me," and she quickly added, "to hear what Nonno Tony has to say."

"He'll be embarrassed enough without having me there."

"It's too bad if he's nervous. Another set of ears is always good. Besides, they already know you're bringing me. Will you come?"

"Damn straight I will."

When Giulia and Chuck walked toward Nonno Tony's room, Nonna was pacing in the hall outside while the nurse was with him. Nonna grabbed Giulia into her arms and kissed her. "You came! You really came." Then she looked at Chuck and whispered into her ear, "Is this beautiful man your friend?"

"Yes," she whispered back and turned toward Chuck. "Nonna, this is my friend, Major General Novak, from the base where I work."

Nonna spoke haltingly in English, thanking him for bringing Giulia. He responded in Italian and asked her to call him Chuck. Nonna beamed.

"Nonna, how bad is he?" Giulia asked.

"He has two broken ribs and is bruised all over. They kicked him when he was down! His knee's swollen, his shoulder was dislocated. And black and blue marks all around his blue eye. But as usual, he says he's fine," she said with disgust and a little grin of pride.

"When can he go home?"

"Maybe tomorrow. *Oddio!*, Oh God! You didn't go to the house did you?"

"No, no. We came straight here."

The nurse, dressed in lavender scrubs, came out and said they were free to go into his room. Chuck stood in the doorway while the two women entered. Giulia hurried to the side of Nonno Tony's bed. Using the arm without an IV, he pulled her close enough to give her a hug—not as powerful as usual—but he murmured he loved her and was sorry he had dragged her into his mess.

"Don't worry, Nonno Tony. You need to heal, we'll talk later."

"We talk now. You didn't go to the house?"

"We came straight here as Nonna said. But why not go to the house?"

"Who's that?" Nonno Tony asked, noticing Chuck across the room.

Giulia wasn't aware that Chuck had hung back; she motioned him to come to Tony's bedside. "Nonno, I want you to meet my friend, Major General Novak. When he heard about you, he offered to drive me here."

Nonno opened his good brown eye wide and appraised Chuck. "Big man," he grunted. "Thank you for bringing my Giulia."

Chuck put out his hand. "You're welcome, sir. Please call me Chuck."

"Gladly. And you will call me Antonio—no, make that Tony."

They shook. Some sort of meeting of the minds happened between these two men. It was subtle, but a rapport had been established. Strange, Giulia thought. She'd expected Nonno Tony might not want Chuck anywhere near her. She was pretty sure, however, that Nonna would be thrilled she had a male friend who'd drive her all the way to Vittorio Veneto.

"Chuck," Nonna said, "would you please find more chairs so we can all be comfortable while Tony tells his story."

Chuck made an almost imperceptible bow and left to find chairs. Nonna caught the bow and smiled.

"Oh my, Giulia. Your young man is so handsome and polite."

"He's not my young man, Nonna. Just a friend."

"So far, *tesoro,* darling, so far," Nonna murmured. "I saw him look at you the same way Tony looked at me once."

"He still looks at you that way, Nonna."

"Yes." She dipped her head, then smiled back up at Giulia.

How interesting, Giulia thought. Nonna wants to include Chuck in her husband's story. She looked over at Nonno Tony. His eyes were closed, maybe painkillers made him drowsy, but it was more than that. He seemed shriveled and frail. For the first time, she acknowledged him as a seventy-seven-year-old man. But this couldn't be her Nonno, who had always vibrated with life. My God. He could die! Her chest clenched and she felt short of breath.

Chuck came back carrying two plastic chairs with arms, and Nonna directed him where to place them. He insisted Nonna and Giulia take the plastic molded ones, and he took the wooden straight-back already in the room. Nonno Tony opened his eyes and assessed the situation.

"Chuck, whatever your intentions are with our Giulia, for today, you're part of our family. That means what I have to say stays here. Understood?"

"Absolutely, sir, uh, Tony."

"Good. First shut the door and if anyone tries to come in, even the doctor, you will deal with them. Va bene. Here's what happened."

"Not far from home, two cars blocked my way and four men leaped out." Tony sighed and continued. One thug yanked him out of his car and punched him in the face, then tossed him on the pavement where he struck his knee. He had presence of mind to act as if it were broken and hoped they wouldn't try to break the other. He heard them discuss the possibility. "For once I was glad to have this white hair, because they decided one broken knee was enough for the 'old coot.' So they merely kicked me in the chest."

"Oh, Nonno Tony!" Giulia cried. She'd almost said "poor Nonno" but that would hurt him more than the beating. "What happened then?"

"They had a message from their capo. 'Fake granddaughter. Fake gems. Don't snivel for payment. Don't work in Vicenza. Not in Verona. Not in Padova. Be glad you're alive.' I remember trying to say not fake granddaughter, but I must have passed out."

"They left him in the street," Nonna snarled in outrage, "his car engine running. Someone came by and called the police." She went to him and kissed his hand. "Promise me, Tony, no more." He squeezed her hand, nodded his head with a sigh and closed his eyes.

"Let's take a break," Chuck said. "I'll go find some coffee. Or tea?" and he looked at Nonna and Giulia.

Tony roused. "Let the women go, Chuck, I want to talk to you."

After the women left, Tony called Chuck to his bed. "I'm weak now, but don't count me out yet, big man."

Chuck laughed. "That thought never crossed my mind."

"Good. First off, those gems weren't fake but Botteri took the opportunity to grab them for free. My fault. I shouldn't have brought Giulia into it, and I should have listened to her when she said she'd go in disguise. That gave him an excuse to renege... and attack. Those diamonds were legit. I've had them stashed from way back. Thought it'd be a good time to break into the jewelry business in Vicenza. Whatever I broke into was not *il mio piano di battaglia,* my battle plan." He shifted in bed and heaved a sigh wincing as he did.

Chuck wisely dismissed Tony's wince of pain, and asked, "What can I do?"

"I need someone to go to the house and assess the damage. Those hoodlums wouldn't stop with me. Thank God, Maria Grazia was with her weaving group, or they might have hurt her, too. So far, I've kept her from going there until I could find someone to check the whole place out. My friends would do it and they'll help me restore it, but the instant you walked in—*che diavolo,* well hell—I knew you were the man for the job."

"Absolutely." Chuck caught himself from saluting. "Tell me what you need and consider it done."

"You're a man of action," Tony said as a statement not a question. "But be careful. You've been in combat, right?"

"Special Forces." And before Tony could continue, "Relax, Tony, I'll check for possible explosives."

Tony took another painful breath and settled back. "I like the way your mind works. My keys are somewhere around here. Ask Maria Grazia. Unless they destroyed everything, you'll find a good flashlight and tools in the shed. Look in every room, even the little attic room where Giulia always stays. Those thugs will have made an unholy mess looking for more gems. Fools! I never keep valuables on the premises. Hope they didn't destroy Maria Grazia's loom."

"Do you have a truck in case I need to haul anything?" Chuck asked.

"Yes. Thank God my neighbors were unloading gravel the day before. It's parked across the street. Those animals wouldn't have known it was mine. Get *those* keys, too." He leaned back and closed his eyes.

Giulia and Nonna came back with coffee and sandwiches. Tony was snoozing or feigning sleep to prevent Nonna from arguing about not going home yet. But when Chuck told them what he'd be doing, Nonna relinquished the keys without a word.

As he went out the door, Giulia handed him a packet wrapped in white paper. "Take a sandwich."

He took it, smiled, holding her gaze for an extra moment.

* * *

Two hours later, Chuck came back. "It's a mess, for sure, but I think it can be set right in a few days. I'd like to help, Tony. I don't have to be back until Wednesday."

Giulia added that she'd left a message about missing her Monday class. "I don't teach on Tuesdays so we have some time."

Tony roused. He and Chuck talked in more detail about what needed to be done. Chuck was able to board up a window and reset the hinge on the front door left hanging askew.

"Giulia, you and your nonna can stay at home tonight," Chuck said.

"Young man, I want you to stay in our home, too." Nonno Tony said.

"Yes. We have plenty of room," Nonna said. "You are most welcome."

"Giulia?" Nonno Tony croaked. His voice sounded raw.

"I'm here, Nonno Tony. What can I get for you? Water?"

After a few sips, he said, "What did Botteri say? What did you say?"

She told the story again with as much detail as she could remember.

"Tell me again about the person who tried to sign you up to be Botteri's kept woman."

Nonna gasped and Chuck rose up, then sat back feeling betrayed. He thought she would have told him all that on the way here. She'd been more frightened than she'd let on. Obviously, he didn't have her full trust—yet.

Giulia felt uneasy, but she told about Laura, the tea, the fact that a certain gentleman wanted her exclusively and the contract offered as Giulia had dashed from the hotel.

"Does he have your name?"

"No. I used Nonna Mirella's name." Giulia felt comfortable to talk about the name business. "At the time, I thought I was being clever, but now I can't go back to him and explain I am your—"

"Never go back to that man, precious. Never!" Tony began coughing. It was obvious each movement was painful.

"Calma, Nonno Tony, calma. More water?"

After another sip, he leaned back. "Avoid him. He wouldn't believe you, and you'd be looking over your shoulder the rest of your life."

"What a mess I made."

"You? I'm the one who pulled you in and to make things worse, didn't take you seriously. I'm sorry, little one. In any case, his kind would have cheated me anyway. Those gems were real. On the phone, I told that thief I couldn't remember how many were in my safe box but I'd send about fifteen or twenty for his appraisal and possible purchase. I trusted he was a legitimate business man. I'm the one who messed up." He slumped back and was quiet.

"It's all over, Tony," Nonna said, but he had drifted off again.

Nonna turned to Chuck. As soon as we set up the kitchen, you're invited for dinner."

Chuck had recovered and stashed Giulia's lack of trust in him away for now. "Allora," Chuck said. "I was thinking of taking you ladies out tonight."

Nonna smiled but began to protest.

"The only place I know is Trattoria alla Cerva. Ever since I knew I'd be coming here, I've been hankering for their pasta with bolognese sauce made from the local deer." He stopped. "Or, is there another place you'd rather go?"

"I'll go with you," Nonno Tony said rousing himself to a sitting position with the help of the mechanical lifter. Nonna rushed to him and gently pushed him down, whispering, "Not this time, *mio leone*, my lion. Not this time."

He muttered that the bolognese was his favorite too, but in the end he acquiesced. The three left, promising to bring him pasta and sauce.

As they drove away, Nonna was sitting beside Chuck in the front seat. Giulia, who had crawled into the small area behind, began to reassure her grandmother about her loom.

"Nonna," Chuck said turning to her, "your loom looks doable. It lists to one side, but the hard wood and sturdy hinges held. We can set it right."

She nodded. It seemed to him that Nonna's mettle was plenty strong to handle a damaged loom. He didn't mention the extra time he'd taken in the small attic room that had been Giulia's ever since she'd been little. It still held a young girl's feel. Most of the available wall space was filled with posters of Venice. One depicted a charming *putto*. The chubby cherub held a book in his hands. A natural choice for a young girl who loved to read. Another poster puzzled him. It held a prominent place on the slanted roof at the foot of her bed. Must have been there a long time because the edges were curled and tattered. It showed a stone lion as big as a horse—a horse with a huge lion's head and frowsy mane. More humorous than frightening.

Sitting sideways on the creature's back was the goddess Minerva, helmet and all, including her symbolic owl perched on top. Odd. Why had that fascinated Giulia? And where in Venice was it? Then it came to him. The lion had to be in the *Giardini,* the Public Gardens, because green shrubs grew around the sculpture as well as gnarled oaks and large Spanish chestnuts. He'd ask later. He'd also ask more about the business of Botteri wanting Giulia to be his exclusive mistress. Jeez!

After dinner, they dropped by the hospital with food for Tony. But too groggy to eat, he sent it on home and bade them a drowsy good night.

Nonna and Giulia showed Chuck to his room. Giulia was ready to drop in her tracks and they all said goodnight. But Maria Grazia seemed energized and began to tackle her kitchen. Because his room lay close by, Chuck heard her humming as she worked. Maybe she felt relieved that Tony's sporadic lifestyle was coming to an end.

Chuck grinned to himself. Tony might be in his late seventies, but as he had said to Chuck, he wasn't down for the count yet. Right away, he'd liked the guy and right away wanted to know more about him. Even in his weakened state, Tony showed signs of being a forceful leader. Chuck wondered about an Italian Resistance connection.

Soon his thoughts turned to Giulia. Yes, he wanted sex with her, but with this woman, he wanted more. He wanted to see her let go of that iron coil wound around her. He wanted to know if she had any girlie bones in that sensual body? Did she squeal at a spider or water bug? Did she read in bed? Did she sleep on her stomach or back or on her side? Nude? He could almost feel her soft body beneath him. Oh yeah, he wanted her. And thinking of that wild-maned lion, he wanted to be her lion the way Tony was to Maria Grazia. Lots more work before that can happen, he thought.

* * *

Exhausted, Giulia stretched out on her attic bed and thought of Chuck's full, sexy lips tucked into that half smile. She remembered the feel of his rock-hard thigh under her hand as they'd driven here. *Oh God.* She shuddered, imagining another part of him that might be equally as hard.

CHAPTER FOURTEEN

Oliver knew all about Pensione Luciana, having driven there while still smarting from the insult of Giulia's knee in his groin. Ever since that afternoon, he often parked across the street behind her pensione hoping to figure a way inside. He needed to punish her for what she did—not to mention that self-righteous prig, Novak, finding out about it. Oliver got hard thinking about that day when he saw her breasts jiggle as she kneed him. He moved his seat back, reached to unzip his pants and grabbed his erection. He wished he had one of her bras. Yeah. Panties to match would even be better. *Was Novak already into hers?*

He cleaned up with a towel kept under the driver's seat and relaxed. That's when he noticed steps leading up to what might be a first-floor apartment. Through the early-evening shadows, he focused intently on the four doors at ground-floor level. Pensione Luciana must also have apartments for rent, he thought. Her landlords were bringing in a nice income. Did they declare the apartments? *Never know when such info will come in handy.*

He'd need a damned clever story to get inside one of those rear entrances. But then what? Her file didn't show a room number. A couple of times he had followed Cavinato, but that proved a dead end because he couldn't enter that front entrance with her. He *would* enter her place. Maybe even her. And with that thought, he felt his blood heat up again.

After he discovered those rear doors, locating her bedroom took up all his free time. Except for important meetings, he made it a habit to swing behind the pensione to watch for a chance to get inside. One evening, he sat at his usual place across the street out of the lamppost's circle of light. He'd been ready to call it a night and reached to turn the key on his sleek Mercedes, when he saw her walk up those steps.

Gotcha!

* * *

It was late Sunday morning, and Tony had stationed his wheelchair in the sunshine between the back of the house and the shed to direct Chuck and friends gathered to help. When Giulia brought him a cup of coffee, he urged her to sit beside him. She'd been helping Nonna prepare lunch for everyone. Chuck came from the driveway carrying wood from the local lumberyard.

"Chuck take a break and come sit," Tony called.

"Be there in a second," he yelled.

"Giulia, bring yourself coffee. For Chuck too, *va bene?*"

When the three were settled, Tony launched into his fear for her safety in Vicenza. "Giulia, now's the time to make your move to Venice. You should have gone directly there in the first place." He held up his hand. "You think you need to work and save a tad more—always more. I understand. But you must leave. That *brutale mascalzone*, vicious villain, will keep looking for you if only to get back at me. It's just a matter of time before Botteri or one of his henchmen spots you in Vicenza."

"Maybe so." Giulia said, thinking of the thug who'd followed her.

"Maybe? No maybe about it," Tony said.

Chuck said, "Someone did try to follow her home after—"

Giulia jerked her head toward him and scowled.

"Lord!" Nonno thundered. "What's that about?"

Giulia sagged back in her lawn chair and told how a man plodded behind her after she'd delivered the gems. "I managed to hop on a bus the moment it pulled away leaving him no chance to follow."

"That was quick thinking, coccolona, but we can't wait for the next time."

"But I wore my wig."

"*Pollastrella!*, chickie," he said taking her hand. "It takes more than a fancy wig to disguise your *forma divina.*"

"Nonno," Giulia said, blushing. She released her hand and lifted her cup.

"*É vero*, Chuck?"

"Si, si, Tony, it's true," Chuck said, hoping to catch her eyes.

"Allora. You must find that place of your dreams as soon as possible. I want you to disappear into Venice away from Botteri's territory—at least I hope his territory hasn't reached Venice." He turned to Chuck. "You live in Venice, don't you?"

"I do." Chuck turned to her, "I'd like to help you find an apartment if... if you want." He took her hand and this time, captured her eyes.

"I would like that," she said.

Chuck nodded, taking that as a sign she'd forgiven him—maybe.

"Good," Tony said. "I'll pay the first month's rent and whatever deposits are needed to get you in fast."

Giulia started to protest, but Maria Grazia came out to see what their confab was about. When Tony explained, she nodded her head in agreement.

"Chuck, maybe you can help Giulia find a place?" Nonna asked.

"Already settled," Tony said holding Maria Grazia's hand.

"*Perfetto*. Now, Tony, come lie down before we spread lunch. You'll wear yourself out. You want to be in good form with your friends, eh?"

He submitted to her and said he'd come in a moment and Chuck could push his chair to the door. Giulia left with Nonna.

"I don't need you to push this rig. I can manage, but I want to ask you something personal-like," and he looked directly into Chuck's eyes.

"Okay," Chuck said.

"Have you slept with her?" Tony asked, still looking straight into Chuck's eyes with his own so incredibly like Giulia's.

"Not yet," Chuck said, grinning.

Tony grinned, too, and held up a finger. "Don't wait long. She's got barriers. I hope you're the man to break them down. Something happened but she won't talk to me. If Maria Grazia knows, she's not talking either."

"I'm working on it, Tony."

"Good."

"Toneee," Maria Grazia called from the kitchen window.

"Coming." He grinned at Chuck, "The lioness is getting restless."

* * *

They accomplished a lot during the rest of Sunday and Monday. By Tuesday noon when Giulia and Chuck left, the house looked much better and so did Tony. Giulia said she'd come back the following weekend, but both grandparents insisted she spend time looking at rentals in Venice.

On the way back, Giulia seemed more relaxed and thanked Chuck once again for all the help he'd been to her and her family. "I appreciate your offer to help me find an apartment, but I can't let you give up your free time for me."

"Giulia, don't you know by now I *want* to spend my free time with you?"

She looked out the window at a fast-moving stream tumbling over small boulders and downed logs. "I did notice. Guess it's me; I'm out of practice in the relationship thing. I… I've been closed down," she said. "After a long—"

"You could practice on me," he said reaching for her hand and holding it on his thigh again as they drove on through the forest of pine, fir and cedars.

"Giulia?"

"What?"

"Tell me more about the woman named Laura. How'd you meet her?"

She took her hand back and gripped it in her other hand as if to steady herself. "First, you understand that Botteri was the same man who'd sent a drink to me in the bar almost a month before I delivered the gems to him."

"Men in bars often send drinks to pretty women. Been doing it forever."

"Yes. But when Laura caught me in the lobby and invited me to tea, I had no idea she was connected to him. Her invitation seemed odd but I was curious. We went to a tearoom off the lobby and tea arrived as we sat down."

"No waiter took the order? Strange."

"I think we were expected. She began to explain about her escort service and that a certain gentleman had seen me recently and wanted to be my exclusive client. In that moment, I put it together and jumped up to leave, spilling my tea. The waiter arrived immediately with a towel and a fresh pot."

"That sounds even more suspicious."

She nodded. "Laura chased me through the lobby and handed me a contract. She looked desperate. I took pity on her and stuffed it in my purse."

"Do you still have it?"

"No! I destroyed it at home after ditching that creep."

"I'm curious. Why'd you go to that bar in the first place?"

"Why not? Are you saying I shouldn't have gone?"

"Not at all. Just wondered how it happened."

"I'd settled into the pensione before classes started and felt lonely. Thought I'd look for a glass of Prosecco. Didn't want to buy a whole bottle. It'd go flat before I could..." She stopped. She felt as if she were confessing to a parent. "Chuck, I've been traveling alone to Italy for years. Taking a walk at dusk seemed like a pleasant thing to do. What's your problem?"

"No problem. Giulia, I'm sorry about your being followed after you left Botteri. And I apologize for telling Tony about that thug but thought—"

"It's okay."

They were both quiet, then she added, "This time," and looked over at him with a little gleam in her eyes.

He took back her hand and held it again. They didn't talk much on the rest of the trip, and she noticed how comfortable their silences were.

CHAPTER FIFTEEN

After her classes, office hours with students and a long departmental meeting, Giulia finally got to her work email. She found four messages from Oliver Ogle wanting an answer about teaching Italian. The first two were reasonable, but the third and fourth, "Do you want to teach or not?" and "I'm a busy man. Get in touch with me!" were downright grouchy. She felt cranky, too, and decided to let him wait until tomorrow.

At home she shed work clothes and pulled on sweat pants and shirt and slid into her slippers with Goofy's head and floppy ears, a kooky gift from Nancy—but they were warm. She poured a glass of red and called Chuck. His phone went to voicemail. She asked if any women had requested protection while they'd been gone then carried the wine to her computer and started searching for apartments.

* * *

Oliver felt frustrated when he left his office. The bitch hadn't answered any of his emails. Then his spirits lifted when he saw Novak climb into that yellow piece of junk he called a car. Oliver hurried to his sleek navy-blue Mercedes and followed him into town. He waited across the street while the hulk came from a pizza shop carrying a box. *Bet that's going to signorina snooty with the big boobies.*

When Oliver saw Novak stand at the front of the pensione waiting for the door to open, he was beside himself with glee. Novak didn't know about her apartment in the rear. *Secretive little bitch.*

Oliver had no intention of trying to get in with Novak around and didn't bother to watch her outdoor steps—this time.

* * *

"Ciao, Giulia," Chuck's velvety voice over the phone sent sparks of excitement to the pit of her belly.

"Ciao, Chuck. How was your day?"

"Been like drinking out of a fire hydrant. How about you?"

"The same." She started to mention Oliver's pouty notes but he cut in.

"Have you eaten yet?"

"No, but—"

"I'm outside your door with hot pizza, and contrary to most Italian pizzas, this one's loaded with melted mozzarella. Interested?"

"You ought to be in advertising, my stomach's suddenly wide awake. I just opened a bottle of red. I'll meet you at the stairs."

For a second, she wished she was wearing something more attractive but the sweats would have to do. She did put her bra back on. Her apartment in the rear of the building would no longer be a secret, but she didn't want to hide from Chuck anyway.

* * *

On the way to her pensione, Chuck had thought about how to help Giulia find an apartment. Okay, he admitted, he'd been thinking more about sex. But not just any sex. He imagined slow, unhurried lovemaking with her. Damn, he hadn't been so turned on since—couldn't remember—and wasn't sure he could take it slowly the first time. After that, though, he'd make love to her for the rest of the night. Tonight maybe?

With those thoughts whirring in his head, when he saw her at the top of the stairs in a sky-blue sweatsuit, Chuck's brain exploded. For a moment, he couldn't decide which way he liked her best. In that sexy skirt and top or in those soft sweats. Damn. She looked delicious, why ask for anything more?

As she led him to her apartment, she said, "My secret's out. From the front entrance, this building is deceptive. Several two and three-bedroom apartments are in the back. Shortly after I arrived, I shifted into one but didn't change my status at the base. Now with Oliver's antics and maybe Botteri searching for me, guess I did the right thing." She unlocked her apartment door and they walked inside.

"Deceptive indeed," he said as he laid the pizza on the kitchen counter and walked into the spacious living/dining area. Carefully crafted moldings framed the high ceilings and a smoothly plastered rosette formed the center from which hung a simple, but elegant, light fixture. "You made a good choice here. It's obviously well maintained. Too bad you'll be leaving soon."

"I know." A small sigh escaped. "But it does seem necessary and Venice has been my goal all along. Shall I put the pizza in the oven?"

"Sure, that sounds good." He walked toward the sliding glass doors. "You have a balcony and separate entrance."

"I do. You're the only one who knows about that, too, except my sweet landlords who agreed not to tell anyone." She slid the pizza into the oven. "They seem to want to take care of me."

"Who wouldn't?" he said walking toward her as she turned from the oven to face him. He opened his arms and sighed with relief as she moved into them. "Mmm. You know what?"

"What?" she said turning her head up to look into his iceberg-blue eyes. Tonight, they were far from icy.

"You feel like you belong right here." He pulled her closer.

"Maybe so."

He lifted her up and kissed her lightly, letting her slide down his body knowing she'd feel the beginning of his erection. He waited. He wanted her to have the chance to pull back in case she might have spoken in haste. After a few seconds of silence, he slid his hands beneath her shirt and put them around her small waist.

Oh God. So smooth and warm. He leaned down to move his mouth across her lips sensing her excitement. *Does she like the feel of my mustache?* He pressed his tongue inside. When her tongue met his, his cock jerked and swelled until he feared he'd go off right then. He tamped down as much as he could but needed to taste more. Slowly, he thrust his tongue deeper. When he began withdrawing it even more slowly, she gasped and put her arms around his neck.

Keeping his tongue in her delicious mouth, he bent to pick her up and went looking for her bedroom. Like a homing device, he seemed to know where to go and pushed open the right door on the first try. He stood her beside the bed and continued to kiss her, letting their tongues enjoy their sex dance. Her breath came faster. He tried to slow his own down. When she unbuttoned his shirt enough to run her hands over his chest, he almost lost it again. He stopped kissing her and yanked off his shirt. Then slowly—still wanting to give her a chance to stop him—he lifted *her* shirt. Her rib cage was slender but her breasts were full and almost over-flowed the lacy pale-blue bra.

He sucked in his breath and leaned back to feast his eyes be-fore running his fingers over the swell of soft flesh rising above the lace. Sliding both hands to the sides of her breasts, he pressed those tempting swells toward his mouth and slid his tongue un-derneath the lace.

Her breath hitched and he heard her hum a little sound of desire. Slipping the straps of her bra down her shoulders, he found the clasp and let it fall away. He lifted her breasts in his hands and felt their luscious weight. Their softness. *I could hold them forever. Bury my face in them. Protect them forever.*

"Ah," he sighed. Lush. Succulent. He kissed her again, still almost tentatively. When she responded, he deepened their kiss. While their tongues touched and teased, he slid her sweats and panties down her silky smooth thighs. Already he imagined how they'd feel wrapped around him.

He laid her on the bed. "Nice footwear," he murmured as he nudged off the silly slippers. He stood to open his belt, holding her gaze while she watched him with those bewitching eyes. He unzipped his pants and kicked them off. *God, she was lovely. Like an angel with soft, dark curls framing her flushed face.* He struggled for control determined not to rush or force her. Hooking his thumbs in the waistband, he pushed down his black briefs and stepped out of them. Her eyes widened at the sight of his erection. He hesitated. Then she reached for him.

That's all it took. He was on the bed, bending to kiss her neck and breasts again. The rosy-brown nipples were already hard peaks and he took one into his mouth. He sucked gently. Then harder. His large hand moved down her smooth belly to lay cupped over her mound. He opened his mouth wider and took in more of her breast.

Instinctively, she arched her back in that ancient response of female to male. While he held the other nipple in his mouth, he eased a finger into her hot, moist body. And suckled again. When he inserted two fingers into her heat, a honeyed response bathed his hand.

"Wait," he said, scrambling for the condoms in his pants somewhere on the floor.

"I'm wearing a patch," she said in a hushed voice.

"And I'm tested regularly at the base. But it's up to you."

"Chuck, I trust you, but maybe—"

"It's okay," he said. He found the condoms, covered himself and began kissing her again, trying desperately to take it slowly. He pushed into her little by little. She was tight. It had been awhile for her. He withdrew, grabbed a pillow to place under her bottom. When he entered again, he also let his thumb move in light circles searching for her clitoris. Warm liquid covered the pad of his thumb again. Her body opened. She was ready. But still, he moved slowly, continuing to brush his thumb against that sensitive nub.

She quivered. Kissing her mouth deeply, he continued to caress that knot of sensitivity. Again she trembled as if hovering on the brink of release.

"Let go, angel, let go," he whispered and drew her breast into his mouth tugging hard. As if a dam had burst, she gasped out, "Yesss." She stiffened, arched and her body shook. Her orgasm shook him as well. His hold-out time was gone! He wanted to wait, but instead, he increased the depth of his thrusts while she was still pulsing from her release. Then she began to respond anew! When he withdrew, he lifted her legs over his arms allowing him to deepen his next thrust. He drove in again, moving faster until she orgasmed once more. This time he was lost. Surging forward, he found his own seismic release and collapsed onto her.

* * *

She'd forgotten how good it felt to have the weight of a man pressing on her. He shifted and began smothering her with kisses and nips along her neck. When he nibbled the lobe of one ear, she felt a tug deep within. How could that happen so soon? She'd felt satisfied only a moment ago, twice. Three times? And now a stirring again? He must have sensed it because he deepened his kiss. But when he withdrew his tongue, she whimpered.

"We'll get back to that, angel. Don't go away, I intend to explore all of you." He ducked into the bathroom to get rid of the condom. As soon as he came back to her, he began kissing her again from head to foot. He sucked her nipples as he molded and gently kneaded her breasts humming to himself as if enjoying a rich delicacy. His fingers probed between her legs again as he moved his kisses and caresses farther and farther down her body. He nudged her legs apart and nuzzled her open with his mouth. Before she had time to think about it, she climaxed again, moaning from the intensity of the sensations. He continued to tongue her clitoris.

"Wait. I can't take any more."

He raised his head. "Yes, my angel, you can. We've only begun."

He was right, she *could* take more. His tongue was relentless.

She felt frantic with mounting desire as he continued to lick and taste the inner folds of her center. To orgasm again so soon was a new sensation. She couldn't believe she was ready for more. And more than anything, she wanted him inside again. She'd never wanted such a deep connection before. His breathing shifted into heavier panting. When he sipped her clitoris, she thought she'd break into pieces. Then he drew slightly harder and she erupted, flooding his mouth with her unique essence.

"Yes," he breathed. Rising on his knees to cover himself with another condom, he slid his hands under her bottom and brought her toward his waiting shaft. And plunged. Again. Fast and carnal. He came in the most explosive release he'd ever experienced, more than when he'd been fourteen and thought the only way was fast and furious. His last thrust carried her with him. They collapsed in a sweaty heap.

They dozed. Briefly. Without a word, he rolled her over on her stomach, lifted her onto her hands and knees. He was gentle when he entered her from behind. Her vagina was hot and juicy, and the angle allowed him to penetrate. But this time, he moved slowly, and withdrew in an even longer, slower slide. He pumped fast, then slow until she felt dizzy and aflame from the intermittent friction. But it must *not* stop. His hard belly slapped against her soft bottom. Leaning on one hand, he took a breast in the other, holding her aroused nipple between his long fingers. With each thrust, he tightened his fingers. She climaxed again.

As she pulsed around him, he gasped, "Now, love. I can't hold…" He plunged once more, and this time she took all of him. He went still. For a moment, she felt him swell even more inside her and then his hot release pumped into her and pleasure continued to burst over and over. The sensations seemed to go back and forth between them. She couldn't separate whose throb was whose. Is this what the ancients meant about two becoming one?

When their hearts slowed to a steady thumping and their breath was easy again, he eased her onto her back and nestled her head in the crook of his shoulder. He lazily stroked her breasts, her waist, her stomach, back to her breasts and even played with her belly button. It seemed he couldn't get enough of her. After a while, he rolled onto her again and said, "Do you need to sleep? If so, tell me."

"Mmm. Maybe later."

The truth? She felt slightly sore but also slick and hot and did *not* want sleep. She wanted Chuck again. As he slid gently into her, something clicked. She'd never imagined this kind of lovemaking, and she couldn't get enough. They made love into the night. Even when not moving, they stayed locked together.

It was a closeness she'd never felt before. She had no idea what would come next. Her emotional life had been a desert before Chuck. He was like long-promised rain falling on one of those desert plants that only get a chance to bloom every seven years.

CHAPTER SIXTEEN

The pizza!" Giulia yelped and sat up in bed.

"Oh yes, the pizza," Chuck said. "Wonder if it's edible."

She punched him on the shoulder as he lay looking more than self-satisfied. "Was the pizza your ploy to make wild, wonderful love."

"Maybe," he said gathering her back down beside him. "Hungry?"

"For what?" she said.

"What appeals to you?"

"Hmm. Whatever I'm hungry for, at least I ought to turn the oven off."

"No problem. I turned it off when we left the kitchen about . . ." He turned his head to look at the bedside clock, "About six hours ago."

"Oh."

"'Oh, she says," and he rose up on his elbow to look down at her. "Is that all you can say for my fabulous foresight?"

"Something fabulous happened here tonight." She sighed pulling him down again to scoot into the hollow of his shoulder.

"I do believe I could eat a bite or two, though," he said. "Shall I go take a peek in your oven?"

"Might as well. You've peeked into every other place in this apartment," and she couldn't keep from giggling. When was the last time she giggled? Twelve maybe?

"So I have, love, so I have," and he turned toward her for a deep kiss that once again expressed a gentleness she'd not expected or ever known.

When he came back from the kitchen, she was in the shower. He slid back the shower door and stepped inside. "We can save time by showering together, and then the pizza will be done perfectly."

"You think so?" she said, knowing her smile was a coy one. And when did she learn coy?

He grabbed the soap from her hand and washed her all over paying close attention to her rich breasts and round ass. She grabbed it right back and began to make suds all over his chest, enjoying the feel of his hard pectorals and the slight roughness of black hair that lightly covered him. The warm water accented the dark path leading from his upper chest to the black, heavy bush encircling his penis. She spent an inordinate amount of time sudsing that area and soon his cock was so stiff it curved upward at a painful angle. His body quivered as he braced himself against the tile wall, but when she put the soap in its dish and started to crouch before him, he stopped her.

He knew where this was going. Yes, he wanted her mouth on him. Oh yeah. He'd fantasized that. But did she think she ought to do this? Hell, he couldn't hold out much longer either way, and in one swift movement, he jerked away from the wall to haul *her* up against it instead. Pinning her there, he shoved into her again and again, making no apology for the roughness. They both exploded at the same time.

"Ohmigod," he whispered as the water continued to pour down on them. He held her to him, grateful for demand water heaters in Italy. "Are you all right?" Before she could answer, he said, "Giulia?"

"Yes?"

"I forgot a condom."

"I know. It should be fine."

He relaxed but wondered why she'd asked for one in the first place. He opened the shower door and grabbed towels. "Let's dry off and see about that pizza," he said with a slight roughness in his voice.

Giulia, seemed overcome and said nothing. She pulled on a deep-blue oversized Tee-shirt and wrapped up in a pale-blue robe of terry cloth. Chuck pulled on his pants but left off his shirt; he was still overheated.

While Giulia set a couple places at the table, she said, "Chuck?"

"Yeah," he answered, turning from the sliding glass door to the balcony where he'd been checking the lock mechanism.

"I want to tell you something."

He walked toward her holding his arms out to her as he'd done earlier in the evening.

Lord, he was magnificent, all broad chest and hard body. "Stop," she said, "I need to see your face when I say this."

"Okaaay."

She inhaled deeply and spilled out the story about Ricky and her abortion at twenty-four, about never telling Ricky or anyone else, and also about learning too late, that she couldn't rely on birth-control pills if she was taking antibiotics.

He stepped up again and put his arms around her. After a beat or two, he asked "Are you on antibiotics now?"

"No. I know it's not reasonable to be paranoid—"

"Shhh. I get it," Chuck said. "We hardly know each other. Although, if you were to get pregnant, I'd want to know about it. My marriage ended before we had kids. The idea of making a child with *you* sounds... right to me."

She tipped her head to look at him. He hadn't been shocked or appalled by her abortion. And what was that about a child? This was the first time she'd told anyone except Nancy, ages ago, and recently, Nonna. In that moment, those taut bands that had bound her chest for years lost a lot of their power.

"Pizza?" he said. "Shall we see how this thrice-baked pizza tastes?"

"Thrice? That rhymes with mice," she said, feeling giddy.

"And lice," he laughed.

"And nice and rice and vice!"

"Heist?" he said.

"Hmm. There are those who might call that a slant rhyme. Enough. Thrice will do. It's a good word. Besides, cardboard with melted cheese sounds good." She grabbed two wine glasses from the cupboard, forgetting the glass left at her computer table a lifetime ago. And at 3:30 A.M., they were at her dining table gobbling pizza and drinking wine.

"Chuck, may I ask you a personal question?"

He laughed. "I'd say you've earned that right."

"I've never seen a man wear black silk underwear before. When I watched you take them off. Zowee."

He burst into a guffaw. "Were you shocked?"

Only by what rose up underneath. "Just surprised," she said. "Are sexy briefs the norm now?"

"Sexy, huh?" His dimple began showing again. "I started wearing them after my first trip to the Middle East. Saw a couple of other guys wearing silk. Sand doesn't cling, and in that part of the world, they dry in minutes. And... well... they feel nice."

"Why black?"

"Hmm. They come in all styles and colors, but I noticed the light-colored ones fade and look grungy. After that mission, I ordered a couple dozen. Wouldn't wear anything else."

"You sound like a walking commercial."

"I do, don't I? Maybe that'll be my next job when I retire from the Air Force. Selling silk briefs." With that he jumped up, unbuckled his belt, slid his pants down and took a stagy stance."

She clapped her hands.

Then he stuck his thumb in the waistband of his briefs and slowly nudged them downward.

Her eyes widened and her eyebrows rose. "Whoohee! You've got the moves. You could be their top model."

Her look of approval made his cock start to grow. But he readjusted his clothes and sat beside her to pour more wine into their glasses. "More pizza?" he asked.

"What? Oh. One small slice."

She doesn't miss a thing. "I'm free to go apartment hunting this weekend. How about you?"

She nodded. "Nonno Tony lit a fire under me… seems more than one fire's been kindled around here."

Holding her hand to his lips for a beat, he said, "It does seem like that spark—we both felt from the start—has come alive."

She smiled into his eyes, but eased her hand from his. Giulia seemed to love everything she knew about him, but old, cautious habits must have crept back in. And he noticed she turned the conversation to the apartment search.

"When you called with the pizza, I'd just started an internet search. By Saturday, I should have a list of names and maybe appointments. No doubt many will be dead-ends. Are you sure you want to take all that time looking at rental properties?"

"Sure, sure, sure," he said punching the air with his fist three times. "I think you understand those words."

"Even so, house hunting can't be high on your list of weekend pleasures."

"Angel," he said, wrapping a tawny curl around his finger, "being with you is all the pleasure I can handle."

He knew she had relished their sensational love making as much as he had, but she still seemed unsure and continued to skirt his personal remarks.

"Nonno Tony has a good point. After the beating he took, Botteri must be a ruthless man."

"I'm sure he is. So far no one knows you live back here with your private entrance, but I don't have much confidence in that door to your balcony. It's only a matter of time before the wrong person notices you walk down those steps. Tony's right about getting you out of Vicenza—and soon."

"Maybe I'll find the ideal place this weekend," she said raising both thumbs up in a pre-victory salute.

They both continued to eat and drink, thinking their own thoughts.

"I know this sounds presumptuous," he said, "but you could move in with me until you find what you want."

Before she could do no more than straighten her spine and swallow the mouthful she'd taken, he put up his hands. "Wait. Hear me out. I have a large apartment; you could have your own space."

"It's a generous offer, but, as you said, we barely know each other."

"Can't think of a better way to remedy that situation." He put his hands on the table and leaned across to nuzzle her nose. "Think of it as temporary. Hey! If I were a woman, would you consider it?"

"Maybe."

"Well, no worries tonight. But keep in mind, it's as much about your safety as my desire to have you nearby."

Again, they were quiet. She poured the last of the wine in his glass. Chuck said, "Do you have to go to the base tomorrow morning—today, I mean?"

"It's Thursday now isn't it? Nope. Was planning to organize lessons at home and do more online searching. You?"

"I need to go in for a morning review, but we could get the jump on the search by going to Venice this afternoon. Check out the areas you've already picked as possibles. What do you think?"

"It *would* help narrow down the choices before having to deal with an agent," Giulia said, thinking aloud. "I like that idea. Are you sure?"

"Babe, a long time ago, I quit offering things I don't want to do. Unless my combat group gets a sudden order to lift off, let's meet at two at the train station. Tell you what, I'll reconfirm with you around one."

"Sounds good." She yawned. "Maybe we could get some sleep?"

"Maybe." *Sleep is important, but damn . . .*

CHAPTER SEVENTEEN

It was misting when they met in Vicenza's train station. Giulia wore waterproof walking boots and her full-length, cobalt-blue raincoat with a hood.

"Hey! That coat, matches one of my favorite eyes!" Chuck said when he met her. "You may need that coverup with these rolling clouds overhead."

She nodded pulling the fastener of her hood closer around her neck. After settling on the train, she asked if any women had called for backup while they'd been gone.

"I did get your call about that. Planned to tell you when, or *if*, you let me in with pizza last night. Then… I forgot."

She smiled, thinking about why he forgot.

"Two called. Each of the guys reported that Ogle noted their presence, then pointedly ignored them."

"And the women's reports?"

"Smooth with no slimy innuendos. Maybe this plan will be enough."

"Hope so, but I'd still like to tutor and teach basic Italian and need to discuss the pros and cons with him."

"And *la mia micina,* I plan to be there whenever you go into his den."

"Micina? Why micina?"

"A couple of reasons. When Dad grew up, 'kitten' was Czech slang for a pretty woman. And," Chuck hooked one of her tawny curls around his finger, "it fits. You have tawny streaks in your hair like the stripes on Mom's Tabby cat."

"What'd your mom call her? Assuming it was a her."

"Oh, definitely a her. Mom called her Smartypants, and

Smartypants was a lot like you. Intelligent, beautiful and always one jump ahead of me. I never could figure that cat out."

Giulia laughed feeling a little embarrassed that he'd chosen a pet name for her. "So, would next week be good for my appointment with Oliver?"

"Yes." He noted her quick change to the business at hand. "Try to make it toward the end of the week. Friday if possible. The lock on the door is already taken care of. Enrico Zava, a skilled carpenter in the maintenance shop, has agreed to work on the mechanism for closing the door. We want it to not quite snap shut unless someone gives it a push. Ogle will notice it and request repairs, but in the meantime, he'll get used to it and may ignore it. It's one more precaution in case he goes off the deep end."

"Surely he's getting the message that he's in trouble," Giulia said.

"Yeah. It'd be best if he'd decide to slither away. We could all forget about any charges and counter charges. If he feels cornered, it's a sure thing he'll play out the legal card as far as he can take it."

* * *

As the train moved across the causeway and quietly slid into Venice station, the city looked more ethereal and seductive than usual. When they reached Chuck's *sestiere*, called San Polo—one of the six original districts of Venice—they could only make out fuzzy outlines of buildings.

The first apartment on her list overlooked Rio della Madonnetta and was in his sestiere. It didn't have a grand water view like the one she'd dreamed about. It's windows didn't look at the lagoon toward Murano or across the large Giudecca Canal where all kinds of water craft passed. But, she thought, an apartment overlooking a quiet canal might suit her better. Grand views draw tour groups for at least nine months out of the year.

They checked out an interesting prospect that overlooked Rio di Angelo Raffaele in a quiet area of Dorsoduro, the sestiere that included nice shops and the famous *squero,* where gondolas were built and repaired. The Academy of Art was also in Dorsoduro. After visiting the Academy, tourists often went to photograph the squero, but seldom ventured on to the Raffaele area. Another listing was in an ancient palazzo overlooking the lagoon that faced the *Cimiterio.* The cemetery was a beautiful place in itself both from afar and within its soft, red-brick walls that were accented by tall, dark cypress.

Those were only three of the listings she'd found, but already Giulia was ready to stop for the day. This project gobbled time and energy. Nonno Tony had been right, she needed to move with it. She wasn't ready to admit to Chuck or Nonno that she'd been feeling uneasy walking in Vicenza. At odd times, the tell-tale trembles in her stomach seemed to warn her of something or someone. More and more often, she had cut short any errand not absolutely necessary in order to hurry inside the safety of her building.

"Okay, Micina, time for a break. You're starting to fade. And I can smell the rain coming. Could I treat you to a meal at Da Carlo?"

"Don't believe I've eaten there. What is Carlo's specialty?"

"He does a mean Torta Verde, made with spinach, rice, eggs and Parmigiano Reggiano. Sound good?"

"Fabulous, but right now all I can think about is putting my feet up."

"You can do that too. Let's hurry. The rain's moving in fast." They ran, ducking under roof overhangs and dodging people with umbrellas. Da Carlo's happened to be Chuck's apartment. His given name was Karl but schoolmates had dubbed him Chuck early on. He told her he'd preferred it because he fit in better; Novak was bad enough since most kids had Italian or Irish names in his neighborhood. He settled Giulia on a Chuck-sized leather recliner which, when stretched out, left her with inches to spare.

When he brought her a glass of wine, she asked, "Do you spell Da Carlo with a C or a K?"

He looked at her. "Yes," he said as that dimple appeared.

She waited, then said, "I'll call you Karlo with a K." And she took a sip.

He went to check his larder. In a few moments, he came back to say he had to go out but found her eyes closed, the glass of wine still in her hand. He smiled, lifted it gently and covered her with a faded afghan left by his Czech grandmother. It was made of green granny-squares, some kelly green and some lime. He remembered being dazzled by the bright colors. She'd even taught him how to crochet similar squares. He'd been her first and maybe favorite grandchild. She always had time to listen to his boyhood dreams.

He left a note for Giulia on top of the afghan and headed out. When he slipped back inside, she was still sleeping. *God, how lucky I was to find her. Now, can I hold her?* At least he didn't have to gain Antonio Tuon's approval about their relationship. And her father and brothers were far away in the States. Old-world thinking, he knew, but then, both of their families came from the Old World.

He went into the kitchen and began assembling ingredients while he listened to an aria from Bizet's opera "The Pearl Fishers" coming from a small DVD player mounted on top of the fridge. The beautiful blending of the tenor and baritone voices in the famous duet got to him every time. Typical of most operas, it had an inane plot.

Chuck always thought of his grandmother when he cooked because she had taken time to teach him how to handle himself in the kitchen. Now, though, he didn't seem to find enough time to deviate from the few simple recipes learned all those years ago. He melted butter and added sliced leeks. When they were soft, he added chopped garlic and pancetta. Before the garlic turned dark, he added fresh chopped spinach, salt and pepper. After the liquid from the spinach had reduced, he stirred in rice and added boiling stock, one ladle at a time. He didn't make his own as his *Babička* did, but it was still a tasty dish.

In her stocking feet, Giulia slipped in silently and watched. When the rice had absorbed the last of the stock, he removed the mess from the heat and stirred in beaten eggs, grated cheese and a grind or two of fresh nutmeg, then dumped all of it into a shallow oven dish. He topped it off with breadcrumbs and dots of butter. Just as he slid it into the oven, he noticed Giulia.

"Hey there," he said as he straightened up.

"Karlo's with a K is a special place," she said. "Great music and the promise of good food."

"Feeling better?"

"Oh yes. Guess I needed that nap. You have a perfect place here. Hope I can find one as comfortable. Was that marvelous baritone with Bocelli the one from Wales?"

"Yes. Bryn Terfel. Fantastic isn't he?"

"I had no idea you liked opera."

"Nor did I know *you* do. Lots of unknowns, Giulia, but I have no doubt about one thing."

"Oh. What's that?"

"I already find you endlessly fascinating."

"Sometimes you overwhelm me with statements like that, Karlo with a K. But the feeling might be mutual, and with the aromas in this kitchen . . ."

"You stinker. You're only after my cooking," he said swinging her around and moving out of the kitchen. "No peeking for forty-five more minutes. Now what could we do in that amount of time?"

They found something to do while the rain pounded down outside his bedroom windows. Later when Giulia was gathering her clothes to get dressed, he handed her one of his Tee-shirts. "If you want, you can wear this for now."

But maybe that wasn't a good idea, because she looked too enticing, and he wanted to throw her back on his bed. The rain continued to blow outside the kitchen window while they ate the cheesy spinach tart and sipped white wine.

"This is beautiful, like golden water." She held her glass to the light.

"It's from the area over toward Slovenia. They've been making wines since Roman times. Most were destroyed in World War II, but the vines are coming back." He took a mouthful and slowly savored it. "Isn't there a famous quotation from Galileo about wine?"

"Something about sunlight?" she asked.

"Yes. Now I remember. 'Wine is sunlight held together by water.'"

"I do believe you're a literary airman," she said.

"Hardly. Now tell me about that picture of the lion and the goddess in your attic room. It's obviously been on that slant wall a long time."

She was surprised he'd noticed. "Not much to tell. After I saw the huge sculpture in Giardini when I was about nine, the image stayed with me. For a while, I'd tried to count all the lions found in Venice, thanks to dear old Saint Mark's influence, but that wild-maned one with Minerva riding side-saddle was the one that grabbed my imagination. I suppose part of it was that I had dreams of being a famous poet one day and wanted to learn more about Minerva." She held out her glass for more wine.

"Lion and goddess are getting a good wash tonight. When the rain stops, would you lead me to it, say this coming weekend?"

"Happy to. I haven't been out to see how they're faring since I've been back. Beside the goddess-of-poetry thing, that silly lion has always tickled my funny bone. Remember Bert Lahr, the disgruntled lion in The Wizard of Oz?"

"Of course."

"Well, this lion is saying, "I'll maul the hairdresser who did this to me."

Chuck leaned back and roared. "I knew he was pissed about something. "

"Could I have one more slice of that scrumptious tart you labored over while I lazed away in your chair?"

"Absolutely."

"You must have gone out for fresh spinach and leeks. I don't remember seeing a market nearby, and I've spent lots of time in San Polo, usually lost."

"There's one left. Tucked in a dark space only the locals know about. So far, it's still thriving because the nearest supermercato is toward the station in Campo San Giacomo dell'Orio, and that one barely ranks as a supermercato. But most Venetians hate leaving the city, if only to the giant markets on the mainland, so they usually make do with what's here."

She shook her head sadly. "Even though living here is harder and harder for residents, I still want to stay in Venice."

"Yeah, me too. I never want to go back to the hurry of America," he said getting up to put away leftovers. "We better be moving toward the train. The next one for Vicenza leaves at nine-thirty. It's eight forty-five now. By the time we get dressed, we should make it."

She got up to help clear the table, putting dishes in the sink to soak.

"Give me ten minutes. I can't travel to Vicenza in your big brown Tee."

"Looks good to me." And with one hand, he lifted the shirt to kiss a breast while holding the baking dish and serving spoon aloft with the other.

* * *

Chuck knew all the meandering calles from his place to the Scalzi Bridge. The station steps were almost at the Scalzi's feet. Whenever Giulia had aimed for the Scalzi from this area, she found herself taking wrong turns and circling back on herself. She usually got there but hadn't yet found a sure route. One day, though, her feet would lead her straight there.

On the platform of the track, people were saying how unusual it was to rain so hard and last so long this time of year. Chuck and Giulia found an empty compartment toward the back of the train, and he began talking about how impressed he was with her grandfather. "I wonder if your original assessment of him as a careless scoundrel is accurate."

"I'm thinking you're right and feel guilty to have jumped to conclusions based on hunches. Still I have a feeling he may have been unfaithful to Nonna."

"Hmm. I got another impression, but how can we know? People in the community might, but you and I will never know, will we?"

Giulia nodded. "You're right, but I do know he adores Nonna and she him. Maybe that's all that matters. They've lived a long life together, and it seems to me their flame still glows," Giulia said.

"I felt that warmth, too. He hinted that most of his life he's been known as carefree and hopeless about money. But I'm guessing he's been the opposite. Most older Europeans have been savers by nature and often invested in mobile assets, like gems, rather than banks. I wouldn't be surprised if the Italians who survived the last war still have gold and gems buried in their backyards or sewn into mattresses. From what Dad told me, my Czech grandparents never trusted banks for fear a corrupt government would swoop in and confiscate it."

"I think Nonno Tony had those diamonds tucked away for a long time."

Chuck nodded. "He did mention, though, taking them from a box."

"I'm so sorry that shyster took advantage. Maybe if I hadn't worn a disguise—"

"Hey. Are you trying to pile blame on yourself?"

She was quiet. "Guess so."

Chuck hit his forehead with the heel of his hand. "You know, when Tony said box, your nonno may not have meant a bank box at all."

"I'm surprised and a little jealous that he told you so much. More than he's ever told me." She sighed. "I suppose it's because I'm female; my dad confided in his sons more than me, too. Obviously you impressed Nonno Tony in a huge way. But why should I be surprised. You impress—"

A loud, tinny voice overrode Giulia's and announced they'd be going back to Venice because of a washout ahead.

CHAPTER EIGHTEEN

It was nine P.M. They'd almost reached Padova, and now the train was inching backward. Rain pounded against the windows. The sheet lightning that had followed them for most of the trip had now become electric forks streaking toward the earth. A crack of thunder followed each fork and Giulia scooted closer to Chuck. Finally, at Dolo, one of several small villages between Padova and Venice, the train came to a switching area and stopped. The conductor came through to explain that the engine would be unhooked and moved to a siding where it would hitch onto the other end of the train. Soon they were on their way again, facing forward.

"Good. It won't be long now," Giulia said. "Do trains ever get hit by lightning?"

"Never heard of it."

"Why is it moving so slowly?"

"Maybe the engineer is being overly cautious—I would be."

Whatever the reason, they didn't arrive back in Venice until almost eleven and had no idea if they'd make it to the base the next morning.

As they neared Chuck's building, Giulia felt uncomfortable— shy even. Should she opt for the spare room? Did he still want her to share his bed? *Foolish woman. He seduced you.* No. It was time to be honest with herself. She hadn't been seduced. It was obvious he wanted her from the moment they met, and she could have taken a firm stand as she'd done many times with other men. As long as she was being honest, why not admit she'd wanted him from the first? Ever since she bumped into him, restless feelings kept pushing against her carefully constructed shield. She felt torn. Should she step on through or try to rebuild?

She felt almost naked without that shield, and now that Chuck had managed to have his way with her... *Holy moly, where'd that come from?* But what if he *didn't* want her anymore?

In spite of his large umbrella and her long raincoat, they were both soaked and shivering when they reached his door. "Does a long, hot bath sound good to you?" he asked.

"Oh yes. I've been thinking about that big tub in your bathroom. But could I wash out some things for tomorrow first?"

"Sure." They left their shoes and coats hanging on hooks above the stone floor at the entryway, and he led her to a small laundry area where she saw a compact washer, dryer and a utility sink. "Wait a sec," he said. "Let me make sure this isn't full of grit: sometimes I rinse hiking boots here." He also extended a wooden rack mounted on the wall for drying things.

This man is organized. "Did your mom teach you how to cook and keep things in such good order?"

"She didn't have time." He checked the dryer and turned it on. "She had four kids to raise—actually five, counting Dad, the sloppiest of all. Dad's mother took me under her wing. She didn't live long enough to give much to my siblings... Guess the military did the rest."

"Did your Czech grandmother speak English?"

"Babička? Hardly any. She had her ways with a kid though. You know. Cookies, getting to lick frosting bowls, stirring stuff on the stove. Didn't take long to catch on to kitchen Czech. Later I studied a little on my own."

"Ba... bitchka?" Giulia said. "Is that spelled with odd marks over the consonants and no vowels?"

He laughed and hugged her. "You're cold. I'll explain later. I better check that bath water. When you finish, bring the warm towels out of the dryer."

The bathroom was steamy, and he was already in the oversized tub when Giulia entered wrapped in one of the warm, giant-sized towels. She tried to climb into the tub while holding the towel around herself. Chuck leaned back, watching. Grinning. They'd made love a few hours ago, and here she was all modest and maidenly.

"Give it up, Micina. Can't be done. I've seen you naked you know."

"You're right," she dipped her head, smiled through unruly curls flopping onto her forehead and dropped the towel.

Which was more beautiful, he wondered? Her face and unique eyes? Her soft dark curls with those tawny glints? Her full breasts with pinkish-brown nipples? Her soft, sexy little belly? Or that curly dark triangle at the juncture of those beautiful firm thighs?

"God, Giulia. You're so beautiful. Quick, climb in and get rid of those goose bumps. I want to be the one to put them there, not the storm."

She slid slowly into the hot water. With a huge sigh, she visibly let go, dropping her shoulders and easing the tensions in her neck. He still didn't know what triggered these times when she pulled into herself as if trying to disappear. He couldn't believe it was about that long-ago abortion. But he knew from talking with his sister that women who chose that route didn't always find it easy to live with. *Time. She needs time. And I need time to move closer.*

Both of them were relaxed and drowsy when they reached his larger than king-sized bed. They slid under the sea-green duvet, and Chuck wanted to make love to her so gently she'd never have doubts about trusting him. Maybe he could hold off, not climax if that's what it took. In their short time together, her genuine response to him had been intensely arousing and gratifying, but this time, he wanted it to be all about her.

As he kissed her mouth, he caressed her warm breasts, stroked down her sweet belly to the velvety folds between her legs. He continued kissing her neck, all around her ears and nibbled her left ear lobe to see if she'd have the same reaction as before. She squiggled and arched into him. He grinned to himself, then shifted on top of her, parting her legs with his knee and eased between them. He guided himself to her opening and pushed in—but only a little. It took all the control he could muster not to pound into her, but instead, waited for her body to adjust.

Gradually her hips began to move to meet him, then she dug her fingers into his shoulders. God he loved when she did that. He scarcely moved. But when her inner muscles tightened around his cock, he felt his own hot blood on the move. The pulse in her throat was hammering, but he wanted this to last all night. As his own orgasm began to build, he slowed even more and conjured dull service reports until the urgency eased a bit.

To gain her trust, he wanted to establish a strong bond. A bond of unconditional acceptance. It might only be a hunch, but he sensed Tony was right, something dark had caused her to withdraw and guard herself from everyone—even her parents and beloved grandparents. Chuck believed the joining of their bodies was a way to forge that bond. Not only a sexual binding, he thought, but maybe a primal pathway toward comfort and connection.

He noticed tensions loosen. They seemed to slide down her torso inch by inch. He even felt it in her legs wrapped around him. As if her body was saying she trusted him to pleasure her with no pay back. He thrust deeply and held until he felt her climax building. He'd been on the edge too long. When her inner muscles tightened around him, molten lava gathered at the base of his spine and hot, stinging streams began to move. He resisted the powerful urge to thrust again and again. Instead, he held deep and steady for her. When she cried out his name—like a stranger sneaking from behind—his own pleasure spread slowly through him like hot, thick honey.

* * *

As he showered and shaved Friday morning, Chuck couldn't

stop thinking about what might have happened last night. Had she let down some barriers as they made love? Or had that perceived openness been merely his wishful imagination? Her response to his every touch made him feel like the greatest stud in the Western world. Even if she had felt some sort of bonding, he vowed to not push her to discuss it. Time. Maybe time would work its magic.

"Hey there, sleepy head," he said carrying a cup of coffee with a few drops of thick cream stirred in the way she liked it.

"I've been sleeping a lot lately. Do your walls exhale magic vapor?" she asked, reaching for the cup and grabbing the sheet to cover herself as she sat up. He wanted to snatch that cover and slip back in with her while her hair was tousled and her skin rosy.

"Could be," he said. "Something magic seems to be happening." He tried not to look like a supplicant who had crawled on his knees over jagged stones to her altar.

"Mmm, the coffee at Karlo's is outstanding like all else offered here." Her smile was radiant. She turned toward the windows. "Is it still raining?"

"Nah. Just the normal Venetian mist. By the way, I called the base. All classes—except a few military procedure sessions—have been cancelled. If you need to get back, the road by car may be passable, otherwise we could hang here and continue searching for apartments."

"Might as well. I need to do a bit of personal shopping, though."

"No problem. We can do that."

"I can do my own shopping for a blouse and underwear, thank you."

"Si, si, Signorina." He grinned, swept his arm in a grand arc and bowed as he backed out of the room. He heard her snickering as he went down the hall to swing by the laundry room for a new bottle of dish detergent. At the sight of lacy lingerie draped on the wooden rod, he felt a surprising contentment.

After breakfast, they printed out more listings and plotted the best course to avoid backtracking. At the first address, the person let them in. But Giulia knew immediately it wasn't for her. With a slight roll of her eyes toward Chuck, they were out of there in minutes. No one answered at the second. At the third, the person who came to the door wasn't at all happy to learn that her place might be rented out from under her.

By mid-afternoon, Giulia had narrowed the listings to two apartments, both near the church of San Raffaele. The small church had been closed for inside restoration for two or three years. Soon, she thought, she'd get inside to see the famed frescoes by the Guardi brothers, depicting the apocryphal tale of Tobias and the Archangel Raffaele.

As they sipped coffee in a quiet bar, Chuck suggested it might be quicker to deal with an agent who would have better information than the tenants.

"Do you know any agents who deal in rentals?" she asked.

"No, but Marc's more of a wheeler-dealer than I am. Let's see if he's in town and what he knows." He pulled out his cell.

"While you do that, I'll look into that small shop on the other side of the rio and pick up a couple of items."

"Good idea." He grinned and tried to make his eyebrows dance as he'd seen Marc do so effortlessly. "By the way, pale blue is nice."

She laughed. "Blue, huh?" and walked away.

* * *

The next morning they reached an agent, who Marc had suggested. She agreed to show the two apartments and met them in the afternoon at Campo Santa Margherita, the amoeba-shaped campo frequented by students from the nearby University of Venice. The first property wasn't bad, but the view mentioned in the ad was non-existent. The other, though, was much more enticing. But the woman who owned it lived in Calabria, and before the agent could go further, she needed to be contacted. Giulia left her cell number and they called it a day.

After showers and leisurely lovemaking, he took her to a small restaurant called *La Zucca*, the pumpkin. It was only a few steps from the large Campo San Giacomo dell'Orio where Giulia had often sat on a bench to watch children kick a soccer ball against the back of the old church. She'd thought about living near that campo because it was quiet. Each time she'd gone there, she'd seldom seen bothersome tourists. Back then, she'd felt like a snob to think that way, since she'd been a tourist herself. But now she'd be a resident and maybe a citizen. Surely she'd have a legitimate reason to complain about the hoards who descend on the city year after year.

Zucca was not strictly a vegetarian restaurant, but it was clear from the menu that serious attention was paid to veggies. Giulia decided to order their specialty, a flan made of zucca, potatoes, broccoli and smoked ricotta cheese. Chuck ordered rabbit cooked in prosecco. That sounded strange but they both found it to be delicious. A side dish of candied squash similar to Thanksgiving-style candied sweet potatoes came with his order. Chuck passed on the *dolci,* but Giulia ate every bite of a cake made with pear and ginger.

When they returned to Chuck's apartment, she washed her face, brushed her teeth with a new toothbrush and fell into bed. When he joined her, she had already drifted asleep. He slid in beside her, gently turned her on her side and spooned around her soft body, once again feeling a serene contentment.

* * *

Sunday the trains were running again. As they settled into a crowded compartment, Giulia sat in a window seat with him next to her.

"Suppose my students will have their essays finished given all the extra time they've had?"

"Don't count on it."

"By the way, you still owe me an explanation of how the Czechs spell grandmother."

"Sure. The spelling is b-a-b-i-c-k-a. But the cee has a small accent over it like a little smile. I don't know what to call that mark, but when it's there, the cee sounds like tch, thus babicka becomes babitchka. Once you learn the sounds, the rest is easy."

"Yeah sure," she said with a little snort. "Those diacritical marks used in Slavic languages seem so... foreign." She twisted her hand in the air.

"Well... yeah," he said chuckling.

She laughed, too. "You've described your Czech nonna as forgiving and tolerant, like lots of grandmothers."

He sat back and sighed. "Not all. My Italian nonna never quite forgave my mother for marrying a Czech or maybe anyone not Italian. She and my sister were on good terms, but she didn't have much use for us boys. Maybe we reminded her too much of Dad."

"It's never fair to blame children for parents' foibles."

"Foibles! My dad's treatment of Mom was more than foibles."

"Tell me."

He turned his broad shoulders and back to the rest of the compartment creating a sort of barrier and put his arms around her as they faced the window. "An old story," he said in hushed tones. "I guess Dad was bitter about how his life turned out. I never knew. But he drank too much and took it out on her."

"Did she ever report him?"

"I wish she would have. Maybe if her father had been living... no, probably not. She wouldn't have wanted her family to know."

"That's a familiar story, too," Giulia said.

"He beat the shit out of me and my brothers at times, but to hit a woman! A woman you claimed to love? One good thing about him, though, he was a great teacher."

"Teacher? I thought he worked in a factory."

"He did. He taught me how NOT to be."

"Oh Chuck, I'm so sorry." She turned to face him and gently touched the sides of his cheeks.

"Don't be," he said and looked out the window at the marshes and tidal flats of the Venetian basin as they chugged toward Padova and Vicenza. "It's over. A long time ago."

She was quiet, wondering if something like that is ever over.

He took her hand and held it between both of his, "I thought it was over until I met you,"

"What do you mean?"

"When I knew I wanted you, suddenly I was scared I'd turn into him."

"But you've been with other women. Your were even married and—"

"Yes. But I never felt the same jolt until you ran into me."

Giulia was speechless.

"Sorry, Micina. Didn't mean to come on so strong."

"No. I'm... I'm honored that you felt comfortable to tell me about it."

"Not overwhelmed?" he asked looking into her eyes.

"A little. Not because of the information about your mom and dad, but that you told me. Not many share with me. Maybe because I've closed myself off. Even as a child. And you know, Psych 101 preaches you have to share to get others to share. What have I ever shared with you?"

"Did you forget about your abortion?" he whispered.

"But you treated that as if I'd mentioned a fender bender."

He pulled her toward him. "Sorry, Micina, I do know it was more than that." He tipped her head up to look into his eyes. "But what happened doesn't make you wrong. And it was a long time ago, too."

She turned back toward the window. He folded around her again and she felt safe and warm. *Could I share my worst with him?*

She flinched as a voice boomed from the speaker directly over their heads announcing the approach to Vicenza.

CHAPTER NINETEEN

The sun was brilliant as they approached her apartment. Giulia was eager to be in her own place again. She needed alone-time to process all that had happened during the last week. Botteri and Nonno Tony and Chuck. With Chuck, she had no regrets—none. Still, she wanted to discover how she felt away from him. No matter how gentle he'd been with her, he *was* a force to deal with.

Her musing was cut off when Chuck suddenly dropped her bag and pulled her close. He'd seen a crime-scene tape across the bottom steps to her apartment. Then she saw it and looked up to see her glass doors boarded over.

"Let's go to the front and find your landlords."

* * *

The police had come and gone, Luciana explained, as she handed Giulia coffee with hot milk and sugar. Giulia never used sugar but drank it without complaint. Saturday afternoon a passerby had noticed the windows smashed and called the police.

"The break-in must have happened during the rainstorm on Friday night," Luciana said. "The police have already surveyed the damage, and no one is allowed to enter, not even you, Giulia, until the police are here. They boarded up the glass doors, hung the crime tape, and told us to call them as soon as you arrived. Gino is going down to meet them now."

Giulia and Chuck waited in the sitting room of the pensione.

"Chuck, I don't want the police to know about Botteri," she said, "even though he may have sent someone to do this."

"It might be considered obstruction of justice, but with his possible Mafia connection, I have to agree with you. Seems best to treat this as random vandalism. Maybe it is." He put his arm around her.

"What about the people at the base? How much will they have to know?"

"Very little, I'd guess. They may not ever be informed except as part of a routine police report for statistical reasons."

"Statistical reasons?" Her face screwed up into little lines of anxiety.

"Yeah, like maybe quarterly or annual reports as to crimes in the city that affect non-citizens who work at the base. Hell, I don't know. Italians are known for loads of bureaucracy and God knows the military is. But, you can't hide where you work, love. Just answer their questions. No need to embellish."

"Right," she said, sighing deeply. "Will you stay with me?"

"You need to ask?" He settled her into the hollow of his shoulder.

Two plain-clothes men arrived, introduced themselves and showed their credentials Luciana served more coffee and left the room. The detectives switched to Italian when it was obvious both Chuck and Giulia were fluent in the language. After the questions were over, they all moved to her apartment.

It was worse than she had imagined. Cushions were torn, objects thrown down, drawers emptied, books and work papers strewn about, dishes and glassware smashed. In the bedroom, her clothes were thrown on the floor, some of her underwear had disappeared, what was left was ripped and torn. In the bathroom, cosmetics were deliberately spilled into the shower stall—even a couple of books and loose papers were soaked.

"My copy of Harold Bloom's *Shakespeare: The Invention of the Human!*" she cried holding what was left of a large reference book with ripped-out pages. "Why would Botteri's thugs do this?" she said in a low voice.

"Doesn't make sense," Chuck said.

Then Giulia looked up at the mirror and her face paled to see "*Puttana*" scrawled on the mirror with lipstick. Whore. She shrank in on herself.

Chuck saw it at the same time and pulled her close saying, "The bastards! Don't let them get to you." But she couldn't stop a few tears from gathering.

The police asked again and again if anything was missing, but she couldn't think. She mumbled she didn't think so. She had little jewelry of value. The small, black-velvet music box with a little jewelry drawer, given years ago by Nonno Tony, was unbroken. With shaking hands, she opened it to the tune of "Somewhere My Love" from *Doctor Zhivago*. Her pearl earrings and Nonna's ring lay in the drawer. Clutching her only real keepsakes, Giulia managed to pull herself together.

"Commissario?" Chuck said to the detective who seemed to be in charge, "could she give you a more detailed report later?"

He agreed. "What about a computer?" the other asked.

"Oh, I forgot. I do have one, but it's with Roberto, the landlord's son. It jammed on me, and he thought he could fix it."

"When did you take it to him?"

"Around noon on Thursday before I left for Venice. He must still have it in his apartment."

At last, they left, and Giulia crumpled. "What now? Where do I start?"

"We lock up—for what that's worth—and find food. Then we'll come back and make lists."

"I couldn't eat a thing," she said picking up and putting down one damaged item after another.

"Yes, Micina, you could. I'll feed you if necessary. Remember what's important."

"What?" she said hearing a whine build in her voice.

"You're safe. Thank God you weren't here. All the rest is only stuff."

After eating a small dish of pasta with tomato sauce and drinking a little red wine at a nearby trattoria, her face took on more color. When Chuck broached the idea of going to his studio apartment in Vicenza for the night, she agreed without protest. It was obvious she wasn't up to making any other decisions. He'd follow up later and try to convince her that now was the time to move in with him in Venice. If not on Wednesday, for sure by the end of the week. She couldn't stay in the pensione's apartment with that worthless balcony door. In fact, he wouldn't allow it.

Whoa! Listen to the caveman.

* * *

After her classes on Monday, it didn't take long for them to finish going through the wreckage of her apartment.

"Giulia, what about your passport and other important papers?" Chuck asked while he piled broken furniture and crockery in a corner.

"In the bank. It's an old habit, I guess. All the years I traveled here alone, I kept IDs, credit cards, even my return tickets, in my money belt. I always thought of it as my portable deposit box. That way I had necessary documents with me no matter what happened to the rest. So, the first week I was here, I opened an account and stashed that stuff in a real deposit box."

"Good. We don't have to worry about identity theft."

"I don't think so." She sighed. "Botteri might learn my real name from my books and guess that I teach at the base. Oh Lord!" She turned to him. "Do you think he'd go that far to get at me?"

Chuck put his hands firmly on her shoulders and looked straight into her eyes. "Calma. I'm sure he wouldn't want to tangle with the U.S. Military. If he was the one that sent people here, I'd guess they were looking for diamonds. Think of the ripped cushions and all."

She grabbed him and seemed to be trying to crawl inside his skin. He pressed her closer and rubbed his hands in circles on her back. She took a big breath, pushed back and said, "I'm ready to leave." As they left the apartment, she said, "Wait, I need to check on my computer. Hope Roberto's home."

He was. Her computer was not "sick" anymore, he'd said smiling. That was a relief because her notes for classes were on it. They made little jokes about him being an excellent doctor, but when she tried to pay him, he claimed it was nothing. He asked her to tell people on the base about him. She assured him she would. Finally, they left for Chuck's studio apartment. She'd return later and settle up with her landlords. The police had her cell number and she didn't intend to divulge another piece of information.

After spending most of the day helping Giulia, Chuck was back at the post taking care of his own business. She took a long, hot shower and tried to rest but no luck. Her mind raced from one worrisome idea to another. They'd leave for his larger place in Venice tomorrow, Tuesday, but then she remembered they had to report to the police one more time. They'd already given their fingerprints for elimination purposes, but there were a few loose ends, the detective had said. She smiled, policemen really did say that. Surely tomorrow night, she and Chuck could go back to Venice.

Too restless to sleep, she called Nancy and brought her up to date, telling her all about the destruction of her apartment.

"Ah Squirt, I'm sorry your place was trashed, but look at it this way, you're staying with Chuck."

"I do feel safe with him. My sweet apartment—it's a scary place now."

"It's strange to me that this Botteri guy and his henchmen would care about your books and papers. I can understand jerks playing with your underwear, but your Shakespeare? Doesn't make sense. But, Squirt, I need to change the subject I have more details on the rest of your Aunt Loretta's bequest."

"The rest? I thought the money she left me and the twins was it."

"It seems her husband had a bunch—I mean a bunch—of Fiat shares accumulated over the years from when he worked in Turin. And your aunt Loretta left all of them to you."

"To me?" Right away Giulia felt alarmed. "How are my brothers going to feel? And Dad? He might not like it that his sister left it all to me. And he'll assume I won't know how to manage a big influx of money." Then Giulia's backbone stiffened, and for the first time, she felt indignant—even angry—with her dad, about his lack of faith in her. She had demonstrated over and over she could manage her money just fine. She put herself through school and grad school, but the boys got help all through their schooling, and as far as she knew, were still in debt.

"Guess your dear auntie figured since they were male—your dad included—they'd always be the favored ones. They'll have to accept her wishes, kiddo. It's a solid legal document."

"Oh Lord. This is overwhelming. Not so much that Lettie would want me to have it—she knew my dreams about Venice—but how do I handle my family?"

"Relax for now," Nancy said. "The shares haven't been worth much for several years. Fiat's had its problems, but rumors indicate that the company's coming together fast with their re-tooling of the popular *Cinque Cento,* Five Hundred, and that cute Fiat Punto."

Giulia thought about Chuck's little yellow Punto.

"You may be a rich heiress yet! This windfall ought to come in handy when you're ready to invest in Venice."

"Got to find something first. That's what I'll be doing while I stay with Chuck. He's already been helping me look for a place even though I'm pretty sure he wants me to settle in with him."

"'Of course he does. Oops! Got a call. Have to take it. Keep me informed."

"Love you," Giulia said.

"You, too. Byee."

Shew! Too much. Can't think about Fiat shares now. Yes, she was glad to be staying with Chuck, but, she'd make it absolutely clear it was temporary. No matter what developed between them, she still had to have her apartment in Venice. After that? Time would tell. And then, would she tell Chuck everything?

CHAPTER TWENTY

"I still want you in my bed every night," Chuck said, squeezing her hand as they walked into his apartment. "But this second bedroom is yours to use however you want." He carried most of his stuff out and left a few things on a closet shelf too high for her to reach anyway.

He'd seemed surprised that she agreed so easily to move in with him. She smiled. Should she have put up more of a fight? No. No games. But she did make it clear this arrangement was temporary. He just pulled her into his arms.

"You don't believe me, do you?" she said leaning back to see his face.

"Micina, I do. But you're here now." He began sliding the vest off her shoulders. "Let's get rid of this damned thing you wear to work." And he tossed it on a chair. When he started unbuttoning her blouse, she responded by working on his shirt.

"You've had a helluva week. I know exactly what you need," he said.

"Let me guess," she grinned. "You'll toss me onto your monster bed and have your way with me."

"You're going to have a Swedish massage."

"Oh." Her eyes widened and her cheeks flushed.

"Disappointed?"

"Of course not." He was teasing again and she loved it.

"Good. My license isn't current so I can't charge a *monetary* fee."

"But you'll collect another way?"

He ignored that but his dimple did deepen. "In heavy combat

situations, the best relief from tension and fear often comes by relieving pressure on over-taxed muscles. I felt good helping men in my unit, and a few of them learned how to help others. Massage can release extra adrenalin too."

As he talked, he continued to remove her clothes and eased her onto the bed. "On you, I'll use a few sliding and gliding strokes unless I find extra tight knots. Then maybe a little kneading. Sound good?"

"Sounds divine."

"I hope so."

"And later?" she asked.

"Don't worry about later. If you unwind into sleep, go for it. I'll collect my personal fee another time." His voice was husky and he leaned over for a kiss. It started as a light kiss, but when she responded, he probed her mouth with the tip of his tongue and slid it along the sensitive underside of her lip. He felt shivers dance through her body. She was now totally nude, and he barely managed to break away. "Now turn over on your stomach while I warm this oil."

Stripping down to his black briefs, he straddled her body and picked up a bottle of oil, pouring a small dollop into the palms of his hands. He began rubbing them together, and the fragrance of lavender filled the bedroom. She inhaled deeply and sighed. Before touching her shoulders, he could see the tension loosening in her small body with its perfect, round bottom. He knew this would be a self-imposed test because seeing her lying there, so trusting, was a huge turn on. Already he was hard as stone. He concentrated on naming the muscles in the back.

His large hands moved slowly and firmly around her neck and shoulders, down her spine, over her buttocks onto her thighs and calves and lingered at her feet. He massaged each foot separately, toe by toe, before working his way back to her torso and upper back where she carried most of her tightness. He shifted to one side of her body and began the glide strokes across her torso in a gentle, horizontal pulling motion. She sighed again. Continuing with more emphasis on her shoulders and neck, he concentrated on each arm and hand. He was about to ask her to turn over, when he noticed she was sound asleep. He muffled his laugh and inched off the bed, laying the cover over her.

As the door closed, Giulia stirred. She lay indulging in a heavenly out-of-the-world sense of euphoria. Without opening her eyes, she turned on her side, yawned and stretched to reach for him. Not there. She sat up. Was that the shower? And another sound? Almost like an animal in pain. She threw on his discarded shirt and went looking.

She peered into the bathroom and saw Chuck's shadow in the shower stall. He was groaning softly. She slid the shower open and felt icy drops spraying. She stuck her hand in the water.

"Why are you standing in cold water? What happened to the hot?"

"Did I wake you?" he said, shutting the water off.

She noticed his cock and guessed the problem. Dropping the shirt and stepping inside, she took his cold penis in her hand. "Does this want my attention?"

"It's in dire need and may never come to life again."

"Hmm. Maybe we can resurrect it, but let's get you warm first." She switched the handle to hot. They soaped each other, played awhile and when he showed excellent signs of recovery, she gently grasped his cock and led him toward the bedroom. He stumbled after her, laughter bubbling up in his chest.

She turned to him. "Do you have any of that special oil left?"

"I do. You like?"

"Oh yes. My turn, though."

"I'm ready."

Chuck enjoyed her efforts at massage. When she asked him to turn on his back for a thorough oiling, as he did so, he whispered, "Climb on." He lifted her onto his erection, and inch by inch, she began a slow descent, adding quirky little circular motions.

"Oh - my - God," he said.

"Goddess. Remember to whom you're speaking."

"You imp." He rolled her onto her back. "Now you're going to get it."

"Promise?"

He thrust and retreated slowly. Penetrated and withdrew, then thrust again. She wrapped her legs around his waist and shuddered. He sensed her body being claimed by wave after wave of ecstasy. In a ragged breath, she called his name. He had meant to wait until the last pulses of her orgasm faded, but that wasn't going to happen. He plunged once more, and a hoarse cry tore from his throat. Then a hot rush of golden pleasure coursed through every vein in his body lasting for what seemed an eternity of bliss. They both fell asleep.

Later, however, she woke to him groaning, twisting and flailing. She rolled off the bed and slipped around to the other side watching his suffering in the dim light slanting through the blinds. When he calmed somewhat, Giulia crawled on top of him stretching out full-length. She put her face in the hollow of his sweaty neck and crooned softly, not wanting to wake him abruptly. He groaned once or twice more, then taking her with him, he rolled onto his side, curved around her, sighed and slept.

* * *

When they woke, the grey light in the sky had faded into night. She didn't mention his earlier distress.

"Hey there," Chuck said raising up on an elbow to look at her. "Was that your stomach or mine?"

"Mine for sure," she said. "What time is it?"

"It's only eight fifteen. Do you want to try an osteria not far from Fondamenta del Vin?"

"Del Vin? Hmm. Is that near the Rialto where they string colored lights over café tables for tourists?"

"Yes. *Osteria al Diavolo e L'Aquasanta* is down Calle Madonna,

one of those narrow paths going off the Del Vin quay. Ever been?"
He wrapped a strand of her hair around his finger and watched the
silky curl slide away.

"Never. Intriguing name, The Devil and Holy Water."

He nodded. They don't take reservations. People are willing
to line up in all weather for a table. This is one place," he snorted
softly, "where even The Marc can't get in without waiting."

"The Marc? Do you call him that to his face?"

"Of course."

"What does he call you?"

"Can't say."

"Hmm. You do know you've thrown down a gauntlet?"

"I'm not worried. He'll never reveal what he calls me—on pain
of death."

"You've got something worse on him?"

"Something like that."

She laughed. "Is Diavolo outside like those tables on Del Vin?
Shall I wear heavy layers and warm socks and boots or do I need
to freeze my feet in more stylish shoes?"

"Neither. Diavolo is small and cozy, but we may have to wait
outside a few minutes so do dress warmly. The temp's supposed to
drop tonight, and I don't want to be attacked by someone's icy feet
later." *I sound like an old married man.* Then it struck him. Married
to Giulia might not be such a bad idea. Wait a sec. Is this the same
guy who swore he'd never commit again?

CHAPTER TWENTY-ONE

Thursday before the storm, Oliver lucked out when Novak walked past his table in the coffee bar. He spoke softly into his phone but Oliver's hearing was acute. 'All set, love? I'll meet you at the station. We'll start your search this afternoon.'

"All set, love?" he mimicked. The big oaf had to be cooing to Cavinato. What was she searching for? No matter, she'd be away—probably with him somewhere in Venice, maybe for the whole weekend. *It'll be easy to find out if she misses her classes tomorrow. If so, I'll slip into her place Friday or Saturday night. Easy peasy. I can hardly wait.*

* * *

Late Friday night, with wind as a cover, Oliver saw the perfect opportunity to break into Cavinato's apartment. All classes had been cancelled and he counted on the storm to keep her in Venice. The rain drove across his field of vision, but he parked his dark Mercedes in the usual space, a half block away.

He wrapped a scarf around his neck, stuffed a pair of thin rubber gloves in a pocket of his dark trench coat and reached for his wide-brimmed rain hat. He was all set when lightning flashed, and he saw two men creep up her stairs. When the thunderclap followed, they broke the glass door and lights went on. *Stupid jerks.* After about twenty minutes, the lights went out, and the thugs ran down disappearing into the night.

Another downpour dumped a flood of water, but Oliver pulled the collar of his raincoat up and tied the hat's string under his chin. With no one around, the rain created a perfect screen as he lumbered up the steps into a trashed apartment. He didn't turn on lights but used his large flashlight, heavy enough for a weapon. What in the devil were they looking for? Cushions ripped and drawers dumped? *What is that cunt into?*

He went looking for her bedroom where *his* interest lay. Her top lingerie drawer wasn't upended but had been pawed through. It bothered him that those ignorant brutes had touched her delicates. He lifted a handful to his nose and inhaled. Jasmine! He always ordered jasmine tea when he visited Signora Sylvia's establishment.

He craved matching sets and found two tasty ones: pale blue trimmed in lace and pristine white, entirely lace! He placed them gently in a plastic bag and stuffed it into the deepest pocket of his coat. He dipped into a rainbow of panties in the second drawer and couldn't wait another minute. Snatching up a pair of bright red ones, he tore off the gloves—had to feel the silk—and threw himself across her bed, unzipped and slowly masturbated into them.

He couldn't leave his own precious essence behind. He ripped them into three scraps of lace and stepped onto the balcony. "Let the rain wash these pretties," he howled into the thunderous night and tossed them over the side.

Back in her bathroom, he grabbed cosmetics and dumped them into the shower stall. Some broke and dribbled out their contents. He giggled while squeezing the toothpaste tube out on top of the mess then decided to leave a choice word for her on the mirror. He found a dark-red lipstick. *She'll understand that. She, the Italian expert.*

After that bit of fury, he calmed down, pocketed the lipstick and put his gloves back on. Back in the living room, her books had been shoved around by those cretins. A few lay on the floor. Poetry books and a big one about Shakespeare. She'd written side notes in that one. Now she's a Shakespeare expert. In another rage he began ripping its pages when an ingenious idea struck. He carried the tome to the shower stall, turned the water on and threw page after page into the mess already there.

Back in the living room again, he snatched up a small book of poetry called *Strong Is Your Hold*. Oh yea, missy, I want your strong hold on my rod. He read the poet's name, Galway Kinnel. Who the hell was that? No doubt someone she admired. He shoved it in another pocket. Maybe they'd read it together. But then he recalled her hiss when he touched her arm. She'd tell him he wouldn't understand. He'd been so gentle with her that day, he'd only taken her arm to calm her. Talk some sense into her. They could have been friends. Buddies. But she had overreacted and drove her knee into his privates. It was all her fault. She had to be punished.

Oliver marched back to her bedroom, looking, looking until he found another pair of untorn panties. Bright blue, like one of her eyes. He sniffed, sighed and reached for his zipper, but changed his mind. Time to leave. He'd save the bright blue for later. Rain still pounded against her window. He had his trophies, and the storm covered his escape. It had been an excellent night.

CHAPTER TWENTY-TWO

On the way to the Diavolo restaurant, Giulia reminded Chuck of her coming appointment with Oliver only three days away. "Are things ready?" she asked. "I want to catch him and be done with it."

He stopped, put his hands on her shoulders and turned her to face him. "You sure about this? We can keep wearing him down with our guard service."

"It'd be marvelous if he went to another post, but, Chuck, a creature like that won't stop preying on women no matter where he is."

"Something is not right about him, about the whole thing. I've been thinking about the break-in. The underwear—some ripped, some taken—fits Oliver. But… but what about the other destruction?"

"The thought of him fondling my underwear is beyond creepy. Nancy reminded me that sleazebags enjoy messing with women's underthings. But would Botteri's thugs—or random vandals—bother with class notes or my Shakespeare book? It could be Oliver's way to get back at me for kicking him."

"Yeah. That's true." Chuck said, "I'd like to sneak into his office and find out what he keeps in there. Better yet, into his house on Viale Camisano."

"That's dangerous thinking, Chuck. If you got caught, you'd be in a lot of trouble with all kinds of authorities."

He looked at her with a grin that said getting caught was not an option. And arm in arm they continued toward the restaurant.

"Micina? I need to ask one more time. Do you still want to keep that appointment on Friday?"

"Absolutely."

"Okay then, here's what we've got. The lock doesn't work from the inside even though it sounds as if it does. As far as I know, he hasn't noticed. He did notice the jimmied door that doesn't always close all the way. It seems the maintenance people are too busy to come adjust it. He'll drive them crazy, but they'll still be too busy."

"Good," she said. "I'm not seriously afraid of him, but I like all the precautions you're taking."

"You can still back out."

"No." She shook her head in one firm jerk to the side.

The calle had become extra narrow, and Chuck turned himself and Giulia flat against the wall to let people coming toward them pass by.

"I'll be wearing a listening device that has voice-activated recording ability," he said. "It won't be admissible in court but I have a hunch it'll be powerful way to convince skeptical officers on the base. More important, though, is I'll know what's going on while you're in there. Do *not* hesitate for one second to scream or scram out of there. Devices can always malfunction."

"I'll be fine," she said. The rain had stopped and fog drifted back into the city. As they turned into the shadowy Calle Madonna, golden halos formed around overhead streetlights spaced along the way. Here, the upper floors of the buildings were very close together. Each light hung from a rod going from one upper extension of a building on one side to another on the opposite side of the calle. Although she knew they must be secured with bolts, to Giulia they looked as if the rods holding the lights had been wedged against each wall like the chin-up bars her brothers used in their bedroom doorway at home.

Throughout the city, calles were lit by lights that pierced the darkness every twenty to thirty feet. It had been this way for centuries, first with torches, then gas and now electricity. Giulia had read that the Council of the Republic believed in the adage that most crime happens in dark places. She agreed with the old leaders and always found those circles of light comforting.

The glistening walkway reflected the soft lights from above, and as they neared their destination, the wet paving stones seemed to emit an orange glow of their own. The mystical illusion came from the flickering neon flame-colored symbol of the devil's fire that "raged" above the osteria's doorway.

"Many upscale restaurants in Italy use the old-fashioned term 'osteria.'" Giulia said. "What did osteria originally mean, do you know?"

"It meant a rustic place where wine and snacks were served. But now the term has a bit of cachet, and restaurants use it to get away with higher prices."

"But I saw a simple osteria over on Larga Gallina."

"I know the one. It's good, maybe the only authentic osteria in town."

Outside Diavolo's door, a few people stood along the walls or sat on benches beneath the neon fire waiting their turn. It didn't take long before Chuck and Giulia were seated and had ordered a bottle of Pinot Grigio from the vineyards north of Venice.

Giulia looked at the menu. "I want to try the *Bigoli in Salsa*. I keep hearing how delicious it is but never ordered it in all the times I've been in Venice."

"It's a Venetian specialty for sure, and I can recommend it here. Do you like anchovies?"

"Uhm, in moderation. Is that what's in the famous sauce?" she asked. "Bigoli are those large, thick noodles, right?"

"Right. The anchovies are in an onion sauce. This Pinot ought to be dry enough to go well with the saltiness of the sauce. Maybe the onions absorb the salt because Babička always said to add extra salt when using onions. I'm skipping the pasta because I want the large appetizer plate *Frutti di Mare,* with paté of cod, and—"

Giulia wrinkled her nose.

"Don't knock it until you try it." He gently pinched the end of her nose.

"We'll see," she said. "What other delicacies from the sea will be on your plate?"

"Can't remember it all. Marinated octopus, for sure, and maybe pickled sardines. You might find a tidbit you'll want to sample. What's your entrée choice?" he asked.

"The pasta and then a mixed salad will be plenty, but maybe I'll decide on something later. Is that allowed at Diavolo's?"

"Of course. It's allowed anywhere. But Italian waiters like to get people to order everything first while they're ravenous."

"I suspected as much."

After she gave her order, he said, "Instead of an entrée, I'm going to order another appetizer. The musetto sausage. I'm sure you'll want a taste of that. It's a rich pork sausage spiced with cinnamon, nutmeg, a touch of chili pepper, and . . ." he turned to the waiter and asked, "and coriander?" The waiter nodded. Chuck told him they'd decide later on other orders.

Here comes our wine and bread. Just in time. I'm starved."

After their wine was sampled and poured and the waiter gone, Chuck leaned across the table and said, "That's what spending time in bed with you does for my appetite."

She blushed, and for a crazy reason, he wanted her even more.

CHAPTER TWENTY-THREE

In "her" room in Chuck's apartment, Giulia was using the top of a large dresser to organize papers for tomorrow's class. She sensed Chuck's presence a moment before he slipped his arms around her using his nose to push her hair aside and nuzzle the back of her neck. "I've been thinking," he said.

"Hmm?" She turned to lay her head against his chest and threw her arms around his waist.

"That, too." He pulled her closer. "But first I have a proposition for you."

She leaned back, looked up to his serious blue-grey eyes and waited.

"Tomorrow night, I'm going into Ogle's office and maybe his house if the timing works out."

Giulia stiffened, took a small step away but laid her hands on his hard, muscled forearms. "Chuck, your career is too important to risk."

He continued. "Doubt if I'll find rings or jewelry. He'd want more intimate things. Are you missing any sexy scraps of lace?"

"Most of my lingerie was ruined, but come to think of it, the blue bra you liked so well is missing."

"Not the blue one!" he shrieked.

She laughed and this time it was a full-from-the-bottom-of-the-toes laugh. He laughed, too and rocked her back and forth. Then, with a soft nudge to her chin, he tipped her face to his, meeting her eyes.

"It would be easier to stay at the studio apartment because

I can't go into Ogle's office until people have left the building. There's a dinner meeting in town that *I think* he'll attend. If so, after his office, I hope to go on to his home. Otherwise, I might have to wait until Thursday, or later, to do his house, but I *am* checking his office tomorrow night."

"You're determined aren't you?"

"Yes. I want to know just how sick this bastard is. If he does have your missing underwear, my guess is he'll have other women's, too. If so, I'll have more confidence about pushing for search warrants. Want to stay with me?"

"I can't talk you out of this?"

"Nope."

"Of course I'll stay."

"Good. If I manage to get in and out of both places, we could drive back here late tomorrow night, but it makes sense—"

"We should stay both nights," she said. "I can be a lookout for you."

Her voice sounded breathy with excitement.

"Giulia, no. Please understand. Not that you couldn't help, but I know me. If you were along, I'd be distracted. My hope is to get in and out fast and take as many pictures as I can with my mini camera. I want you waiting at my studio apartment. That way, I can show you whatever I find immediately. Hell, I want you there anyway," he said with a dimple-deep smile.

"Chuck, I do know how to be quiet. Sneaky, too. As a kid, I snooped in our parents' place, the grandparents' too. They never knew."

"*Maybe* they never knew. And maybe they didn't want to spoil your fun."

"Oh no. My dad wouldn't have put up with it, and now, I agree with him, sneaking is not nice. But," she laughed softly, "the boys always got caught. They left trails a mile wide."

He hugged her again. "I'm not one bit surprised about your sneak-skills, but angel, this will be breaking and entering and—"

She sighed. "Okay. You're the expert. I'll wait... this time."

"Good. Got that settled. Now, when you're finished packing, do we have plans for the rest of *this* evening?"

* * *

After work on Wednesday afternoon, Giulia noticed a pizza shop not far from Chuck's studio and called to tell him she'd bring supper. It was the same place from which he'd brought pizza the first night they'd made love. His apartment had no oven to keep it hot, but they made do and ate picnic style on top of his king-sized bed.

"This pizza's okay but not as good as the thrice-baked kind," he said leaning over for a kiss. "Now, before I go, I need to refresh my memory on how to use this digital camera so if I find 'contraband underwear,' I can —"

She stifled a giggle.

"I can take fast photos and scram."

"I like the scram part," she said.

About eight, Chuck left for the post. He slipped in a side door of the admin building, took the stairs to the top floor—the third—and walked silently along each hallway looking for lights and listening for voices. Ogle's office was on the first floor. When he reached that landing, he stopped to pull out a pair of thin rubber gloves. He felt certain the building was empty, although a cleaning person could appear any time. Or Ogle.

As soon as Chuck got inside Ogle's office, he checked for a possible exit. The office was larger than most and had a private half bath with a window. He opened the window wide and leaned his head and shoulders out making sure he could squeeze through if he had to. It would be a bit of a drop, since the first floor was at least ten steps from the ground, but he could hang from the sill and then drop. He left it wide open.

Back in the office, he pulled out a penlight and began his

search. He was almost finished when he heard footsteps coming down the hallway. He froze. He closed a desk drawer without a sound and holding his breath slipped down the short hallway toward the open window. Then he heard the squeak of wheels. A janitor's cart? With his hands on the sill ready to hoist himself through it, he waited. The squeaking wheels moved past Ogle's door and stopped. A door opened from what sounded like a couple doors down. Wheels squeaked again, and a door closed.

Chuck went back to the desk, pulled out the top right-hand drawer again, picked up the folder marked Cavinato that he'd seen when he'd heard the noise. When he opened it, the local information page was on the top and a blue pencil circled the words Pensione Luciana. He took more photos. He put the folder back and closed its drawer. He'd already snapped pictures of black panties scrunched under folders in the bottom drawer of the desk. The last sound heard in Ogle's office was the bathroom window easing shut.

On his way across the street toward the parking garage, Chuck glanced at his watch. Nine ten. According to a friendly secretary in charge of coordinating events, two visiting administrators from the University of Maryland were being wined and dined at Hotel De La Ville. The dinner would have barely started at nine. If Chuck knew anything about Oliver Ogle, he would not miss an opportunity to suck up to any perceived power. Confirming this notion, Ogle's calendar had indicated he planned to be there. Written in a small, controlled hand in blue pencil were the words "Cocktails, 8:30." Chuck grimaced at the irony of both Giulia's nemeses hanging out at the same hotel.

He found Rob Ryland's dark green Fiat Pinto where he'd said it would be. They had exchanged keys that afternoon. Chuck's car was great for spotting in a crowded parking lot, but canary yellow did not make for a good getaway.

"Ciao. It's me. I'm moving on to the next location. Wish me luck."

Giulia sounded frustrated and pleaded again to join him. He replied, "Wait up for me, love."

"You think I'd sleep?" she said in a hoarse voice.

"Calma, per favore!" he said and closed the phone.

Chuck had been to a boring function in Ogle's house once. *Villa,* Ogle called it, as many did who had houses outside the center of town. Viale Camisano was easy to find. It was an ancient—but still used—road leading to Padova. He parked the little car behind a grove of trees across a plowed field at the rear of Ogle's house.

First he switched off the dome light, then pulled on a new pair of surgical gloves and covered them with leather ones in case he needed to climb trees or fences or other obstacles. Dressed in black cargo pants, heavy black sweatshirt and black running shoes with soft leather soles, he set off toward the house.

Once inside, he located the security panel. The system was a farce, and in minutes Chuck was glancing around the main floor. He sprinted up the steps to the bedrooms, figuring Ogle would want his souvenirs in a private area. He entered the master bedroom. When he closed the door on a large walk-in closet and found the light switch, he sucked in a breath. No racks for hanging clothes nor shelves for hats, gloves, or shoes were visible. Instead, a metal panel about three and one-half feet wide was mounted along each of the walls facing each other. The entire space was designed for his collection. A *large* collection of feminine under garments. Mounted on the metal surfaces were sets of matching bras and panties. Ogle had used colored magnetic circles: blue ones, brown ones, and green to mount his trophies. The circles were part of a coding system because each carried a tiny date printed in indelible ink. Chuck needed to break the code, hoping he'd find it some-where in the house.

Then he recognized Giulia's light-blue, lace-trimmed bra and panties to match, the ones she'd worn their first night of love mak-ing. They were attached with one brown and one blue magnet. Ah ha. Eyes. Another set, which was also held in place by the dual magnets in her colors included a bra made completely of white lace with white lace panties to match. Damn! He hadn't had the pleasure of seeing her in those.

He wanted to snatch them off the wall and get the hell out of there. *Get a grip, man, calm yourself.* He needed to leave them here for the search warrant. *Which I WILL get.* The code system was obvious. Now he needed to find the filing system with names and maybe pictures. Oliver would surely want to gloat over them. First, though, he took pictures of the entire closet museum.

It was 10:30 P.M. when he finished shooting all the items. That dinner might be over soon. Where would Ogle keep folders with personal information? He turned off the light, closed the closet door on the hidden trophies and left in search of a filing cabinet or safe. Four other doors were on this floor. He opened each one. Two were furnished as bedrooms, one was a small bathroom and the one across from Ogle's master suite held a home office. Chuck pulled the drapes closed. To save time, he switched on the overhead lights. It didn't take long to find a cabinet with file folders also colored to match the blue, brown, and green of the magnets. All the blues were bunched together as were the browns and the greens. A few tabs were colored to look like hazel and two were grey. Only one had both blue and brown.

He snatched that one first, and sure enough Giulia's sweet face looked at him. Her name, height, weight and. . .bust size, waist size, hip size—what the fuck! Where did Ogle get that information? Bastard!

Chuck couldn't stand it. He hurried back to the trophy closet and carefully removed Giulia's bras and panties and stuffed them into the deep pockets of his cargo pants. If all this made it as evidence in a court, he would not allow his woman's intimate wear to be on display.

Back to the cabinet full of folders. He felt uneasy prying into other women's information but needed to verify Ogle's system. Sure enough, it included dates and locations of where the prizes had been "collected" as Ogle phrased it. Chuck photographed the insides of enough folders to document that most of these were

U.S. citizens. If Ogle were ever arrested, that information would be valuable because the arrest would go through the U.S. court system.

I've been here too long. He closed all the cabinet drawers. Turned off the lights in the home office, opened the drapes to where they'd been before and was starting down the stairs when he stopped in his tracks. If Giulia's underwear wasn't here, how could she prove Ogle had ransacked her apartment? Shit! Dammit to hell! They *had* to be on that infernal wall. He raced back up the stairs. His fingers fumbled as he foraged in his deep pockets for the magnets that he'd dropped in with her things. They might not be arranged exactly as they had been but, hell, who was Ogle going to complain to?

On the way downstairs again, he heard the distinctive sound of a diesel engine. Ogle was home. When Chuck was on the bottom step, the lights of the Mercedes flashed through the front windows of the house as Ogle pulled around to the back. Chuck had planned to leave by the rear entrance in order to re-set the alarm system. That wasn't going to happen. He'd have to leave by the front. Surely all the doors were on the same system. Worth trying.

As he was about to open the front door, he heard Ogle muttering to himself as he walked past a front window coming straight for the front door. What was that all about? He didn't wait to find out.

Moving with stealth and speed, Chuck reached the rear door, opened it, re-set the alarm and raced across the field to the grove of trees. His heart was thudding. *I'm getting too old for this stuff.* He didn't remove his rubber gloves until he was inside the little car. Gloves? Where were the leather ones? He stepped out of the car to reach into his deep pockets. Ah. There they were. He'd worried he hadn't followed his time-honored pattern of never laying a tool or personal item down. When he turned toward the villa, a light appeared on the main floor. By the time he settled back in the car, that light was out and another came on upstairs. The monster was in his lair. Does he visit his trophies every evening?

On the way into town, Chuck made a mental note to clean Ryland's car for him since he'd crashed through a muddy stream to get away.

* * *

"He's the one, isn't he?" Giulia said. Her eyes looked haunted after seeing the pictures Chuck had taken.

"Yessss." Chuck dragged the word. "Still don't believe he's the only one."

"What?" she said looking up from his camera.

"You saw the destruction that day. Broken furniture, cushions slashed, crockery broken. Ogle *could* have done all that, but I doubt he'd waste time on that stuff. His goal was on these," and he pointed to the pictures.

"It was smart to put my underthings back on that... wall. They need to be there if he's ever investigated. I'd never touch them again anyway."

"Oh sweetheart, I understand." He pushed the camera aside. "Come here."

Later, lying together spoon fashion in his bed, Chuck said, "Damn."

"What?" Giulia said, drowsing against his warm body.

"Do you suppose we could find you some more frothy, white things?"

CHAPTER TWENTY-FOUR

Friday morning—Giulia's day to go to Oliver's office—Chuck stopped her as they left his studio for the post.

"Micina? One last time. Are you ready to go into Oliver's alone?" He knew she'd been restless all night.

"As ready as I'll ever be." Her voice sounded chipper, even flip.

"Thank God, you won't have to wear a wire. Yesterday I stood outside Ogle's office wearing the voice-activated system, and I could hear him loud and clear. I'll hear every word you have with that creep."

She took his hands, kissed his palms and held them. "Karlo."

No one had said his name with such compassion and sweetness since his mother had died.

"Thank you for all you're doing," Giulia said. "You're a mensch. With you nearby, I'll be fine."

*** * ***

"As Giulia stepped into Oliver's office that afternoon, he leaned out the door and looked both ways.

"What? No guard standing by?"

She ignored that and casually took her usual seat in front of his desk. "We have much to discuss, don't we?"

"We do. We do indeed little lady. Let's get this special session in gear," he said, turning the deadbolt mechanism behind her.

The clunk made Giulia's heart pound. She "knew" it wasn't locking, but it sounded so solid. So final. Nevertheless, she waited as calmly as she could for Oliver to settle behind his desk and fuss with his papers.

"You're certified to teach Italian as a second language?"

"I am. You'll find a copy of the certification attached to my resume."

Rubbing his hands together, he opened a folder making clicking sounds with his tongue as he ran a finger down one of the papers. "Certified to teach English as a second language, but—"

She held her position and did not lean over his desk to show him.

"Oh yes. Here it is. My, my. And what else are we certified for?" He looked straight at her with his pale, reptilian eyes. "Certified to suck me off?"

She did not blink. Instead, she stared him down and hoped Chuck's high-tech device was transmitting this horrible man's words onto tape. Oliver's face and neck were flushed and his breathing seemed labored. From the moment he'd sat down, he'd been casually rocking an oversized mechanical pencil held between his thumb and forefinger. The tips of the pencil click-clacked against the metal desktop. The clicking seemed to increase in speed.

Lord, I need to calm him down. "Do you have an idea how many military personnel will be in the Italian class?" she asked. "Has an announcement been published about it?"

Miraculously, the pencil slowed. "So far, we have eleven who have signed up. It would depend on the schedule and location of the class, of course."

"Eleven is a good size for a class to make progress."

"Yes. Progress. Yes indeed. Well, no doubt faster progress could be achieved if you held smaller classes—maybe in your nifty apartment in town, say, in your bedroom?" He looked up at her with predatory eyes.

For a moment, she felt shaken but clamped her teeth and sat up straighter. *He wants me to know.* She said nothing and sneaked a deep breath.

His pencil rocked steadily, and she noticed his other hand move beneath the desk.

"What is the pay scale for teaching extra-curricular classes on the base?"

Again, he seemed to switch into a business mode and turned to his computer, tapping the keys with both hands. He began discussing pay scales for various extra teaching duties. But he jerked his head up and suggested private classes. He bobbed his eyebrows as Chuck had done once in jest, but on Oliver, the action was ugly, menacing.

"Mr. Ogle, I'm not interested in private classes. Studies have shown that students usually do better in a small class of peers. And I don't have time to accommodate eleven students on an individual basis. I could teach Italian on Friday afternoons, unless students would prefer another day because of the weekend." As if she'd just thought of it, she said, "Or, if not Fridays, Monday or Wednesday afternoons would be good. I'd prefer not to hold night classes."

"Found someone to fuck every night, eh?"

She stared at him. The air was thick with an electric charge. She'd had enough. "Do you speak to all your personnel this way?"

"Only those with cunts." The pencil began to drum faster, and more red spots mottled his face.

"I see. Does that work for you?"

"It's a numbers game, dolly, a numbers game. With all your education surely you understand the laws of statistics." Sweat beaded on his forehead and around his upper mouth. A strange odor filled the space between them. Strange and unpleasant. Was she sensing her own fear?

She jerked to her feet. "Please send me suggested times. I'll e-mail back my availability." Gathering her purse and scarf, she said, "After we settle that, I'll come in to sign a separate contract."

For once he didn't comment but she heard a zipper slide.

Still standing, she said, "I want to teach this class, but I need to keep the same working days as specified in my present contract.

If afternoons don't work, I could come in early any of those three days."

Out of nowhere, he sneered and said, "How about using your place behind Pensione Luciana for private classes?"

She staggered back. *He's bragging about stalking me. About breaking in.* She whirled toward the door. As before, he moved fast and reached her just as she got her hand on the door.

"You cock teaser! You're not getting away this time." He grasped her blouse. She screamed. Thank God the door opened in her hand but not before the cloth ripped.

"What the fuck? I locked that. Knew something was off with that door." He charged after her. His foul breath hot in her face, Oliver managed to grab hold of a breast and squeezed. Hard. At that moment, Chuck and Colonel Ryland crashed in with Marlowe behind them. They'd decided at the last minute it'd be good to have a female witness along. Marlowe pulled out her brand-new camera phone and started snapping pictures. Chuck pulled Giulia away growling, "Get out of here! Now!"

At that same moment, Ryland, almost as big as Chuck, yanked Oliver away from her and the front half of her blouse tore away. As soon as Giulia was out of harm's way, Chuck helped Ryland restrain Oliver. Both men took particular pains to use no unnecessary roughness, although Chuck longed to break the bastard's neck. Marlowe continued to take pictures until she noticed Oliver's fly was unzipped. She caught a couple shots of light-green fabric poking out before Ryland turned him toward the door. Through her lens, she noticed Giulia's state of undress. After shooting a picture, she removed her own jacket and wrapped it around Giulia's shoulders then hurried back to take more shots. Giulia staggered out the door and stumbled along the wall of the corridor.

Colonel Ryland led Oliver away in white-plastic handcuffs but Oliver shouted, "Puttana! You'll pay for this!"

It was late Friday afternoon, but two people poked their heads out of a door nearby. One of them gave a thumbs up when he saw

Oliver being led away. Chuck rushed to find Giulia cowering in a far corner of the hallway.

"It's over, my angel." He shoved each of her arms through the sleeves of Marlowe's jacket draped over her shoulders. He buttoned the jacked closed and saw she was trembling. Then, holding her in his arms, he rocked her back and forth, but she remained tense. Frozen. "I heard every word," he said. "What a sick bastard. But, damn, you were good in there." Still, her body remained stiff and felt cold. He held her a little apart to look in her face. "What's wrong, Micina?" *Oh hell. Is she going into shock?*

"Over?" she said, staring past him.

Putting his hand on the nape of her neck and tipping her head up with his thumb. "You pulled it off, kiddo." He kissed her. No response. "What's going on? Look at me." He saw only vacancy. "Talk to me!" he almost shouted. Then he reined back and spoke softly, slowly, all the while stroking her back.

"Going on?" Her eyes were unfocused, and she began to shake.

"Let's get you out of here.

"Out of here," she repeated, nodding her head. "Out of here."

Her voice had sounded so confident through the listening device, but this whole operation had taken more from her than he expected—more than a big blockhead like him could imagine. All along, she had outsmarted the bastard. Had kept her cool with the despicable monster. When it was over, Chuck—her white-knight rescuer—was rough and only focused on dealing with Ogle. Hell. Ryland could have handled him. Damn.

Marlowe came rushing up to them and pulled Giulia into a hug. "Hey, girl. It's over. You did it! Let's go celebrate. Marc's on his way. I've been wanting to try that restaurant called Zio Zeb ever since you told me about it. Okay?" She hadn't noticed yet the uneasy cloud hovering around Chuck and Giulia.

When she got no response, she finally focused. Giulia's face was pale. Her eyes, dull and spacey. Chuck was holding her with a helpless look on his face.

"Sounds good, Marlowe," Chuck said hoarsely and caught her

attention by twitching his head toward Giulia. "Might be good for *some* of us to stop at the Greek place here on the base for a shot of ouzo or grappa, if they have it. Warm us up. Calm us down, right?"

"Yesss. Super idea," Marlowe said.

* * *

Giulia shivered uncontrollably and her legs weren't cooperating. Chuck supported her as they walked across to the row of fast-food spots. He could have carried her, but walking might help work adrenalin out of her system. She seemed caught in a trance when they entered the taverna. As he guided her to a booth, he noticed the bar board showed only cheap brandy or ouzo.

"Do you want ouzo or brandy?" He didn't ask *whether* she wanted a drink, hoping the pressure to make a choice would pull her out of the foggy cocoon that locked her away from him.

"Ouzo."

He sighed with relief, slid into the booth beside her and chafed her hands. He and Marlowe talked softly to her as they waited.

When their drinks arrived, Marlowe raised her glass to Giulia, "We did it. *You* did it, Giulia. Bottoms up."

Giulia tipped her shot glass. She sputtered and coughed and broke into laughter. Laughing hysterically, she held out her glass for more. Chuck signaled the man at the bar for another. When it arrived, Chuck offered her the second shot, but she was still laughing too hard to take it. He set it down, grasped her shoulders and held her in a steely grip, not wanting to slap or shake her.

"Giulia, stop!" he ordered. Her head snapped back. With one hand he held the back of her head, with the other, he touched the glass to her lips. She looked at him with recognition in her eyes. *At last.* She took a sip. Marlowe and Chuck were quiet while Giulia continued to sip the strong, sweet liquore.

"Ouzo. Haven't had any for years. Strong isn't it? Guess I needed that."

"Guess so," Chuck said. "Are you cold?"

"A little, but mostly I'm starved."

Chuck and Marlowe grinned at each other, knowing the worst was over. "Let's get going," she said. "Marc will take a cab to Zio Zeb."

"Sounds great. What are we waiting for?" Giulia said.

Chuck and Marlowe looked at each other again and laughed with relief.

Later while eating, they re-hashed what had happened. Giulia was calm and in control again as she answered Marc's questions. "I don't quite understand my crazy reaction afterwards. But the best part... it's over."

Chuck pulled her into the shelter of his shoulder.

"What happens now?" Marlowe asked.

"Ogle will be held by the military until American civilian authorities arrive, probably from Padova," Chuck said. "He can't be tried under military law, and he'll raise a huge stink the entire time. Ryland and I will be called to make our statements to the military tribunal—Monday if not sooner. I'm sure we'll also be required in the civilian court. Won't be pretty. But the end result's bound to be good. Oliver won't be working here anymore."

"That's good news," Marlowe said, "it should never have gotten this far. I still don't understand why the women on base let it go so long. Wonder how many other places he's shifted out of?"

"He was already here when I arrived almost eight years ago," Chuck said.

"More likely, women transferred to get away from him," Marlowe mused.

"A lot of what went on is my word against his," Giulia said.

"That's why he's gotten away with his abusive behavior for so long," Marlowe said.

"Exactly." Giulia shook her head back and forth biting her lower lip.

"Don't forget three of us saw him tearing your shirt and grabbing your breast," Marlowe said.

"Let's hope his inevitable accusations of entrapment won't stick," Marc added.

They all looked at Marc. "Yeah," Chuck said nodding his head. "The waters could be muddy on that subject."

"But other women will testify about being afraid to go in his office alone." Marlowe said. "I wonder how many other women have been molested in that office with no witnesses?"

"If they'll testify," Giulia said.

"They will," Marlowe said. "What's to fear now?"

"Hey guys," Marc said. "For now, it's out of our hands. Shall we all head home?"

CHAPTER TWENTY-FIVE

As they stepped out of the Venice station, Marc and Marlowe saw their vaporetto approaching. Marlowe gave Giulia a quick hug. "Gotta go. If we miss this, we'll have to wait another hour." Marc called out, "We'll be in touch."

Giulia and Chuck hiked the fifty steps up and fifty down of the Scalzi Bridge, putting them into Santa Croce. Chuck's feet guided them seamlessly into San Polo where his quiet apartment waited. As they hurried through the dark calles with buildings close on either side, Giulia said, "There's no doubt that Oliver was the vandal who broke in."

"Oh, he was in there for sure. But all that violent destruction?" Chuck took Giulia's arm, guiding her to the right. "This way, it's quicker even though it seems wrong."

"He's stronger than he looks."

"Oh sweetheart, I'm sorry he touched you. Are you hurt?"

She ignored his question. "Writing Puttana on the mirror, makes me think he was the only vandal."

"That doesn't mean a lot. Filth comes out of his mouth every other word. He probably calls any woman a whore if she doesn't kow-tow to him."

"But he hadn't used Italian with his other vulgarities. Why that one? I think he wanted me to know who wrote it on my bathroom mirror."

"For sure he wanted you to know he'd been there. But he can't reach you anymore." Chuck opened the door to his building. "He couldn't get to my address files like he did yours, but God help him if he *ever* follows you here. He wouldn't have Ryland to protect him from me."

"Believe it or not," she said, while they climbed to his first-floor apartment, "I'd prefer it was all Oliver's doing. Oliver might be dangerous, but he'll be out of the picture soon." She sighed. "Won't he?"

"He'll be off the post, you can count on that. I'm glad I got into his office and villa before this happened." After a moment, Chuck said, "Damn!"

"What?"

"I hope he won't have time to move his trophies before he's shipped off to the States." Unlocking his apartment, he said, "Well, let's give it a rest."

"Yes. I do crave peace and quiet. Tomorrow I'm going to call my grandparents to see if I can visit them for the weekend. Want to come too?"

"Yeah. I'd like to find out how Tony's doing in his retirement."

"Retirement? That's doubtful. But maybe his adventures will be a little more cautious. No more talk of Oliver tonight, but I do need a hot shower after being around that slimy toad."

"Go ahead. I'll check on a couple of things," Chuck said.

In her room, she stripped quickly, pulled on her ratty robe and rummaged in the drawers where she'd stashed clothes brought from her apartment. Still unnerved and exhausted, she couldn't find her over-sized Tee-shirts. She went looking for Chuck who was sorting mail on the kitchen counter.

"Excuse me," she said.

He looked up and smiled. *Oh Lord, that smile.* "I can't find any of my sleep Tees, could I borrow one of yours?"

"You don't need to wear anything in bed." *I'll haul it off anyway.*

She waited.

"Okay," he said. "Check the middle drawer of the large chest." His eyes followed her hips as she walked away.

She chose a faded green Tee, soft from many washings, it would feel perfect after the rough handling by that creep. After a long, hot shower she lay fatigued, but unable to relax. What was taking him so long? After Jason's lies and before meeting Chuck, she'd been sure the internal switch she'd flipped to "off" had shut her down for good. But when Chuck walked in from his shower, she noticed a big bulge tenting the towel around his waist. *God, I'm glad I was wrong about that switch. Here's a man made for loving and loving and loving.*

"How're you doing?" he asked.

"Not good. I need you. Now!" She switched off the bedside lamp, but not before he'd dropped his towel and she'd seen exactly what she wanted. He flipped the light back on and sat down beside her, splendid in his nakedness. All man.

"I want to look at you," he said and pulled back the duvet, grasped the hem of the green shirt and dragged it over her head. He gazed down at her then drew in his breath. "Your breast. Your beautiful breast. It's turning blue. That miserable bastard. I'll see him rot in hell yet! Oh, my angel." He leaned down and kissed the bruise with feathery kisses moaning softly. "Does it hurt? Are you all right?"

"Never mind that. Come here," she hooked her arms around his neck and pulled him down crushing his mouth hard on hers. Her tongue pushed into his mouth, and she dug her hands into his back trying to pull him closer. Chuck resisted letting all his weight down although by now she had her hands fisted in his hair as if she'd never let go. He didn't want to crush her and tried to slow her pace. He straddled her hips and began kissing her neck slowly. But with her hands still in his hair, she forced his mouth back to hers and into another ferocious kiss. He loved kissing Giulia so he gave in and let her indulge her frenzy. After a few more wet kisses, he worked his tongue into a slower motion seeking to turn things down a notch. He rolled onto his back—worried about that bruised breast—to offer her more control. She took it. Her hands went straight to his cock and began guiding it into herself.

"Hold on." He grabbed her hands and held them in one of his while he gently slipped a finger inside to be certain she could take him without pain. Not surprised, but needing reassurance, he found her slick and fiery hot. *Lord. This is happening too fast, but if it's what she wants, I'm her man.* He released her hands and she pressed her palms on his upper chest for support. He grasped her hips helping to lift her all the way up to begin an excruciatingly delicious slide down his shaft. At this point—*finally*—she slowed her pace. Her female scent enveloped him. Her face was flushed, her upper body rosy. God she was beautiful. Her head was thrown back and her brown nipples were hard points begging for his mouth. He curled upward, took one and sucked. Hard. She gasped and began her descent.

"It's absolute heaven this way," he said.

"You mean when I'm up here?" she panted.

"That, too, but I'm thinking how good you feel when I'm not wearing a condom."

"Yes. Oh yesss." And she added a little circular motion to her slow slide.

The sensation was incredible. He couldn't hold back much longer, but she'd made it clear she was in need tonight so he thrust his hips upward to meet her and they found a rhythm that grew in intensity until they both dissolved into a sweaty heap of mutual ecstasy.

"Better now?" he asked.

She sighed. "Was something wrong?"

"You *are* a vixen." And he switched off the lamp.

* * *

Giulia opened her eyes to a clear morning. Ouch, her breast was more tender than last night. It would heal. Chuck's warm hand cradled it. For all their softness, boobs were pretty tough. Chuck stirred and his morning erection poked her.

"Mornin'," he whispered. "How do you feel about using this?"

She turned over to face him and said, "It'd be a shame to waste it."

"Waste not, want not, Babička used to say."

So they obeyed his grandma's admonition, but in a more leisurely manner than the wildness of the night before.

Later as they drank the last of their coffee, Chuck's phone rang. When he finished the call, he told what she had surmised from his side of the conversation. He needed to go in for an acknowledgment and signature on the report he had e-mailed sometime last night. "Have you spoken with your grandparents yet?"

"Yes. They want both of us to come. They already know I've moved in with you—temporarily," she emphasized again. "And they're delighted. But I haven't told them about the vandalism. And… I'd rather they didn't know."

"I understand. The best thing that could happen," Chuck said, "would be for Oliver to let it slip during interrogation that he was the vandal. We'd know for sure Botteri hadn't been involved. *Then* we could tell Tony. That way, he wouldn't feel extra guilt."

"I'd love that outcome."

"Want to go back to Vicenza with me this morning? We could take my car directly to the grandparents."

"Good idea. While you're at the base, I'd like to visit Luciana and Gino. You could pick me up at the pensione or in town when you're finished."

"Perfect. Let's do it."

On arrival in Vicenza, Chuck carried their overnights to his car, and she caught a bus to the pensione. After visiting her former landlords, she'd leave a message on his phone as to where she'd be.

Luciana had brought in coffee and apricot-filled croissants. And Giulia had offered, again, to pay whatever the insurance company wouldn't cover. But Gino waved that off saying it'd be months before all that was settled. Weekend guests would arrive soon and she knew they'd be busy, but before leaving, she offered to pay something up front until the settlement. Neither would listen to her offer and simply gave her a big hug saying to stop by soon for a visit.

Figuring she had plenty of time, she walked toward the town center and strolled among the many graceful buildings Palladio had designed. She left Chuck a voice message about her whereabouts and asked him to call her when he left the base. Then she meandered into the grand piazza of the ancient city hall. The design to renovate the old hall had become Palladio's stepping stone to fame and fortune. His idea had been to cover the old gothic building with classical columns reminiscent of ancient Rome. In the mid-1500s, this idea was considered innovative, maybe even avant-garde.

She remembered buying her first ripe *cachi* at the outdoor market held beside the building. Not having eaten a persimmon before, she had assumed it was an exotic fruit typical of Italy and bit right into it. It had been like eating pudding with her fingers, and the sticky stuff spread all over her face and hands. On that trip, her new friend, Pamela, teased her, but neither of them had more than a tissue or two. Then Pam spied a spigot with water running freely at the side of the building. "Saved again!" Giulia had said laughing. She'd referred to the time when Pam helped Giulia elude an unwanted Romeo in Verona, where the two had met in a cheap hotel for women.

As she moved on through the grand piazza, she noticed a man who looked familiar. It was the second time she'd seen him that morning. He moved gracefully away from her toward one of the small shops. The way he walked... *Oh Lord. He served tea and works for Botteri!*

Her phone vibrated in her pocket and she ducked behind one of the huge support columns of the Palladiana. Chuck was leaving the base. When he got her location, he said, "Why are you whispering?"

"I saw one of Botteri's men. He may be following me."

"Exactly where are you?"

When she told him, he said, "Get out among people. Now! I'll be there in ten-twelve minutes. Keep on Corso Andrea Palladio heading toward the River Bacchiglione. Wait in the middle of the bridge where people can see you until you spot my car. Then come across, turn right and go to the cloister of San Pietro. I'll find you."

"Will do. I might be wrong, you know, but…"

"Don't chance it. Go!"

She stood on the bridge, ostensibly gazing at the fast-moving river, but out of the corner of her eye, Giulia watched for the slender man who had served tea. No sign of him. Then she saw Chuck's bright yellow car and breathed again. She turned toward him at the same moment he spied her. He double parked and ran to her. He scooped her up, and they held each other until both hearts slowed down.

"I haven't seen him since before I spoke to you. Either I was mistaken or he's a better tracker than the first one."

"Either way, sweet angel, let me get you outta here."

CHAPTER TWENTY-SIX

Chuck leaned over to kiss her lightly and fastened her seatbelt.

"Okay already. Enough fussing," she said. "I'm fine. Tell me how your interrogation went?"

"About as I expected." He began winding his way out of city center. "The AFOSI guys were suspicious about how it all came down. Why was—"

"AFOSI?" Giulia interrupted.

"Air Force Office of Special Investigation."

"Of course. Another alphabet moniker. Sorry, you were saying?"

"They asked why Ryland was there. Why was Marlowe taking pictures? Marlowe was easily finessed. The four of us were planning an evening together, and I honestly had no idea she'd have one of those new camera phones. Damn. I need one of those."

Giulia laughed. "Does Marc have one?"

"No doubt. He always has the latest."

They were quiet while Chuck maneuvered past a tricky intersection onto the road toward Vittorio Veneto.

"How did you finesse Ryland?"

"I said I'd been waiting for you and he happened along. The truth was he *had* planned to pick up brochures and school schedules from Ogle for a comrade and family arriving soon. I saw no need to mention I'd asked him to stop by at that exact time."

"I'm curious. Did you expect so much resistance from Ogle that you'd need another man there?"

"Him?" Chuck took his eyes from the road for a moment and gave her a look that said you've got to be kidding. "I was worried my anger might get out of control and thought it'd be best for Ryland to do most of the taking down."

"Do officers usually carry those plastic handcuffs around on the base?"

"Jeez! You ask tough ones. You could have been one of the men leaning on me this morning. But I'd worried about that too and e-mailed him last night to get in touch with me ASAP. He called this morning. It happened that Ryland had been demonstrating the proper use of plastic flexi-cuffs to a couple of new MPs on the post. The cuffs were still in his pocket. We lucked out on that. But..." He shook his head back and forth.

"What?"

"It shows me that our little operation wasn't so well planned after all. We were more interested in catching Ogle than how to explain ourselves later."

"Did they question your use of the listening device?"

"Not at all. I'd already told them you and other women were nervous about entering his office alone so when I knew you were going in, I wanted to be damned sure I could hear what went on. I said, 'What if she hadn't been able to scream?' So far nothing has come up about the door. I need to get it back into proper operation."

"Hmm." Giulia said, "Even if Ogle thinks the lock had been tampered with, what can he say? He'd have to admit he locks women in."

"Good point. But I'll make sure Enrico puts it in working order when he gets to the spring-loaded door he jimmied for me. He'll take his sweet time, though, it seems he hates Ogle's guts."

"Do you suppose anyone likes the guy. Poor man."

"After what he did to you? Don't waste any pity on that predator."

They didn't speak of the incident any more. Shortly before they took the exit into Vittorio Veneto, Giulia said, "Even though my grandparents know I've moved into your place—temporarily—I'm sure they'll want us separated when it comes to sleeping under *their* roof. At least Nonna will."

"I understand." And as he slowed into the exit, he said, "And Giulia?"

"Yes?"

He looked directly at her as he stopped at a light. "I do get that your stay with me is temporary."

"Okay," she said, tipping her head down to study her feet.

To their surprise, Nonna led them both to the large bedroom where Chuck had slept before. When she left, they looked at each other. Giulia raised her shoulders and hands in surrender. Chuck just smiled.

The weekend was pleasant; exactly what they both needed. Nonno Tony knew the location of Giulia's new place and claimed it to be not only an elegant area but safe for his precious grand-daughter.

"You'll be surrounded by churches, coccolona, if that ever made anybody safe," he grumbled.

"Now Tony," Maria Grazia said.

"Your rio is named for the Archangel Raffaele and his church sits beside the water. Are you across from it?"

"Yes."

He closed his eyes for a moment. "So. San Sebastiano lies behind Raffaele, and the ancient church of San Nicolò is down to the right of your apartment, and on your left, toward Campo Santa Margherita, is *Chiesa dei Carmini,* Church of the Carmelites."

"You really know Venice," she said.

He grinned. "Sometimes I feel almost Venetian. I spent a lot of time there as a young turk on the prowl. You might be able to look out your window and see that nice sculpture above the church's front door."

"Yes, I can. It's rather sweet. The Archangel Raffaele bends toward the little boy, Tobiolo, whose dog holds that big fish in his mouth. It's a fascinating story from ancient scriptures. The apocrypha, I think."

"Lots more interesting than most tales churches like to preach," Tony muttered.

"I had no idea you knew that much about the famous Hebrew

story," Giulia said. "Some claim Tobiolo and Raffaele were around before the Hebrews came on the scene."

Chuck looked at her with a question wrinkling his brow as if amazed at her knowledge of old religious stories. She merely shrugged.

"Is your loom working right, Nonna?" Chuck asked, hoping she wouldn't mind him calling her grandmother.

"Oh my yes. After you put it back together, it works beautifully. Come, Giulia, I'll show you a couple of new scarves I've designed."

As the women left, Chuck said, "Tony, your home looks as good as new. And so do you. Now tell me what you've been up to."

Tony seemed somewhat subdued but mentioned he still attended estate sales to find good buys for the twins' import business in Portland. He confessed he had no more plans to break into big-time gem operations.

"By the way, I picked up interesting news about that shyster Botteri. He got into big trouble."

"What happened?" Chuck asked, leaning forward.

"Don't have details, but the rumor is the Carabinieri's Vice Squad was trailing him. About the time they swooped in, someone took a shot at Botteri. It seems he's been taken into a hospital at an unknown location. Heard they caught a few of his followers, too."

"Maybe they'll try to extract information about bigger connections," Chuck said, "but it's good news for both you and Giulia."

"What's good news?" Giulia asked as she and Nonna came back into the dining room.

Nonno Tony told the story again.

"Stupendo!" Nonna said and went to the cupboard to get aperitif glasses for a toast. Afterward, they enjoyed white bean and kale soup laced with plenty of garlic, topped with shaved Parmigiano Reggiano cheese and accompanied by hot bread and salad.

On Sunday morning, they all took a long hike, returning to a huge brunch Maria Grazia had organized. After stuffing themselves, Chuck and Giulia left for the drive back to Venice.

"Maybe I was wrong about the man I saw Friday afternoon. Why would he trail me if his boss was being held by the police?"

"Good question. Maybe he hadn't been called off? How sure are you?"

"I felt positive at the time, but it was more a feeling about the way he walked than a clear certainty."

Chuck parked his car in the parking garage at Piazzale Roma. "Shall we catch a vaporetto down to Rialto?" he asked.

"Let's walk. Do you mind carrying your duffel that far? I can pull my small carry-on."

He hoisted his bag onto his shoulder. "After all Nonna's food, walking sounds perfect."

* * *

As Giulia was organizing her notes for class, she had to admit the notes saved from the shower stall proved worthless. To her, that was one more clue it had been Oliver. He would have known those papers were important to her. Thugs would have ignored them.

Chuck had gone on an errand. She finished up and stepped into the shower. April twentieth and it was Easter Sunday. Tourists had begun to flood into Venice; many were Italians. She hoped most would wash back out again after the holiday, but merchants were gearing up for the coming months. Soon, the most popular areas would be crammed with visitors.

There was no doubt in her mind that come May first—less than two weeks away—she'd move into her own Venetian apartment. *Girl, are you sure about this move?* Already the idea of not waking up in Chuck's arms gave her a lonely chill. But this dream had been the focal point of *all* her goals. To give it up would feel like a betrayal to the little girl who created the fantasy, but another reason was becoming even more important. It might be a survival thing.

She was crazy about Chuck. He was a good man inside and out. He cared about her. Oh yes, she knew that. He cared for others too—for his young men who went into dangerous situations. And she and Chuck had a lot in common. They both had immigrant parents and both loved Venice. Certainly, his words and actions told her he wanted her for more than short-term rolls in the hay.

But. . . the big *but*. In case he turned his back on her when she told him about the escort service, she'd need her own place. She had never expected to reveal that part of her life to anyone. But now, the idea of having a secret from him plagued her. She reached for a towel and doubted she'd ever feel alive again if he . . .

"There you are," Chuck said peeking around the edge of the bathroom door. "Am I lucky or what? To have this vision of loveliness in my lowly abode." He wrapped his arms around both her and the damp towel. "Mmm. You smell good enough to eat. Speaking of which, are you as hungry as I am? We could re-heat your nonna's venison stew as our first course. I picked up a ready-made salad at the deli for the second, and then... who knows?"

CHAPTER TWENTY-SEVEN

Monday evening Giulia felt frazzled when she got home from work and poured a glass of wine before considering dinner. Her phone rang the moment she stretched out on Chuck's plushy, leather couch.

"Micina, I'm not going to be home to eat with you."

"No problem. I was wondering whether to bother anyway."

"Tired?" he asked.

"A little. Sometimes petty departmental stuff wears on me more than all the rest. Is anything wrong at the base?"

"No. An impromptu round-up of team leaders. We'll bring in beer and pizza. Shouldn't last too long. Keep the doors locked and our bed warm, okay?"

"I can handle those instructions. Might be awake when you get here."

"Go ahead and fall asleep. I won't disturb your slumber... too much."

She felt better just hearing him make a sexy promise. In the end, she pulled out a couple eggs, a small tomato, a piece of cheese and found tiny, green onions and parsley to stir into an omelet. Compared to her usual fridge, Chuck's was always stocked with little extras to make a dish special. She dropped a small glob of butter in the skillet when the intercom buzzed. She flicked off the fire and hurried to the control panel.

"*Chi è?* Who's there?" she asked.

"*Sono il Tenente Armando di Stefano dei Carabinieri sono venuto a parlare con Ms. Giulia Cavinato.* This is Lieutenant Armando di Stefano with the Carabinieri to speak with Ms. Giulia Cavinato."

"What is the purpose of your visit?" she answered in Italian thinking it strange that he used the American title "Ms."

"May I come in?"

"I'm sorry… not at this time." She'd almost said she was alone, but thought better of that. "Could we set a time for another meeting? Tomorrow evening, maybe?"

"Yes, of course. You may call me about that. I'll give you the office number. That way you can confirm that I am who I say I am. Let me give you my direct number as well."

She took down both numbers and said she'd call first thing in the morning. She could hardly wait for Chuck to arrive so they could speculate together what this was about.

Later. Chuck ran his hand through his hair. "God, I'm glad you didn't let him come up while you were alone. This is the nudge I need to get a video system installed. Not that I'd want you to let a stranger up even if you could see him, but it makes sense to see who's ringing before answering. You're probably not in any trouble or he would have demanded to come in."

"That's good news," she said. "It must be about Botteri. But how would he know I'd gone to see him? Could it be about the vandalism? But the federal police wouldn't be in on that, would they?"

"Guess we'll have to wait 'til tomorrow night to find out. In the meantime, after a long shower, I'm going to hunt you down."

"Do you need a talented back scrubber?"

"My back doesn't need much attention, but… I'll take what I can get."

* * *

Tuesday evening, the intercom buzzed exactly at eight—the time Giulia had suggested to the lieutenant's receptionist.

"Let me get it," Chuck said.

Before the tall, slender policeman crossed the apartment threshold, he asked, *"Permesso?"* The time-honored question voiced before entering the home of anyone except family or good friends.

Chuck replied, *"Certo,"* and the officer held out his credentials for them to inspect. When Chuck stood aside for him to enter, Giulia gasped, "You!"

Chuck looked at her in alarm. "What's wrong?"

"He's the one who served tea in the hotel."

"Yes, Ms. Cavinato, I am." He ran his hand through his wiry blond hair, a motion reminding her of Chuck's habit. For some reason she relaxed a little.

"Please let me explain. I've been working with a task force for almost a year now and—"

"So you're undercover?" she blurted.

"Si, si. Un agente segreto."

"It *was* you last Friday afternoon at the Palladiana."

He sighed. "I'm embarrassed you caught me. I felt like a beginner. Maybe we should hire you to help train me and the rest of our squad."

"She does have a special sense for stalkers. She caught me when I pursued her, too."

Both men chuckled. "I'm sorry if I frightened you, signorina."

She waved her hand as if it had been nothing when in reality her heart had pounded into her throat that day until she'd spotted Chuck's yellow car.

"May we offer you something, Lieutenant? Tea, coffee, wine?" Giulia gestured for him to follow her into the living room.

"Nothing, thanks. I won't take much of your time. My assignment these days is to track *you* ."

"Me?" Giulia gasped and looked up at Chuck.

"The reason is complicated. First off, I'm happy to report that Signor Bernardo Botteri has been apprehended and is in custody. But until his more zealous *gallopini,* errand boys, are convinced that he's lost his power, they might continue to try snatching you. He controls by fear but rewards richly for jobs well done. Until they back off and move to another boss—or are apprehended themselves—a small team is organized to protect you."

Giulia's face went pale. "Why would he want them to grab me? I have nothing he wants."

"Oh, Ms. Cavinato. It's you he wants. In his 'private stable' as he calls it."

She shuddered and Chuck moved closer to her.

Lieutenant di Stefano pulled out his business cards and gave one to each. "If either of you see *anyone* that looks like they might bother you, call immediately."

"How will I know whether they are the good guys or the bad ones?" She couldn't stop a little grin from sliding across her lips.

"I hope you won't see the good ones," he snorted, "but I can send you photos of my team. Do you have a fax?"

"We don't," Chuck said. "We have email, but pictures aren't always clear or small enough to carry in one's pocket. How about I pick up actual photos from your office in Campo San Zaccaria?"

"Excellent idea, but not at the Zaccaria site. The fewer people handling pictures of undercover operators the better. I'll organize two packets for you and deliver them myself. But it'd be best if I deliver them to you, Major General Novak. Until we nab these goons, the less open contact we have with Ms. Cavinato, the better. I'll call later and arrange a place to meet. Va bene?"

"Shew!" Giulia said after the policeman left.

"He's impressive. It's going to be okay." Chuck kept his arm around her as they stared at the stairway di Stefano had taken to the ground floor.

Turning back inside, Giulia said, "I don't usually have premonitions, but I had an uneasy feeling when Nonno Tony asked me to take those gems. I'm sorry I suspected *him*, though. I sure don't want him to know all the troubles they've brought me."

"I agree. Let's not let him know."

* * *

Chuck was easy to be with. He was more meticulous than she was and kept his place tidy and clean with little effort. She tried to comply with his sense of order although he didn't seem bothered if she left a book or scarf lying in the living room. His kitchen cupboards were orderly but the products weren't lined up like soldiers with all the labels in "alpha-fucking-betical" order as a friend in Eugene had reported. She'd told Giulia that after watching her husband re-arrange canned goods in the middle of the night, kitchen chores were all his.

Giulia didn't enter Chuck's study unless he was there to invite her in. Everyone needed privacy. He'd seemed pre-occupied lately but she didn't pry or ask over and over if he was all right. Lord knew she was preoccupied with her appointment on Thursday to give a deposition to Oliver's lawyer. She'd already given one to Rafe Lyne, the lawyer Chuck had hired for her. Rafe was a transplanted Englishman and located in a small office in the clock tower at Piazza di San Marco. He wasn't a stiff-upper-lip kind of Brit, and they were on a first-name basis which eased her nerves a lot. He'd given her advice on what to expect and how to respond.

Wednesday evening, Chuck and Giulia met Marc and Marlowe for an early pizza at the trattoria Serenissima in Cannaregio. The first whiff of garlic as they entered caused Giulia's mouth to water. For sure, Serenissima's pizza rated tops in the city for her. They passed the tables near the front windows and went on beyond the central cooking area where a monstrous jar of oil filled with peeled garlic cloves sat on the counter. They found a table in a rear corner for a little privacy. After ordering, Marc and Marlowe began giving Giulia advice. It was similar to Rafe's. She should tell the truth as she saw it and nothing more. Giulia nodded.

"Take all the time you need. Don't let the opposing attorney badger you into answering too quickly," Marc suggested. Giulia nodded.

"Ask for a repeat of any question that seems strange or off the mark," Marlowe said. Giulia nodded and began to see herself as one of those bobble-head dolls mounted in the back window of cars in the States.

Chuck had a copy of the tape and its transcription from that horrible meeting. Giulia had already listened to it at least three times and read through the report to refresh her memory. At the time, she'd thought she'd been alert but after it was over, details had blurred. If this went before a jury, the recording would not be allowed, but Rafe knew the judge and Oliver's attorney—possibly Oliver, himself—would have heard it so she wanted to have it in mind, too.

"My fear," she said, "is blurting out words that could be construed as having been a purposeful entrapment."

"Enough!" Marlowe said. "We need to give it a rest. Besides, you don't blurt, Giulia. Go home, take a hot soak, relax. You'll do fine tomorrow."

Chuck and Marc signaled for the check. The four friends walked out together and went their separate ways. But as Giulia and Chuck walked back across the Rialto Bridge toward his apartment, she couldn't leave it alone.

"If he asks if I instigated Oliver into assaulting me, I can easily answer no. If he asks if I went there to catch him? How do I answer? You know I wanted him caught and was willing to be bait." She hesitated. "I know it's semantics. Truth to tell, I think *he* was trying to trap me."

"That's the way I see it."

"I think he wanted to get back at me for kicking him after his first assault. So, in a way, we were both setting a trap for each other."

"Hmm. You might be right," Chuck said as he opened the outer door to the apartment. "Don't forget he locked the door, or thought he did, and you were there at his request. Remember his emails urging you to come? Sure, we all wanted to get rid of him, but you had a legitimate reason to be there."

"Yes, but—"

"Would he have been willing to discuss by phone or email whether you would teach Italian? I think not. And at some point, you would have had to go to sign another contract. Having backup nearby was merely the same precaution other women were taking. Oliver was aware of that. Remember him checking up and down the hallway looking for possible guards? He just didn't happen to see us that time."

"You're right," she said feeling more positive as she hung her jacket in the hall closet. "He believed I was locked in with him and thought he had the cards stacked against me." She shuddered. "Jeez. When I heard that click, it sounded so final."

"Ah Micina. I hate you went through that." Unbuttoning her shirt, he said, "Maybe I can find a way to take your mind off tomorrow."

She slid her hands under *his* shirt moving up his solid chest and stopping to feel the strong throb of his heart. He had *all* her clothes off by the time they reached the shower. In bed, he kissed her from her nose to toes and slowly back up her body, bringing her to a long climax only seconds before his own. Later in the night, she woke feeling restless and worried, but Chuck's arms around her put the whole ordeal in perspective. She felt loved no matter what would come later.

* * *

The deposition with the opposing attorney was as nerve-wracking as she had expected, but after their talk the night before, Giulia felt confident about her role in that sordid meeting with Oliver Ogle. Not once did Oliver's lawyer manage to trick her. And when he asked if she had "instigated" the assault, she felt the tightness in the back of her neck let go, releasing the dull headache she'd carried around for a week. She answered no with easy conviction. After that, she relaxed enough to focus on Oliver's attorney, who seemed to be struggling to defend Oliver.

Marc and Marlowe came to Chuck's place that evening to celebrate Oliver's downfall. It wasn't over, but in the end, they'd never have to deal with him face to face again. At Giulia's request,

Chuck made his Czech grandmother's leek, spinach and cheese tart. It wasn't too different from a favorite tart Marc's Italian nonna made for him. Marc mused aloud if he might try it himself.

"Hey ol' man, are you ready for a tart standoff?" Chuck challenged, holding a serving spoon out as a mock sword.

"Great idea," Marlowe announced. "Giulia and I will be impartial judges."

And both guys blew out big raspberries.

Marlowe carried in a tiramisu she'd brought to the celebration. Rich with heavy cream folded into whipped raw eggs, plenty of Vin Santo and curls of dark chocolate on top. The evening was a fitting tribute to their joint efforts to free the area of Ollie the Ogre.

CHAPTER TWENTY-EIGHT

After her class on Friday, Giulia visited Saint Francis again. She continued to wrestle with how and when she should reveal her past to Chuck. But convincing arguments for *not* telling him flooded her thoughts instead. First, Chuck didn't know. Second, he didn't need to know. And most important, her escort activities were long before they'd ever met. But when she looked up at the serene face of Francis, he seemed skeptical. The truth—he seemed to say—was she did not want to lose him. Maybe when they were old and grey, she'd tell him. *Where did that come from?*

That evening, Chuck headed straight to the fridge, opened a bottle of beer, sank onto his huge recliner and took a long pull.

"What's up?" Giulia said, coming to sit on the wide arm of the chair.

He pulled her onto his lap. "Have to replace another officer who has an emergency. I'll be at the base tomorrow morning until Sunday night or possibly Monday morning." He took another swallow and sighed. "It's odd. B. G., I never minded. But damn, I've grown accustomed to lazy weekends with you."

"I'm disappointed too. What's bee gee?"

"Before Giulia." He put his beer down and kissed her.

"You're funny. Sweet, too." And she snuggled closer.

"We ought to make the best use of our time while we have it. I have a sneaky hunch I might be called out sooner." Before she could comment, he lifted her sweat shirt and began to bury his nose between her breasts.

The phone rang around nine P.M., rousing them from a blissful snooze after languid lovemaking. Chuck had to leave. His own team had been called up. He needed to brief himself *and* his men on their mission. He couldn't tell her anything and she didn't ask.

"Thank God you don't have to go with them," she said as they hugged at the door. She looked up. "Or... do you wish you were going?"

"A little part of me does, maybe always will. But no," he shook his head. "I don't want that mind-numbing responsibility anymore. It's enough to send them off, hoping to God they're ready."

* * *

Saturday morning, Giulia felt bereft. The night alone in Chuck's big bed had been a sample of how lonely she'd feel after she moved out. Was she crazy? She ought to be glowing with excitement, instead, she felt off kilter. This should be an excellent time to shop for all the items needed to make the new place hers, but the idea of shopping seemed too trivial.

She wandered aimlessly across the Rialto Bridge. But after she turned left toward Cannaregio, she knew where her feet were taking her. The narrow calles were filling with people doing their Saturday shopping and meeting friends at little tables outside the coffee bars. She maneuvered past them until she reached Fondamenta Nuova where she looked for Vaporetto Thirteen's landing stage. Her regular pass didn't allow her on number thirteen. She bought a ticket, forgetting to ask when it would depart but waited and stared across the vast expanse of the lagoon.

It was a lonely ride into the far northeastern reaches. The craft's destination was Treporti. The town was on the lagoon side of the broad peninsula that reached out from the eastern mainland. The peninsula almost touched the northern tip of the Lido. Together, these two landmasses usually held back stormy waters of the Adriatic Sea.

The sky, heavy with grey clouds, colored the water almost black. Sky and water matched her state of mind. She glanced around, wondering if Botteri's goons were on this boat, and idly hoped di Stefano's team was, too.

A handsome man with thick, salt and pepper hair and a dark, shapely mustache tried to engage her in conversation. He resembled one of the five or six top politicians in the central government in Rome who changed places frequently. Each time she visited Italy, the same ones were doing their musical-chairs routine. What was his name? D'Alema. Yes, Massimo D'Alema, an intelligent speaker, but she dismissed this man with a distant smile.

Water almost covered small, barren islets. Had there ever been life on any of these? For a moment, she thought they might be cruising on the back side of Torcello Island but then noticed they were nowhere near the first beginnings of Venice. She was jerked out of her musings when the craft slammed into a huge bricola at Punta Vela, the dock for Sant'Erasmo. The pilot must have been distracted to make such a rough landing.

Huge chains wrapped the three stocky tree trunks that formed the bricola they'd just rammed. This sturdy structure was surely made to withstand more than a careless bump from a vaporetto. To hold the boat steady for people to get off and on, the *marino*, ship's attendant, threw his rope around a smaller post, also part of the pier.

Of all the different wooden configurations in the lagoon used to buttress piers or guide pilots through the shallows, the triple cluster was her favorite. No doubt there were hundreds—maybe thousands—of bricolas throughout the Venetian Lagoon; most were much smaller than the giant one at Sant'Erasmo. To form a bricola of any size, three poles must be set deep into the mud beneath the water's surface and placed in such a way that their feet are spread apart at the bottom with their shoulders leaning together above the water line. One or two steel bands bind them in what seems to be an eternal embrace.

She had watched a small bricola installed near the Arsenale once. The men who placed it had the advantage of a mechanical aid to pound the wooden beams into the sandy bottom. Centuries before, of course, men would have used their own muscle power. She pondered on the fierce determination those ancients must have had.

In the evenings, amber lamps mounted on small bricolas guide water craft across the dark waters like golden stepping stones. They had a beauty all their own. To Giulia, bricolas were as much symbols of Venice as the towers and domes. *So much beauty here. Why must I feel so heavy?*

No one got off or on at Sant'Erasmo, the largest island in the lagoon. It was considered the vegetable garden of Venice. Some day, maybe she and Chuck would attend the Artichoke Festival she'd heard about. Then her throat thickened, and she found it hard to swallow. Chuck might have nothing to do with her when she told him. Dread moved through her like a poisonous venom.

The vaporetto backed away with its usual grinding of engines thrown into reverse and turned toward Treporti. It was a different world out here. Could she live in this desolate expanse of water and sky? Probably not. If Chuck were with her? Maybe. When had she begun to measure every thought against whether Chuck would be involved? Whether he'd want to do this or that with her? Strange how her ideas of not wanting a man in her life changed when she stumbled into him.

Two men in a small motorboat whizzed by. They wore camouflage suits and had a pile of reed in their boat. Were they going to a duck blind? Hunting now? In the spring? No. Must be off to build a blind, but why then camouflage? Maybe they liked to pretend to be military. She'd gone with her dad to a huge gun show in Eastern Oregon once. Many men—even their little kids—wore camouflage outfits. She thought of Hemingway, who went duck hunting in this lagoon. Men were strange creatures, eager for war or pretending to be warriors. Hemingway was one of those and wrote about them.

Again, she thought of Chuck. Conflict was *his* chosen career. Would he have chosen it if not for his need to escape a hopeless future? She'd never known anyone like him in her life. Someone she respected and enjoyed bantering with. Someone who seemed to adore her. Would he feel the same if he knew?

After stopping at Treporti, the boat turned back. She checked her pocket compass. It indicated they were heading southwest, back to Venice. Good, she thought, at least that's working. Then the tears came. She couldn't stop them. Already sitting in a corner next to a window, she huddled closer against the glass. Few people were on the return trip and none had ventured near her. Maybe they sensed a deranged woman. After the politico look-alike had left, no one else had acknowledged she was on board.

The marino came through again and he, too, passed her by. Her ticket must have been good for the return. She pulled it out and sure enough it said round trip. The ticket seller hadn't asked what Giulia wanted. Obviously, he knew she didn't belong out here. "Live and learn," she thought. How would she live without Chuck? Yet, she must take that risk. Otherwise, her past would always shadow her and be between them. He was the most sensitive man she'd ever known. He'd feel that shadow. Maybe already did.

The tears had drained her. She slipped into a doze while the vaporetto chugged slowly back. When the sound of the engines changed from their steady thump to a resounding roar, she opened her eyes and saw they were about to dock at Fondamenta Nuova. She gazed behind her still not sure what to do. The brooding clouds that had hovered during the entire trip were now luminescent. Glowing. The afternoon sun pierced through the last of the clouds almost blinding her. She shaded her eyes and looked down. The water was no longer murky. Instead it reflected back the brilliant blue of the heavens. The truth of the heavens? Will Chuck still want me when he knows my truth?

* * *

Saturday night. Another night without Chuck. She hated it. She'd grown accustomed to his strength and heat curled around her. How did people endure the loneliness and fear when their loved ones were sent into war zones? *And here I am about to send him away when I don't need to!*

She turned on the light and picked up a book, hoping to stop the thoughts from running round and round like her gerbil, Rodolfo, did when she was ten. But soon she gave up and snapped off the light. She'd felt strong when she had signed up for the escort service. In control. Imagined herself as taking advantage of men instead of the other way around. Many women had been involved because they had nowhere else to turn, but she'd done it for a crazy, perverted idea of vengeance.

What a joke! Ricky and Jason weren't aware she was striking back at them. And neither one had used her—not really. But she worked too much, studied too much and in the end, their love for her wasn't enough to overcome the twitch in their cocks. Most hurtful, though, was Jason's lies from the start. *Stop it! You've been over this same ground too many times.* She punched her pillow, flopped onto her stomach and felt better.

Then she remembered the greasy little man in the restaurant. Her defenses had been down when he'd grabbed her hand, and the floor had tilted beneath her feet. She'd barely recovered before Chuck appeared.

Is that it, girl? You've decided to tell Chuck out of fear of getting caught?

Oh God. Of course. And he had a right to know up front before their relationship went where they both wanted it to go. Why was she struggling? If this dilemma tortured a friend, she'd have seen the answer long ago. She knew what she must do and slid back under the duvet, breathed deeply a few times and drifted off.

* * *

Giulia's eyes popped open. Her body went rigid with the strain of listening. Had she heard something? The numbers glowing on the bedside table read 3:10. She'd slept three hours. Someone was in the apartment and moving toward the bedroom. Slowly, stealthily. She held her breath. A large, dark shape filled the open doorway.

"Chuck?" she whispered.

"It's me," he said. His voice softer than usual, almost hoarse. "Sorry I woke you."

She released the breath she'd been holding and said, "Don't be sorry." And held out both arms.

He sat on the side of the bed and scooped her against his chest. "You're trembling. I scared you. Next time I'll make more noise so you'll know it's me."

Next time? *Would there be a next time?* And without warning, she burst into sobs. "What's happening to me?"

He was quiet and continued to hold her. She could stay in his arms a hundred years. His shoes were already off and his clothes, too, by the time he'd reached the bedroom. He rolled onto the bed to embrace her. They lay without speaking. Eventually, she began to relax.

"Sorry I frightened you." He gathered a strand of her hair and let a silky curl slide through his fingers. " We need a plan, in case it hadn't been me. Do you know how to use a gun?"

"No."

"Do you want to learn?"

"No."

He snorted. "We need to come up with an idea. We'll talk later."

She said nothing and pulled his mouth to hers.

Soon they fell into a deep sleep, but this time *his* body trembled, and he growled. He seemed to be telling someone to do something, but she couldn't understand. Giulia crawled on top of him as she had once before, but he raised up, grabbed her and roared, "No!" His hands on her upper arms felt like vises. *I need to wake him up. Now!* She yelled his name over and over, but he rolled over onto her. For the first time, she felt afraid. He wouldn't intentionally hurt her, but... she screamed, "Chuck! Wake up!"

At last he let go and fell onto his back panting, still agitated. From the ambient light coming through the blinds, she could see that his eyes were closed but his eyelids quivered. Then, she eased on top of him again, cradling his head in her hands. She feather kissed his eyelids and spoke in a low, soothing voice. "It's okay. It's okay. It's over."

When his eyes opened, he was instantly awake. "Whoa. That was a bad one. Did I hurt you?"

She shook her head and hoped bruises wouldn't appear on her arms for him to see. They curled together. The rest of the night, he seemed to hang on tighter than usual. She didn't mind. Not at all.

* * *

Giulia woke to an empty bed. Remembered his nightmare. Remembered he was supposed to be at the base all weekend. Had he gone back already? Then she heard a crash. She scooted out of bed, grabbed her robe and found him on his knees wiping the kitchen floor.

"What happened?"

"Nothing," he said, reminding her of her brothers.

"I see. Is nothing the reason you're scrubbing the floor?"

He looked up and there was that grin with the deep dimple. *Oh. That does it. I CANNOT chance losing him.*

"Can I help?" she asked bending over.

"Nope. All done. When I woke this morning, my fingers had all turned to thumbs. If I have enough eggs, I'll start over and make you an asparagus, tomato frittata."

"Yum, that sounds good. But why are you here?"

"Got my own unit off in good time and the other emergency was handled sooner than expected, so at least we have today to fritter away."

"Good. Shall we see a flick?"

He laughed. "What's on?"

"That just popped out. I ought to go shopping for my apartment."

His face sagged. Then he said, "Sure." He opened the fridge, pulled out ingredients for a frittata and began chopping. "Ouch!" He grunted and reached for a clean towel to wrap his bleeding finger.

Giulia came up behind him and put her arms around his narrow waist. "Oh Chuck. I'm sorry." It wasn't the cut she was sorry about. "Come sit."

He did. "It's nothing. I forgot old Remo came by to sharpen my knives."

She sat across from him and held his hand. She opened the towel; his finger was still oozing blood but didn't look bad. She wrapped it up and ran to the bathroom to look for adhesive bandages. "First shelf on the left," he called.

"Now," she said when they'd managed to get the finger wrapped after some jostling and laughing. "We need to talk."

He nodded but said nothing.

"You know I plan to move on Thursday. But after two nights alone in that bed… well, one and one-half actually. I've been torn."

"Don't be," he said taking both her hands in his. "Stay with me. It doesn't have to be permanent, you know. Give us a chance, Giulia. Let's see how things go. There'll always be another apartment."

Oh Lord! His feelings are right out there, loud and clear. She felt herself wavering. Through all the years of working toward her own Venetian place, never had she expected a man like Chuck to come into her life. The way he'd been there for her, he should have ridden in on a white horse. What would her grandparents think if she changed her mind? *Ha.* She knew that answer. Maybe she could get some of the money back for them. But what about that little girl in the attic? What about Aunt Loretta?

But that little girl and Lettie are both gone. What about the grown woman sitting right here? The woman who wants this man?

Chuck was quiet. He seemed to sense a turmoil raging inside her head.

"Have you ever had an idea or dream that spurred you on year after year?"

"Yes." he said. "But, you can't touch a dream. Can't see it or hold—"

"I know. Believe me, I know," she said, "But I-have-to-do-this. If I don't, I'm afraid I'll lose a piece of me."

Chuck sat up taller, inhaled and pressed both palms down on his thighs. "So what can I do? To help you leave me, I mean?"

"Chuck. Don't play dirty. I'm not leaving you."

"Feels like it. I thought we had something worth holding onto." He stood up, looked at her, dumped the chopped veggies in the trash and left the room.

His reaction was like a slam in her chest. This tender, sensitive man had just walked away from her, obviously fed-up.

She hadn't handled anything right. She was crazy about him. Didn't want to lose him. But, dammit!

CHAPTER TWENTY-NINE

Late Thursday afternoon, all her stuff had been lugged up the thirty-two steps into her new apartment. Chuck was ready to treat his two protégés who'd helped with the move. They were already out the door. He turned to her. She knew he expected an invitation to come back later.

"Chuck, I… I need to be here alone tonight. Can I see you tomorrow?"

His eyes widened, then narrowed into a cold glare. He shrugged his broad shoulders, turned and slammed the door in her face.

She felt shocked, but she'd written the script for this moment years ago and had to go with it. After she heard his heavy steps fade away, she leaned her back against the door of her new apartment, closed her eyes and shouted, "I'm here. I did it!"

She felt nothing. The feeling of elation didn't come. But she wasn't ready to give up. She had waited all her life for this and rushed to one of the living-room windows overlooking the rio—her rio now—still expecting to feel exhilarated. But the water wasn't rippling to catch the dying light of the day; it seemed stagnant and sluggish. *Tomorrow. When the sun comes out and people are out and about, then the euphoria will come.*

She got busy. Unpacked clothes and books, and started on the kitchen and remembered she hadn't shopped. Didn't have one coffee bean. No bread, no cream, no yogurt or fruit. She jogged to Campo Santa Margherita and made it into the COOP Supermercato ten minutes before closing. Rejuvenated, she decided to hurry home, do a few more chores, and maybe wander back for a bite at one of the cute cafés clustered in the campo.

After organizing the kitchen, though, she felt exhausted. Maybe a slice of toast after her shower. Then she entered the bedroom and saw the bare mattress. She'd forgotten to make up the bed first thing as she'd always done when moving to a new place. No. She hadn't forgotten. She'd put it off because part of her hadn't wanted to consider crawling in alone. She threw herself across the cursed thing and wept. Had the years of working toward a bright, shiny dream all been for this? This empty illusion of success? Empty because Chuck was not here?

The last few nights in his bed, they'd made love but only when she initiated it. Had he pulled back to protect himself? Did he doubt her love? Or? *Oh God.* Did he doubt *his* love for her? She scrambled for her phone and called him. Maybe he'd come back if she begged. It rang and rang but he didn't pick up. She almost hung up, but he'd see her number so she left a pitiful plea for him to come back. She dragged a quilt and pillow onto the couch in the living room and sobbed herself into a stupor.

* * *

It was late when Chuck put the guys on the train for Vicenza and headed home. His phone had rung while in the bar, but it was too noisy to do more than look at the ID. He hadn't expected her to call and wouldn't have talked to her with the young fly-boys around anyway. No doubt they speculated about him, but that wasn't a big concern; newbies always speculated about officers. At home, when he finally listened to her message, he threw the phone on the bed and said, "That little bitch!"

He felt jerked around. He'd felt that a lot lately. But... hot damn. She wanted him with her in that damnable place after all. Maybe this could all work out if only he could be patient a little longer. *How much patience do I need with that tawny kitten?* As he slid into bed, he felt more lonely than he'd felt since Babička died. Since he'd been a child, she'd been his best friend, but as he rolled over, he knew he'd really prefer a certain curvy body to spoon around.

* * *

It was dark and quiet in her new neighborhood, but Giulia roused enough to drag herself to the bathroom. A glance in the mirror showed puffy eyes and sallow skin. After a scalding shower, she made up the bed and crawled in. And cried. Again! So many tears after years of none. She had not allowed time for relationships. Certainly not for tears. She'd held out for the glowing dream.

To hell with dreams. *But, girl, one thing is certain. If you want to stay in this town, you've got to show up for work tomorrow morning.*

Yet, there she lay, straining to hear Chuck's key in her door. After an eternity, she quit listening and drifted off.

* * *

Giulia's place was not as convenient to the train station as Chuck's, and she needed to allow time to catch a crowded vaporetto. Would she see him at the station? Maybe after her classes she might find him and invite him for coffee. She'd use the same words about the enticing variety of coffee drinks offered as he had used that first time with her. Whatever method, it was up to her now. He must feel used. All her doing.

Dreams. Bah, humbug. Scrooge? Should she offer Dickens to her students? Maybe they could analyze his quirky characters? Which ones? But instead of Dickens' characters, thoughts of Chuck kept moving through her mind all the way to class. Lord, how she missed their morning joshing.

There were few absences on Fridays—it was a military base after all—but most students' minds had flown elsewhere. Usually her Friday class read scenes aloud from plays, but with the Ogle deposition last week and her move with all its upset, she'd forgotten to assign work and prepare.

"I have a confession," she said. "A crisis or two landed in my lap the last few days, and I'm not prepared. Have any of you ever experienced that phenomenon?"

Of course, they enjoyed a good laugh on her.

"Today, I'd like to hear how you think books, plays or movies affect your lives." After a few minutes of awkwardness, they opened up and seemed to forget she was in the room. Their opinions about the mess "so-called leaders" had made of the world surprised her. She'd expected young military people to be brainwashed to accept authority not only in their immediate units but in political officials as well. What astounded her even more, was that to bolster their opinions, many cited bits and pieces from Shakespeare, Whitman, Dos Passos, Hemingway and authors she wasn't familiar with. The time flew.

Fifteen minutes before the end of the period, she asked, "How would you like to continue the discussion next Friday, but with a central focus?"

"Could the focus be our suggestion?" a student asked.

She laughed, "You read my mind." She closed her briefcase and said, "Take the rest of the period, and when you have a consensus, let me know by email. No later than Tuesday, please. I'll re-confirm the same way, and we'll see what happens next Friday." She left them buzzing together.

As soon as she was out the door, she tried calling Chuck. No answer. Maybe he'd left for the weekend. She left yet another forlorn message and started for home. Home. The only "home" was in his arms.

* * *

Her new apartment needed lots of tender loving care, but she dumped her stuff and went out. Where? Anywhere her feet would take her. The city was hers now. She could meander with no return flight schedule lurking over her shoulder. Soon she found herself at the far end of Piazza di San Marco leaning against a pillar of a bookshop that displayed large art books. A small basin, almost like a cul-de-sac-pond, had been created by the dead end of a narrow canal. A gaggle of polished, black gondolas jostled each other gently.

Gently was the operative word here, she thought, as she watched the action. The slightly-asymmetrical boats were decked with brocaded cushions in exotic colors and embellished with fringes and tassels of golden threads. Gondolas were prized possessions. She'd heard that gondoliers treated their unique boats with more tenderness than they did their wives or girlfriends. With a phone mounted on a short pole, a dispatcher handled calls as they do at any taxi station anywhere in the world. No one seemed conscious of the beautiful buildings around them that represented varying centuries of architectural designs. All attention was given to the excited customers eager to board.

A polite twitter of Japanese tourists waited in line two by two, the way they tended to walk through the city. One gondola nudged forward and a ganzer—a retired gondolier—hooked a curved stick to the inside gunwale and helped pull it to the steps for the animated travelers. He held it steady and offered his arm to passengers as they stepped in. A gondolier could easily manage this maneuver, but she guessed they sympathized with these old fellows, who probably had trouble leaving the only environment they'd ever known. But she noticed most tourists did tip the ganzer.

A gondola ride was expensive—last time she checked it was seventy-five euros for forty-five minutes—about ninety dollars. The new euro had gone into effect in January of 2002, a little over a year ago, but already the dollar had lost ground. She'd ridden once with her dad and brothers, but the boys had acted up, so that didn't count. Would she ever ride with Chuck? Would he ever call?

She turned away telling herself to go back and work on her apartment, but instead she moved into the maze of streets leading in the opposite direction. Soon she stood beside the Grand Canal near a station for *uno traghetto*, a bare gondola with no chairs and no glitzy decorations. This boat was used solely as a ferry to cross the Canal and manned by two gondoliers, one in front and one behind. It bobbed waiting for more passengers.

Three people were already standing in the ferry-gondola to

make the short trip across the busy waterway. It had been awhile since Giulia had done this, but now that she lived here, she might as well get in the groove. She gave a fifty-cent euro coin to the gondolier in the rear and as soon as she stepped in, he shoved off. Smoothly, thank God, because at first, her knees felt unsteady and she worried that she'd embarrass herself, but the old balancing trick came back. In no time they were on the other side at Campo San Silvestro. And now, she had to acknowledge her true destination. Her heart raced and the lump in her throat was about to choke her, but she would not back down. Soon, she was pushing the button on Chuck's intercom.

"Si?" he answered.

"*Sono io*, it's me," Giulia said in a breathy voice.

"*Chi è?* Who is it?" He sounded impatient.

"Sono Giulia," she said.

The door clicked. She started up the stairs. Would this be her last time? He was standing at his open door when she reached his floor.

"Ciao," she whispered. "*Permesso?*" she asked, feeling that he might refuse her entrance.

"*Certo,* " He stepped back to let her in.

"I've missed you," she said raising her eyes to his face.

"I see."

His face looked hard, stony. They were barely inside his apartment and stood within touching distance. "I was wrong last night; I didn't want to be alone."

"I got your call but couldn't take it until the boys were gone. It was late and… wasn't sure exactly what you wanted."

"Wanted you," she said. She was looking at her feet but felt his body heat.

"Me or sex?"

Her head jerked up. For a moment, she thought he'd been joking, but his jaw was set and his lips—those lips—had tightened into a hard, tight line.

"You!"

"I needed to be sure because... Giulia? I want a lot more from you. So I'll ask again, only me?" and this time she detected a slight curve to his lips.

"Sometimes it's hard for me to separate the two," and a little smile crept across her lips, too.

He opened his arms and she flowed into them. "Now, tell me what's going on." And he nipped her neck.

"I can't say for sure. But it's not working. When I walk into my apartment, it feels like a Christmas morning that Santa forgot."

"I'm sorry." Against the side of her neck, he whispered, "I wondered."

"You know I had mixed feelings about going ahead with this," she said, "but felt too committed to stop. All the scrimping I've done. All the free time I've given up to work extra hours toward this... this damned dream—"

"How can I help?"

"Hold me."

"That's easy, angel, but I need—"

"You need?" again Giulia felt afraid.

"I meant what I said, Giulia. I want a lot more than sex. If you can't give that, I need to know it now."

She melted against him. "I want more, too," she whispered.

"Good! But before anymore talk, how about we take care of the sex first."

She laughed with such relief that for a moment she feared she'd slip into hysterics. He took her hand and led her down the hall. Lowering his voice into an authoritative tone, he said, "I've always found when planning crucial strategy sessions, it's best to get complex pressures out of the way at the outset. And recently, I've had pressures building that need to be handled."

"Handled?"

"You are a pill." And he swept her up and tumbled her onto his bed.

"Chuck?"

"Yeah," he said beginning to undress.

"I've been walking and fretting and feel grungy. Could I shower?"

"Of course. I'll join you."

She felt at peace. All the apartment hassle could be sorted out. She was at home with Chuck, and that's all she cared about. After teasing in the shower, they moved to his bed. His cock had risen in the shower, but now they lay together just holding and holding. He seemed unwilling to start anything. She reached to stroke him, and before he could restrain her, she was kneeling over him with her mouth around his penis. He gasped and raised his head. "You don't need to do this."

She looked up surprised. A little frown creased her brow. "But I want to. I want to taste you, love you this way. Lord knows you've tasted me. We *are* talking about some sort of partnership, aren't we?"

"Hope so."

"Well then, it's only fair for me to have my way this time, right?"

"Right," he sighed and let his head fall back onto the pillow.

"I'm not an expert at this, but I think I can figure it out as I go," she said letting her tongue flatten along the underside of his stiff penis.

"You're doing... just... fine," he gasped sounding short of breath.

A glistening drop leaked out, and her tongue curled around it. She liked the taste and his special scent. What was it? She ran her hands gently over his shaft that pulsed with heat. She closed her mouth over the head and half sucked and half tickled.

"One problem with you tasting me," Chuck panted, as he raised his head again, "once I explode, we have to wait. With you, we can keep on going."

"Hmmm," she said. "Are we in a hurry?"

Not waiting for an answer, she continued, and he was past stopping her.

"Micina, climb on. I'm close. So close."

"In a sec."

Then he did exactly what she wanted. He erupted into her mouth. She swallowed as much of his primal offering as possible and grabbed up a bath towel to catch the rest. Her heart was pounding, and she was pleased with herself. Anise! His special scent was anise. Immediately, he began to caress her. She stopped him. "Take your moment, Chuck. I'll be here."

They lay together a long time, dozing. Then he roused and knew exactly how to give her the most pleasure. They made love again until they were both sated and content to fall asleep in each other's arms. An evening meal had been forgotten.

CHAPTER THIRTY

"Pronto," Chuck said coming out of a deep sleep.

"Hey man, sorry to call so early, but . . ." Chuck slipped out of bed and crossed the hall.

A short time later, Giulia woke to the smell of coffee.

She cinched the belt of a robe she'd left behind and followed her nose. "Do I smell freshly brewed coffee?"

"Perceptive of you," he said and wrapped his arms around her. She lifted his Tee-shirt, insinuating her nose into his chest hair to inhale his scent again. She'd never get enough and her tongue skated across a nipple.

"Hey, we don't have time for that and breakfast too."

"Why? What's the hurry? Do you have to go back to the post?"

"No. We are going to the airport to meet Tom, an old comrade. Need to be there in ninety minutes."

He told her about Tomasz Makowska. He spelled the name and said Tom's Polish name was pronounced Tomahsh. He was coming in for a couple of nights on his way from a weather conference at CERN. With his Ph.D. in Atmospheric Physics, Tom was a specialist in meteorology and global weather patterns. Tom had also begun his education at the Air Force Academy, and they'd met in Special Ops training. But when time came for re-upping, Tom had opted out. His wife had given him an ultimatum.

"Now, though, he and Teri aren't together anymore. Anyway, I want him to meet you. We can show him the Venice we both adore."

"Are you sure? Maybe you'd rather spend catch-up time alone?"

"I'd like to have you with me—sort of show you off—if you would?"

"I can't wear the clothes I wore yesterday, they're in bad shape." And she thought of the bad shape her emotions had been while wearing them.

"No problem. I'm hiring a taxi to pick him up anyway. Let's have a quick breakfast. Then we'll zip over to your place, you can change, and we'll make it in time."

Giulia hurried to take a quick shower and when she came back into the kitchen to grab a piece of toast before dressing, Chuck said, "Have a quick question for you."

"What is it?"

"Have you gone back on the pill?"

"No. Why?"

"Earlier I noticed the patch on your hip was gone. I admit, though, I wasn't all that lucid at the time."

Giulia reached under her robe and felt for the patch, first one side of her hip and then the other. "It's not there. I have no idea when it came off. I'll be right back."

Chuck took a cup down and poured steaming coffee into it for her.

"No sign of it," she said when she came back. "Don't know when it came off. When we stop at my place, I'll put on another one to start a new cycle. It should be fine because the hormones stay in my body for a while."

He handed her the coffee. "How's the patch different from pills?"

"Not much. Both release certain hormones for three weeks and not for one week—to simulate a woman's normal cycle. Some programs use blank pills for the fourth week. Makes it easier to take one every day rather than remember to stop and start again. With the patch, you wear it three weeks and leave it off one week."

"That makes sense." He looked at his watch. "Can you be ready in ten minutes?"

"Fifteen?" she asked.

* * *

When Giulia saw the tall, blond man lift his bag from the moving carousel, she flinched. She remembered him from the last escort service she'd worked for. In fact, he'd requested her on his second visit. Both times he'd been a total gentleman and made no sexual overtures.

The two big men embraced and pounded each other on the back. "Hey weather man, what's comin' at us this year?" Chuck quipped.

Here it comes for me, she thought. No more luxury to debate with myself. He'd know it all today. She straightened her spine and inhaled deeply.

Chuck reached over and pulled her under his arm. "Tom, I want you to meet the most important person in my life, Giulia Cavinato."

Tom turned to her smiling and stuck out his hand to shake hers then leaned in to look into her eyes. "Don't I know you?" he said.

She nodded. "You knew me as Juliette back in Eugene. When I was your escort, I had two brown eyes."

"Ohhh yes. Have to say, I like 'em better this way. I requested you when I went back to hear Dr. Goswami, the 'guru' physicist. You live here now?"

Chuck's mouth was hanging open. "Escort?"

"Yes." Giulia looked straight at Chuck but couldn't quite stop tears from welling in her eyes. "I worked for an Escort Service that catered mostly to visiting scholars. After all, the University was the main industry in Eugene."

"I see," Chuck said.

Obviously he didn't. Most people assume an escort service is a cover for prostitutes. Mostly they're right. Who'd believe a company that did not condone sexual encounters? One look at Chuck's face and she knew it was over.

"Well," Chuck said, and swallowed as if his throat was closing on him. Then he seemed to recover and hustled them to their waiting taxi. They climbed in and sped across the lagoon. The two men chatted but Giulia couldn't hear them. The roar of the boat's engine and slap of the waves covered their conversation. She was sitting across from them and could barely see them because the sun glared off the water behind them and directly into her eyes. She needed to distance herself anyway. She sighed. Strange how life works. The action she'd taken to get here, was now the reason for her despair.

When they dropped Tom at the side of the Hotel Gritti Palace on the Grand Canal, he said, "Soon as I'm settled in, I'll call. We can take that long walk you mentioned."

While the taxi backed again into the Grand Canal, Giulia said, "You can drop me at Ca' Rezzonico, I'll walk from there."

Chuck moved forward to give the pilot instructions. But soon it was clear, they weren't stopping at Rezzonico. Giulia started to go forward, Chuck held her back. "You're not escaping so easily, Micina."

"From the look on your face at the airport, I wouldn't be surprised if you had dumped me straight into the lagoon."

"You think? As I remember, we didn't finish our talk last night about apartments." He sighed. "Now we have more to wade through."

She assumed he meant wading through more of her shit but was too much of a gentleman to voice it. After passing Rezzonico, the water taxi continued following the curve of the backward S up the Grand Canal, aiming toward the Rialto. Just before reaching the bridge, the boat slowed and dipped left into Rio della Madonnetta, slid under a low bridge coming from Campo San Polo, turned right onto Rio di San Cassiano and swerved to stop in front of Chuck's place. For the pilot, it'd be a quick trip onto the last of the S where, in no time, he'd be in front of the train station waiting for the next fare.

Chuck's having a hard time. Although I was only arm candy, I had sold myself. Tom might defend her, but Chuck would assume he was saying what he thought Chuck wanted to hear. No doubt, Chuck's pride had been crushed to think she had fucked Tom, not to mention countless others.

He took her arm and tugged her—gently as always—into the building and up to his apartment. Neither said a word. When they entered, he led her to the living room couch where he sat beside her. "Got a couple questions."

She couldn't speak. Her mouth was dry. She now understood when people said their mouth felt full of cotton. Should she give him a list of reasons why what happened years ago had nothing to do with today? She waited, determined not to shed a tear. There'd been enough of those lately.

"Did you fuck Tom?"

"No!"

"That's what he said. Why do I want to believe you?"

"Because it's true."

"Was that creep in Corte Sconta a visiting professor?" he asked with the beginnings of a sneer on his lips.

"No." Then Giulia collapsed back into herself, thinking, what's the use?

But then Chuck's voice softened as if he were trying to pull back from his inquisitorial stance. Maybe he was trying to believe her.

"Talk to me, Giulia. Tell me your story."

"May I get a glass of water first?"

He nodded and watched her move as she went toward the kitchen. She was wearing that same swirly skirt she'd worn when they'd gone to Sconta with Marc and Marlowe. No boots today, but pale, sexy leather sandals. And with that turquoise top showing a hint of her breasts... God help me, he thought.

She came back with two glasses of cool water. They both drank deeply. *Anxiety was thirsty work.*

"Okay," she said. "You know about the dream I've had since I was seven."

He nodded.

She told of working as a waitress before and during undergrad school. It was stressful and didn't pay much. She received small stipends for graduate work and tutored in Italian but needed more work. Needed the kind of work that wouldn't take so much energy. For a few hours here and there in the evenings, when her brain was used up anyway, escort work paid much more than waiting tables.

She stopped.

He said nothing but listened in that focused way that left no room for subterfuge. She wasn't trying to prevaricate anyway. Like lancing that boil on her heel once when she couldn't afford to go to a doctor, she just wanted to get it all out—pain and all.

"And?" he said.

Giulia described the first service she'd joined with its two levels of pay. He seemed fascinated. She sat up straighter—feeling hopeful—and continued to explain how it worked, wanting him to sympathize.

"Some men signed agreements for Level A—no sex—but a few always thought the rules didn't apply to them. I had trouble with a couple. One was that horrible man at the restaurant. He was the only time I'd forgotten to wear my brown lens. Soon after him, I quit. Later I heard of a different service that offered only companionship and strictly stated no sex."

"An escort service offering no sex?"

"Yes. It was called Unique Escort Service. They catered to visitors coming to university conferences who wanted arm candy. It was like the A Level I mentioned. And it paid much more than waitressing."

"No doubt even visiting dignitaries tried to break the rules, huh?"

"A few. But by then, I was pretty well tuned to recognize them quickly."

"I just bet you were," he said.

She heard a snarl in his voice. Her hopes had been high for a few moments, but when she heard that tone, she knew it was over. She couldn't continue without his trust.

"I sense there's nothing more I can say." She started to get up to leave.

The phone rang. Chuck took her hand and tugged her back down.

"Good," he said into the receiver. "My place is difficult to find. We'll come to you. What room? Four ten? See you soon."

"Chuck?"

"Yeah," he said as he closed his phone.

"You don't want me along. I'll bow out rather than go through a charade for Tom's sake. He'll understand. He's a good man."

"He is that."

"I'll pick up a couple things and be out of your. . . life."

"Giulia?"

She turned back to face him. His eyes were drawn together and a crease of what looked like pain formed between his brows. "Do you want out?"

She took a deep breath and stood as tall as she could. "If you can't trust me?" She exhaled and felt her body deflate. "Yes."

He ran his hand through his hair and heaved a sigh. "It's your *past*, I know. But it's a lot to process. I wish," his voice sounded hoarse, "Lord, I wish you'd told me sooner."

She nodded crumpling and sat on an ottoman across from the couch. "It's been weighing on me—"

"I often wondered. From the first, I've known a barrier hid part of you. Kept hoping it would come down."

"Well, it came with a crash today," she said in a thready voice.

"Thanks to Tom. Were you ever going to tell me?"

"I tried. But one thing or another kept... No. That's not true. It was me who kept waiting for the perfect time. I didn't want to lose—"

"I don't want to lose what we had either," Chuck said leaning toward her.

"I should go to my place. Give you time to—maybe after Tom leaves—"

"No need for a charade. While Tom's here, I want you with me."

"I see," she said. Her eyes were dull. Her shoulders sagged.

"No, you don't. What I mean is, I want you with me while he's here."

"How is that different?"

"God, I don't know. Let's go." He took her hand and pulled her up. "Maybe I'll work it out."

CHAPTER THIRTY-ONE

Giulia had never been inside the famous Gritti Palazzo, former home of Andrea Gritti, one of the strongest *doges*, rulers, of old Venice. The silken lobby walls of the hotel shimmered with reflected light from the Grand Canal flowing outside the open door. On the back wall was an excellent copy of a portrait by Titian of Doge Gritti. It was mounted in an ornate gilt frame. From her only trip to the National Gallery in Washington, D. C., she recognized the doge's proud, fierce face that oozed power.

A large bouquet sat on an ornate table beneath the portrait and hid the lower section of the painting. Would Titian hate having that display of flowers hide any part of his painting? From what Giulia had read about him, he wouldn't care as long as he'd been paid. He was known for demanding and getting high sums for his portraits of important figures.

Ordinarily, this would have been a thrilling moment for her, but today was not ordinary. Her nerves were frayed. When Chuck and Giulia arrived at Tom's door, he greeted them with hair damp from the shower. But its bright gold color was barely darkened, and his butterscotch-chocolate brown eyes shown with mischief. For a moment, Giulia was back to being twelve years old at summer camp when the first male she'd ever fantasized over was in charge of the waterfront. Bill Fear—a name engraved in her memory—was gloriously blond with the same teasing brown eyes. But he was seventeen and absolutely unattainable.

With a grandiose sweep of his arm, Tom welcomed them inside his sitting room which also had silken walls, a glittering chandelier suspended from a high ceiling and large, ornate chairs with bronze, velvet-covered cushions. He snagged Giulia's hand and swept her to the open window that looked across to *Santa Maria della Salute*, Saint Mary of Health. The church, together with the former *dogana*, customs house, overlooked the most picturesque part of the basin and was probably the most photographed of all churches in Venice. To her, it was the most beautiful. Chuck came behind her and said, "What a view."

Tom looked at Chuck and said, "Yes, she is." Not one to dance around an issue, he said, "In my usual suave manner, guess I blundered into something, didn't I? Sorry. Hope it won't plague the two of you like Pandora's box."

"I do too," Giulia and Chuck said almost simultaneously.

"That sounds hopeful," Tom said, and his warm brown eyes almost twinkled. "You do know, don't you, that when she let all the evils into the world, one thing was left lying in a dark corner of that box."

Chuck and Giulia both seemed too stunned to respond.

"Hope. It was hope!" Silence prevailed. No one spoke. "Listen. You two aren't obligated to cart me around. You need to be alone to sort things out. I'm a big boy. I can poke around Venice myself."

"You can, but you won't. We've talked some, and for my part, I could use a break to focus on something else. And you, ol' buddy are it." Turning to Giulia, Chuck said, "How about you, love?"

She nodded, speechless. Still shaken by the last two days' events. Giulia felt as if she'd stepped off a wobbly roller coaster. Dashed to the bottom when Chuck hadn't answered her calls. Carried to the highest peak by their passionate reunion last night. Then at the airport, the coaster had collapsed.

"I've never been to Torcello or to Cipriani's famous restaurant on that island," Tom said. "I tried to get a room at that little inn, but it was full. I'm on a generous expense account as you can see from these digs. God, I have to pinch myself. Me, a kid from Poland Street in Detroit in this palazzo on the Grand Canal," and he spread his arms wide to the view again.

"I think we can swing a bite at Cipriani's," Chuck said. "Wanna go tonight?"

"Anything works, friend. I've missed you. If we can get in, we can catch up and eat good grub at the same time. I promise to use the proper fork."

"Maybe it'd be best for you two to go without me," Giulia offered. "I'm sure you have tons to talk about."

"Oh no you don't. Without *your* class, they wouldn't let us past the front door, reservations or not," Tom said.

Giulia laughed for the first time in awhile. "You *are* a charmer."

"Naw, just quick to observe the obvious."

Giulia had to admit she could use a light touch, too.

* * *

They took a vaporetto to Torcello Island and strolled past the two grand churches near the restaurant until time for their reservations. Both were closed. The small area around the churches was well maintained and dedicated to what was left of the first settlement of Venice. Tom found a primitive stone seat under the shade of a tree and plopped onto it.

"That's called Attila's Chair," Giulia said smiling, "because legend blames Attila the Hun for driving mainland people out here."

"When *did* the first people come?" Tom asked.

"Exact dates are lost, but experts think those brave souls first ventured out here in the middle of the sixth century. Each time the huns swooped in from the North and East, people fled into the lagoon to hide. Finally some stayed and lived mostly on fish and sold their extra catch back on the mainland. They must have roamed all over the Lagoon because they also sold salt mined in the southernmost part, all the way to Chioggia. To answer your question, all I *know* is shown on the small plaque in the duomo that claims it was built in 639 A.D.

"Those first people must have been a lot like American pioneers trying to find a better life by moving into the wilderness," Tom said.

"Tough people for sure," Chuck added.

"Was history your major?" Tom asked her as they walked past an ancient palazzo that housed a small museum—also closed for the night.

"No," she laughed softly. "I teach English but have been crazy about all things Venetian since I was a kid." She looked up at Chuck who was staring at her with what seemed to be adoration or... was it disgust? *Maybe thinking how that damned dream brought me here at any cost.*

She turned back to Tom. "Too bad we can't get in the duomo," she said. "The mosaics are magnificent especially the one of the Teotoca Madonna."

"Tayo what?" Tom asked.

"Teotoca," and she spelled it out for him. "In ancient Greek it means God Bearer. She stands tall and elegant in the apse, which is entirely covered with golden mosaics. A lot of other interesting art in there too. She oversees it all. She holds her child triumphantly, but if you look closely, you can see one tear falling on her cheek—an amazing mosaic tear."

"Wish I could see her, Giulia. Obviously, she made a huge impression on you," he said.

She nodded. Chuck put his arm around her and pulled her close. "Anyone hungry?" he said. "We can go in now."

* * *

Giulia was excited to see the inside, but wished it were a happier moment for her first time. She'd been to Torcello often, but never felt she could afford Cipriani's. From the outside, the little inn was not nearly as imposing as The Gritti. Bright red geraniums in huge terra-cotta pots stood in front of the entrance and added color to the dull beige stucco of the plain building.

The maître d' led them past the main dining room with walls of rich, burgundy-red bricks. Pale pink cloths draped to the floor covered round tables. Each table boasted scarlet napkins and a bouquet of scarlet roses. Giulia looked longingly toward those colors and the elegance. In a few moments, though, she was thrilled to see the majordomo pulling out a chair for her at a table decorated in the same rich hues. It, too, held a bouquet of crimson roses. Their table was nestled in a secluded alcove formed by small ficus trees.

Flutes of Prosecco were poured for each of them and menus lay beside their places. While Giulia excused herself to the restroom, the two men looked at each other. "What's going on in that thick skull of yours?" Tom asked.

"Brain's churning for sure."

"She's a gem, you know."

"I do. It's a lot to digest. Last night—" Chuck stopped. He'd almost blurted to Tom about the incredible head she'd given him saying she wasn't an expert but would figure it out. Man did she ever. But he couldn't do that to her.

Tom looked and waited.

"Making love with her has been beyond fantastic. From the first, she's been right there with me. Then this morning, when you dropped that bomb, all at once I began wondering if it had all been technique? And how many others? Even you."

"Whoa!" Tom leapt up from the table. "Thought on the taxi this morning you got it that nothing happened. If you can't trust me, I'm outta here."

Chuck was up and around the table in a split second, grabbing Tom by the shoulders, "Sorry, man. I'm an idiot."

"I'll shake on that," Tom said. Both men sat down facing each other again, touched glasses and took a swallow, never breaking eye contact.

"Are you able to listen for a minute without jumping to conclusions?"

Chuck sighed and nodded his head.

"Here's what I think. You're mixing apples and oranges."

"How so?"

"Step back—if you can—from this latest news. How do you feel about her? Not her past. With Teri, I learned too late that the here and now is what it's about. Has to be. If you dwell on what happened before… " Tom threw his arm back in an arc, and stared down at his hand for a long moment. His voice came out deep and gravelly. "That shit'll drag you into the pits." He looked straight into Chuck's eyes. "You'll never crawl out."

"I'm crazy for her. Fell like a ton of bricks the first time we met. And, man, the way she responds to me, but then—"

"For God's sake. Every time you think she's responding to *you*, are you going to wonder if it's the sweet apples you had before I upset the cart, or all bitter lemons?"

Chuck was silent. "Oranges."

"What?" Tom asked, frowning.

"Bitter oranges."

"Oh… yeah."

Chuck looked more miserable than Tom had ever seen him, even during their worst scrapes together.

"You're letting your dick rule. If she means *anything* to you—and the way you look at her says she does—watch out. If you keep this up, you're gonna lose her."

Chuck nodded, remembering Giulia admitting she wanted out if he didn't trust her.

"She's one fine lady. Great conversationalist. Quick mind. Great listener. That's why I requested her when I went back to Eugene. I wasn't looking for a lay either time. Too damned twisted and torn over Teri. I opened up about that with Giulia. She tuned in but didn't offer a shitload of advice like many do."

"Still, wish she'd told me."

"Sure… I can imagine why she didn't though."

"Said she wanted to. Waiting for the right time. I've known something's been bothering her. Said she was afraid of losing me."

"Somewhere above your dick-brain, do you believe her?"

"Think so. Want to."

"What about your own past? You want her to know everything you've done and been through?"

Chuck stared into his drink, his mind falling backward in time. Finally he took a sip of Prosecco and looked back at Tom with bleak shadows in his eyes.

* * *

Giulia sat in a stall wondering how she could possibly eat a bite. She was sure the men were talking about her—almost hoped so. But it was foolish, to hope Tom could convince Chuck to believe her. Trust. Faith. Strange how they worked or didn't. She stood up, flushed and went to the sink hardly daring to look in the mirror. Her eyes were hollow, her skin sallow. She pinched her cheeks. Took a deep breath and knew she had to leave it all to the universe. At least she'd fulfilled her dream. But that apartment could be a palazzo along the Grand Canal, and if Chuck didn't believe her, it would feel like a hovel.

* * *

"Here she comes." Tom said and began to tell a story of how they'd made fools of themselves letting off steam in a crappy dive after bad breaks during Desert Storm. As she arrived at the table, Tom summarized his story for her saying, "Pure junior high stuff." They all laughed as she sat down.

"We better order, I'm hungry. Don't look at the prices. Remember my expense account."

The moment Giulia sat down, a waiter came to remove her untouched flute of Prosecco and place a fresh one before her, then topped up the men's drinks. "My goodness. The service here's amazing," she said lifting her glass.

"Wait, wait," Tom said. "A toast to all of us together in Venice."

They touched each other's glasses and drank. "And Tom," Giulia said, holding out her glass again, "another to your next visit."

"It might be sooner than you think. I'll be settling in Brussels soon. It'll make it a whole lot easier to drop down to *La Serenissima*. Ah yes. The most serene of all. Let's toast the city." They took another sip.

"What's in Brussels?" Chuck asked.

"Belgian Institute for Space Aeronomy and Weather-Modeling Physics. I'm looking forward to it. Need a change work-wise and... for sure life-wise."

"Sounds good. You've been wanting to do more atmospheric modeling for a long time, right?"

He nodded. "Maybe a bit of solar work, too. But right now, my stomach wants those antipasti heading our way."

A young waiter staggered toward them with a huge platter of raw veggies, various sea critters fried and pickled, an array of salamis, cheese and olives. Another, brought hot puff pastries in various shapes and fillings.

"We won't need to order anything else," Giulia said reaching for one of the delicate breads. Maybe she *could* eat a bite or two.

The size of the platter was deceiving because each small item was nested into an artful arrangement of delicate greens. The men managed to devour every morsel with a little help from her.

For their *primi*, Chuck ordered *gnocchetti di patate con pomodorini*, little gnocchi made with potato flour and tomato sauce. Giulia ordered *ravioli formaggio di capra con melanzane e timo*, ravioli stuffed with goat cheese, eggplant and thyme, and Tom ordered the most exotic item, *strettine al ragù di seppie e fiori di zucca al profumo di limone*, linguine made with stinging nettles and a sauce of cuttlefish and squash flowers flavored with essence of lemon.

They tucked in and shared bites. Not quite what proper Italians would do when eating out, Giulia thought. The night was warm and since Tom ordered both red and white wines, they soon relaxed and enjoyed the evening as if no tensions existed around their table.

For the main course, Tom ordered *filetto di branzino con finocchi e olive taggiasche e pomodoro candito,* filet of sea bass with fennel and olive tapenade and candied tomatoes. Chuck ordered *filetto di angus argentino,* filet of Argentine beef, and Giulia passed, happy to wait for a simple green salad. Of course, both men offered her tastes of their entrées. No one wanted dessert but all enjoyed espressos accompanied by minuscule biscotti and chocolates. Truly an expense-account repast.

CHAPTER THIRTY-TWO

Chuck and Giulia left Tom, promising to have breakfast with him the next morning. Chuck invited her to his place; she invited him to hers. He hesitated. He liked his better, then felt selfish and agreed. "I even have an extra toothbrush," she said.

He laughed and pulled her into his arms. They caught a vaporetto to Rezzonico. "We haven't talked about our apartments have we?" he said.

"We've had other things on our minds," she said so softly he barely heard.

"Here's what we'll do," he said. "We'll shelve everything for tonight. Maybe get some rest. Okay?"

Her apartment was still bare and didn't feel much like home, he thought. What did home mean anyway? A place where you knew exactly where your favorite paring knife resided? Where your books were lined up on the shelves not by size but by favorites? Maybe home was having Giulia in his arms. He'd never once thought about this in his first marriage.

She suggested he go ahead and shower first. When she slipped into bed beside him, he was naked. She wanted to feel his skin against hers and slid out of her sleep Tee to snuggle close to him. They held each other, but neither one wanted to start anything. He loved every second of their lovemaking, but this was heavenly, too. He always slept better with her in his arms. The nightmares seldom came when the girl-weight of her arm or leg lay across his body.

By morning, though, Chuck took a chance and curled around her moving his hand to hold a lush breast. He couldn't keep from humming low in his throat. She turned toward him letting her hands skim his chest and on to his aroused cock. His big hands encompassed her rib cage, moved over her belly until one hand lay on her mound. She trembled and when he discovered she was ready, they made slow, silent love. Nothing special. Nothing unusual. And for him, it was one of the best sexual experiences he'd ever had. *Seems like those words slip into my head a lot lately.*

* * *

After their breakfast on the hotel balcony outside Tom's lavish suite, he gave them a tour. Every inch was over decorated, but when he opened the door to the bathroom, he reared back and laughed. "Whooee, take a look at this," and Tom pointed to the gilded mirrors, golden faucets and exquisite marble sinks and counter made of a rich, bronze-streaked marble. "Tour's over. Let's get out of this stifling excess."

They walked and talked all through the rest of the day, grabbing pizza at Serenissima, their favorite pizza shop with its multicolored carnival lights that glowed night and day, every day. More talking and walking and finally back to Tom's balcony. Soon, Giulia excused herself to prepare for Monday morning classes. Chuck walked to the door with her to get a whispered assurance that he could drop by after an early nightcap with Tom.

But Tom followed to say goodbye.

"Come back soon, Tom, expense account or not."

He bent to kiss her on the cheek and give her a gentle hug. "I plan to. I'll see *you* in spite of what this lug does with himself. In the meantime, take my card in case you need anything." Then he punched Chuck in the belly. "Hey, man, you're getting soft."

With that Chuck put him in a headlock, and said, "Soft eh?"

She left, not needing to find out which one would cry uncle first.

* * *

The two good friends sat on the Gritti balcony of Tom's room and sipped four-year-old Cognac. Tom lit a cigar but Chuck passed. He wasn't crazy about them and didn't want it on his breath for later with Giulia.

Tom wanted to know more about the Ogle mess that Chuck had alluded to as well as the Botteri business. Chuck summarized what had happened from the time she kneed Oliver in the balls and ran straight into Chuck's arms. Also about the break-in of her apartment in Vicenza.

"She's convinced Ogle did it," Chuck said, "but I think Botteri's thugs had been there, too.

"She's been through a lot."

Chuck nodded and sipped his brandy.

As usual, Tom didn't let the subject go. "You don't ever need to know what she did years before you. But as I said, for the record you have nothing to worry about. All you need to know is who she is now. Right, ol' man?"

"She charmed men, whether for sex or not. How do I separate that from who she is with me... or seems to be."

"Jeezus! You've had plenty of women. If you can't tell whether a response is genuine or fake—in bed or out—then you're... you're a hopeless case."

He poured a little more brandy into Chuck's snifter. "This woman rings as true as an Indian temple bell. Look how she stepped up and admitted to her past the minute I thought I recognized her. She's the genuine article. When we first met, she was kinda on stage trying to cater to my wishes."

"That was her job, to cater to your wishes."

"Not sexual wishes. Christ, you cannot get off that horse can you? Your poor dick has taken a hit. I thought it was tougher than that."

Tom kept talking while Chuck brooded over his brandy, but he listened. Chuck thought back ten years. He remembered waking once in the middle of the night while visiting his sister, trying to decide about Special Ops. Fame. Medals. Glory. That's who he was back then. Is he still that man greedy for praise? Does he still need to prove to his dead father he's not a failure? A man who needs a pure-as-snow woman? Does he want a woman who acts like his mom did? Afraid of him?

Chuck came out of his reverie and noticed that Tom was staring across the water looking forlorn himself. He might have a drop or two in his eyes. Was he still suffering over what he'd lost with Teri?

"What's going on in your love life lately?" Chuck almost whispered.

"Not much. Go out some. Seldom repeat more than a time or two. It's all over with Teri. Her problem with me wasn't my commitment to Special Ops after all. It was my commitment to *anything* that didn't focus on her. I've been grieving for something I never had." He heaved a huge sigh. "We never were soul mates."

They were quiet. "I think Giulia and I could be," Chuck said almost under his breath.

"I have a hunch you're right. That seldom comes along. If you feel lost without her—I'm not talking sex here—you need to grab on and hang tight."

They watched the moon's reflection on the water flowing beneath the balcony. "I could get used to this peacefulness," Tom murmured.

"Better let you get some sleep," Chuck said. "You have an early flight."

"Yeah. Have to wrap up the project at the Smithsonian Center for Astrophysics in Boston. But when I'm in Brussels, we're going to connect more often, man. The years are going by."

Chuck put his hand on Tom's shoulder, "I'd like that... a lot. As usual, you've given me much to ponder. Next time, though, stay with me."

"Sounds good. In the meantime, scout someone for me exactly like Giulia. This could be a pleasant place to settle. More and more I'm thinking... quiet. Is that old age or what?"

"Could be." Chuck stood. Tom did, too.

"Going back to her?"

"Yeah."

"Good."

"Good luck on your new project. But Tom, keep your heart open."

"I will, man. Hope it works out for you and Giulia."

"Thanks. I'll need all the help I can get."

CHAPTER THIRTY-THREE

Giulia, already in her sleep Tee and robe came to the door. "Don't you have a key?"

"I do, but... thought you might want me to knock anyway."

She puzzled over that but didn't reply. "Would you like a drink? Are you hungry?"

"Nothing. Wait, I could use water. Not used to drinking brandy even if it was an exclusive brand I've never heard of before," he snorted half-heartedly. Both seemed unable to slip into their former casual banter.

When she brought a glass of water, he was sitting on the oversized, rather lumpy couch. She joined him to sit at the end to lean back facing him.

"Did you get your class notes ready?"

"I didn't have much. Guess I needed space."

"I kind of guessed."

"I wanted to give you guys space, too."

"He thinks the world of you."

"Can't imagine why, considering my past profession."

"Semi-profession," Chuck added.

"Still I took money from men even if only for arm candy."

"*Some* arm candy." He moved to pull her into an embrace beside him.

"Giulia?"

"Yes?"

"Tom's talk about hope in the bottom of Pandora's box... I want there to be an 'us.' I don't want us to split over your past."

"But?" she said, waiting for the qualification.

"Tom would bust my ass if he heard what I'm about to ask. And I think I know your answer, but I have to ask anyway."

"Sure." The word slid out on a ragged sigh as she eased out of his arms.

"Did you ever fuck a client?"

"No." She stood up and walked toward the kitchen.

"Hand job? Blow job?"

"No, and no!" Then she whirled back to face him. As a hunky military man, you've probably fucked more women in six months than I have in my entire life. Marlowe said you took a gorgeous woman to the New Year's Gala. Should I ask if you fucked her?"

He put his glass down and walked toward her. "Giulia, I'm—"

"Why care about what happened before we met? You'll never let it go."

"Hunky?" he said as he took her into his arms and kissed her hard and long. He took her hand, led her to the couch and pulled her onto his lap.

"I'm sorry, Giulia. I knew better. Had to stomp down that last—"

"And how many more times will you need to stomp—"

"*Never. Never again.* No more doubts." They sat without speaking. The tick of the ornate clock on a wall shelf dominated their space.

Finally, he broke the silence. "What's the time period on this lease?"

"Six months. I would have signed for longer, but you and Nonno urged me to sign for less until I knew how this place would work out."

Chuck nodded. "I could suggest one thing that isn't working out."

"Oh. What's that?"

"That lumpy mattress. Haven't you noticed?"

"Those lumps *are* awful. They are hard and don't give an inch. I spoke to the agent, and she said she'd contact the owner down in Calabria."

The place is spacious, though, with high ceilings and the view of a rio," he said. "So, how are you feeling about your dream place?"

"Confused. I keep thinking if I'd take pains to make it mine, I'd feel better." She leaned against his chest. "Guess it's the old expectation upset."

"How's that?"

"Like anything you build your hopes up for, the result falls flat. The apartment doesn't have the tinsel and sparkle of a seven-year-old's fantasy."

"Nothing could." He pulled her closer. "But, Giulia, leases can be broken."

"Yes. But it might be best if I stay right here. As you said, we haven't known each other long."

"Hey! Why don't you move back in with me until the new mattress arrives? You can come visit your place any time."

She laughed. "Oh Karlo with a K," and she put a hand on each side of his face locking his eyes to hers. "I think you agree we need more time in separate places, but you're struggling to give up your side of the argument. Right?"

His smile was wistful. "Maybe. But that mattress is—"

"You're right, it *is* horrid. I'll grab what I need for work and we'll go to your place, at least for tonight."

"Are you sure?"

"Sure, sure, sure."

* * *

"You can still stash stuff in your room," Chuck said when they walked into his apartment.

"My room?"

"I'm in no hurry to place my things back there, Micina. I'm hoping you'll soon clutter it with your stuff."

"I see," she said, "You *place* your things, but I *clutter* mine."

"Yes. Exactly. I know I have a little problem with order."

She gave a small snort.

"The truth is, I like seeing your stuff around. I can't explain it, but when you were living here, if I walked in and saw one of your scarves or a book lying around, I felt like I'd come home."

She dropped her briefcase on the floor and put her arms around him. "Oh Karlo, my love."

He wrapped his arms around her. "Let's forget about leases and apartments tonight. Okay?"

"Let's!"

* * *

Chuck lay atop her body breathing hard. His weight felt good. It anchored her and she was right where she wanted to be. He rolled onto his side, carrying her with him, staying deep within.

"That's one way to forget about who lives in which apartment," she breathed.

"Yup. One way. Wait a sec. We'll try another way."

"A second?"

"Well maybe a minute?"

"You think so?"

"Know so."

She played with the dusting of hair on his upper chest. Lazily followed the dark path down to his navel where it circled around. She feathered a finger around his belly button and into it. He chortled. When she moved slowly on to the thicker, black bush at his penis, she felt a thickening inside her body.

"You might be right," she whispered.

"Damn straight, I'm right," he said as he rolled onto his back and slowly lifted her up to straddle him. She whimpered her pleasure. Those whimpering sounds had a way of pushing him beyond his limit. He thrust upward once, rolled her onto her back again, and drove with a wildness she hadn't expected. But she welcomed each plunge until he roared out her name, and together they dissolved into bliss.

They lay side by side, hearts pounding, gasping for breath.

"I think I've found *il mio leone,* my very own lion."

"Hmm," he sighed. "And are you *la mia leonessa?*"

"Si," she growled softly. "Do you think Nonna and Nonno Tony came up with their pet names this way."

"I have no doubt," he said turning her on her side to curve around her. "And now this contented lion is ready for a nice, long snooze."

CHAPTER THIRTY-FOUR

The following Saturday evening, Giulia and Chuck met Marlowe and Marc at Peggy Guggenheim's Museum with plans to go on for dinner at Ai Gondolieri nearby. The two couples wandered through the museum that had been Peggy's home for about thirty years. Giulia had always thought Peggy had led a fascinating life although maybe not a contented one. She had been a child of one of the incredibly rich Guggenheim sons of New York city. But her father had been a black-sheep playboy, who lost a huge fortune by gambling and also his life on the Titanic. While living in Europe before the Second World War, Peggy began collecting Modern Art and lovers, some of whom were the very artists whose work she collected. After the war, she moved to Venice permanently.

"This building's still listed on local maps as *Palazzo Venier dei Leoni,*" Giulia said as they walked through the rooms. "Supposedly the Venier family kept lions in the huge garden in the back."

"I've always thought the building looked more like a sprawling ranch house than a Venetian palazzo," Marlowe said.

"Me too," Chuck said. "It's squat and ugly and doesn't fit in with the other masterpieces along the Canal."

"The original design was supposed to have several upper floors," Giulia said. "Imagine how big and ugly it would have been if the family hadn't lost their fortune? Lucky for Peggy, though."

"Why lucky?" Marlowe asked.

Marc chimed in. "Since it wasn't finished, it's never been listed as a national monument, right?" he said turning to Giulia who seemed to be up on details about Peggy Guggenheim.

"Exactly," Giulia said. "That way she could make all kinds of changes inside to show off her art collection." They entered Peggy's bedroom. "She did it her way," Giulia said with a glow in her eyes. "Imagine having this mobile by Alexander Calder hanging over your bed."

Chuck put his arm around her as they all walked out to the front courtyard to inspect the famous equestrian statue. It had been part of a sculpture exhibition held by Peggy in her backyard. Each of them had seen it whenever they cruised past on a vaporetto. Before entering the museum, they had speculated whether the phallus would be in position. Marc saw it first and gave a thumbs up signal to the others.

Giulia may have had more details on Peggy and her eccentric life, but they all knew the story of the famous phallus. When Peggy was planning the exhibition, she'd gone to Milan and ordered the sculpture from Marino Marini. It's an exuberant statue of a horse and rider, and Marini christened it *The Angel of the Citadel*. The nude rider's arms are spread out in ecstasy and to emphasize the rider's euphoria, Marini added a phallus in full erection. When he cast the figure in bronze, he made the phallus separately so it could be screwed in or out depending on who might be attending the exhibition.

After they strolled through the gardens, Marc asked, "Anyone hungry?"

* * *

Ai Gondolieri was one of the few restaurants in Venice without fish or seafood on the menu. They ordered wine, pasta, entrées and salads, then Marc asked Giulia how she liked her apartment. She sighed and made the famous Roman emperors' signal of thumb down. "It has its problems."

"I'll say. Oh my aching back," Chuck said, trying to lighten Giulia's mood.

"It's the mattress, mostly," Giulia said. "But there've been other reasons for complaint. After the first few days, I went to Aletta, the managing agent, with a list. First, the pillows provided were those huge, hard foam ones."

Marlowe groaned in commiseration.

"Not only that. No bread knife, no breadboard, no garbage pail, no towel hooks or toilet-paper holder in the bathroom." Giulia threw up her hands in disgust. "And the teapot leaked!"

"An impressive list," Marc said with a bit of a grin emerging.

"I've asked myself at least fifteen times why didn't I lie on the bed before I signed the lease. Why didn't I inspect the kitchen? I was too excited about the location on the Rio di Angelo Raffaele."

"Raffaele *is* a fabulous area," Marlowe said. "Quiet, too. Few tourists make it that far from the Academy of Art."

The waiter brought them all flutes of sparkling Prosecco and a plate of crudities to dip in individual bowls of olive oil that held a dollup of brown mustard. A strange but interesting combination.

"What did this Aletta say?" Marc asked.

"She's unflappable. She suggested I buy the items I needed and submit the bills. I asked if that included pillows and she said, *'Certo, Certo.'* She says certo a lot to let me know she understands, but so far it hasn't taken the lumps out of the bed. When I asked if she'd spoken to the owner, who lives in Calabria, she assured me she was trying to reach her."

"I'm sorry, Giulia. You'd been counting on having your own apartment here for so long," Marlowe said.

"Maybe I wanted it too much," she said, glancing at Chuck.

His eyes softened.

"Three days after I told her about the lumpy bed, Aletta came to see it." In a high, sweet voice, Giulia mimicked Aletta, *"Ah si. È vero, il materasso è terribile!'* Ah yes. It's true, the mattress is terrible.' Well, I already knew that!"

Chuck snorted. The others did too.

"By the way," Marc asked. "Is Aletta an Italian name? It could be I suppose, but I've never heard it."

"Dutch. Her mother's from Holland, but it seems to me Aletta's more Italian than Dutch. For example, five whole days after pronouncing that the mattress was horrible, she called all excited to tell me that the owner would pay for a new one but didn't want to replace the bed since it was an antique. That's fine, I told her. All I want is a good night's sleep." Then Giulia grinned. "Aletta doesn't need to know I have another place to lay my head."

"Of course not," Marc added, glancing at Chuck.

"Then what happened?" Marlowe asked.

"Two days later, she called to say she had specific directions for measuring the odd-sized mattress and needed to come by. I told her to come anytime and use her agent's key. Aletta is often an hour or more late or calls to change the time. I know she has other duties, but my time is worth *something*."

"Take a break, love," Chuck said, "our pasta's here."

Giulia exhaled a big breath and slumped back onto her chair. "Good idea. Enough of my woes."

"When it's finally settled, I hope you'll be able to laugh about all this," Marlowe said.

"Someday, maybe," Giulia said. "Let's enjoy our meal."

For a while, they were quiet as they ate their small plates of pasta.

"Marlowe and I have finally settled on a date to celebrate our wedding back in February," Marc said. "We want you to be there."

"Marc's family wasn't all that happy with us for slipping away to Las Vegas." She looked at Marc, whose large, grey eyes seemed to shower rays of adoration onto Marlowe.

Marc turned to Giulia "After Chuck helped her get the interview for the job at the base, she had to go back to sort her belongings. And I had to make sure she'd return. We took a detour to the Little White Chapel."

"It sounds tacky," Marlowe said leaning in, "but the thing is, we got to do it our way. For me," she looked at Marc again, "it was perfect."

He laid his hand on her shoulder and gave it a gentle squeeze.

"But, the reception's another story. It'll be what everyone else wants!"

The pasta plates were cleared, and the waiter had no problem sorting their entrées because they had all ordered the same thing, *una braciola di maiale con salsa di pere e finocchetto selvatico,* a pork chop with pear sauce and wild fennel. Marc leaned over his dish and inhaled, giving a huge sigh of pleasure. "Buon appetito!" he said and waved to the waiter making a pouring gesture that they needed more wine. They all tucked in.

"This chop is superb. Tender and succulent," Giulia said, and took a sip of wine. "When is the reception? Can I help?"

"Saturday, the fourteenth of June," Marlowe said. "We hope to hold it outdoors but with the crazy rain patterns, we need a place where we can duck inside if we have to. Until that's settled, all we can say is the date. As for your help, I'll let you know, but I have a feeling there'll be so much family help that I might just disappear until the fourteenth."

* * *

Later they all strolled through the calles leading to *Santa Maria della Salute*, the gorgeous church across the Grand Canal from the Gritti. Marc and Marlowe said goodnight and boarded a vaporetto destined for Murano.

"Do you feel like walking or shall we wait for a vaporetto going the other way?" Chuck asked Giulia.

"Walk. I ate a lot and also need to work off more frustration."

They backtracked across a bridge and caught a traghetto over to Campo Santa Maria di Giglio. In the quiet evening, they were the only two standing in the bare-bones gondola that made the trip across the Canal. They moseyed slowly through the quiet streets, crossed the Rialto and on to Chuck's place.

"Do you realize it's been almost three weeks," she began again, "since I first complained about that darned mattress?"

"That long?" he commented. Chuck listened with supportive grunts here and there but was glad it was dark enough that she didn't notice him grinning. It was fine with him that Giulia spent most of her nights on his mattress.

"For a whole week, I was under the illusion it had been ordered until she brought a mattress person to get the exact measurements.

She apologized profusely but as far as she knew, I was still trying to sleep on those lumps."

"So far, I haven't noticed any on your side of *my* bed."

"Oh you," she said punching him in the belly. "I'm being crazy over this. Guess it's not only the mattress that makes me crazy, is it?"

"Probably not," he said as he opened the outer door to his building. He knew she still worried about Botteri and his thugs and, of course, Oliver Ogle's trial loomed in their future.

"It's hard to stay angry with Aletta, but it's obvious the owner hadn't maintained the place before turning it over to an agency."

"That's for sure." *Still focused on that damned apartment.*

"It's also obvious that either Aletta or someone in her agency had been negligent. No one even visualized how it would be to actually live there."

"I'm sure you're exactly right."

"You're patronizing me. I don't blame you. Let's change the subject."

They entered his apartment, and he crooked his arm around her neck, pulled her close, and said, "What shall we talk about?"

"You're choice. I'm all talked out."

"I have a project in mind that doesn't require talk."

"Let me guess," she said.

"You'll never guess."

"Oh?"

"Before I left for the museum, I put bedding in the laundry, " he said, "and rather than talk, you could help me make up the bed. And then—"

"Then we could take a bath together and settle in for the night," she said reaching up to feel the raspy growth of his beard, running her finger across his mustache and full lower lip. "Why is it I like the feel of your stubble?"

"Interesting question. Come on, let's do our chores, then we'll concentrate on your beard question."

CHAPTER THIRTY-FIVE

Sunday morning, Giulia filled a breakfast bowl with strawberries she'd found at the Rialto market. She added a dollup of plain yogurt and felt satisfied, but Chuck whipped up a three-egg frittata for himself. As he drank a third cup of coffee, he looked up from the Gazzettino, the Venetian paper, to watch Giulia twirl a strand of hair while working on a crossword puzzle from the International Herald Tribune. He wondered when this fly-boy had ever felt such pleasure in doing nothing?

"Do you have big plans for the day?" he asked.

"None. I'm sick of fretting about that apartment. And you?"

"It's a glorious day out there. How about a walk along the Lido's sea wall down to Pellestrina?"

"Perfect. But I'll need hiking clothes and boots from my wretched place."

"While you're doing that, I'll go to Antonio's. I've been hankering for his fabulous panini. You know his place on Frezzaria?"

"I know Calle Frezzaria, but Antonio's?"

"Antonio is the main man there, can't remember what the shop's called."

"What shall I bring?"

"Yourself will be plenty. Can you meet me at Piazzale Roma in front of the bus ticket office?"

"Sure."

"I'll get my car from the garage and we'll catch a ferry to the Lido."

"Good idea. The Lido bus takes forever and hardly makes any stops." She carried her bowl to the sink. "Okay Karlo, I'm off."

When Chuck drove to where Giulia stood waiting, he felt a little hitch in his chest. She looked so small standing in baggy, navy-blue cargo pants and clumpy walking boots. She wore a loose Tee-shirt to match the pants, but there was no way she could disguise her sweet body. *Oh Lord. How lucky to have her in my life. Now, can I keep her? If I play an entrapment game like old Peter the Pumpkin Eater did, I'll lose her. The only way is to somehow make sure Giulia believes it's her idea to move back into my pumpkin shell.*

* * *

All day long the weather had been perfect. But it began to rain while they were on the number eleven bus traveling back north from Pellestrina to the Alberoni inlet where they'd left Chuck's car. When the bus stopped, the rain was coming down hard and gusts were blowing in from the sea. They dashed for the safety of his little Fiat minutes before the sky opened up with a thundering torrent. It was slow going north along the two-lane road. But, they were in luck, because the lights of a ferry were approaching just as they drove onto the Lido's dock.

As they stood at the window of the ferry while crossing the lagoon to Venice, Chuck held her from behind. "It's been a great day, Micina. We goofed around, got a little exercise and—"

"And?"

"Nothing, just rambling."

"You don't ramble. And what?" She faced him.

"It took your mind off that… apartment."

"You bet it did," she said, turning back toward the window. "And now the perfect ending to our day is to watch the magical skyline of *our* Venice emerge through the mist."

His chin rested on her head, and he took in the scent from her hair: part sea-salt, part jasmine shampoo and part sexy woman.

Giulia had already planned to stay at her place. But, on one of those hunches that Chuck often had, he followed her up the stairs to her apartment.

"I want a decent kiss before I leave you tonight."

They put their sandy boots outside her door on a mat of woven rush she'd found in a flea market. The minute they opened the door, they felt a cool, damp breeze ruffling the gauzy curtains in the narrow entry way. Giulia started to rush down the hall toward the bedrooms where the gusts came from, but Chuck held her back.

"Let me go first," he whispered.

She waited, trusting his instincts.

He was back in minutes. "No one's here," he said, "but you left a window open in the spare room and the rain's blowing in."

"I did *not* leave that window open. Two days ago, the handle came off in my hand. I called Aletta, but, of course, she had to arrange for its repair."

He said nothing.

"Oh no. Look at this bed," she said. "Soaked. I bought new sheets and pillow cases with lacy tatting on them because Nonna's planning to come for a visit." Her voice had risen into a whine. "I wanted it nice for her." She began ripping the bed apart. "This is the last straw!"

Chuck stood in the doorway. With her arms full of bedding, she wheeled toward him when her stocking-foot slipped on the wet floor. He lunged and caught her before her backside hit the tile. But he lost his own balance and they both ended on the floor in a heap of wet linens.

"You okay?" he asked.

"No, I'm not okay. What do you think?"

He waited.

"I wedged a broken broom handle between the window and the bed."

"That was a good plan."

"Yeah, so why didn't it work?"

"Guess the force of nature was too much."

"Some kind of force is working against me here."

"Might be a good time to break your lease. Seems to me you'd have every right without having to pay a penalty."

"I should never have rented a furnished apartment. Should have found something else. Should never have rented a place with the owner all the way down in Calabria."

He got up and lifted her to her feet. She sighed. "All I saw was the canal."

"I know." He gathered up the wet linens. "Where shall I put these?"

"I'll take them."

He followed her and closed the door to the small room. There'd be less chance of gusts from the window. After she slammed the laundry-room door, he said, "Sit in the kitchen. I'll fix tea and we'll make plans." He pulled out the new teapot and dumped in a few loose tea leaves.

"I need to clean up the mess, first," she said with dry towels in hand.

"It's only water, angel. You make the tea and let me take these. Maybe I can find something more substantial than that light-weight cot to wedge the window closed. Okay?"

"Okaaay."

She heard a loud screech, two thumps and a bump and he was back with damp towels in his arms. "The window won't open again until it's repaired properly. Were these towels okay to wipe the floor?"

"Sure. The whole mess'll need washing anyway. What'd you use?"

"A large wooden dresser that stood in the corner. It's heavy enough, but it needs work. For a second, I thought it was coming apart but it held."

Giulia sighed. "What a jerk I've been and—"

"No reason to blame yourself. Come sit while we wait for the tea."

They sat but Giulia still seemed wound up tight.

"Who would expect an apartment run by a reputable agency to be in such terrible condition?" he said.

She got up and walked around, still agitated. "I didn't tell you about the crazy doorbell. I leaned out the window and felt like one of those old Italian women who watch the street all day. Finally a man came and fixed it."

"So?"

"The next morning, a horrible buzzing woke me. I wandered around in a stupor until I discovered it was coming from the bell mounted at my front door. I could *not* make the thing stop. If I'd had a hammer . . ."

Chuck smothered a laugh.

"I got the cover off and located the part making the noise, but when I let go, the racket started again. With that sound battering my brain, I managed to close the door to the hall and call Aletta. Had to leave a message, of course."

"After an interminable ten minutes, the clever girl called to suggest I go downstairs and push the button. Maybe it was stuck. Maybe a mail carrier had pushed bells at random to get into the outer door. I threw on clothes and ran down leaving that screech behind. And guess what?"

The tea kettle shrilled. He poured boiling water into the tea-pot.

"Sure enough, a new brass button was all the way in its socket. I pushed. Nothing happened. I shoved again, hard, and finally it popped out. She was right. When I got up here, the noise had stopped. Peace at last, but no more sleep."

"You've had your share of problems, for sure."

"The problems are endless. A lamp in the spare room was no good so I bought another one and added it to my list. The cord on a heavy floor lamp in the living room was frayed. After it sparked the second time, I dragged it into the far corner of the entryway and exchanged it for a table lamp that sat beneath the stairs to the loft. Don't ask what junk is stashed up *there.*"

Giulia plopped down, deflated, and he poured the tea. "Thanks for your patience, Chuck."

He sat down and lifted his cup to smell the brew.

She did the same. "Ah jasmine. You found the good tea."

She began again. "Don't know if you noticed the door into my apartment is oily around the strike plate."

He shook his head.

"I swab it with olive oil daily. It was giving me trouble and I worried that I couldn't get inside some cold, dark, rainy, stormy, miserable night."

At this last complaint, he couldn't stop a big chuckle from rumbling out. She saw his face and broke out laughing, too. "You're right, I need to get out of here. Do you think The Marc would know a real-estate lawyer?"

"We'll call him tomorrow. How about leaving this miserable place?"

"Thought you'd never ask."

CHAPTER THIRTY-SIX

Marc did know someone in real-estate law, and late Monday afternoon Giulia started the lease-breaking process. All parties knew she was moving out, but the lawyer urged her to maintain a semblance of possession until papers were legally filed. She'd grown to hate everything about the place and didn't want to stay another day. Earlier she'd been determined to stick out the six-month lease to give Chuck time. But in spite of her tantrum when the rain blew in, he'd made it clear he wanted her with him. The truth? She was the one who felt conflicted. Did he truly accept her in spite of her past?

Then Aletta called and asked Giulia for a huge favor." The new custom-made mattress would be delivered from Milan on Wednesday, the fourteenth of May, but she couldn't be there. Could Giulia do that for her? Giulia agreed without much grace, but Aletta didn't seem to notice.

On Tuesday she called again announcing in her cheery voice that the mattress had arrived in Venice, but with heavy rains and a high tide, boats were having trouble getting under low bridges. She still expected delivery on Wednesday. "Thursday for sure," she sang out and hung up.

Giulia had been noticing water sloshing onto the fondamenta when boats went by although most pilots moved cautiously during high-water times. Wednesday morning, Aletta called saying, "Maybe late in the afternoon, when the tide and wind go down. Even though you're moving out," she trilled, "at least you'll have a few decent nights in the apartment."

It didn't matter a fig to Giulia anymore, but it did sadden her to think of the fate of Venice. The old Venetians didn't expect high water to come so often and certainly never in the middle of May. In the old days, *acqua alta* came only in November.

At 4:42 P.M., the doorbell rang. The mattress had arrived. She responded over the intercom but leaned out anyway to see the mattress man below. He looked up, waved and smiled. She liked him right away. His smile reminded her of Brian Dennehey, the stocky actor she'd always respected. And better yet, the man's daughter came with him.

Together they carried the mattress to her door. She was pleased to see a father/daughter company in Italy. They set to work speaking quietly to each other. They'd been instructed to put the disgusting, floppy abomination up in the loft with all the other useless items stored there. So much for the "bonus space" advertised on the internet.

They installed a new frame made of handsome pieces of blond, polished wood. He demonstrated how Giulia might move leather straps on the slats to give them more or less support. Had Chuck ever seen a mechanism like this? She wanted to show it to him before she moved out. Should she make the bed? They might try it out before she vacated her "dream" apartment. But there was no time to make the bed, because, after the delivery people left, Chuck was at her door, maneuvering a borrowed handcart out of the freight elevator.

"What a clever idea," she said and gave him a hug. "Are you still sure you want me moving in with you lock, stock and barrel?"

"I'm sure," he said, holding her.

"It will be awhile before I get my apartment-hunting energy up again."

"Maybe you won't need to go hunting."

"So you're willing to take a risk with me, considering my past?"

Chuck's eyes flashed and he dropped the handle of the cart on the floor. When it struck the tile, the sound rang out as angrily as the look on his face.

"Why the hell can't you trust that I believe your explanation?" He held her away from him and looked straight into her eyes. "Methinks you protest too much. Which is it, Giulia?"

"So you *do* doubt me!"

"Not until sixty-seconds ago. What's going on?"

"Well, you did have doubts about whether Tom was telling the truth."

"Don't even go there," he snarled. "Tom and I have—we're solid."

"I thought you thought he had said what you wanted to hear."

"You think too much."

"I'd never heard you speak of this wonderful trustworthy friend until you insisted I go to the airport to meet him."

"You weren't reluctant about going until you saw who he was. Then the cat was out of the bag and you had to fess up." Suddenly, Chuck heard his father's voice arguing with his mother.

Giulia's body seemed to crumple and turn in on herself. "I struggled a lot about when and how to tell you. It seemed best to do it right there at the airport." She spoke so softly he could barely hear her.

"Yeah. Maybe so. But... hell, we're veering off." He didn't want to be like his dad but couldn't let it go. "I'm thinking you have the biggest trust issue here. Maybe the lumps in that bed are the perfect penance you've been looking for." He turned, walked out and didn't look back.

She stood stunned. What had she done? He'd been honest about how he felt. He'd shared his struggle over the whole thing. He'd given her every chance to explain. But she kept making him jump more and more hurdles. And he'd jumped them. Why had she goaded him... again? She'd gone too far.

She ran to the window overlooking the street below and leaned out. "Karlo, don't go."

He was walking away fast, but turned and jammed his hands in his pockets. He'd never felt so furious with her and knew his face was flushed. He was tempted to say for all the neighborhood, 'Need one last fuck?' But he couldn't bring himself to do it. Instead he said, "What do you need?"

"Please wait. I... I love you," she yelled.

He stood speechless, and she gasped herself. But hearing those words shouted for all the world to know told her they were the truest words she'd ever uttered. A couple of people walking by stopped to look at Chuck then up at Giulia. They shook their heads, smiled and walked on.

In a quieter voice, she asked, "Can we talk? I'll be down in a sec."

When she came out the door onto the sidewalk beside the canal, his dark eyebrows formed straight lines over those pale, wolf-like eyes. "Is this a game with you?"

"No! No game. I need to explain even more," she said putting her hands on his forearms. "Somewhere else?"

"A public place," he said, not wanting cozy intimacy.

"Of course."

* * *

Giulia wrapped both hands around the stem of a glass of chilled white wine, and Chuck sipped a beer. Made in Sicily, Birra Messina had less than five percent alcohol. He was pleased this little bar near Campo Santa Margherita had it on tap. It was the only thing that pleased him at the moment. He needed to focus one more time on this complex woman huddled across from him.

She reminded him of the relationship with Ricky that ended in abortion.

He nodded, but felt exasperated. He took a small sip of beer.

She had avoided men for a year until she met Jason. She told about him lying from the first and his estranged wife showing up pregnant.

"I knew he wanted children, but I hadn't been ready while in grad school. After that, I swore off men and wanted revenge."

Chuck started to interrupt but sensed she needed to tell it all before she lost her courage. He sat back, drained his glass and signaled for another. Giulia lifted her glass to take a sip, but her hand shook. She set it back down and looked scared. Tears formed in her eyes but she blinked a few times obviously determined not to break down.

"I feel embarrassed. It was stupid to think I could get revenge against Ricky and Jason by taking money from strange men. When I first got the idea, I'd planned to go all the way. What did I care? My life was over anyway. Whatever they wanted, I'd give. But—"

Chuck put his untouched second beer on the table and leaned forward. "Maybe you had more self respect than you realized?"

Shaking her head, she said, "I doubt it. My studies suffered. If it hadn't been for the old Italian Professor Emeritus, who reminded me about all the work I was throwing away, I would have dropped out." She sat up straighter and this time managed to hold her glass steady enough to take a sip.

* * *

The wine was no longer chilled, but the dry, tart taste felt good going down. *I can't lose this man who's good inside and out, but I must tell it all.*"

"After several bad experiences, I finally understood how reckless I'd been. I wasn't hurting Ricky or Jason. Heck, they had no idea what I was doing. And they weren't bad, just two young guys not ready for real relationships."

She was sure Chuck wanted as far away as possible. He leaned in to speak. She held her hand up palm out, asking for one more moment. His mouth tightened and his pale eyes radiated icy shards of silver.

This is my last chance.

"Chuck, I trust *you* until the sun expands. It's me, not you. You said it. I'm the one with trust issues. For too long, I've expected betrayal by men, and my behavior came out in unpleasant ways.

No, change that. It came out in crappy, selfish ways, and I'm sorry. So sorry."

* * *

She looked limp and drained.

He was quiet. *She's an enigma. She responds to me like a lioness but withdraws and becomes distant. She wants a place of her own yet wants to be in my bed. She has a lot to learn about herself. But damn, she's working on it. And... that's enough for me.*

He set his beer down, leaned forward and took both of her hands.

"Giulia, do you think you're the only one ever betrayed by a lover?"

She snatched her hands back, sat up and stiffened her back. If she'd been a cat, he would have sworn she was arching her back, with her fur standing on end, ready to hiss and scratch. Then her body deflated. And her lips curved into a small, sheepish smile.

"How self-centered I've been. So afraid to be hurt. There's no guarantee is there? It's part of life," she said.

He moved around the table dragging the spindly little chair with him to sit beside her and hold her. "I had to say it."

"I had to hear it." She put her arms around his neck and threaded her fingers in his thick hair. "Oh Karlo. I love you so much."

"Those are the only words I've heard all day. Nothing else matters."

CHAPTER THIRTY-SEVEN

Chuck was spending longer hours at the base mostly working out at the gym. That gave Giulia time to adjust to being back in his apartment. At times, she thought he was over-protective. She struggled to get used to having him, or anyone, worry about her—except for her parents, who still fretted about her choice to live in Venice. But she was loving the quiet evenings with Chuck.

Saturday night Giulia poured them each a glass of red wine and sat at the kitchen table while he chopped garlic and tomatoes for what he called a simple pasta sauce. And for what she knew would be elegant in its simplicity.

Oliver Ogle's trial continued to loom over their heads, but it was out of their hands. All they knew for sure was it would be held in Baltimore, maybe mid-September. Chances were that both Chuck and Colonel Ryland would need to appear—Giulia for sure—but either way, Chuck said he'd make the trip with her. And because the situation had developed on a military post, her travel costs would be taken care of. They had bothered her, but they were the least of her worries.

"Rafe Lyne told me Oliver's out on bail," she said to Chuck's back.

"No doubt he's trying to ruin as many lives as he can. What a piece of work," Chuck said.

"Can he come back here, do you think?"

"Don't know. That's a good question to ask Lyne. As your attorney, he'll know about the conditions of Ogle's bail or can find out."

"Yes." She heaved a huge sigh. He turned his head to look at her. "The idea of testifying at Oliver's trial is haunting me already. How will I ever say out loud what he said and did to me?"

"No use to start worrying now, Micina. As time draws near, Lyne will help you prepare for that. And I'll be there with you all the way."

"You will, won't you. That means so much." But she stared into the distance. "If only I hadn't kicked him. I should have somehow twisted out of his grasp and run out the door that first time. You know he'll make a huge to-do about that. *Assault* he'll call it."

This time Chuck turned abruptly from his chopping with the knife still in his hand. "Giulia, stop it! The operative word is 'somehow.' *Somehow* you should have been able to twist out of his grasp. Marc was right, you reacted in self-defense."

"But only I know that."

"Wait until the search warrant for his villa is executed. And all those women's intimate things and all their names will be found in his dirty little file. Wonder how many of *those* women kicked him?"

"Did you get a warrant signed?" Giulia asked, straightening up.

"Didn't I tell you? Jeez, I'm sorry." Chuck lay down his knife, turned the stove off and sat at the table across from her.

"I didn't have to do anything about the warrant. When my superior officer saw the photos of all that lingerie, he was livid that it happened on his watch. After that, strings were pulled. The Italian judge wouldn't allow a search of Ogle's office because, legally, his office is the same as being in the States. The U.S. judge from Padova said no because of personnel records of U.S. citizens. Hell, they could have gotten around those objections by inserting someone from the university during the search. A shame because finding a pair of panties in his office desk would be one more nail in his coffin."

"Probably doesn't matter." Giulia said. "I met Susan Riggs, the interim director of Human Resources yesterday afternoon. She'd found my folder in Ogle's top drawer just where you said it was."

Giulia related the meeting. After Ms. Riggs had read through Giulia's material and Ogle's notes about her teaching Italian to cadets, Riggs asked Giulia to come in to discuss also teaching Italian to military families' children enrolled in American-style classrooms.

"It seems the powers-that-be had been pushing toward this. Of course Ogle acted as if it was all his idea after looking at my resume."

"Micina, you may end up spending more time on that 'dreary post,' as I've heard you call it, instead of in Venice." He stepped back to the counter.

"You're right, it could be a problem. The thing is, I'd like to establish myself on the post as a teacher of Italian to English speakers and English to Italian speakers. That carpenter, Enrico Zava, asked about lessons, and lots of Italian workers on the base might want to learn. Eventually I hope to set up a business here in Venice with excellent referrals from there."

"You're a constant surprise," Chuck said and stopped his food prepping again to swoop her into his arms. "That goes along with my thoughts about retiring. I can rely on you to take care of me."

"Don't get ahead of yourself big man. But wait. You haven't heard the most interesting news about what Susan found."

"And?"

"She said there were indications in Ogle's office, suggesting he might have serious mental or emotional problems. When I asked her what she meant, she said she'd been warned to say nothing. But she could tell me that the top sheet of my folder which showed my personal information had the address where I lived circled in blue pencil."

Chuck nodded. He'd seen that.

"Ms. Riggs said, 'Mr. Ogle seemed to prefer blue pencil to emphasize something important to him.' That could be another nail in Ogle's coffin. And we know what she found in his bottom desk drawer."

"Yeah. I'm guessing that pair of black underwear was still there just as your folder was where I left it," Chuck said. "So you're right, it probably doesn't matter that we didn't get a warrant for his office."

"So, when *will* the villa be searched?" she asked.

"Any day now. Unless Oliver carted his souvenirs away, the villa will be enough to indict him."

"That's such good news. What about your commander?"

"That's what's so incredible. I took a calculated chance showing him those pictures. I didn't say I took them. Didn't say I didn't. Just that they were from Oliver's home. He never asked me directly and didn't want them in his possession. In fact, he hinted I keep them a secret. I've always had a good feeling about him. All along, he's consistently advocated for pursuing and prosecuting sexual harassment on the post."

"It sounds unusual for a man of his high rank to not stick strictly to the book," Giulia said.

"Thank God a few like him are around. I hope Oliver didn't destroy all his booty before they hauled him off to the States."

With that reminder, Giulia crumpled in her chair and began to twist the stem of her wine glass round and round.

"Giulia?"

"I almost wish he had. I can see it now. In front of the whole courtroom, my attorney and his team will display the garments on a huge screen for all to see." She spread her arms wide. "And then, with one of those laser pointers with a red light, he'll identify mine." She slashed her arm forward, narrowed her eyes to fix on the tip of her finger jabbing it at the imaginary display.

"Aw, sweetheart." He came around the table and took her in his arms. "Maybe the pictures the search-warrant crew takes can be shown only to the judge and jury." He waited a beat, tipped her chin up and said, "But yours were the prettiest."

She couldn't quite stifle a snicker. "You're crazy. Sweet, too."

"I know. Can't help myself," he said. "We'll get through it, Giulia. When it's over, we'll come back and enjoy our life in Venice. Right?"

She nodded, burrowing into his chest, inhaling his warm, man smell.

He turned back to finish smashing herbs and garlic together in his mortar and pestle, and she gathered plates and cutlery for the table.

"Giulia? How would Ogle know the measurements of all those women?"

"By the label sizes, or maybe he studied size charts in a catalogue."

"So, how'd he do on yours?"

"You're incorrigible. Wait a minute." She left the room, coming back in a moment to toss a pile of colorful lingerie on the table. "Here. Make your own estimates."

He leaned back in a deep, rumbling guffaw which tickled her into laughter herself.

"Take 'em back. I'd rather handle the real thing." He pushed her glass of wine toward her. "For now, drink up. Then, milady, if you have any strength left, I could use help with the salad."

* * *

On Sunday, Chuck had gone to the post for a few hours. When he came in and plopped down on his recliner, he heaved a sigh and said, "I know I can't compete with the young men under my command, but I've been lax on that front lately." She laughed and punched his abs which felt as hard as ever to her small fist.

"Don't laugh. It's serious."

"I won't laugh. I've also been flexing muscles. Basic Italian-grammar muscles. Wednesday afternoon, I'll start my first class of third-graders. I've never taught little ones and I'm nervous. Old Ollie would be upset if he knew I was getting my teaching objectives met."

"I'm thinking of other objectives." Chuck pulled her onto his lap.

"Mmm," she said, and slid her hands under his shirt, scrabbling them up and down his chest. He moaned softly. She slipped her hands under his jeans waistband trying to grab his firm buttocks.

"Didn't know you were an ass woman," he said and grasped *her* rear.

"Mmm," she answered.

"Me? I'm an all-body man." He began untying the belt of her bathrobe while pulling her into a kiss. "You're warm from your shower and smell delicious. Jasmine?"

He didn't wait for an answer and pushed the robe from her shoulders to take her breasts in his large hands. He lifted one, plumping it up to meet his lips, kissed it as he ran his tongue around the nipple. She sucked in a breath.

"You like that?" he said. "How about this?" and he began suckling on one as he stood her up and walked her backwards down the hall. "Or this?" By then she was laughing as she fell onto the bed.

He crouched beside her while he undid his belt and slid his jeans down his long, muscled legs, kicking the pants free. When he pulled his briefs down, his cock jerked free and grew larger by the second. She reached for it, but he pushed her hands away.

"Later, Micina, later," he whispered. "I want to pleasure you. It's been too long since we've spent leisurely bed-time."

"Yes," she sighed.

God he loved her response. He wanted to taste her again—honey mixed with jasmine. His cock twitched at the thought. Could he hold off long enough to take her further than ever? He nibbled down her body, wanting to make sure she'd always wait for him. Her body trembled, then stiffened. She was coming already! When he made her come, he felt like a conquering hero. Her essence emptied into his mouth as she called out "Karlo!" He knew he'd never forget her taste. Never.

After she wound down, he began to take her slowly. But when he felt her clamping around him again, his own muscles spasmed into the deepest pleasure he'd ever known. It lasted and lasted. Before he collapsed, though, he rolled her sideways staying locked inside.

They both lay in each other's arms panting. She whispered, "I've never felt anything like this. Never felt so loved before. So desirable."

"More?" he whispered.

"Maybe when my heart stops hammering at my ribs."

"Yeah. A minute or two might be good," he said as he drifted off.

CHAPTER THIRTY-EIGHT

Monday morning, when Giulia stretched awake and lazily reached for Chuck, he was gone. Before she had a chance to look for him, she found a note on his pillow:

Giulia, wait for me.

I love you, Karlo.

What did he mean, wait for me? Like an afterthought, he'd scrawled *I'll call later.*

But he didn't call, and it wasn't long before she felt frantic. She called his cell and his office. No answer on his cell, and no one could tell her a thing at his office number. Or wouldn't. After classes, she caught up with Marlowe and told her, "I can only think of one reason. He's gone on a secret mission."

"But he doesn't do missions anymore," Marlowe said.

Giulia nodded, her eyes felt burnt from too many tears. "He said once that it was enough to prepare his men for *their* missions."

"Come over for dinner tonight, Giulia. Let's talk with Marc about it. Maybe he has an idea of what's going on."

Giulia shook her head. She wanted to be home in case Chuck called or came home. But when he didn't show up or call by Tuesday, she called Marlowe, and almost begged to be with them.

The moment she walked into their apartment, Marc looked shocked at the changes in Giulia. Dark circles under her eyes gave her a bruised look, and she'd lost weight since they'd been together at Guggenheim's not quite two weeks ago. He hugged her and put a glass of red wine in her hand.

"Drink up, Giulia," he said, "you've been through a lot lately.

Ogle's attack, your dream apartment a nightmare and now Chuck dropping off the face of the earth."

At that, she burst into tears. *And they didn't know about Botteri. Or the worst, her past.*

"Aw Giulia, I'm sorry," he said putting his arms around her again and led her to one of the couches facing each other in front of the fireplace. "I was trying to sympathize and only made it worse. Come. Sit and eat a few of these tasty *cichetti* Marlowe brought from the bar around the corner."

She sipped the wine, but didn't touch one tidbit lying on the platter in front of her. Gradually, she relaxed and leaned against the couch.

"Has Chuck been doing anything different lately?" Marc asked. He picked up one of the savory morsels and touched it to Giulia's lips. She smiled and took into her mouth a small slice of salami wrapped around an olive.

"Now she has a mouthful and can't answer your question, you big oaf," Marlowe said, popping a round of provolone with a piece of anchovy into her own mouth. Giulia chewed the delicious morsel and decided maybe she could eat after all, but she answered Marc before trying another cichetto.

"The only thing different was staying later and going in earlier, saying he needed more exercise. What else could it be but a mission?"

"Knowing Chuck, he may have thought he might have to go and didn't want to worry you. You know, don't you, he wanted to be finished with all that."

Giulia nodded and her lip trembled as if she'd start weeping again. "He still has nightmares once in a while."

"Maybe he knew someone over there—wherever 'over there' might be," Marc said taking a healthy swallow of wine.

"Yeah. Maybe he was the only one that person would trust," Marlowe said as she sat on the couch opposite Giulia.

"That makes sense," Marc said. "Hell, I don't know. I do know these ops can be tricky, and if it's a hostage situation maybe more so. Who do you know that might tell you without breaking some fusty military rule?"

"Maybe Colonel Ryland, the one who helped with Oliver that day," she said. "Do you know him?"

"We've met. Chuck and I played doubles tennis with him and another colonel or maybe a major. Why don't you call him tomorrow and see if he can meet with you?"

"Good idea," she said draining her glass and holding it out to Marc for more. He grinned and poured. "Drink up, girl. We've got a guest room."

"Let's change the subject," Giulia said. "What's going on in your lives?"

Marc had crouched down to get a small fire going but turned to look at Marlowe, tipping his head slightly and raising his eyebrows.

"I was going to tell you tomorrow at our regular Wednesday lunch, but maybe you'll be seeing Colonel Ryland instead," Marlowe said.

"Tell me what?"

"I have news, or maybe non-news about my long-lost son."

Marc took Marlowe's hand and slid next to her on the couch facing Giulia.

I visited Sister Fiorenza, the only person left at the convent who was there when Tomaso was born." Marlowe inhaled, sat up straighter and continued. "She's pretty much bedridden but has kept her sneaky sense of humor. When I got to her bedside, she took my hand and told me she had an incurable disease. When I leaned closer and asked about it, she cackled and said, "Old age! Then she rang her bell, and a young novice tripped in full of eagerness to please. Sister Fiorenza asked for her bottle of Christmas brandy, reminding her to bring two snifters. She said it was good French brandy and old friends have a right to luxuries from time to time."

Marlowe took a sip of her wine. "I wish I'd thought to take her a bottle of brandy for Christmas."

"You can still do that," Giulia said.

"I won't wait until Christmas. Anyway, she told an interesting story. When word got out that a young woman—me—was pregnant and couldn't keep her baby, couples approached the convent. Sister Fiorenza bragged that gossip like that traveled faster than any news on that 'internet thing.'"

They all chuckled.

"One couple came more than once. That young wife had just given birth to a stillborn. When she heard about me, she began pumping her breasts hoping to get my baby and nurse him as her own."

"Shew! To do that while grieving the loss of her own child, that's—"

"Evidently she'd already suffered two miscarriages, so, I'd say she was motivated."

"Bet that tipped the scales for the convent officials making the decision. Someone that dedicated would surely take good care of your baby."

Marlowe nodded slowly. Marc took her hand and held it in both of his.

"So does Fiorenza think that's where your baby went?"

"She wasn't privy to that information but guessed the administrators would have covered their asses. She said 'cover their bases,' but she'd had a twinkle in her eye." Marlowe sighed. "I'm afraid there may never have been a legal adoption recorded."

"But how could that be?"

"Hunh! Many ways, considering the convoluted machinations of both the Roman-Catholic hierarchy and the Italian government."

"Did Sister Fiorenza know anything else about that couple?"

"They looked great. She was about twenty-five. Her husband was older and established on the academic track at the University of Padova."

"Padova's close, maybe you can find them," Giulia said.

"I asked Sister about papers."

"The child had to have an official birth record," Giulia said.

"Of course. But why couldn't a helpful bureaucrat—whose pocket had been enriched—easily create such papers?"

"'Maybe the parents made a gift to the convent that got partially transferred to that bureaucrat," Giulia said.

"Good thinking, Giulia," Marc said.

"I asked about a donation. Again she had no idea but thought there'd surely be a record of one about that time."

"Would your Padre Tomaso have any information?"

"If so, he's never indicated such. Surely he'd tell me if he knew. I've been leaving messages on his phone about our reception. He loves parties. If he's alive, he'll be there and I'll corner him."

The timer rang on the stove. After an old-fashioned American meatloaf dinner, Giulia felt better having shared her worries with them. She helped Marlowe clean up in the kitchen and Marc and Marlowe went with her all the way to the door of Chuck's apartment. She still thought of it as Chuck's although she'd finally moved all her stuff in. Then he vanished! They hugged good night and left. Marc and Marlowe were fast becoming two important people in her life.

She made it through another night, and the next morning, she called Colonel Ryland's office.

CHAPTER THIRTY-NINE

Wednesday morning was Giulia's usual day to teach, but all classes had been cancelled for required assemblies. "Bullshit military stuff," according to what students said in the hall late Monday afternoon. She didn't need to be there but was willing to make the trip to learn whatever Colonel Ryland might know. He had suggested lunch at the Greek taverna on the base. Her memory of being in the taverna was hazy, but she would have eaten a sandwich made with mushy buns at McDonald's to hear anything about Chuck.

After they met and shook hands, he said, "You're looking better than the day we met in Oliver Ogle's office."

"Thanks. That's a day I'd like to forget. But I sure want to thank you, Colonel Ryland, for coming to my rescue.

"Please call me Rob. Colonel sounds stuffy."

After they were shown to a booth and had ordered, she said. "Rob, I hope you can come to Chuck's rescue this time.

"Nothing I'd like better, but I have no intel on where he might be. The scuttlebutt says his unit was called up for a super secret mission."

"I guessed as much. But I'm puzzled because usually he didn't go with his unit. That's why I'm so worried." She looked at his handsome dark face and wondered how much she should tell him about how Chuck didn't want to deal with the horrors of missions anymore. She worried he might consider that privileged information. She focused on this officer for the first time. He seemed as fit as Chuck, and she figured he was almost as tall. His hair was cut close to his head, but instead of Chuck's silvery eyes, Ryland's were brown on brown.

"Has he told you about his former missions?"

"A little. We've shared our war stories over beers. Like me, Chuck has had his fill of that kind of trouble."

She nodded and swallowed hard. Their lunch was served. She hoped she could eat a little of the Greek salad put before her. He dived into his plate of moussaka as if he hadn't eaten for a week.

When he stopped to drink, he asked, "How long has Chuck been gone?"

"He left early Monday morning, so this is going on the third day." A frown pinched her brow. "How long do these trips usually take?"

"That's a tough question. Three days is a bit on the long side for a routine rescue mission. But . . ." as if to brighten the mood, he added, "It could mean it was supposed to be a long mission in the first place."

Or that something went wrong.

"Sometimes," he said, "it's a quick in and out and the team is back in a couple days. Other times, it takes longer to get the lay of the land and set up contacts. So, to answer you, I haven't a clue." He shrugged and spread his hands up and out in the universal gesture of helplessness.

"Is there any way you can find where he is and why?"

"I doubt it, but I'll give it a super try. You need to know that Chuck has a rep for success throughout the entire 273rd. He's one of those unit commanders well known for bringing all his men back."

"That's good to know," she said taking another bite of salad, hoping he'd bring *himself* back. When the waiter came to remove her half-finished plate, she ordered an espresso.

At last, the lunch was over. She called for the check and thanked him for coming. He offered to pay, but she insisted and thanked him again for coming. "If you hear anything, would you let me know?" She gave him her cell number.

"Will do," he said, and they parted heading in different directions.

* * *

On the way back to Venice, Giulia continued to worry. She felt so helpless. This waiting was hell. She wanted to talk to Nonna and Nonno Tony. What she really wanted was to catch a train to their place and crawl under the covers in her attic room. But fear and worry would go with her. Not wanting people on the train to overhear words of a mission gone wrong, she held off calling them. She couldn't deny anymore that something *had* gone wrong. As soon as she got inside the apartment, she called to invite them to Venice.

"I need to be with you, Nonna, but I'm afraid to be gone right now."

"Certo, certo, I understand sweetie. I want to come and so will Tony. Are you sure about us staying in Chuck's apartment?"

"Absolutely. He thought it was a fine idea when we talked of you coming after that last disaster in my so-called dream place. It'd be nice if you could stay over the weekend, but anytime. Anytime."

"Va bene, I'll call you when we know our schedule."

"*Grazie mille,* thanks a million, Nonna. I feel frantic."

"*Ho capito,* I understand. It's horrible, the waiting."

* * *

Friday afternoon, Giulia met her grandparents at the train station. They traveled light, and it took them no time to settle into the guest room. When they came into the living room, Giulia was carrying wine, bread sticks and olives to the coffee table. While she poured their wine, they asked more questions about what had happened. She re-told the story. Her hand trembled when she showed them the note.

"Oh Giulia, your young man cares so much for you," Nonna said.

"I think so," Giulia said as she blinked back tears. "I don't want to lose him," she said, her lips quivering, and she couldn't stop the tears. "He's the best man I've ever known." Nonna moved to hold her close.

"If what that Colonel Ryland says is true about Chuck's record, he'll come back to you," Nonno Tony said and embraced both women.

"That man has his wits about him. He'll be back. But for now, I'm taking my favorite ladies to a cheery place for dinner. Wear your jackets, we may have to stand outside in line. It's a no-reservation place."

He hustled them out the door and across the Rialto, leading them behind the famous old church of San Marco. They walked a little farther and came to a small bridge that led across the Rio San Provolo. At that point, however, they didn't go up and over the bridge, because tucked beside and almost under it was a little place called Trattoria Rivetta. Sure enough five people were waiting in line to enter. They held glasses of red wine in their hands and smiled to Giulia and her grandparents.

A jovial waiter dressed in white shirt and red-sweater vest came out carrying a bottle tucked under his arm and holding stems of glasses for Giulia and her grandparents. He guaranteed a table within ten minutes as he poured wine for them and topped the glasses of those already waiting. Someone yelled to shake his tail inside. He laughed, hollering a retort and trotted away.

Nonno had a broad grin on his face. This was his kind of place. Soon they were led inside and seated where a basket of bread and a bottle of red and one of white were already open on the table.

"They have their own vineyard in the Veneto. It's always been a secret about that vineyard. Sometimes the wine's great and sometimes pretty good but always decent. Unless they've changed, it's also on the house."

It was a noisy place with a lot of friendly teasing between the waiters and the manager, who stood at the cash register near the entrance. All the waiters wore red-sweater vests, the manager too. At times, a waiter would put a patron on the spot pretending to find fault or maybe make a derogatory comment about one of the Italian soccer teams. Anything to get people to participate and have fun. Giulia smiled but didn't feel a part of it. Then a waiter filled her wine glass to the brim and asked if she was a Comunista? She was shocked to be the center of attention and answered, "*Non lo so*, I don't know." He started to tease but was called away.

Nonno Tony whispered, "Don't forget, cara, Venetians are known for voting left." Giulia nodded. Of course, she knew that. After the waiter took their orders, he turned to her again and said, "Allora, Signorina. Comunista or no?" This time she said, "*Certo. Sono comunista!*" Everybody cheered and clapped and a genuine smile spread across her face. After much joshing, Giulia found herself eating more than she'd eaten since Chuck had disappeared.

"Coccolona, when that man of yours gets back, you can surprise him and bring him here." Nonno shouted over the din.

"I will, Nonno Tony, I will," she hollered. But quietly sent a prayer to all the Gods of *all* the religions that "her man" would just come home safely.

* * *

Late Saturday morning over a leisurely breakfast in Chuck's kitchen, they talked about the situation with her apartment. "I knew better. I'd rented crummy apartments when I was in college, but none had so many problems. I didn't use my head on this one. All I thought about was the location."

"Enough lamenting," Nonno Tony said. "The best part is that you got away from that criminal, Botteri."

"Have you heard anymore about what happened to him?" she asked, feeling deceitful for not mentioning the undercover agent's news. But they didn't need to know she'd been tailed again. She hadn't had that shaky feeling in her stomach for a while, so maybe coming to Venice had worked.

"Not a word," Nonno Tony said. "Maybe no news is good news. But I'd like to hear he's locked away forever."

While making another pot of coffee, Giulia told them about breaking the lease on the apartment. "The real estate expert thinks I'll be able to get my deposit and the last-month's rent back. As soon as all that's settled, I'll pay you back, Nonno, every penny."

Nonno Tony waved his index finger back and forth clicking his tongue in time with the motion and shaking his head. Nonna shook her head too. "We wanted you out of Vicenza fast. After Tony's beating, who knows what a man like that would do to you. It was money well spent and you can use it for your next one. Or . . ." and Nonna's lips curved into a little smile, "Are you thinking of staying right here with Chuck?"

"Let's hope he gets home safely, then we'll see. He seems to want me to stay, but we still have things to talk about."

"Of course," Nonna replied. "I don't mean to stick my nose in."

"Nonna, don't even think that. It's so good to have you both here with me. I'm so scared he might be lying injured somewhere or worse."

Nonna put her finger to her lips. "Don't say such things."

"It's another nice day," Nonno Tony said, "let's see what's going on in the calles of Venice."

"While you're here, what would you like to do?" Giulia asked Nonna.

"Allora," Nonna said, reminiscing. "Years ago, I sat in a boat in the basin and was fed a delightful supper as we watched fireworks over the water at the Festa del Redentore. You know, the July celebration to honor the end of one of the plagues centuries ago? Now, I'd like to see the inside of that votive church, but I don't think Tony would be interested." She looked at him as he refilled their cups, and he shook his head. She laughed softly. "Maybe we could do that tomorrow because Tony needs to go back for an important estate sale."

"For now, let's walk and see what we see," Tony said. "Maybe we could end up at the Zattere for lunch." But it was almost one when they finished their coffees and cleared away the dishes. By the time they wandered all around Dorsoduro and passed her cursed apartment, the sun was beginning to set.

They sipped coffee as they sat at tables on the Zattere and gazed across the deep Giudecca Canal at two of Palladio's white, temple-like churches. Redentore was near the eastern end of the long Giudecca Island. And from where they sat, San Giorgio—on its own island—appeared to be floating off the tip of Giudecca. Both took on a faint pink glow in the lowering light.

For dinner, they went back to the apartment and Nonna pulled out a dish of lasagna she'd slipped into the fridge to thaw the night before. Later as Giulia pulled up the duvet in Chuck's big bed, she drifted into sleep believing Chuck would make it back.

CHAPTER FORTY

In the morning, Giulia found Nonna drinking coffee alone. "I didn't get a chance to thank Nonno Tony for coming. For everything."

"He knows, Giulia. He knows you love him."

"I hope so. I'm thinking I've been too self-centered to let people know how I feel."

"Are you thinking of Chuck?" Nonna whispered.

"Maybe I am. He's been so supportive of my problems about the apartment and... other things."

Nonna was quiet. She went to the counter and sliced bread for toast.

Giulia heaved a sigh. "Nonna, I need to share more stuff with you."

"Va bene," she said leaving the bread to come sit with Giulia.

"I've never told anyone—anyone—what I'm going to say. Not until I was forced to tell Chuck."

She began where she'd left off on their hike when she'd told of breaking up with Jason. She explained how she had joined two different escort services with the foolish idea of getting revenge from men who used women.

"Then Tom recognized me. After all my struggles trying to decide whether to tell Chuck and how to do it, it took a stranger!"

Nonna said nothing.

"I could tell Chuck wanted to believe me, but he had a hard time. Who wouldn't?"

Nonna still said nothing.

"Nonna, I never had sex with any of those clients."

"Oh child, you didn't have to say that. I believe you. Always have." Her mouth twitched. "You never could lie to me."

"You're right." And Giulia thought of times when she'd tried to fib as a little kid. "Nonna, I accept that Chuck had been with other women before we met. Why is this such a difficult thing for him?"

Nonna got up to put the bread slices in the toaster. "A man is fragile, Giulia. So fragile when it comes to his... *pene*."

Giulia's head whipped around. Nonna's back was to her when she'd said the word for penis. Giulia grinned but said nothing.

"You have brothers. Even when they were babies, they grabbed hold for security."

Giulia snickered softly. "Yes. I remember that."

"Although it happened long before he met you, Chuck still felt threatened." Nonna turned to face her and said, "And surely you've noticed that men often think with their penis before their brain?"

Again Giulia was surprised—pleasantly so—to hear her nonna talk plainly, woman to woman. "I have noticed," she said on a breathy laugh.

"Do you think he's come to terms with the idea now?" Nonna asked.

"Yes. Oh yes. I know so. The last time we spoke about it, I was foolish and tested him one more time about his trust in me."

"What happened?"

"He was furious that I still doubted him and turned it right back on me. He said maybe I *did* have something to hide and stormed out. Oh Nonna, I almost lost him."

"What did you do?" Nonna placed buttered toast in front of Giulia.

"I ran after him and begged."

"Good."

"Good? It was awful."

"But there was fire, right?"

"Yesss," Giulia dragged out the word.

"And later you made up and it was better than before."

Giulia got up went around to hug her. "Nonna, you do understand."

"I do. Now eat up, you'll need strength to guide me over to Redentore."

* * *

As they stepped off the vaporetto in front of the church, Nonna said, "It's funny, Tony still doesn't like it that I was invited to the Festa by another young man. And that was before we began to see each other!"

"The fragile thing, huh?"

"Guess so," Nonna said, laughing and put her arm around Giulia's waist.

It was one of those dazzling mornings in Venice that come when the sun lights up every surface. The ruffled water sparkled and sent glittery shards of crystal into their eyes. The gleaming white facade of Redentore looked like a temple out of old Rome, or, more appropriately, old Greece.

Nonna said, "The door's open, we ought to go in before they close it. You never know when those sacristans will decide to lock up."

"That's for sure," Giulia said. They hustled up the steps and inside.

"What a huge space," Nonna said in a hushed voice.

Giulia spoke in a soft voice, too. No one else was there but the white stucco and grey stone walls seemed to require hushed tones. "I read that Palladio designed this for crowds of pilgrims who'd come for the celebration. I want to attend the event this summer. Want to come with me?"

"Maybe I could. And maybe it's time for Tony to accept my past as well as Chuck has accepted yours."

"Yes." Giulia said, and for the first time, she saw her grandparents as real people with real relationship problems. "I can't imagine a pontoon bridge all the way across the wide Giudecca. It must be a sight," Giulia said.

"I suppose it was amazing back then, but I was so enchanted with the young man who took me in his boat, I don't remember much else," Nonna said with a dreamy look on her face.

"That's the way it should be, right?"

"Right, but don't tell Tony I said that. Now what shall I look for?"

"In my opinion, the artwork isn't as spectacular in here as in other Venetian churches."

They strolled around in the vast empty space. Giulia let Nonna take the lead.

"Finished? Giulia said.

"Yes, I expect so."

"Before we leave, I want to show you something strange in the sacristy."

"Va bene. Let's find it."

No one was in the large room either. Giulia followed along waiting for Nonna to stop in her tracks. When Nonna did, she gasped.

Eleven life-sized wax heads of brothers of the Order of Capuchins were arranged on the top of a large cabinet that ran along two sides of the room. The individual faces had realistic, glass eyes and thin beards that looked like real hair. Each one—encased in a glass capsule like a bell jar—had a title card attached.

Even though she'd known what to expect, Giulia still shivered, seeing the strange heads. She remembered the crypt of a Capuchin church in Rome decorated with skulls and bones from thousands of dead monks.

"Mio Dio!" Nonna stopped when she came upon a head of a woman, Santa Veronica di Giuliani. "She must have been outstanding to be honored here among all these 'worthy' men," and Nonna made quotation marks in the air. "Her title card reads," and she spelled out the letters *Ord. Capuccinarum abbatissa.* "An abbess?" Nonna asked, turning to Giulia.

Giulia nodded. "After seeing all this, I read up on her. She *was* an abbess of her convent. You know about Saint Francis's sister order?"

Nonna nodded. "The Poor Clares."

"Veronica joined the Poor Clares at a very young age and was about seventeen when she suffered stigmata. The wounds were almost exactly the same that Francis had, except hers appeared five hundred years after he died."

"Enough," Nonna said and shivered.

"What do you say, we find a steaming cup of cappuccino in honor of the Capuchins and this macabre place? I know a little bar here on Giudecca. From there we can sit and look at the fantastic skyline of Venice."

"Excellent idea," Nonna said.

* * *

Monday morning, Nonna's train was scheduled to leave twelve minutes before Giulia's. They hugged one more time.

"Thank you for coming. Will you thank Nonno Tony again for me?"

"Of course."

Giulia pulled back to look into Nonna's eyes and said, "Thank you most of all for listening. I'm sorry I dumped on you like that."

"Dump? No, child. We all need someone to share heavy times—happy times, too. For years, I've had my friend, Angelina." She looked straight into Giulia's eyes, "And you can rest easy, your story stays with me."

"Thanks, Nonna. I've needed to tell someone for so long. Even with special friends, I resisted letting my barriers down."

"You've told Chuck and now me, those walls may keep tumbling down."

Giulia nodded slowly. "Old habits are hard to break. But maybe."

"Best I get on board. Call me the minute you hear about that wonderful man in your life."

* * *

As soon as her classes were finished, Giulia hurried toward the bus for Vicenza to catch the next train to Venice. Her head was down, and she didn't hear her name before she ran right into Officer Ryland.

"Sorry to block your path, but it seemed the only way."

"Oh, excuse me, Colonel Ryland."

"Rob, remember?"

"Yes, Rob. I was hoping to catch the 12:12 for Venice."

"How about I drive you all the way? I've got some news."

"About Chuck? Is he safe? Is he alive?" She barely stopped herself from grabbing Ryland by the collar. "Where is he?"

"He's in a rehab center in Venice."

"Rehab? What for?" She was gasping for breath. "Is he okay?"

"I - don't - really - know," he said spacing his words. "But I'd think so if he's in a rehab."

"Why not a military hospital? How can that be? What does that mean? Is the military giving up on him?"

"No. God no. It wouldn't mean that. There's got to be a good reason why he's in a private facility. I'll take you there. Let's get to the parking lot and be on our way. I'll answer what I can. You want to see him, don't you?"

"Oh yes. Yes, of course."

He led her to a dark-green Fiat Punto like Chuck's. In spite of her worry, she smiled at how Chuck looked whenever he crawled into his canary-sized car.

"So?" She said as Ryan pulled onto the highway for Venice.

"This morning the base commander received a call from Landstuhl saying that Karl Frederick Novak was being transported from their trauma center to the Elena Cornaro Recovery Center in Venice." He handed her a copy of the message. "It's my understanding that this rehab is in Campo San Zaccaria. Do you know it?"

"I know San Zaccaria, but the only place I've seen that could be anything like that is a *casa di cura,* a nursing home."

"I sure don't know. Someone dragged me to Zaccaria once but

don't remember much about the campo."

"Strange."

"Yeah," he said. "Wait a minute. There's a facility for the Italian Military Police in that campo."

"Yes, the Carabinieri. I've always thought it ironic that when Napoleon suppressed the San Zaccaria nunnery, their quarters went straight from being female religious cells to male military ones."

"Hunh! I'll bet a lot of snide jokes still make the rounds about that," Ryland said. "We'll know more soon. I have a permit to go check on him, and I'm taking you in on my permit."

"Thanks, Rob. Thanks for thinking of me."

"I'm sure Chuck would rather see your pretty face than my mug." He fished a card out of his shirt pocket and handed it to her. "Take a look and see if you can make out exactly where it is."

She studied it as they drove. It gave the name and address of the facility with a little map sketched on the back.

"It looks like the place I thought was a nursing home." She sat back and stared at the card.

"He means a lot, huh?"

She nodded. Her voice was raspy. "We've had ups and downs lately but now this . . ." and her voice trailed off.

"Hang in there, hon. It won't be long now."

She looked at him and smiled, but her eyes were filling. She blinked hard and turned to the window, straightened her spine and took a deep breath.

"What's Landstuhl? A German hospital?"

"No, American. In the city of Landstuhl, Germany. The biggest military hospital outside the States. Has a great reputation for trauma cases, coming from the Middle East mostly."

"Was he in Afghanistan? Iraq?" she asked.

"Honestly, no clue. Maybe neither. Sorry, I still don't know."

"So the hospital on our base isn't much, huh?"

"Nah. It's little more than an infirmary. Maybe you've noticed earth movers tearing up the ground beside it. A bigger, better one's scheduled to open in 2006. Not likely they'll make that date, three years isn't much time for the government. Hey!" He struck his forehead with his palm. "That might be why Chuck's being sent to the rehab."

* * *

When Giulia entered Chuck's room, she sucked in a breath and almost staggered backward. He was so thin and ashen with IVs attached to his hand and arm and a monitor blinking beside his bed. She felt relieved he couldn't see her shocked face. He looked wasted. Would she lose him now that they'd found each other? She pulled up a chair and sat beside his bed, taking his hand and began to squeeze his fingers.

Chuck's eyes fluttered when she squeezed them. "That's good," the nurse said as she came in on silent rubber soles. "Keep doing that and talk to him. He's not in a *deep* coma."

She talked about his score on something called a Glasgow Scale. Giulia had been squeezing different fingers off and on since she'd come in at one o'clock. It was four-thirty now. She hadn't noticed when Ryland had left. She should have let him know how grateful she was. She'd be sure to call him; he'd want to know Chuck's progress. Or lack of it. *Oh no! Can't think that way.*

There didn't seem to be a hard rule about "family only" here. There'd certainly been no problem with Chuck going into Nonno's hospital room. *I should call them. Marc and Marlowe, too.* She hated to leave his side for a minute but slipped out to make quick calls. She didn't want to miss the doctor who was expected around five.

Giulia grabbed a cup of coffee and went straight back to the room. She held the cup close to his nose, hoping the aroma might stimulate him. So far, nothing. He remained quiet. She talked to him, telling about Ryland bringing her here and about Nonna and Nonno Tony staying at the apartment. But no response. A different nurse shooed her out to take his vital signs and test him again on that scale. She heard violent coughing from his room and started to go back in. The nurse was firm and said, "*No, no, signorina, non ancora.* Not yet."

Finally, his coughing subsided and the nurse came out carrying one of those small metal pans used for people to spit or vomit in. Giulia followed her down the hall and asked about the coughing.

"He's been in an explosion," the nurse said. "Suffered from smoke inhalation with possible damage to his bronchial tubes. Every couple of hours, we try to aspirate *porcheria,* gunk, out of his system."

"So that's what made him cough?"

"Yes."

Giulia's face crumpled.

"It's going to be all right, signorina, coughing is good even if it sounds horrible. His points on the Glasgow are pretty good, and the doctor thinks the lingering coma is more about the smoke damage than the head injury. He's probably not getting enough oxygen."

That was scary. Giulia knew the brain needed oxygen. When she'd first arrived, he hadn't had oxygen cannulas in his nose, but now he did. Was that a bad sign? She felt frantic and couldn't leave his side. Finally, the doctor came in to check him and sat with Giulia.

She introduced herself as Dr. Cornaro. Tiny, not five-feet tall, with short blond hair and dark brown eyes. She didn't look much older than Giulia, maybe in her late thirties. Energy radiated from her wiry body.

"He's had a head injury but the results of a CT indicated no bleeding in the brain. The swelling has gone down and his Glasgow scores are improving." She frowned a little. "Of course, we can't ever know for sure, but things look good for your husband."

"He's not my husband, but… I care for him."

"I can tell." She put her hand on Giulia's shoulder. "And from my nurses' reports, you've been diligently squeezing his hands and talking to him. Smart to change his hands from time to time. Those are important stimulations for him right now. We all try to do that for our patients but with your perseverance, well, I can't tell you the *good* you are doing."

"What else can I do?"

"You can get a bite to eat and take a walk. Then come back and start all over again."

"Please. Can you tell me what this scale is, and what's a CT?"

"CT merely means Computerized Tomography. As I said, it's a test to measure bleeding in the skull. And the Glasgow Coma Scale is a very useful tool. If used correctly, it's an excellent way to assess the level of a coma. Even better, it's non invasive. For example, when you squeeze his hand and his eyes flutter, he gets two points. If his eyes open or move to a loud voice, he gets three, and if he does it spontaneously he gets four. There are points for various verbal and motor responses. When you squeeze each finger separately, as I saw you do, I'd say he gets four more points when he reacts to the pain—no matter how slight. And his toes. Clever! "

"How many points does he need to be awake and oriented?"

"A fully awake person has a score of fifteen."

Giulia stood up and looked down at him. She heaved a big sigh. "He's a long way from fifteen isn't he?"

"Right now, yes, but occasionally patients wake up all of a sudden and we can stop counting. I've used this scale for many years. You might say it's my specialty." Her brown eyes shone with what Giulia thought of as a dedicated light. She moved closer to Giulia and touched her shoulder again. "Go now. Eat and walk. We need to aspirate him."

Giulia started to rise but stopped and said, "He didn't have oxygen going into his nose when I got here at one. Later, when I came back in, he did. What does that mean?"

"That you're too observant for your own good." She smiled. "It means that we use oxygen for a time, then take it away, then bring it back. That way we can assess his situation and also stimulate his bronchial tubes to function better on their own."

"I see."

Dr. Cornaro smiled. "No, you probably don't, but it *is* standard procedure. Now go. Come back in an hour. We'll take care of him."

CHAPTER FORTY-ONE

"Marlowe! Thank you for coming." They hugged outside the front door of the rehab.

"How is he?"

"About the same. They asked me to leave for a while and assured me he's moving in the right direction, but I hate not being beside him every minute."

"I can imagine. Come on let's walk, you look pale," Marlowe said. When they sat on a bench along the Riva overlooking the basin, Marlowe handed her a package. "I brought you the latest Donna Leon to read while you're with him."

"Oh thanks, Marlowe." Giulia hugged her again. She appreciated Marlowe's gift but couldn't focus on anything but Chuck's situation. "Chuck's doctor measures his progress with something called the Glasgow Coma Scale." She explained what she knew about it.

"Marlowe, when you get time, would you find out more about his doctor, Luisa Cornaro? Does she know what she's talking about? When I get home, I can't seem to concentrate on the computer."

"I'll get on it right away."

"Maybe more about the coma scale too?"

Marlowe nodded. "Glasgow, right? Scotland?"

Giulia just shook her head. "I'm going back. It's been almost an hour, I doubt *they* need an hour. The doctor probably thought I did."

"Shall I come sit with you?"

"Yes... No... I don't know, Marlowe. All I want to do is talk to him, pinch him, squeeze his hands... maybe later, okay?"

"Sure. Marc will want to come, too. He's in Germany working on a construction-equipment deal, but he'll be back tonight. He'll be thrilled to hear Chuck's good news. It sounds encouraging."

"Maybe."

"I'll print out whatever I find about his doctor. Surely she knows what she's doing or the military wouldn't have sent him to her."

"I hope so," Giulia said, but her shoulders drooped.

"Hang in there. Tomorrow, I'll drop by as soon as I finish classes. Agree?"

Giulia nodded and watched her leave, but felt alone and helpless. No, not alone. Her grandparents would be with her in a minute, and Marlowe and Marc, were "with her" too. But squeezing fingers didn't seem enough. What *else* could she do? She stayed beside his bed until the doctor woke her out of a doze at nine and insisted she go home.

As she walked through the quiet calles, she breathed in the chilly air. Then all at once, she turned and ran back to the rehab. She'd forgotten to tell him she loved him. She wanted him to hear it no matter what level he'd comprehend it. The nurse at the door didn't want to let her back in, but when Giulia told her why, she smiled and opened for her. Giulia felt much better on the way home knowing she'd left him with a positive thought. She needed to stay positive herself until Chuck was really back with her. At least she knew he was safe and good people were caring for him.

She stood on the top of the Rialto Bridge for a moment and looked at the Grand Canal as it wound toward the most elegant palazzos in all of Venice. She thought of the Gritti Palazzo at the far end. Tom! She'd forgotten to get in touch with him. She hurried home to find the card he'd put in her hand the day he left. If he's in Brussels now, he might come here soon. She hadn't used the small purse since Tom was here. She grabbed it off the shelf in "her" room and looked in the small pocket with a zipper. There it was. She dialed the number.

"Giulia! To what do I owe this call? Everything all right?"

"No, nothing's right. Tom . . ." the words stuck in her throat but she choked them out, "Chuck's in a coma."

"How did that happen? Where is he? What's the prognosis?"

"He's here in Venice at a private Rehab in Campo San Zac-caria. Can you imagine the military shipping him here from a big hospital in Germany and—"

"Landstuhl?"

"That's the one." She told him what she knew hoping he could come.

"Of course, I'll come. You needn't meet me, I'll find my way to Zaccaria. Give me the name of the facility again."

"Thanks. I know he'd want you here, and I could use a big shoulder."

"You've got it. I'm guessing things are better between the two of you."

"Yes. We were still working on... but yes, definitely better."

"That's good. Okay, let me get on the horn for reservations. See you soon. Hold on, he's a tough one. He'll be grabbing you before you know it."

* * *

It was Tuesday. Giulia hurried to the rehab. *No negative thoughts. He needs positive energy around him.* She got an idea and began to jog. When she arrived at seven, the nurse, who usually took care of Chuck, told her he'd uttered a few words.

"They weren't understandable, but—"

"What were they?" Giulia interrupted.

"One sounded like 'Chools.' *Senta,* what is your name?"

"Giulia."

"That could be it. The "chu" could be "giu," don't you think?"

"And the other word?"

"'Zomash' or maybe 'Zahmash.' Does that mean anything to you?"

"Zahmash? His best friend is Tom. His Polish name is To-masz," and Giulia pronounced it the way Chuck had taught her, "Tomahsh."

"Hmm, pretty close. Maybe he'll say them again."

Would Chuck say Tom's Polish name? Then she remembered hearing him call Tom a "blue ass." A private joke. *Close enough.*

"The important thing," Doctor Cornaro said, walking into the room, "is he's trying to speak. Makes no difference whether it's comprehensible to us. This is terrific news!"

"I hope so. I called his best friend, Tom. He's coming from Brussels."

"All good. Now you step out for a few minutes, while we check him out and see if we can aspirate more residue from his bronchial tubes."

It seemed she had to step out a lot. But the doctor had been so cooperative and supportive, Giulia didn't want to rock the boat. As she walked down the hallway toward the small cafeteria, the aroma of fresh coffee floated toward her. She picked up her pace, realizing she'd forgotten all about eating this morning. She carried a cup of coffee and a brioche back to Chuck's room.

Finally, all the medical people had left—at least for a while. She put down her coffee and half-eaten pastry and moved her chair close to his bed into a position where she could see anyone coming down the hallway.

"Okay, Karlo with a K," she said in a loud voice. "It's time you do something to let *me* know *you* know I'm here!"

Did he squeeze her hand? Did his eyelids almost open? She wasn't sure. She didn't have much time. She slid a hand under the covers and gradually moved along his thigh toward his cock. She was determined to find out if he'd react if she touched him there. She placed her fingers lightly on his soft, lifeless penis. She didn't remember seeing it—or feeling it—this soft before. Then it changed. Only a little, but there was a definite quiver. Was it only an involuntary response or did he sense he was being fondled? She caressed him again, and knew for sure.

She heard him drag in air and wheeze out a word that sounded like "Sahyaz." She leaned closer and squeezed his cock a little more. He rasped again, "Sahyaz."

Was that "say yes?"

"Karlo," she almost shouted. His eyes opened for a second. "Karlo, what's the question?"

With great effort, he raised off the pillow—his bed was already inclined—and rasped out "Chulsa! Chulsa?" And he coughed violently.

A nurse came rushing in and shooed her toward the door. "Chul?" he coughed out again.

Another nurse came in and pushed her toward the door. But before going out, Giulia turned and yelled, "YES! YES! YES! " Maybe that would revive him even more. Was he asking if she loved him? If she'd stay with him? Her mind was going crazy. But for sure, he was *not* injured in that part of his anatomy!

Giulia hovered outside the doorway and heard the ugly sucking sound of the aspirator. She could almost feel that dreadful tube going down his throat and needed to gag. She swallowed hard and took a deep breath.

"Whatever you did in there," his nurse said as she came charging out, "he coughed up what we'd been trying to get out of him since he's been here." The nurse carried the metal pan again, this time with a cloth over it. "A big, old black hunk of stuff. Want to see it?"

Backing away, Giulia put out both hands. "No!"

The nurse laughed. "Don't blame you. He'll sleep easier now. We shot him with a mild sedative. You can go in but he won't be aware for a few hours."

Giulia slipped in and stood as close to him as possible. She leaned over to listen to him breathe. Then straightened to peer intently. He did look different, didn't he? He seemed to be breathing easier. She inhaled deeply herself then checked the color in his cheeks. She kissed one lightly. There *was* more color wasn't there? She stared down at this big man who had stolen her heart.

She stood that way for a long time. Finally, someone touched her shoulder. The doctor again.

"The worst is over. He'll make it now. Go home and rest."

It was eleven in the morning. She didn't know how long she'd stood there immobile watching him sleep. If she didn't move soon, she'd keel over like a dying tree in the forest.

"When you come back this afternoon, we'll talk." The doctor gave Giulia a gentle shove. "Now go."

Giulia leaned over one more time, slipped her fingers through his hair and lightly kissed his lips. "I love you, Karlo with a K."

Maybe there was a slight smile on his face as she dragged herself away.

CHAPTER FORTY-TWO

Giulia dropped everything, stripped, showered and fell into bed but not before setting her alarm. She didn't want to miss Doctor Cornaro at three.

At the sound of both alarm and phone, she dragged herself awake. It was two already. She punched the alarm off and lurched across the room to grab her bag. Had something happened to Chuck? She fished out the phone but the call had already gone to voicemail. She let out a breath of relief to see it was from Nancy. Two other calls were also from her. Coffee first.

It would be five in the morning in Eugene, but Nancy often went in early to call the East Coast for the latest data. She'd have her favorite croissant and latte from The Beanery across from her office.

"Tell me your story," Nancy began as she always did.

"Oh no you don't. You're the one who called three times within one hour."

"Yes, but I have a hunch you've got the best story. So?"

"Where to start? Too much since we last spoke."

"Start with that hunk of yours?"

"The truth is, Nancy, he is my hunk. I've fallen hard."

"Tell me what I don't know."

"What? Last time, I told you I had no intention of getting involved."

"I know. So, what's happened since you insisted you weren't involved?"

"You smartass," Giulia laughed. "So. You knew I'd moved in with him until I found my own apartment. Right?"

Nancy made a yes sound while chewing.

"Well, I found my so-called dream apartment and—"

"On Rio what's it Raphael?"

"Oh Nance. That was a nightmare, and I'm back with Chuck. But in the meantime, we had a bad fight and... Oh geez, I don't have time right now. I'm due at the rehab in twenty-five minutes."

"Rehab? What kind of fight was it, for God's sake?"

"Not that kind. Chuck left on a mission and came back in a coma. Been that way for at least a week, but I only found out yesterday. Today, what's today?"

"Tuesday, May twenty-seventh according to my calendar," Nancy said.

"Yes, Tuesday. This morning he started to come out of it. Anyway, I've got an appointment with his doctor at three and—"

"We *do* have a lot to catch up on. I'll be quick. Your Fiat stock is rising, and I recommend you sell some if not all. Papers are coming by Fed Ex. The gist of my call is that you are a rich woman!"

"That's nice," Giulia said. "I'll call you later. My... my man needs me."

"Zowee! Never thought I'd hear those words from your mouth. I'm thrilled for you. Have you told him everything?"

"About the Fiat shares?" Giulia asked.

"Not exactly. I mean . . ." Nancy hesitated for a moment and then charged on, "I mean did you tell him about Julietta?"

"W-w-hat?!" Giulia screamed into the phone. *How'd she know about the Service?*

"Calm down, sugar plum. You weren't the only one doing the vetting when we first met. I checked you out, too."

"Oh." There was a long pause. "You've known all along?"

"The important question is does *he* know?" Nancy asked.

"Yes. He knows."

"G-R-R-E-A-T! That's all I need for now. Go see your man, but don't you dare forget to call me back any time day or night."

"I will, Nance. I will. So you've known all this time?"

"Of course. My momma didn't raise no dummy even if we

were trailer trash. I knew you couldn't be depositing that much money as a student just from scrimping and saving. I wished you'd felt you could tell me back then, but what the hey. You had your reasons."

"Thanks for hanging with me, Nance."

"What are friends for, huh? Go to him. But this time I get all the info straight from the horse's mouth. Every juicy morsel."

"Love ya," Giulia said but already the line was dead. Tears rushed into her eyes, and this time, she didn't fight them. Not tears of grief or guilt, but tears of a different kind. A joy she never imagined she'd have. People loved her just as she was.

* * *

In the rehab cafeteria, Dr. Cornaro was gentle but continued to press Giulia to find what she'd done to cause Chuck to cough so violently. When she finally told her, the doctor seemed disappointed as she lifted her cup of tea. "I'd been hoping it would be a method we could use with other patients." She grinned, set her cup down and laid her hand on Giulia's. "It might not be considered accepted practice by most of my colleagues—particularly the male ones." She lightly pinched Giulia's hand and laughed aloud. "But in certain cases, I'll probably encourage the... *the procedure.*"

At that, Giulia laughed for the first time in days, weeks maybe? After a moment, though, she sobered. "You said it was about over, but he's still not really awake."

"*Pazienza, cara, pazienza,*" the doctor said. "It all takes time. This can be the most difficult period for the patient and loved ones."

* * *

Wednesday morning. Ordinarily she'd be leaving to teach, but instead, she was heading back to the rehab. A friend had agreed to fill in for her. She'd told Giulia that most people on the base knew about Chuck and his coma. That meant they also knew about their relationship. They hadn't exactly tried to keep it a secret, and the Camp Ederle community—including those off the base—was like a little town. Few secrets can be kept in a village.

Rob Ryland told her the men in Chuck's unit were chafing to come visit, but their superiors wouldn't allow them yet. They'd all made it back, although Gene Linch had a broken leg. He was the man Chuck had dragged out of the building moments before the final explosion. No wonder he had so much gunk in his lungs.

When she reached his room, he wasn't in his bed. It was empty and the bedding all gone. In a panic, she ran toward the nurse's station. On her way, she bumped into his regular nurse. She steadied Giulia and said, "*Calma. Non si preoccupi del Generale Novak.* Relax, don't worry yourself about General Novak. We moved him to another room for his final recovery. Come along."

Giulia let out a huge sigh of relief. "How is he?"

"Agitated. In and out of consciousness. That happens. He's asking for you. I said you'd be here but I'm not sure he believed me."

When she got to his room, he was propped up and wearing the pajamas she'd bought after the doctor said he'd need them for walking the halls. They were crummy because she'd rushed into Standa—the K-Mart-style department store—and grabbed the first ones large enough. At least they were pale blue and not a horrid orange plaid, but to her, he'd look marvelous in anything.

His eyes were closed and his mouth was hanging open a little, but those lips—those full lips— begged to be kissed. So she did. His eyes flew open, looked straight into hers and kissed back.

"You're back," she said leaning over him.

"Giulia! Giulia!" He took hold of her hands and held them tightly, too tightly, but she wouldn't have pulled away for any reason. He looked into her eyes, sighed and closed his.

She waited. After a moment, he opened his eyes and squeezed again.

"Chuck, don't you dare disappear on me again." She was

certain he could feel heated daggers burning into him. His eyes looked like a startled woodland creature caught in headlights.

"I... I left a note," he stammered.

"Thank God for that. I was frantic. Your note said you'd call."

"I couldn't. Couldn't say more—still can't."

"Of course I know *that*. But you *knew* it was coming. You knew for a few days and didn't trust me enough to—"

"Nothing to do with trust," and he coughed, but struggled through more coughs to say, "protect you."

Coughing or not, she didn't let up. "Some protection! If I'm going to live with you, it's only fair—"

"Absolutely. As my roommate," and it seemed he couldn't keep a little grin from emerging, "as my partner, that is, you have every right to be on a need-to-know-basis."

"More!" She grabbed his face and forced him to look straight into her eyes. "If we're apartment partners—bed partners—surely I rank higher than your unit members. They're the ones on a 'need-to-know-basis.' And she spit out those words in a brittle voice.

"I love it when you're bossy."

"After the best lovemaking ever, you left me with a... a damned note."

"Best... YET," he said. "Come here." He dragged her onto his bed to lie beside him then gave a huge sigh and dropped into a deep sleep. She lay in an uncomfortable position but felt content. She tried to lie quietly but finally had to re-adjust her hips. He opened his eyes and pulled her closer.

She squirmed up to straddle him, and said, "It's been a long, *long* ten days since you vanished, and *Mister* Novak, you've got lots of explaining to do."

"I love you, too," he said grinning, and that dimple on the right side of his cheek appeared melting her heart.

"Oh God, Chuck. I thought I'd lost you."

"Bad, huh?"

"Worse than bad." And the tears started to form. "I didn't know how... I couldn't live without you."

"Tell me."

She leaned back to glare at him, "You're a greedy bastard." She sniffled and wiped her nose with her sleeve, then started to grin.

"I am," he said. "But look what I had to do to hear you say those words."

"Do you remember anything?" She worried because what she'd read about comas and post traumatic amnesia said the *length* of the amnesia gave a better idea of brain damage than how deep or long the coma was.

"It's all in the report. Let's talk more about how important I am to you."

She smiled. "There's no report yet, silly, you just woke up. Do you remember where you were and what happened?"

"How can I make a complete report until I get answers from you."

She gave up and leaned down to hug him. "Am I too heavy for you?"

"Nah. Girl weight. No problem."

That did it. Hot tears dampened his new pajamas. They felt stiff and scratchy. She should have washed them first, but when he put his arms around her, she let that go. When she raised her head, she thought she saw tears glistening in his eyes, and she kissed his stubbly cheek.

"Ho there! Is this standard hospital procedure?" Tom said as he walked into the room. "A woman in your bed, ol' buddy? How'd you pull this off?"

"You got here fast." Giulia hopped off Chuck's bed and gave Tom a hug.

"Fickle woman." Chuck grumbled.

Tom and Chuck joshed with each other. But within ten minutes, Chuck was fading. He invited Tom to stay at his apartment with Giulia, but Tom declined. He'd already booked into a small hotel near the Stazione; he knew how fragile a man feels when his body's weak.

"Next time, ol' man. I'm going to take Giulia for lunch, then I'll be back."

"What can I bring you?" Giulia asked Chuck.

"Real clothes. I saw my rear in these PJs. My ass looked lopsided."

Tom laughed. "'Vanity of vanities, all is vanity.'"

She laughed, too, enjoying the novelty of humor.

"Don't forget a belt. I think I've lost weight." And Chuck drifted off before they were out of the room.

"He has lost weight," Giulia said with a little frown on her face.

"Don't worry, he'll be whipping up one of his rich frittatas in no time."

CHAPTER FORTY-THREE

"You're looking better, friend," Tom said.

"Breathing without tubes makes a whale of a difference."

"Was it a bad mission?"

"The worst. But maybe I've seen too much. I'm getting out."

"Interesting," Tom said and pulled up a chair.

"My service obligation ends November first. Thought I'd re-up one more time to train and prep, but no more. They sucked me back in—again. Thing is, my heart isn't in it anymore. I might not make it out the next time, and with Giulia—"

"Yeah, she's a good reason to get out. Teri's ultimatum about Ops was a blessing in disguise. It gave me the momentum to move all the way out of the Force. Like you, I hadn't planned it, but man, I haven't missed it," he said.

"Neither will I. Don't need that adrenalin rush anymore. Got plenty with Giulia around."

"I can imagine."

"Not sure you can," Chuck said with a broad grin on his face. "The nurse assigned to coddle me revealed Giulia's method for waking me up." He laughed then started to cough. Tom hopped up to hand him a cup of ice water from the tray that had been shoved too far from his bed.

After Chuck settled down, Tom said, "And?"

"That little wench slipped in here when no one was around and reached under the covers—"

"Checked to see what other parts were in a coma?"

"Something like that. Medics usually stick your toe with a sharp needle. She had other ideas."

"Hands on approach, huh?"

"What's funny is the doc seemed to think it was a good idea."

"This doctor must be special for the military to put you in her care. What about her?"

"Giulia seems to think she walks on water," Marlowe said as she and Marc came in.

Chuck started to introduce them, but Marlowe took over. "Save your throat, Chuck."

"Your doctor, Luisa Cornaro, got her medical degree from University of Bologna. She'd lost her younger brother to head trauma and was determined to prevent that from happening to others. She worked with the Swiss Air Rescue group for a few years where she got hands-on experience with head traumas and learned about a diagnostic tool called the Glasgow Coma Scale."

Marlowe continued, "She tried to work with the Italian Rescue group but they weren't well organized—big surprise. They used private companies for rescue in the Italian Alps, and she met resistance with these groups because she was a woman—again no surprise."

"Here we go again. Men getting a bad rap," Marc sighed.

"I'm merely stating the facts, Marc."

"I know, Sprout. Just pulling your chain."

Undaunted, Marlowe continued. "Your doctor, Chuck, ended up studying with the people at uh…" From her knapsack, she pulled papers out and read from one. "Here it is. She studied at the Womack Army Medical Center at Fort Bragg, North Carolina. That's where the coma scale was devised." Marlowe gave them a quick example of the point system and put her papers away. "I'm guessing your doc's reputation is why the military experts sent you here."

"Thanks, Marlowe," Chuck said. "I appreciate the information."

"You can thank Giulia. She asked me to research it for her. Where is she?"

"Resting, I hope. She's been here almost as much as I have," Chuck said.

"When will they spring you?" Marc asked.

"Soon, dammit, or I'll spring myself. Giulia agreed to bring real clothes. As soon as I can maneuver these halls without gasping for air, I'm outta here."

"You look a helluva lot better since yesterday," Marc said then turned to Tom. "Tom, your time's probably limited. We can pester Chuck later."

"I'll walk out with you," Tom said. "Back in a jif." But Chuck's eyes were already drooping. They all stepped into the small campo and walked toward the round-shouldered facade of the old church of San Zaccaria.

"Tom?" Marc said turning toward the somber man beside him. "We'd like you to come to our wedding reception on June 14th. Chuck's talked a lot about you, and I feel I already know you. Chuck ought to be up and about by then. Could you make it?"

"Could be."

"We got married in February," Marlowe added, "but Marc's family is planning a whoop-tee-do. Ought to be fun."

"Thanks for the invite. I'm on a new job and need to see what's scheduled. But it sounds grand."

"Guaranteed," she said. "The Baroviers take family festas seriously."

"I'll do my best. That's less than three weeks away. I'll want to check on Chuck anyway. I'm glad to finally meet you, Marc. Even more pleasant to meet *you*, Marlowe." He gave her a small hug, shook Marc's hand and they left.

When Tom slipped back into Chuck's room, he thought he was asleep and started to back out. Chuck croaked, "Don't go away mad."

"How are you doing, really?"

"Gettin' there."

"And Giulia? Your devoted slave?"

"We're in a better place."

"Any doubts left?"

"Not on my part."

"What's that mean?"

"She had—or maybe still has—doubts about my possible doubts. Jeez, relationships aren't easy."

Tom guffawed. "Elementary, dear Watson. What's going on with her place versus yours? Obviously things have changed since she's back with you."

Chuck gulped more water and gave him a recap of her cursed apartment.

"Is she with you permanently?"

"We were working on that before I shipped out. Her enthusiasm for finding another place had waned, and I was trying to take advantage of that."

The nurse came in to check his vitals.

After the nurse left, Tom continued. "Guess she's had this idea of a special Venetian apartment for ages, huh?"

"God yes. Now, though, it seems fruitless to keep looking since it's ninety-nine percent sure we both want to be together."

"It's none of my business, but—"

"You're right. But you won't let a little thing like that interfere."

Tom punched Chuck lightly. "You're going to get my two-cents worth."

"I'm all ears."

"It's simple. When you get back on your feet, why don't both of you search for another apartment—"

"A neutral place?" Chuck asked.

"Yeah. How'd you know I was going to say that?"

"Give me a break. I've had nothing but time to think on this. I like my place but like her better. I'll move anywhere, but first, I've got to pin her down."

Tom muffled a laugh.

"What's so funny?"

"Just thinking about that little gal sneaking a feel to check out your tool."

Chuck raised himself up a little, "And *your* tool will be in great trouble if you let on to her that you know." Then he coughed again.

"Lie down, man. Rest. I need to shop for a couple friends in Brussels."

Giulia walked in at that moment. Tom gave her a brief hug and headed on out. With her back to him, Tom mimed zipping his lips and left.

"How're you doing?" she said. "You've had a ton of visitors. And the guys in your unit are chafing to come. Are you up to it tomorrow?"

"Yeah, I think so. Short visits anyway, except for you."

"Did I tell you Colonel Ryland was a big help? And very kind."

"He's a good man. A loyal friend." He coughed, and she leaned across him to pick up the cup of water. Her breast brushed against him.

"Want a sip?"

He nuzzled her and whispered, "I want a sip of you today and everyday."

"Are you talking about permanent sipping privileges?"

"Damn straight I am." He began coughing, violently.

"Pulling your old tricks again?" his nurse said to Giulia. "Let's see what he brings up this time."

While Giulia waited in the hall, Lieutenant de Stefano of the Carabinieri appeared. After a brief chat, he followed her into Chuck's room.

CHAPTER FORTY-FOUR

I'm sorry to bother you, Major General Novak, but Ms. Cavinato assured me you were well enough for a quick visit."

"Absolutely," Chuck said and raised himself into a more upright position.

"First, Signor Botteri is in custody and won't be free until he and his henchmen are brought to trial. And the men who were trailing you, Ms. Cavinato, have also been captured."

Giulia's cheeks puffed as she blew a big breath out of her mouth. "It'll feel strange to walk around not cringing at every shadow. The thought of being in that man's clutches…" She shuddered. Chuck reached for her hand.

"I'm surprised that a man like Botteri can't pull strings to get himself free or at least out on bail," Chuck said.

"Not this time. As far as I know, he has no access to his many *avvocati*, lawyers, and he and his followers are being held far away. As I mentioned, a task force has been working on an issue that involves more than Botteri and his petty hoodlums."

"Thank you for coming to tell us, Lieutenant," Giulia said.

"And I want to thank you for protecting Giulia until they were all caught," Chuck said.

"You're welcome. Are there any questions?"

"Yes," Giulia said. "Do you know if Botteri's thugs broke into my apartment in Vicenza?"

"Oh. Almost forgot. Other than the fingerprints the police expected to find, like yours and your landlords', there were three different sets. Two were from those men who were trailing you. They've been in trouble time after time. It's strange Botteri used them. But the third set, found on a tube of toothpaste, are unknown." He shrugged in disbelief at that. "The police are still trying to find a match for those."

Chuck and Giulia exchanged glances. They knew whose prints they were but couldn't prove it without admitting Chuck had broken into Ogle's place.

Di Stefano caught their silent communication. He seemed to hesitate but then asked, "Do you know whose prints that third set might be?"

"We only have a suspicion," Chuck said. "No proof." Di Stefano was quick and Chuck hoped he wouldn't think Giulia was involved in another crime he ought to investigate. "He's connected with the American base and is in custody in the States for something else."

"Well, then," the Lieutenant said. "Maybe your lives can return to normal."

"Hope so. And thanks again for your protection," Giulia said.

"You have my card. If you feel threatened again, don't hesitate to call."

"I won't."

"Use this case number." He took another card and wrote on the reverse. "That will speed things up."

He left and Giulia collapsed into the chair beside his bed.

After a long silence Chuck said, "Micina?"

"Hmm?"

"Before I leave here, we need to talk."

"You need rest. We'll have plenty of time when you're home."

"No. I'll be filling out form after form about the mission not to mention going in for oral reports. Then I'll start paperwork to get out of the Force. My tour's over November first."

"So you're going to do it after all? I admit I'm pleased, but aren't you too young to retire?"

"Not too young to get away from more disasters or—like this last time—avoiding one by the skin of my teeth. I've given enough and served more than my twenty years."

"But what will you do with yourself when you get your energy back?"

"I have an idea or two, and I'll tell you about it, but right now, I have a much bigger worry and—"

"In your fit condition, Dr. Cee says you'll be back to normal in no time."

"I know. Soon as I can work out regularly, my lung capacity will be back."

"Then what's your problem?"

"Come closer." She did, and he lifted her up to lie beside him again, putting her head in the crook of his arm.

"What can I do to help?" she asked and squirmed closer.

"You can marry me."

She stopped squirming and lay speechless.

"Will you marry me?" He whispered and raised up to look at her. "I'll get down on my knee—"

"Yes."

"Giulia, if that's what you want, I'll get on my knee right now," and he pushed the cover back to slide out of bed.

"Chu-uck," she said dragging his name into two syllables as she pulled him back. "Yes. Yes. I will. I already shouted yes day before yesterday."

"You did? To me?"

"Of course to you," she laughed. "You kept saying words that sounded like 'Say yes.' You said them over and over, so I shouted back, 'Yes. Yes. Yes.'"

Chuck was quiet for a long time. "I thought I dreamed it."

They lay on his narrow hospital bed holding each other. He nuzzled her ear, she kissed his neck, and both fell asleep.

* * *

When Chuck woke up, Giulia was gone. Dr. Cornaro was leaning over him listening to his chest. He looked around. "Where's Giulia?"

"I sent her home for the night. She's exhausted. She'll be back in the morning. Your evening meal's on the way, and I insist you eat every bite."

"Yes ma'am." And he saluted her. "I do believe I'm hungry."

"That's good news." She left.

As Chuck finished eating, Tom walked in. "Want to spend a few more minutes with you, before I leave. My new assistant called, sounding frantic. But I'm hoping to be back for Marc and Marlowe's big party."

"Good. Maybe I can rustle up a prospect for you by then."

"You still planning to call it quits?" Tom said as he pulled up a chair.

"Absolutely. The Force has been good to me. In the early years, I was inspired to achieve and they rewarded me for some of my ideas—especially on missions. But lately, it seems innovation has become dangerous to career success. Personnel are promoted by years of service rather than merit."

Tom was nodding as Chuck spoke.

"More and more I feel like an outsider. Like Harry Bosch. Have you read Michael Connelly's thrillers about detective Bosch?"

"Oh yeah," Tom said. "He's a memorable character."

"Right now, I feel like Harry. My success rate's been good. Out of countless missions, I've only lost one man—one of my best." He stopped to sip more water and stared out the one window of his room. Not much of a view, but a lone cypress and its green boughs gave him a sense of space. For a moment, he was back there with the man he'd lost. Then he turned to Tom.

"But the damned system keeps investigating my methods. Thank God I brought everyone home this last time." He sighed. "I'm signing off on that."

"What will you do?"

"Back in the States, lots of special-forces guys go into private security or start their own. I have no plans to live there again but been wondering if that could work in Venice."

"Don't see why not. Criminals and terrorists lurk everywhere. And from what I've been hearing, they're all across the Veneto. Maybe even in Venice."

"For sure," Chuck said, thinking of Giulia's experience with Botteri over in Vicenza. "How long do you plan to stay with the Solar Wind project? If I start a security company, maybe you might come in with me?"

"I can see doing that." Tom crossed his arms and leaned back tipping his chair. "After clawing my way up one hill after another, either for the next degree or promotion. Yeah!" Tom said, leaning forward, slapping his thighs as the front legs of his chair hit the floor. "Running our own show sounds good. Real good."

"You've met Marc. He's an expert in procurement and number crunching. He could be our financial officer. We might send him out on some assignments, too. He's agile for such a big guy. Never been in the military but in top form. He does some weird Chinese shit. Think it's called Ba Gua, it's—"

"It has to do with palm and heel strikes," Tom added. "Yeah. Sounds as if he could take care of himself in a blind alley. What would be our territory? What would we call ourselves?"

"Territory? Guess we'd grab as much as we could handle. Name? Been playing around with that. What about Security Solutions?"

"Off the top of my head, I like it."

"Keep it simple. If someone's looking in a phone book or on the internet, the first word in our name says what we do. Or... we could say A-1 Security Solutions, that way we'd be at the top of the list."

"Good thinking."

"I considered using our initials to make up a name, but dropped that."

"We could have a logo made of initials," Tom suggested. "C for Chuck, M for Marc and T for Tom. CMT?"

"Or TMC? Or MCT?" They broke into laughter.

"We've got time." Chuck said. "It can't happen overnight, but hot damn, I'm ready for a change. By the way, Giulia has agreed to marry me."

"Great news, man. But… is she only worth a 'by the way'?"

"'Course not," Chuck growled. "She's worth the world to me. I've just been savoring the idea."

"Worth savoring. It couldn't happen to a finer man. Congrats." Tom stood up. "Your losing altitude, ol' buddy, and I gotta a plane to catch."

"Stay with us next trip, and keep thinking about our security idea."

"For sure. I imagine I'll need to be with the project for a couple years, but after that? It'll take you awhile to fully recover and settle things with the Force *and* with your beautiful lady. Tell her I approve, will you?"

"Absolutely."

"Bounce your idea around with Marc. I like him. Seems a good man. By damn," Tom said ramming his right fist into his left palm, "We'd make an awesome team. I'm feeling pumped." He glanced at his wrist. "Okay. Must go."

Tom held out his hand; Chuck took it. They held their grasp, looked straight into each other's eyes, then Tom was gone.

CHAPTER FORTY-FIVE

Next morning before anyone was moving about in his part of the rehab, Chuck got dressed. *God. Real clothes make a difference.* He carried his shoes and silently manipulated the lock on the front door. Before closing it, he inserted the end of a wooden swizzle stick into the mechanism.

Walking in Venice at night—or predawn—was like nothing else in the world. Unearthly quiet. But once you knew how to listen, the quiet came alive. While still a cadet, he used to slip out with a new friend, who was part Comanche. What Wolf hadn't taught him about stealth and tracking, his Special-Ops sergeant did. This morning, Chuck focused on the murmuring water. Gentle, sibilant kisses against the hulls of boats tied along the canals soothed every cell in his body. These timeless tidal movements, slipping in from the sea far beyond the lagoon, brought him peace. Moments like these washed away any doubts about his decision to remain in this city.

His feet weren't as silent as they should be. His legs felt sluggish, but his throat and lungs began to relax as he inhaled the moist, mystical air. Today's destination was the broad promenade, Riva degli Schiavoni, that runs beside the deep *bacino*. For centuries, Venetian merchants sailed from here, first into the Lagoon, then the Adriatic Sea and the world beyond.

Chuck needed to steal past the Carabinieri facility without arousing suspicion. Except during Carnivale, Venice was not a late-night-carousing kind of town, and any movement at this hour might be noticed. He inhaled as deeply as possible, and while easing it out—hoping he didn't cough—he crept soundlessly past a window where a dim light was burning. A sleepy guard's office no doubt. By the time he reached the Riva, though, the only sound he heard was his own labored breathing. *Damn, maybe I'm rushing things.*

Slouched onto a bench facing the water, Chuck watched clouds sidle across the sky. A thin crescent moon seemed to sneak through them on its way to the western horizon. After a while, he drew in several deep breaths, heaved himself onto his feet and aimed them toward the rehab, counting each lumbering step until he could fall back into bed.

* * *

"Major General Novak?" Doctor Cornaro said as she slid a cold stethoscope under his shirt and laid it on his unsuspecting chest.

His eyes flew open. His arm shot out and snatched her wrist in an iron grip. When he saw who it was, he relaxed his hold and eased onto his pillow.

"Buon giorno, Dottoressa Cornaro."

She rubbed her wrist. "I knew better than to surprise a military man."

"Sorry. Is your wrist okay?"

"It will be. I'm sorry to startle you, but I need a report on your AWOL activity."

"Who ratted me out?"

"Your empty bed."

"Oh."

"How are you feeling?"

"Better for having breathed Venetian air again."

"Good. But please don't do that to us again. I was about to call another military man next door."

"Would have had to wake him."

She laughed. "I've always wondered why they needed an officer to guard a building full of able-bodied young men."

"Bureaucracy."

She nodded. "Now, tell me how your breathing went out there."

"Not bad. Not good either. This moment? Better."

"Let's make an agreement for the next day or two before I release you."

"And that would be?"

"First, I believe your exertion was beneficial, but I need to know when and where you will go next time."

"You want a report? Fine. I walked to the Riva and back."

Her lips quivered and she couldn't keep a small giggle down. "The report must be filed *before* you exit, or I'll bring that sleepy guard over here to stand outside your door."

He gave her a mock salute. "So, I'm stuck here two more days? Not that it isn't marvelous, and I thank you for bringing me back from a living death."

"But?" she said.

"It's not home."

"You are so right."

"One request before I agree to this new arrangement."

"And that would be?" she said, mimicking his words.

"My outside exercise will be unaccompanied by anyone on your staff."

"No problem, as long as you give us an itinerary and estimated time sequence."

"You sound as if you've had military experience."

"In a way. First with the Swiss Air Rescue Teams and later with the U.S. Military at—"

"Womack Medical in North Carolina."

"How did you know?"

"I have my sources," he grinned. "Again, I'll always be grateful for your expertise and support."

"Thank you, Major General Novak."

"Please call me Chuck."

"If you'll call me Luisa."

"Will do."

"And now I'm guessing you're ready for a well-deserved nap. See you later, Chuck."

"Look forward to it, Luisa."

* * *

That same afternoon, Chuck and Giulia walked out of the re-hab and moved toward Zanipolo, the church of two saints. His energy had improved since his early-morning excursion. He said, "Micina, I've seen you look up longingly at *altanas*."

"I didn't know it showed," she said.

"Maybe I see more than most where you're concerned, and maybe some of your walls have crumbled."

"Hmm. I expect you're right. Nonna thought they might after telling you of my past." She almost said shameful past but it had not been all that shameful, and she was determined to stay away from anymore negativity. "I don't plan to broadcast my past, but I do feel easier in my skin."

He snugged her close under the V of his shoulder and arm as they entered the huge campo. A café off to the side had tables spaced comfortably apart. He chose one and pulled out a chair for her leaning down to kiss the top of her head. They sat looking toward the row of three-story buildings facing them from across a canal. A waiter appeared almost immediately.

"I'm thirsty for juice from those blood oranges in front of the café," he said. "How about you?"

She nodded. "They look so enticing piled in that gleaming, copper kettle."

The waiter hurried away.

"I'm glad you feel easier now," he said, "and Giulia, you have nothing to hide—ever. Remember that."

"With you to remind me to let go, maybe I can."

"Oh yeah, babe, I'll remind you. You can let go in more ways than one."

She laughed.

"Now, let's study those two altanas over there. Which one do you prefer?"

They gazed at the pretty buildings lined up along the other side of Rio dei Mendicanti. It was a fairly large canal—and a busy one—that flowed past the front of the church, continuing along the side wall of the large civic hospital that stretched all the way to the long Fondamenta Nuova. From there, the canal emptied into the lagoon. It was almost macabre that the city morgue's doors opened onto this canal because its next stop was the cemetery isle.

Directly across from them, a woman came onto her balcony and watered several potted geraniums lined up on top of the railing.

"Look. She's cut holes in the railing for the pots to fit into. That way, she doesn't have to worry about knocking one off onto a passing boatman's head."

"He might feel the drip of excess water, but all in all a clever idea. Let's keep that trick in mind," Chuck said.

She looked at him, but he continued, "If we ever have a balcony over a rio, that is."

The woman started to go in and then turned back to call to a man below as he chugged past in a flat-bottomed motor boat filled with planks of wood and plaster debris. He looked up and waved.

The waiter brought their drinks that looked like raspberry juice. She lifted her glass to Chuck. They held each other's eyes, clinked and drank. "Every time I see this deep red color," he said, "my taste buds are surprised. Love the tangy flavor of these Sicilian oranges."

"Mmm, it is delicious," she said and pointed across the way. "That altana above the geranium woman is more elaborate than I'd ever want. Those four white pillars and fancy wooden supports make it look like an enclosed room. It looks too formal, too fussy. But that one over there," and she pointed to a small roof-top structure with wire railings tall enough to keep adults from falling off, "is about perfect. I like those giant pots lined up full of greenery; they provide privacy yet surely allow plenty of cooling breezes."

"Up that high, you wouldn't need to worry about privacy, would you? We could have a comfortable bed up there for the dry season, huh?" Chuck was thinking his libido was ready for action. He wanted out of the rehab and soon. Maybe tonight. The doctor couldn't keep him against his will, could she?

"They say people lie out there on hot evenings," Giulia mused. "And that one looks big enough to invite a few friends up to catch the breezes."

"And not too elaborate to require lots of maintenance."

"Which one do you like the best?" she asked.

"Oh, I'd choose the one with the greenery, too. I'd say it's about," he held his hands around his eyes and squinted, "twenty feet across. Can't tell from here how deep though."

"There's a tiny one stuck on a building over on Rio dei Carmini. It's perched way up on top of what was probably added after the building was legally finished. I bet it's not a legal height. That altana must be almost five-stories up. It looks too puny and precarious. I wouldn't want that one on top of my. . . our apartment."

"I think I know the one you mean." He liked her switch of pronouns.

"I wonder how much it would cost to have an altana? Does anyone in your building own one?"

"Nope. I asked once about constructing one on top of my building, but the laws for adding new altanas are Byzantine. I backed off. We should find an apartment that already has one."

"Are we looking for an apartment?" she asked.

"I'm thinking it would be a perfect solution to our apartment dilemma."

"But I've already agreed we'd live in yours. It's a great place."

"That's my point. You'd always see it as my territory."

"How do you know I would—"

"You just did. It's a natural reaction," he said. "Besides, you need more space for a desk. That dresser you've been using doesn't cut it. What do you think about beginning a joint campaign to find a neutral place?"

"To buy, you mean?"

"Yeah. I'd have to sell mine first but think I could get a good price."

"Interesting," she said. "I'd always thought of renting, but maybe buying makes better sense. If that's the case, I want to be a full partner."

"Of course. You'll always be my partner, all the way. And Micina, not only my partner... my soul mate." He tipped her face to look into her eyes. Did that sound too "woo woo" for her?

Giulia put her glass down and set his down, too. Then she grasped one of his hands and laid it on her chest near her heart. "Karlo, you *are* my soul mate, my partner, my only love."

It took all his will power to let his hand lie on her chest without caressing her breast. But he knew this was too serious a moment for her—hell, it was for him, too. She took his hands, turned them over and kissed his palms.

She sat up straight and said, "Now, back to the financial portion of this partnership. I have something to tell you."

"Okaaay."

"I'm about to become a wealthy woman."

"Did you uncover a secret cache somewhere?"

"Sort of. You know Aunt Loretta left my brothers and me each a nice sum."

He nodded.

"But, later I was informed of a side letter to her will where she left a lot more to me in the form of Fiat stock. Uncle Giuseppe had held a lot of company stock. But he died of lung cancer and left it all to her."

In his focused way, Chuck said nothing and took another sip of juice.

"Aunt Loretta was more of a liberated woman than Mom will ever be. Over the years, she convinced Uncle Giuseppe to see their life as a partnership in all ways. She'd thought my dad and mom didn't have an equal set up although they seem satisfied." Giulia finished up her juice.

"Lettie always urged me to hold out for a full partnership when I married. She wanted children, but it didn't happen. In a way, I think she considered me her daughter. After Uncle Giuseppe died, she ended up in Portland to be near her only family. But I think she always wished she hadn't left Italy."

"Why didn't she go back," Chuck asked.

"She could have. She had her own pension as an executive assistant."

At Fiat?"

"No. I don't remember where she worked, but in Torino where they moved for his job. Also, she had her share of the insurance from when Dad and Lettie's parents were killed in an auto crash. She never touched the Fiat stock. And unlike Mom and Dad, who seem to think my idea to live here is foolish, Lettie supported my dream all the way. She planned to join me after I finished school and found a job here. But before that could happen... she died of a kidney condition." Giulia's eyes clouded and she struggled to continue. Chuck put his arm across her shoulders and gave her a light squeeze.

"Anyway, soon after I learned about the first inheritance, I went looking for financial advice. Dad teaches accounting at Lewis and Clark College in Portland, and I knew he'd want to take over for me. But I wanted to handle it myself. He doesn't know about the Fiat stock, and I worry about how he'll feel that Lettie left me more than his sons. Besides, he still thinks of me as his little Barbie Doll."

"Uh oh," Chuck said.

"I found Nancy Metz, a financial planner, who's been cautious and careful with my savings. I've learned so much from her, and we've become close friends. She studied the history of the Fiat company and the founding Agnelli family and urged me to leave the stock alone. The stock has come back. She sent a letter a few days ago suggesting it's time to cash in, saying I'm a rich woman. It came the day you'd been found, and I forgot all about it till now."

"Here I thought I was marrying you for your body and sharp wit and now I'm confronted with a rich heiress."

"And I came for a dream apartment and found a dreamy hunk instead."

"Dreamy hunk, huh? He stood, lifting her up with him. He kissed her deeply and fully not caring who saw them or where they were. He laid money on the table, and said, "Let's get outta here."

CHAPTER FORTY-SIX

Chuck walked into his apartment and there she was—his woman—pretty and feminine in a pale lavender halter dress with a full skirt. *And she's mine.* A wave of desire slid through him. He hoped she wasn't wearing a stitch under that dress. His blood was pulsing, and he felt his loins thicken. By the time he turned her into his arms and settled his mouth over hers, he was as hard as the stone balustrade outside the window.

"Mmm," she murmured and put her arms around him. She leaned back and asked, "Where've you been? Are you okay?"

"Enough with the 'are you okay' questions." He held her away from him and looked her squarely in the eyes. "I've been home from the rehab for six nights and seven days. I'm fine. A little tired, but mostly bored."

"Okay, okay. I understand. Shall I never ask how you are?"

"I wouldn't go that far. You may *always* feel how I am," and brought her hand to his groin.

"Niiiiice," she said. "But I've never questioned that part of you."

"Oh no? Seems to me you did that very thing not two weeks ago."

She muffled a giggle.

"Speaking of being in the rehab, I saw Dr. Cornaro today and she gave me the go ahead on *any* activity I feel up to." He held her away from him again and did his best to bounce his eyebrows.

"Did she check with your eyebrow therapist? Otherwise all appears fine."

He ignored her comment and nuzzled her neck. "And tomorrow, I'll be taking the train with you to the post. I have important appointments."

"What about?"

"Have to finalize details from the mission. And after that, I'll submit the first paperwork to resign my commission."

"A huge step for you," she said putting her hands on the hard columns of his forearms. "Any doubts?"

"Nah. I've been going through the motions for a while. Knew I wanted to stay in Venice, and the agreement I had with the military to train and ship my unit out seemed a convenient gig, but they reneged twice. Well, they've twisted my arm to go back into all that for the last time. The main word here is *last.*"

She looked surprised.

"You know I wanted no more wild adrenaline rushes. And going out with that attitude?" He shook his head holding his mouth in a grim line.

"Oh Chuck!" Giulia said putting her arms around his waist and burying her head into his chest. "I didn't know."

"You didn't need to know."

"Yes. Yes I did. I thought we had this "partnership conversation.""

"*After* I got back. Hell, you may wish I'd stop sharing my thoughts."

"Try me. I'll ask again. How do you really feel about resigning?"

"Ready. My only dread is all those exit forms Tom warned me about. For the immediate future, though, I have a better idea in mind. How about taking a nap with me?" He began to loosen the ties on her halter.

She stretched up on her toes and put her arms around his neck. "That can be arranged." And her pretty dress slid to the floor.

* * *

On the train returning to Venice the following afternoon, Giulia noticed Chuck was visibly weary. *But no more mothering.* She remembered her mom and dad calling each other mommy and daddy instead of their own names. She'd always hated that.

Nonno Tony and Nonna don't forget who they are to each other, and she could hardly wait to tell them the latest news. She hadn't mentioned a word during their last conversation, wanting to tell them face to face. She had a hunch they wouldn't be surprised. Maybe they could go . . .

"Saw Ryland today," Chuck said as they moved closer to the window to allow another passenger in the compartment. "More news about old Ollie."

Giulia roused from her thoughts, "What?"

Chuck lowered his voice. "Someone found him in his apartment in Maryland with his wrists cut. He hadn't slashed them deeply. Like many first attempts, he'd pulled the knife across his veins, not in their line of direction. For now, though, he's undergoing medical and psychological evaluations. I expect he'll be in a hospital for a while."

"I should call Rafe Lyne to see what he knows," Giulia said. "So much has been going on, I haven't thought about Oliver."

"As your attorney, Rafe should have called you. Want me to call him?"

"No. Unless you'd prefer since you insist on paying for his services."

"Nope. It's your deal," he said "Maybe the military legal eagle who represents me will have information. Let's call them now."

They both pulled out their cell phones and punched in numbers. Chuck had to leave a message, but Giulia connected with Rafe Lyne. The train's wheels were hitting seams in the tracks and he couldn't make out much about her conversation. Even after the track smoothed out, she said little. She nodded a time or two, said words like "I see," and "interesting," and "that is amazing." Then she thanked him and asked to be kept informed.

"What's the scoop?"

Giulia turned in her seat toward Chuck, "He told much the same story you heard. For now, he believes the case will be held over until Oliver's pronounced fit to stand trial. If ever. But Rafe feels relatively sure—you know attorneys—that Oliver's attempt at a counter suit will fall flat. Too many women have come out of the woodwork. Once the news about Oliver's arrest went into the university's international newsletter, messages started coming in."

"Did he say whether the search warrant was executed?"

"Yes. Wednesday, May twenty-first. You were still missing." She opened her phone to check her calendar and said, "That's the day I met with Colonel Ryland to find out if he knew what had happened to you."

"What else did your attorney tell you?"

"Rafe wasn't free to tell me what they found in the villa only that it damned Oliver's case. Well, we know what they found, don't we?"

"Too bad the search warrant didn't allow them into the personnel files," Chuck grumbled. "For one thing, they could have communicated directly with many women."

"True, but don't forget what Susan Riggs told me, or rather what she *didn't* tell me, about finding things in his office that damned him."

"Oh yeah, that's right."

"Rafe seemed flabbergasted that U. of Maryland's education programs on military posts are so far-reaching. It was obvious he was reading a report of places the women had written from. He mentioned Garmisch, Mannheim and Stuttgart in Germany. Also Naples."

Chuck nodded. "There's a huge U.S. Naval establishment in Naples."

"And, let's see," she said, "somewhere in the Netherlands. Oh yes, Volkél, is that the right pronunciation?"

"No. Volkel sounds like local, no accent on the last syllable, it's in southern Netherlands. I've flown into Volkel a time or two. It was a Dutch air base before the Second World War, then the Germans took it over, and now it's Dutch again with a big U.S. presence."

"Is there a place you haven't flown into?" she said looking at him with what he "thought" was admiration. Whatever it was, he loved it when her eyes glowed for him like that.

He kissed her lightly and said, "Sorry. What else did Lyne say."

"He said letters had also come from Ismir, Turkey and Kabul, Afghanistan and uh... Camp something in Kuwait."

Ogle's influence was far-reaching," Chuck said.

"It seems Oliver has only been stationed here and at Stuttgart. Evidently women moved on. I had the idea he wasn't finished with the list, but he changed the subject and emphasized that the most destructive part—to Oliver's case—was those events happened over a long period of time."

Chuck nodded slowly. "That would indicate a long-term pattern."

"You know, Oliver might be held in a hospital for the criminally insane," she said. "Remember how Ezra Pound was held in one for twelve years until the political climate changed and he was finally released?"

"It's different. Pound was charged with treason during wartime. Ogle's charged with criminal assault and can't be released on the whim of a politician."

"Well, I hope he's never released and that I'll never have to testify."

"Could he have been faking his suicide?"

"Maybe," Giulia said, then shook her head. "No. I don't think so. If you could have seen him that day. He was agitated. Sweating—shew! The feral odor that came off him was horrible. Not an ordinary gym-shoes-sweat smell, something else. And at times, he bounced that pencil on his desk faster and faster. I think he's probably insane." She heaved a big sigh. "I guess my druthers would be to have him stand trial after all *and be convicted*. I don't want him to get out of facing charges by pleading insanity, only to be a good boy and pronounced fit to start all over again."

Giulia leaned back against the cushions of the train compartment and stared at the flat, marshy land sliding past the train window. Chuck put his arm around her shoulders. "Micina? Thoughts?"

"I'm trying to talk myself out of feeling guilty for his fate. He is rotten. I know that, but, still, I'm the one who brought him down."

"Someone had to."

"I'm thinking I'm a jinx to bad guys. First Botteri and now Ogle."

"Oh yes. This small woman dances into their fine 'upright' lives and wields an overwhelming power to destroy them."

She chuckled. "Put that way, I guess I've given this small woman far too much power, haven't I?"

"Not to me. You have utmost power over me, babe."

CHAPTER FORTY-SEVEN

It was Saturday. They both slept later than usual, but when Chuck woke and reached for Giulia, she wasn't beside him. *What am I going to do with this monster woody?* He heard her talking to someone in the kitchen. *Shit. Who's here on Saturday morning?* As soon as he neared the kitchen, though, he deduced she was finishing up a call with her grandparents. As soon as she lay her phone down, he lifted her into a long, body-hugging embrace making sure she felt all of him.

She tilted her head back and said, "How would you like to visit *i nonni* this afternoon?"

"Sounds good to me. They're one of the best parts of my life, but we don't have to leave yet, do we?"

"No need to rush. I understand your need to catch up on your rest."

"What I need to catch up on is you. Hope you might need more time, too."

"What kind of time?" she asked with a wicked little smile.

Ah ha. She had felt the monster. "Shall I explain or demonstrate?"

"Both. I love it when you tell *and* show."

"How about I *show* first?" And he backed her toward the bedroom.

* * *

"So," Chuck said sipping his second cup of coffee. "How are Maria Grazia and Tony doing?"

"They're thrilled about your recovery and want us to enjoy the fruits of their spring garden. And I want to tell them face-to-face about us."

"Me too. Have you told anyone else yet?"

"No. But as soon as we tell them, I'll tell my parents, and Marlowe and Marc, and Nancy, for sure. Knowing her, she'll want me to force you into a pre-nup."

"Whatever, micina. I know how the burden of wealth must weigh on you."

"She'll want it because she doesn't know you. But I don't because I *do*."

Chuck thought women always rushed to tell friends and family they were getting married. "Giulia?"

"Hmm," she said as she pulled out ingredients to make pancakes.

"Why haven't you told anyone?"

When she turned to see a pained look on his rugged face, she dropped the bag of leftover bread on the counter and wrapped her arms around his waist. "Because," and she drew out the word, "I wanted to savor the idea all to myself for a little while."

"Oh." He let go the breath he'd been holding and remembered that was pretty much what he'd told Tom.

"Have *you* told anyone?"

"Only Tom. Marc and Marlowe and Ryland are next on my list and maybe Gene Linch."

"Gene Linch?"

"The fellow I dragged away from the explosion. He has the idea he owes me big time."

"Does it have anything to do with ancient Chinese legends?"

He snorted. "Nope. He came up with his own version all by himself."

"Do you like him, or is he being a nuisance?"

"He's a good man but seems to have a bad case of hero worship. But what the hell. Life has a way of coming back at you. He might come in handy when we move into our ideal apartment."

"Hunh. By that time, his idol may have lost his glitter."

Chuck laughed. "That's very possible."

"Are you in the market for pancakes this morning?"

"Always."

"These are Lettie's recipe. They're made mostly with bread-crumbs. After I pulverize these hunks of leftover bread, I'll add a bit of flour and cinnamon and a drop or two of honey. You'll like them. Would you be willing to go out for a fresh lemon for the honey-lemon syrup?"

"Consider it done," he said as he stepped close behind her and pulled an appliance from a top shelf. "You might like to use this heavy-duty blender to make bread crumbs."

She arched back against him and waggled her butt. "I do like being near a man equipped for everything."

"You imp. Keep that up and the lemon will be a forgotten fruit."

* * *

"Where will you get married?" Nonna asked. They were still sitting around the kitchen table after eating perfect penne tossed with sautéed red and yellow bell peppers, juicy tomatoes and fresh basil all from her greenhouse garden.

"I've been away too long from Portland to expect Mom and Dad to do a wedding for me. Besides, we want to make our own plans." She looked over at Chuck.

Maria Grazia caught Tony's eye. A swift communication passed between them. Then she stood and began clearing the plates. Giulia rose to help and continued, "Not in a church, neither one of us is religious." She looked at Chuck again. "Right?"

He nodded. He didn't care where or how—as long as it happened. "I'm sure we can find a good setting," he said. "I've been to a couple of classy civil weddings in the city. I'll ask around."

"You could get married here," Nonna said softly, bringing to the table a pear torta. Nonno Tony nodded and put his arm around Nonna's waist.

Chuck saw the torta and sighed. "Nonna, I was told to gain weight, but after this meal, they'll be putting me on a diet. Your entire meal has been fabulous. Are these pears from your tree?"

She nodded with a big smile. "Last year's crop."

"Unless you want to wait until winter," Tony interrupted, "we could have a garden wedding. When *do* you plan to marry?"

"Soon!" Then Chuck knew he sounded desperate. "How about late summer or early fall? Ought to be beautiful out there." He recalled their garden sloped down to a stream flowing through a grove of spindly alders and maples.

Giulia looked at Chuck. Their eyes met in agreement. "Sweet idea," she said. "I hadn't thought that far. Only wanted to come tell you about our decision. Do you think Mom and Dad will be okay with us having the wedding in Italy instead of the States?" She laid dessert plates and silverware on the table.

"Don't think it matters whether they like it or not," Nonno Tony said. "It's your wedding. But I bet they'd love to come back for it. And I'd help the twins on expenses if they want to come, too. Lots of estate sales go on in late summer. I could take the boys to a few."

When they'd finished eating, Nonna said, "Tony, you can tend to the coffee, I want to ask Giulia about a weaving project."

In her workroom, Nonna showed Giulia a piece on her loom. It had geometric designs in the same brilliant blue and old-gold colors as the scarf Giulia had fallen for almost three months ago. "What do you think of this as a winter throw for that big couch in your apartment?

"Did you have to ask? It's gorgeous."

Mostly I want to know what you think of my plan for the final border. The blue in the body is the same as your blue eye, and I'm thinking the border might be a grey yarn with a silvery thread running through it."

"For Chuck's silver eyes," Giulia said softly.

"Do you think he'll approve?"

"I do," Giulia said. They hugged, swaying back and forth. "Nonna, you worked on this before you knew about our plans."

"*Magari!* Tony and I just knew it would happen and we're thrilled for you both. That young man adores you, you know." Nonna's eyes glistened.

"Let's get him in here."

Of course Chuck approved and was moved that Nonna had done so much work for them and would edge it to match his own odd eyes.

They all gathered in the kitchen for coffee and more wedding talk.

"Dino's been wanting to build an arbor out there," Nonno said. "I know he'd like to create one for your wedding. He often asks about you, Giulia. Do you remember the teeter-totter that used to sit under the big oak?"

Giulia beamed at the thought, nodding her head.

"When you were about three, he and his wife, Donatella, took you to the city park once—I forget the occasion—and he couldn't get enough of your giggles on the seesaw. So he built one for you here. Every time he pretended to fall-boom, as you called it, you'd burst into tinkling laughter. Every single time." Nonno Tony laughed at the memory. "Chuck, it was quite a sight. Dino's about your size."

"Dino? Wasn't there a Dino helping out after your break-in?"

Tony nodded. "An old comrade from years back. Seems to think he owes me for something long ago. Dino Salvatore is the town butcher, but his skills are not limited to butchering. He's an excellent carpenter."

"Was he a comrade from the forties?" Chuck asked, wondering again about the Italian Resistance.

Tony looked directly into Chuck's eyes and said, "Something like that."

Chuck held Tony's gaze for a second, nodded and said no more. He understood that some secrets a man couldn't reveal even when the time for secrecy had long passed.

* * *

As they drove back to Venice Sunday afternoon, Chuck said, "It's settled. We'll get married at our grandparents' place. I mean *your* grandparents. How quickly I've adopted them."

"I'm glad you feel that way because, for sure, the feelings are mutual. Guess we need to settle on a date and let people know. I'm going to ask Nancy to be my maid of honor and leave it at that. Don't want lots of fuss."

"Good. Keep it simple. I'll ask Tom to stand for me. I'm kind of torn between Tom and Marc. Both go way back, but I guess I'm bonded—if that's the right word—closer to Tom because of a couple of tight corners we've been through together."

"I bet Marc understands that."

"Yeah, I think he does. And he has Marlowe. Tom has no one right now."

"If Nancy can't come, I'll ask Marlowe. Our friendship has been short, but I feel certain it will last. What do you think about inviting Dr. Cornaro?"

"A grand idea. I think she'd come," Chuck said. "And how about Lieutenant di Stefano? I'm still grateful that he watched out for you."

"Yes. I bet he'd come. And Colonel Ryland and the men in your unit?"

"We better make a list," Chuck said.

"Do you think your family will come?"

"Pretty sure my sister, Anna, and her husband, Andy, will make it. My brothers? Maybe not. From what Anna tells me, though, they're doing really well. Both are in AA and holding firm. When Dad died of liver failure, I think they finally 'got' it. Of course, I'll invite them, you never know."

"Good. I'd like to meet all of them."

"Either way, the next time we're in the States, I want us to visit them in New Jersey—on their turf."

"I'd like that." She laid her hand on his thigh, and he placed his on hers. She remembered how nervous *and* thrilled she'd felt when he had put her hand there on that first trip. Not nervous anymore, but she did wonder what he'd say about her next confession.

CHAPTER FORTY-EIGHT

The following Wednesday after making love, Giulia snuggled closer into Chuck's shoulder. "I've been thinking," she said. "Maybe we ought to set the wedding date back a bit."

"Whatever you say." He wasn't focusing on her words so much as enjoying their comfortable sound.

"It'd be good to have it sooner to avoid autumn rains. They start in early September, don't they?"

"October," he said absently.

"And also because I'm pregnant."

"That's nice," he said lazily stroking her breast. Then he raised up to look at her, "Pregnant?"

Her smile was hesitant as he stared at her. He wrapped his arms around her, rolled onto his back, pulling her with him and rolled back and forth, back and forth on the bed. "A baby. *My baby*. You have my baby inside you?"

She nodded. A grin now spreading across her face.

"Our baby," he said. "I can't believe it. How did that happen?"

"Probably because you put your—"

He roared with laughter. "I did, didn't I? But which time?"

"I'm thinking around the time you noticed the missing patch?"

"Ah yes. And I'm thinking your sweet bod doesn't like pills *or* patches."

"Maybe."

"Whatever the reason, I'm glad. Our baby, you and me. Fantastic. But wait. Are you glad, too?"

"Oh yes I am. I do so want this baby."

"When?"

"February."

After a few moments, Chuck said, "So our August 23rd wedding would put us at about three months, right?"

She nodded, loving that he said "put us."

"How long have you known?"

"Since two o'clock this afternoon. I've been suspecting for a few days, but with the patch, it can be iffy. The doctor estimates the first or second week in February."

"February. I'm going to be a father in February!"

"Guess I'll be a mother, then, too," she said softly.

"Ah Micina. I'm being a selfish oaf. Sorry. But it's… I'd begun to think I'd never be a Dad."

"Don't be sorry. I'm thrilled you're happy about it."

"Beyond happy."

"Chuck?"

"Yeah."

"Will the military allow me to continue to teach next fall?"

"Don't know why not? Pregnant service women stay on the job until they choose to take leave. Of course you can teach. Back to our wedding. Why change the date? Who cares about such things? Haven't people made flight plans?"

"Some have. It could be a hassle to change. I don't mind if you don't."

"Micina, all I care about is that she arrives safe and sound."

"Or he."

"Or he," he said, gently laying his hand on her belly and holding her closer. "But I'm pulling for a baby girl."

FINITO

About The Author

Marlene Hill, author of *Last Fling in Venice,* the first book in her Venetian Waters series, was born in Nebraska. She first discovered the wonders of Italy when her third-grade teacher sent her to the library for a report on Ancient Rome. After living off and on in Italy for many years, Hill now lives in Portland, Oregon.

Made in the USA
Charleston, SC
04 December 2013